IN THE LIFE AND DEATH WORLD OF DRUG TRAFFICKING INFORMANTS ARE NECESSARY TO STAY ALIVE. THE PERFECT INFORMANT CAN ALWAYS BE DEVELOPED BY APPLYING THE RIGHT AMOUNT OF LEVERAGE.

The wife of a Mexican Cartel leader is poisoned while having dinner with her eleven-year-old daughter, and the head of the most violent drug trafficking cartel in the world sets a $10 million reward for the murder of the waiter responsible for poisoning his wife, as well as the unknown individual responsible for ordering the hit. Julian Castro Rodriguez, aka: El Jefe, orders dozens of Cartel members to Sinaloa and offers the reward for information leading to the murderer.

Meanwhile, DEA holds a conference in Southern California which has brought together agents investigating the same members of El Jefe's cartel.

The worlds of both sides collide viciously when Toro, a Cartel assassin, kidnaps a DEA agent and threatens to kill the agent unless law enforcement reveals who was responsible for ordering the murder of El Jefe's wife.

Both sides use a web of informants to obtain intelligence furthering their goals. While the Cartel operates ruthlessly, the agents on the streets balance the scales of justice with integrity and tireless effort. To tip the scales in their favor, the agents must work outside the government's drawn lines of right and wrong, producing results both legendary, and calamitous.

What People are Saying about THE INFORMANTS

"To all who will read this book, remember while reading, fiction isn't far from reality.

In my 30 years working as a DEA Special Agent, Scott Nickerson was one of the best agents I have ever worked with."—*Retired DEA Special Agent Scott Eichenberger, Los Angeles Field Division.*

"Great read with really interesting characters. Highly recommend." *– Retired US Probation Officer James Chappell*

Excerpt

Toro had worked for El Jefe as a sicario, or cartel assassin, for the last 18 years. In his 18 years as a sicario, and the last 10 years as the leader of one of the sicario teams, Toro had never failed to accomplish the objective of an operation, which always ended the same, fear and pleading prior to death.

Today was a special day though. He was waiting for transportation to be taken to an in-person meeting with El Jefe. Most others that received a request to meet in person would be fearful of coming before such a man as Julian, a man that had given the order to murder more people than any living person on the planet. Toro lacked this fear though. After all he had seen and done in his 33 years, he no longer feared anything, to include death. Where Toro differed from others, and what made him so valuable, was that he no longer cared about most things. Right or wrong were obvious, but it did not matter to him, nothing did, other than doing the job that he was requested to do.

As the black SUV with tinted windows pulled up to the parking lot in front of the bar, Toro walked outside and ducked into the back seat of the bullet-proof vehicle, without a word to the driver or the passenger. Toro's reputation preceded him, and there was no need to confirm who had entered the SUV

THE INFORMANTS

Scott Nickerson

Moonshine Cove Publishing, LLC
Abbeville, South Carolina U.S.A.
First Moonshine Cove Edition February
2022

ISBN: 9781952439254

Library of Congress LCCN: 2022900618

Cover and interior design by Moonshine Cove staff, cover images public domain.

About the Author

Scott Nickerson worked as a DEA Special Agent in the Los Angeles Field Division for 9 years of his 13-year career. He was the case agent for multiple international investigations that resulted in seizures of more than 1 ton of cocaine and $30 million cash. He worked closely with members of the District Attorney's Office in Los Angeles County, San Bernardino County, and Riverside County, authoring dozens of search warrants and affidavits requesting telephonic interception during a five-year period. He also worked a 9-month federal wiretap investigation with the US Attorney's Office in Los Angeles.

He developed an area of expertise in the field of telephonic interception, and he worked closely with several agents and detectives that were exceptional at the recruitment and development of informants. He developed a close working relationship with several local police departments in Southern California, to include Pomona PD, Santa Ana PD, and Beverly Hills PD.

Scott currently lives in his home state, Alabama. He has worked as a Sportswriter for the *Elmore Autauga News* from 2018 – 2021, and previously worked for the *Wetumpka Herald* in 2017, publishing numerous articles to both sites.

Scott is a 2003 graduate of Auburn University, where he obtained a bachelor's degree in Criminology. In addition to the articles he has published as a Sportswriter, he has also authored several additional works pending publication, to include the sequel to *The Informants,* titled *No Good Choices.*

theinformantsbook.com

CAST OF CHARACTERS

Cartel de Culiacan

Julian Castro Rodriguez (aka: El Jefe) – Leader of the Cartel de Culiacan

Juan Ramirez Montoya – 2nd in command of Cartel de Culiacan. Responsible for coordinating logistical details of the cartel's drug trafficking operation.

Carlos Montoya – son of Juan Montoya. Exiled from Mexico and surrendered to US authorities.

Toro – Leader of a sicario group, a team of 10 assassins that work for the Cartel de Culiacan.

Leon – 2nd in command of sicario group behind Toro.

Felipe – Corrupt member of the Mexican Federal Police getting paid by the Cartel de Culiacan

Tonio – associate of Felipe.

Chico – Money Collector. Based in Tijuana but responsible for collecting drug proceeds from traffickers based in Southern California, and then coordinating the transportation of the proceeds to the leaders of the Cartel.

Tito - Chico's brother

Guardianes del Golfo (GDG) Drug Cartel

Oscar – operator of stash location in Chihuahua, Mexico. Working for GDG in an area controlled by the Cartel de Culiacan

Blanco – drug trafficker from El Paso, Texas. Customer of Oscar

Pablo Torres – 20-year old drug courier that drives cocaine into El Paso

DEA

Tyler Jameson – Special Agent from the San Diego Field Division. His investigation started Operation Raging Bull.

Reuben Valdez – Special Agent from the Los Angeles Field Division. Has a vast network of confidential informants.

Ana Lucia Rodriguez – Special Agent from the El Paso Field Division. Leader of wiretap and informant investigation connected to Operation Raging Bull.

Rodrick Chambers – Special Agent assigned to the El Paso Field Division. Partners with Ana Lucia.

Trevor Johnson - Special Agent assigned to the El Paso Field Division. Young agent learning from Rodriguez and Chambers.

Brandon Ledbetter – Special Agent assigned to Mexico City. Develops high-ranking confidential informant inside the Cartel de Culiacan.

Daniel Benson – Special Agent assigned to Juarez. Outspoken and brash agent from Philadelphia that has developed multiple informants in Juarez.

Michael Winston – Special Operations Division Coordinator responsible for coordinating different operations within Operation Raging Bull

THE INFORMANTS

Chapter 1

Culiacan (Imala) State of Sinaloa, Mexico
Tuesday, August 22

Toro leaned against the waist high bar and motioned to the waiter that he was ready to pay his tab. He finished off the last bit of his cerveza and proceeded to pull some cash out of the stack that he had bundled together inside his wallet. Despite the earliness of the morning, he had decided to kill some time at a local bar that was open 24-7.

The bundle of cash, consisting of a combination of Mexican pesos and American dollars, had been given to him for the purposes of costs associated with his trip to this location in the heart of the Northwestern Mexican state of Sinaloa.

A Mexican flag, as well as a flag from the state of Sinaloa, were proudly displayed on the wall behind the bar, along with framed photographs depicting newspaper articles documenting the generosity of the state's most famous and wealthy resident, Julian Castro Rodriguez.

Julian was not only the wealthiest resident of Sinaloa, but he was also one of the richest people in the world. The wealth that he had amassed from his drug trafficking empire was as impressive as anybody in the history of the world, and Toro knew from his one brief encounter with "El Jefe," as most referred to him, that he took great pride in that fact.

Toro gave one last glance to the newspaper article reporting the generous donation Julian had given to the owners of this bar for its construction over 15 years earlier and wondered what happened to most of the money. It had not gone in the construction of the bar.

While the bar was nice enough to serve the purpose he was there for, it should have been much nicer. The owner had likely socked away most of the donation, as did most citizens that received money from the wealthiest man in Mexico.

The private citizens had nothing on the corrupt government officials, who he knew took large amounts of the money given to the cities for construction of roads and schools. Everyone had a price at which they would turn their back on their morals and previously held convictions. Toro had seen this firsthand from priests, law enforcement, government officials, farmers, everybody.

The all-mighty cash always gave El Jefe leverage over anybody that might stand in his way and oppose the method which he used to amass his fortune. Toro knew that as well, and had seen it often, but his role in the enterprise usually came when it was too late to win over people with money.

Toro had worked for El Jefe as a sicario, or cartel assassin, for the last 18 years. When Toro's number was called, leverage was no longer being sought. No amount of cash offered by his target could match that which he and his crew of men were getting paid to carry out the execution. Only the allure of beautiful Mexican women had ever been successful in tempting any member of his team to not perform to the standards expected of them, but as the leader, Toro made sure the needs of everyone working for him were met before and after an operation.

He considered that the mark of a good boss. Toro had ten people on his team at any one time, each one with their different vices. Some had to have a snip of cocaine before a hit to get them in the right mindset, some needed it after in celebration. Others preferred to celebrate with alcohol, but the one common denominator that each needed was a bountiful supply of different women at all hours of the night.

As such, Toro had advised his immediate superior of this requirement, and an additional stipend was provided to Toro personally each month, in addition to the monthly salary of the sicarios, that was used to fuel their sex-craved lusts.

He never used the money on himself because he had lost all desires for drugs and sex years earlier. That was likely the reason he was still alive after all these years. He did only what he needed to do to be successful and carry out the mission.

In his 18 years as a sicario, and the last 10 years as the leader of one of the sicario teams, Toro had never failed to accomplish the objective of an operation, which always ended the same, fear and pleading prior to death. Some were more gruesome than others. It depended on the instruction received from his contact with the Cartel.

Today was a special day though. He was waiting for transportation to be taken to an in-person meeting with El Jefe. Most others that received a request to meet in person would be fearful of coming before such a man as Julian, a man that had given the order to murder more people than any living person on the planet. Toro lacked this fear though. After all he had seen and done in his 33 years, he no longer feared anything, to include death. Where Toro differed from others, and what made him so valuable, was that he no longer cared about most things. Right or wrong were obvious, but it did not matter to him, nothing did, other than doing the job that he was requested to do.

As the black SUV with tinted windows pulled up to the parking lot in front of the bar, Toro walked outside and ducked into the back seat of the bullet-proof vehicle, without a word to the driver or the passenger. Toro's reputation preceded him, and there was no need to confirm who had entered the SUV. The vehicle then left the parking lot of the bar, headed to a destination unknown to all but a handful of people in the world, Julian Castro Rodriguez' Sinaloa mansion.

* * *

The passenger's request to put on a blindfold was not met with resistance. Toro knew the lengths that Julian and his staff members went through to keep his location safe. He could not afford to trust anybody for the simple reason that the individual might be arrested at some point in the future, and then attempt to exchange his or her freedom for the disclosure of the Sinaloa mansion of El Jefe. It would not be the first time, and it would not be the last, but the necessary precautions would be taken, and Toro would respect that rule.

His respect lasted as long as he could keep his weapons at his side. The cold steel of the Glock firearm on his right hip, as well as the blades strapped to both legs, left him with a sense of comfort, despite not being able to see his surroundings. Toro's Glock always held 15 rounds, and he always without fail carried an additional two magazines with a capacity of 15 rounds each. He had earned the Glock several years earlier as a gift. The fact that the same weapon was carried by the Drug Enforcement Administration in the United States was one of the reasons that he liked it. He appreciated that it was easy to use, easy to assemble and disassemble, and it rarely malfunctioned. Since obtaining the Glock 12 years earlier, Toro had put over 1000 rounds through this weapon, not to mention the other weapons he had back at his home in Chihuahua, and this weapon had never malfunctioned on him, which he attributed to his dedication to always ensuring that it was clean and well-taken care of. He considered the weapon an extension of himself.

The duties of Toro's job over the previous 18 years had heightened his senses so that he could hear every breath and snort of the driver and passenger, and any conversation between them. He noticed when the passenger shifted in his seat and placed his right arm against the window, and when the driver adjusted the rearview mirror. Toro had judged the distance between his position and the other occupants of the vehicle and trusted his senses to relay to him any aggressive or threatening movement. Although he did not expect it, one could never be too careful. That would get you killed in this line of work.

Toro's senses told him that the driver was performing routine measures to ensure nobody was following them away from the motel. He was confident that they were only a mile or two away from the motel despite 30 minutes of driving. This too, was expected, and used by everyone in the drug trafficking business to make sure they were not being followed. Some people took great pride in their ability to evade the detection of law enforcement, others did not care. The ones that did not care eventually got caught. Toro had seen that as well. He knew that you could never be careful enough, and he leaned back while he waited for the driver to complete his evasive maneuvers before he felt safe enough to finally make the trek to Julian's mansion, which everyone referred to as a "ranch."

An hour after he put on the blindfold, Toro began to anticipate they were almost at their destination, as the vehicle slowed, and he heard the surface the tires rolled over change from pavement to gravel. Toro's hand rested easily on his gun out of routine, prepared to respond if necessary.

The passenger of the SUV opened the front passenger door and spoke with another individual beside the vehicle, who Toro knew was likely the guard at the gate of the ranch. Toro ascertained that the bulletproof windows did not roll down, which caused the passenger to have to open the door so that he could communicate with the guard. The fact that the passenger was comfortable enough to open the door also indicated to Toro that they had reached El Jefe's ranch.

"We're here with the last guest," he overheard the passenger say.

"Very good, they've been waiting for you," the guard responded. "About half a mile down the driveway on the right you will see some other cars. Pull there and somebody will tell you where to go."

The door closed without any further conversation and the vehicle slowly proceeded down the driveway and slowly made the turn into the area described by the guard. Toro heard the driver and passenger exit the vehicle, and a short time later the rear passenger door was opened.

"Come with me sir," a new voice said. Toro felt the man grab his forearm with one hand and place his other hand on Toro's back to help him get out of the SUV.

Toro did not ask to have the blindfold taken off. He knew that when it was okay to be removed, it would be.

"I'm sorry for the inconvenience," the man said politely, "but if you will come with me then we will be inside shortly and can remove this blindfold."

Toro did not speak, or even acknowledge the man, but he complied with his instructions and walked where he was being led. Toro did not hear any additional footsteps and figured that the driver and passenger that brought him to this location were not invited guests.

After almost 100 steps, Toro heard a door open, and he crossed the threshold of an entrance to the ranch. Cool air from the air conditioner greeted Toro as he took a few steps inside. He could hear his footsteps falling on hardwood flooring.

A ding sound indicated that an elevator was available. Toro had not heard the button pressed, so he realized it must have been sent from whatever floor he was about to stop at.

The man pressed a button, but did not enter the elevator with Toro, who was on the elevator by himself for a short time. He guessed the elevator went up two floors when the doors opened, and he was greeted by another male.

Finally, the blindfold was taken off Toro's eyes, and he was led out of the elevator.

Another man looked at him, and said, "Welcome to El Jefe's ranch. He has been awaiting your arrival to begin."

* * *

Despite everything he had heard about El Jefe's lavish lifestyle, he was still impressed when he saw it for the first time. The fruits of ill-gotten gains had paid very well. The ceiling above him was at least 50 feet high, and directly in front of him was the entrance to what looked like an auditorium. Giant marble columns with gold crown molding were littered throughout the giant room.

Two muscular security guards were standing in between Toro and the open doors of the auditorium just behind him. One of them approached with his hand out instructing Toro to stop.

"Hold on, amigo," the security guard said. "Before you are allowed in there, I'm going to need any weapons you may have."

Toro looked at the guard, and slightly shook his head. "Not happening," he simply stated.

"It was not a question," the man countered, puffing his chest out with his pride hurt from being rebuked in front of his co-worker.

The guard proceeded to place his right hand directly on Toro's gun concealed in a holster under his shirt on his right hip. With lightening quick reflexes, Toro grabbed the guard's wrist with his right hand and then yanked it upward away from his gun, as his left hand came down with such speed and force that it snapped the guard's wrist like a rag doll.

Just as quickly, Toro delivered a crushing strike with the heel of his right hand directly to the guard's nose, knocking him unconscious on the ground below, while at the same time reaching across his body with his left hand and drawing his weapon that he leveled at the second security guard that was frozen in stunned silence, unbelieving that somebody this brazen had come into El Jefe's ranch.

"I won't break any of your bones or put any holes in your body that aren't already there," Toro said, "as long as you don't attempt to take my gun. Nobody takes my gun."

"But El Jefe..." he began

"Whatever reason El Jefe brought me here is fine, but he knows I go nowhere without my gun. You can run along and ask him to make sure it is okay. If not, I am not sure why I was even called here in the first place," Toro told the scared security guard.

As the security guard glanced at his co-worker laying on the floor with his right hand bent at an impossible angle, and blood gushing from his nose onto the flooring, he almost tripped on his boots he turned so fast to fetch El Jefe.

"No need to leave your post," boomed a voice from inside the auditorium. Out of the room walked a man that seemed larger than life. Julian Rodriguez strolled into the foyer with the air of confidence of a man who had not smelled fear in a long time.

"This man is precisely right," Julian said. "I brought him here because I trust in his talents." He then turned to look at Toro. "I wouldn't have expected any less," he said, with a smirk and a head nod toward the injured security guard.

"Come, follow me," and he strolled into the auditorium, where he was surrounded by at least 50 other people seated around tables or standing in spaces between them.

"This man, I'm sure, needs no introduction," Julian said as he walked quickly toward the front of the room. "He is the infamous TORO! You distinguished gentleman have the honor of seeing him and living to tell the tale. Most he encounters do not have that option. Now let's begin."

Chapter 2

Los Ángeles (Redondo Beach), California
Tuesday, August 22

Tyler Jameson adjusted the gray tie and his pressed white shirt that was buttoned snugly around his neck. He slid on the black jacket to complete the ensemble. No matter how many times he put on his suit, which he and his co-workers at the Drug Enforcement Administration referred to as a monkey suit, he always felt slightly uncomfortable.

He was used to coming to work every day in jeans and a t-shirt. It was normal attire for the typical DEA agent that might be required to drop everything at a moment's notice and initiate surveillance of a suspected drug trafficker in a middle or lower-class neighborhood. Running around in khaki pants or god forbid a suit like the FBI would be a dead give-away that the individual was a narc.

However, when the time called to put on the monkey suit, big things normally happened, either for the good or for the bad. Tyler could recount each time he had to put on the suit in the last seven years since he left the DEA Training Academy. Most of those occasions were when Tyler appeared in Federal Court, either signing a wiretap for initiation of telephonic interception of a drug trafficker's phone or testifying in court. A couple other times he had decided to don the fancy threads when he was requested to make a presentation at a conference put on by the Special Operations Division for DEA, as was the reason he had it on today.

Since Tyler's case had pretty much developed the information that led to the start of Operation Raging Bull, he decided to look professional and once again bring out his nice black suit and gray tie for his 10-minute presentation.

Tyler was assigned to the DEA's San Diego Field Division Office and had made the trek north up the 405 freeway to Redondo Beach for the Special Operations Meeting for all the DEA cases nationwide under Operation Raging Bull. Even though it was not a long drive from San Diego to Redondo Beach, located just west of Los Angeles, Tyler was approved for one night of per diem. He was scheduled to be the first presenter of the morning at 9:00 a.m., so he decided to spend the night before at the hotel where the conference was being held, and then return to San Diego following his presentation, despite the fact that the conference was a two-day event.

Tyler and the Group Supervisor, Miguel, were the only individuals from the San Diego office present for the meeting. The remaining members of the group had elected to remain back in San Diego and coordinate any surveillance efforts that resulted from information obtained over the wiretap they had recently signed for a money remitter that was based in Tijuana and responsible for collecting millions of dollars of drug trafficking proceeds and then delivering those proceeds to the Cartel bosses based further south in Mexico.

Tyler and Miguel arrived at the conference room of the Hilton located on Marine Avenue in Redondo Beach about 15 minutes before the presentation was scheduled to begin. They did the normal meet and greet with other agents that they had come to know through telephone conversations and de-confliction notices provided by special government systems.

Tyler and Miguel first met with the Special Operations Division Coordinator. They knew he had done a very good job coordinating many different events that were somehow connected between the DEA offices around the western part of the United States. SOD Coordinator Michael Winston had access to information from all kinds of sources, not all of which could be used in a United States court of law. It was information that he used to determine when certain connections existed between the different cases in the United States. Most of the time, those connections existed in Mexico, whether it was a case in San Diego that had the same cocaine source of supply as a case in Phoenix, or a money remitter working for the cartel that collected narcotics proceeds from traffickers in Los Angeles as well as Chicago. It was like a puzzle, and Michael was good at puzzles, and prided himself in putting together the most successful SOD case that was active at that time.

"Ladies and gentlemen," Michael said starting the meeting. "I'm Michael Winston, SOD Coordinator for Operation Raging Bull. I thank everyone who is in attendance today from locations all over the country. I know most of you have active and ongoing cases, and that you may have to step outside during the meeting to take important phone calls. That is completely understandable, I just ask that you do it as respectfully as possible so the agents presenting their case are not interrupted. The goal of these meetings, as always, is to establish any potential crossovers that may exist in your enforcement efforts here in the US. I know of the cross-over in Mexico, but I want to make sure that any enforcement efforts taken in one office do not negatively affect the enforcement efforts of a case in another city. If they do, then we need to figure out a contingency plan and look at the risks versus rewards of carrying out the operation.

"The higher ups in the DEA echelon are particularly interested in this operational takedown, and for the last couple months I have been reporting directly to DEA Deputy Administrator Allen Peterson and providing him with updates," Winston said.

The DEA Deputy Administrator was the second in command of the entire DEA. He had risen from the ranks as a street agent in Chicago, and then promoted to become a supervisor in Phoenix before rising to senior level management in the Los Angeles Field Division, and then being selected as Deputy Administrator. DEA agents looked at him as the true leader of the agency, and the actual Administrator as nothing more than a figurehead, a former CEO of a major cell phone company appointed recently by the newly elected president, despite a complete lack of experience in drug law enforcement or drug trafficking in general.

The SOD Coordinator continued, "When all of you guys send me your case updates and funding requests, just know that the Deputy Administrator is personally involving himself in this mission. He sees this as an opportunity to finally take down Julian Castro Rodriguez, the leader of the Cartel de Culiacan, or CDC. Now, I cannot go into specific details, but just know that DEA in Mexico is working with a source inside the CDC that is providing real time information regarding some of their activities and plans. There is a very real possibility that we will finally be able to catch El Jefe, as he is known, within the next few months, but a lot of that depends on different factors which we all know exist in Mexico," referring to the blatant corruption of Mexican law enforcement officers.

"Brandon, our DEA agent from Mexico City that is here today, will go into that more when he gives his presentation later today, but we are still assessing...how trustworthy this source of information is and if he is truly providing reliable information. The information he has given us so far over the last couple of months gives us optimism that he is being truthful, at least as truthful as crooks can be.

"Now as most of you know, this operation was initiated two years ago with SA Tyler Jameson in San Diego, and it has expanded to include international DEA cases in Tijuana, Juarez, and Mexico City, as well as domestic cases in Los Angeles, Fresno, Seattle, Las Vegas, Chicago, Phoenix, and El Paso, just to name a few. Most of you agents know each other, hopefully there haven't been any fist fights in the parking lot before coming out here today," he said smiling, as a few of the law enforcement personnel in attendance chuckled at the attempt for humor.

"We are hopeful to reach a satisfactory conclusion to this operation in the next two to three months. I realize some cases are prepared to enter the take down phase now, while others are just getting started and are in the initial phases. We can and will work with everybody. Nothing is set in stone. However, the DEA always loves an opportunity for good press, especially when it involves arresting a bunch of drug dealers and showing the public photos of all the drugs we have seized and taken off the streets. Some of the media nowadays does not support what we are doing. They think we're all screwing hookers, skimming money from drug proceeds we've seized, and using government resources to fund extra-marital affairs," Michael said, referencing several recent allegations that had come out against DEA agents worldwide.

Again, a few of those in attendance managed a respectful laugh. DEA agents were always a tough crowd, especially early in the morning before most had woken up and had any caffeine.

"Whether or not those allegations are true, the press will print it with minimal proof, and the public will eat it up. Just ask some of these agents from international locations. Do what you do to the best of your ability, but do it carefully and within reason, because nobody in this agency in untouchable. Point being, DEA likes positive news, so if our takedown can generate that and counteract all the negativity out there nowadays, it will make my job and your job easier in the long run. So, I would like to ask SA Jameson to come up to the front and begin his presentation so that everyone sees how it started, and how it has progressed."

* * *

Tyler walked up to the podium and grabbed the remote that would control the Power Point slides being displayed on the overhead projector behind him. He was normally nervous when asked to speak publicly, but he was much more comfortable when speaking about his case. He knew it so well that he didn't need the Power Point, but he used it nonetheless to give him some key words and events to discuss further, and also to give the audience something to look at besides him.

"My name is Tyler Jameson, and I work in the San Diego Field Division. The origins of this case and operation go back two years when the son of Juan Ramirez Montoya, second in command of the Cartel de Culiacan, surrendered to US authorities un-expectantly. I had worked a previous wiretap investigation that had identified Montoya's son, Carlos, was responsible for coordinating the direction of thousands of kilograms of cocaine into the Southern California area. Because Carlos' father, Juan, was second in command of the CDC, and Juan was best friends with the leader of the cartel, Julian Castro Rodriguez, it had long been considered that Carlos was untouchable. Our DEA investigation had obtained evidence that indicated narcotics proceeds seized in San Diego were being prepared to be shipped to Carlos. This information came in the form of ledgers that were seized during search warrants, as well as admissions from several individuals we arrested."

Tyler clicked the button on the remote, and the slide showed a picture of two different ledgers seized during a search warrant that listed '$1.4m and $800k' with an arrow to Carlos M.

"The information from the ledger alone wouldn't be enough to prove that Carlos Montoya was involved, but information provided by Special Agent Reuben Valdez, from the DEA Los Angeles Field Division, confirmed a couple months earlier that Carlos was being trusted to send his own personal shipment of cocaine into Southern California, and the kilos were imprinted with a stamp, or label, C1, so we knew that cocaine stamped with the C1 label was coming directly from Carlos Montoya. These ledgers were seized during a search warrant which also resulted in the seizure of 125 kilograms of cocaine. Each kilogram had the famous C1 stamp on it," Tyler explained, as he clicked on the next slide that included a picture of the large seizure of cocaine, and a photograph of several of the kilograms that had the C1 stamp.

"Based on that information, as well as toll records which showed our targets in San Diego were in direct communication with a Mexican phone number that SOD indicated was likely being used by Carlos, we believed that Carlos was the head of this particular cell of traffickers that we were investigating.

"In total, over the course of an 18-month investigation, we seized a total of 1373 kilograms of cocaine and $10.75 million dollars in US currency, all attributable to Carlos Montoya. We indicted him out of the Southern District of California, but we doubted that he would ever get captured, much less delivered directly to the United States."

Tyler then clicked another slide which showed a picture of Carlos in handcuffs outside the San Ysidro Port of Entry, "but one day in August, for reasons unknown to us at the time, Carlos surrendered to law enforcement. After a bunch of pissing contests between different law enforcement agencies around the country, it was decided that Carlos would remain in San Diego and that I would be able to interview him based on the indictment that came from our prior case.

"During our interview of Carlos, he was surprisingly forthcoming. We asked him why he surrendered, and he said he was forced to do so, because of recent events in Mexico. According to Carlos, he was responsible for the death of CDC leader Julian Castro Rodriguez' son a few weeks earlier. Carlos claimed that they had been out celebrating his sister's birthday. As the party went on into the early morning hours, Carlos walked in a bedroom to see his sister passed out on her bed, and Julian's son, Victor, on top of her and raping her. Carlos went crazy when he saw that his sister was being raped and beat Victor so bad that he had swelling in his brain and died the following day.

"This event between the two sons of the two top leaders of the CDC obviously strained their relationship, especially after they had successfully eliminated several of their competitors recently, to include smaller cartels in Tijuana and Juarez. Julian and Juan came to an agreement that Juan's son Carlos would not be killed, but that he would have to surrender himself to American authorities and would be permanently exiled from Mexico.

"Carlos didn't think this was very fair, because he had been protecting the honor of his sister who was being raped, but he acknowledged that he knew the consequences of anybody that harmed Julian's son. Carlos also admitted that he was probably the only person in the entire world that would not have been killed for killing the prospective heir of the most powerful cartel in the world."

Tyler clicked the remote once again, and the slide showed an additional seizure of drugs and cocaine. "Carlos knew that he was facing a life sentence at a maximum security prison, and that no amount of negotiating would reduce his sentence, however, he did offer to provide information if it led to him being allowed to be placed in a non-maximum security prison. He offered to provide information which would prove his willingness to be cooperative with law enforcement. Carlos immediately wrote down two addresses. One was a small house in Escondido, a town north of San Diego up the 5 freeway, another was a farm in Perris, a town northeast of San Diego. We went and established surveillance at those locations, and ultimately observed activity which led to a search warrant. At the residence in Escondido, we seized $2.3 million dollars, and at the farm in Perris, we seized 297 kilograms of cocaine. It was the largest single seizure of money or drugs in our case, and they were both on the same day."

Many of the agents in the room nodded their head, impressed at the substantial haul of narcotics and narcotics proceeds.

"Perhaps the more interesting note that came out of our interview of Carlos, was the admission that his father Juan and leader Julian had embarked on a mission to take over complete control of the drug trafficking corridor in the western part of Mexico, which provided them with exclusive rights on all customer locations in the western United States.

"Carlos said his father hand-picked a team of 'Sicarios,' or cartel hit-men, that went around absolutely wiping out rival members from the Tijuana and Juarez cartel. This team also went around wiping out entire Mexican Federal Police teams. While this should have created an uptick in the pressure applied to the drug cartels, it had the opposite effect. The Mexican president at the time declined to focus enforcement efforts on the CDC, leaving them free to carry on without fear of police. Carlos also suggested that a large majority of those Mexican Federal Policemen murdered had been dirty and working

24

for the other cartels they had wiped out. I do not know how they came across that information.

"When we asked Carlos about this team of hitmen, he claimed that all he knew about them was that they were being led by a man nicknamed Toro, Spanish for bull. Carlos said if we used our DEA offices in Mexico to follow up, then they would confirm the information he had provided. We contacted our DEA counterparts in Juarez and Tijuana, and they were able to confirm with the local police the amount of deaths on the dates provided by Carlos, again proving his information as being reliable.

"Carlos said that nobody knew any personal details about Toro, but that he was becoming increasingly popular and that many narco-ballads had been made in his honor, claiming that he was ridding the world of corrupt police and crooked drug dealers. I guess the narco-ballads left out the part that Toro was a murderer working from another drug dealer, but whatever.

"About three weeks after Carlos surrendered, DEA San Diego received notification from the Border Patrol about a seizure of narcotics from a vehicle trying to enter the border. Our case had previously identified the vehicle going to a suspected stash location in San Diego. At the time we weren't sure what was in the house, so we let the vehicle go back to Mexico, and determined to put a lookout at the border that would guarantee the vehicle was stopped and searched by the Border Patrol if and when it returned to the United States.

"The lookout was placed a couple months earlier though, and with everything that happened with Carlos, we kind of forgot about it. However, the Border Patrol agent that made the stop told us to come down and look at the dope which ended up being 50 kilograms of cocaine. Instead of the C1 stamp on the cocaine, the new dope was labeled with what appeared to be an angry bull. Thus, the Operation Name of Raging Bull was born."

Chapter 3

Culiacan (Imala), State of Sinaloa, Mexico
Tuesday, August 22

Toro noticed 10 to 15 guards standing around the walls of the giant auditorium, all which would have prevented him from being able to reach El Jefe if he had come in with bad intentions. Toro knew that there was no way that Julian would have left only two guards out front to protect him. They had been nothing more than pawns used by Julian to determine that Toro was the very man that he was made out to be. Julian's own experience with Toro had happened years earlier. It was an experience that bred an immediate trust and respect for Toro and his capabilities. Julian was pleased to realize that those capabilities had not diminished since the last time he saw them in person.

Julian walked through the crowd and approached a small stage. Seated on the stage was his right-hand man, the second highest ranking member of the Cartel de Culiacan, Juan Montoya. Julian had set aside his anger that Juan's son Carlos had killed his son Victor. Julian had shown mercy by exiling Carlos instead of giving him the death that he deserved, but the fact was that there was simply too much money at stake to risk their relationship.

Juan's role in the organization was simply too important. Since childhood, Julian knew that his best friend's strengths were in his attention to detail and organizational skills. Juan routinely handled the conversations and contracts with their cocaine suppliers from South America, to include number of shipments of cocaine, the number of kilograms included in each shipment and how those shipments got to Mexico. He was also responsible for determining who would be trusted to receive those shipments, and then transport them to other members of the organization based in Mexico that would be able to get the dope into the United States, the biggest consumer of illegal narcotics of any country in the world.

Juan stood as Julian arrived on stage and greeted his old friend in a warm embrace. He always stood beside Julian so that they would be looked at as equals, leaders that were responsible for constructing the greatest single cartel of their generation.

"As you look around today, chances are that you don't recognize anybody around you," Julian began. "That is for a reason. In this room we have very important members of our organization. Some, as Toro, have specialized skills in certain areas, while others provide valuable information that is vital in keeping us ahead of the American's efforts to stop our enterprise. The 'tres letras,'" Julian said, referring to the three letters of DEA, "will always come after us, and they will always fail. They will not succeed in promoting their imperialist agenda into the Mexican culture and society, mainly because we have one thing they cannot match, no matter the quality of agents or the level of dedication to their operations. We have more money than they do. Each one of you in this room has been paid handsomely at some point in your life. That money has come straight out of the revenue produced by our organization, so you should be proud.

"As you all likely suspect, we have hit-men here yes, but we also have members of the organization that receive and then move our product, we have representatives from the Mexican Federal Police in every state in which we operate. We have members of President Lopez' staff that provide us with information," Julian mentioned, referring to the president of Mexico that had taken over after the previous administration was embarrassed over the lack of response to the massacring of so many Federal Policemen.

"And last of all, we have those inside the great beast itself, working inside the United States. We have someone that gets information directly from DEA agents, directly from Border Patrol Agents, directly from the FBI. If the feds are planning something, we usually

27

know about it before most of the agents on the street do. We also have defense attorneys here that represent our organization's members that work for us in the United States and help with distributing our product to our customers. Everybody is accounted for, so do not worry. I have not gotten where I am today without making sure all the...what is that American saying? All the bases are covered!"

Many from the crowd nodded their heads, some even raising their glasses in respect to the most powerful man in Mexico, and possibly the world.

"Now the reason that I've brought you here today," Julian said, with his voice strangely cracking with emotion, "is because of a tragedy that has occurred recently. I...I don't know if I can finish this without...without..." Julian didn't finish his statement, instead pounding his hand on the podium at the center of the stage in a surprising twist of anger that was not expected. The quickness Julian had changed from mild-mannered to rage filled was surprising in person, despite it being long claimed that he was bi-polar and many frequently suffered from his outbursts. Only Juan was there and able to calm him.

Juan put his hand on his friend's shoulder and told him that he would finish for him. The crowd composed of people working at the behest of the Cartel de Culiacan edged closer to the stage as they sought to listen to the second in command, a man that was not known for speaking in public. Indeed, not a single man there had ever heard Juan utter a word, but now he addressed the crowd with a confident assurance that did not indicate there were any nerves in his important statement.

"Everybody, El Jefe's wife was murdered two weeks ago," he stated, as many in the crowd gasped. Even Toro's eyebrows raised at this information, which he had not heard prior to Juan mentioning it on stage. It was common knowledge that El Jefe was on his second wife, having divorced his first wife almost 15 years earlier before he established a firm grip as the head of the Cartel de Culiacan.

28

"She was poisoned, while she ate," Montoya said. "She died right in front of El Jefe's 11-year old daughter. Nobody has taken responsibility for this heinous crime, likely because they know the results that it will produce. But until someone takes responsibility for it, or we find out who it was, then EVERYONE will suffer.

"It could have been DEA, CIA, FBI, but it could have been someone from the Mexican Federal Police. It could have been someone from the cartel on the east side of Mexico, the Guardianes del Golfo, although that would be very foolish of them since we came to an agreement," Juan said, referring to an agreement that the Cartel de Culiacan would control western Mexico, and thus deliver their product into the Western United States, and the Guardianes del Golfo would control eastern Mexico and deliver their product into the eastern United States.

"It is very concerning to El Jefe that we have all of you in this room whose job is to advise of exactly this type of vicious plot against our leaders, and yet nobody knew about it. So, you are all instructed to go out, and find out who is responsible for poisoning El Jefe's wife. The person that brings proof to us of the identification and death of this waiter will receive a $10 million reward.

"We know that the waiter that poisoned El Jefe's wife is not the person, or group, that conspired to commit this murder, so we are also offering a $10 million reward for the identification of the individual responsible for ordering the assassination of El Jefe's wife. Any means necessary is okay, no approval is required, just proceed with what is mandatory to figure it out, and you will be backed up by El Jefe.

"We have set up a way for us to all communicate with each other quickly and in real-time, through an app designed by our own social engineers. I will let Pedro come up and explain the details, but everyone will be provided with a single device that contains an application where we can all communicate with each other. It is requested that you immediately report any information you have pertaining to the murder of El Jefe's wife. We will all have access to this information through the app because information obtained by one person might be beneficial in helping someone else find the killer. Rest assured, any information provided that leads to the killer will be financially rewarded, even if you do not get the $10 million grand prize.

As the young social engineer walked nervously to the stage, a hand raised from out among the crowd of gathered men and women. Juan acknowledged him and nodded his head, giving him permission to ask his question.

"Señor," the middle-aged Hispanic man began. "What if we come across information that indicates the gringos in the US were responsible for the murder, but the only way to elicit a confession is through extreme measures...are we allowed to proceed?"

"Yes," Juan responded, his answer simple and striking.

The question was an important one that most everybody in attendance was wondering, for the last couple of decades there was an unwritten rule that as long as the cartels kept the increasing violence on their side of the border and did not allow it to spill into the United States, the Americans would not use their considerable influence and dogged relentlessness in pressuring the Mexican government to intervene and track down the murderers and drug dealers. Experience had shown that if an American law enforcement officer was killed in Mexico by drug traffickers, like in the case of Kiki Camarena, a DEA agent who was murdered in Mexico in 1985, then a hornet's nest would be stirred and there would be consequences, but that had not happened in many years. There was no experience with Mexican drug traffickers coming into the US and harming American law enforcement officers. Again, it was an unwritten rule that all law enforcement officers realized. While they might be in harm's way against drug dealers located in the US, Julian and nobody from the leadership of the Cartel de Culiacan or the Guardianes del Golfo had ever authorized or given permission to a representative to cross into the US to kidnap, torture, or kill a US law enforcement officer. That option was now on the table, and the ramifications were obvious to all. If it happened, it would start a war.

With that, Juan walked away from the podium, comforting Julian who sat down in the chair seemingly lost in his grief, while the awkward but brilliant young man that had just turned 23 walked to the podium.

"I used to work for WhatsApp" Pedro said, referring to the messaging application that allowed individuals in different countries to communicate simultaneously. It was the preferred method of communication by most drug traffickers around the world that needed to communicate quickly with someone located thousands of miles away. "I...um...was there for about four years.

"I was hired about a year ago to start a new secure messaging application for El Jefe, but after his wife was...um...I mean after what happened to her, he asked, I mean I was asked to create a new way for everyone to communicate to figure out who...poisoned her. I have devices pre-programmed with the app on it and nothing else. There are no other ways to track it. The app is associated with a phone number, but I have been assured that the phone company is...um...going to make sure that the numbers are secure, and if there is any inquiry from the police about certain numbers, it will be immediately flagged and the individual with that number will be advised. So, if you go out to the lobby, and take the elevator down two floors, there will be some people that will set you up with everything you need."

Julian spoke from his seat, having regained his composure. "Do NOT, make me wait long to confront my wife's killer."

Juan stood up and waved his head, and dismissed the crowd with a simple word, "Go."

At the back of the room, Toro turned around without talking to anybody, and walked out of the auditorium.

　　　* * *

"After Toro received his phone containing the messaging application, he was directed into a small room down the hallway. The room was simply furnished, containing nothing more than a wooden rectangular table with two chairs at the sides and a chair at both ends.

Seated already at the heads of the table were two people that Toro recognized, the two leaders of the Cartel. Seated at the side of the table was a man that Toro did not recognize. He was about the same height and weight as Toro, but nice clothes, straight teeth and wavy hair indicated to Toro that the man had money. Montoya made the introduction.

"Toro, this is Felipe. He is an asset for us that works in the Mexican Federal Police Department." Toro gave a slight nod of his head in Felipe's direction, acknowledging his presence, before Felipe began speaking.

"I have a vast network of informants that provide information regarding both American and Mexican law enforcement. Also, I have informants both inside the Cartel de Culiacan, as well as inside the Guardianes del Golfo. Because of the importance to be able to communicate in real time, El Jefe has given me permission to contact you directly, in case information needs to be relayed that you and your team can respond to."

Toro looked over at El Jefe who smiled and nodded his head.

"Part of the information I've gathered is that the GDG has established a stash location in Chihuahua, which is territory agreed to be controlled by El Jefe and the Cartel de Culiacan. If I find a specific address for this location, I will pass it on immediately."

Toro nodded.

"And Toro," Montoya said, "I need not explain the possibility that the GDG might have been responsible for the murder of El Jefe's wife. If Felipe is able to identify this stash location, then it would be very beneficial for you and your team to use your skills to pry out any information possible from any person present."

Chapter 4

Los Ángeles (Redondo Beach), California
Tuesday, August 22

After explaining the origin of the SOD operation that all law enforcement in attendance ultimately became a part of, Tyler began delving into the specifics of his current case. Through his experience, he had seen how many times these types of presentations turned into nothing more than an oratory on how great the agent was and how great the agent's case was, with little to no information provided that might help others or expose some kind of a cross-over with another case whose case agents were present. In an attempt to avoid that sense of grand show-boating, Tyler focused less on the seizures that had been made, which were substantially higher than many other cases represented at the meeting, and more on the intelligence side of things.

Tyler explained how they had examined the telephone of the drug courier stopped with the kilos that had the raging bull stamp, and the information gleaned from that stop led to a wiretap. Information from that wiretap led to another wiretap and so on.

Of note that Tyler wanted to specifically mention, was that at some point his Spanish speaking wiretap monitors, employed by a contracting agency but working directly for the DEA, had informed him of their suspicion that one of their targets in San Diego was in contact with an individual they believed to be a dirty cop in Mexico.

While the suspected dirty cop never spoke of his title, he carried an air of authority in his words, and used abbreviated words common to law enforcement, like op for operation, 10-4 for confirmation of what was said, but the biggest clue was a couple instances when he informed previously identified drug traffickers of different locations where law enforcement was going to be stationed on a road at a certain date and time, essentially directing the drug trafficker on the other end of the phone where not to go in order to avoid detection by law enforcement.

Early in his career, Tyler had learned to trust the judgment of his best wiretap monitors. He had witnessed many agents with Type A personalities that refused to question their own beliefs if presented with information from the monitors that conflicted with their thoughts and suspicions. He had seen many agents that refused to accept the suspicions and instincts of others, only to find out months or weeks later that their own preconceived notions were incorrect and that they should have trusted the judgment of the wiretap monitors.

Many agents took the wiretap monitors for granted, but Tyler truly believed the reason his previous case had succeeded was because of how good those wiretap monitors were. It was these same monitors that were insistent that the Mexican based target that referred to himself as Felipe, was a law enforcement officer, believed to be a Federal Police officer.

With the amount of corrupt law enforcement in Mexico at the time, the fact that a DEA investigation had intercepted a dirty Mexican cop wasn't surprising, but the ramifications of that revelation were important, for Tyler knew that the dirty cop would lead them to more drug traffickers, drugs, and drug proceeds. Little did Tyler know that in less than a month, he would be moments away from death at the hands of this very same individual.

Further, Felipe had also mentioned having friends in Phoenix and Los Angeles. Tyler admitted that he wasn't sure if these individuals were real friends, or if they were drug trafficking associates, but Tyler assured his co-workers in those locations that he would let them know if any information came from the wiretap at a later time that might assist the agents in those locations of making seizures of drugs or money.

* * *

The agents that followed Tyler's presentation were all equally involved and impressive in their own rights. Reuben Valdez from the Los Angeles Field Division was the second presenter at the SOD Conference. Tyler's proficiency in wiretaps was countered by Reuben's expertise with informant handling. Reuben had several factors that contributed to his natural born ability to appeal to drug traffickers and elicit information they otherwise would not reveal.

For starters, Reuben did not look like a cop, especially a fed. He stood 6'4" and weighed 260 pounds, with a big frame that had put on an extra 40 pounds once he reached his 40s a couple years earlier. He had the black hair and dark complexion of both of his parents that had moved from Guadalajara to Los Angeles prior to his birth. His piercing dark eyes and sharp tone and demeanor gave a no-nonsense vibe when it was time to work. However, Reuben was well-known for his love of alcohol, and was very generous with picking up the tab at the bar during his quick meetings with informants bringing useful information.

Most obviously, most of the Hispanic drug dealers in Southern California felt more comfortable speaking with somebody that looked like them and spoke their native language. Reuben's parents had continued to speak Spanish at home while Reuben was a kid. His fluency in both English and Spanish was a huge advantage in Southern California.

Despite all those traits that contributed to his ability to turn drug traffickers into informants, and retrieve useful information that would otherwise be withheld, Reuben's biggest asset was something that could not be quantified. It was the way he spoke to people. He was good at cutting through the crap and telling people exactly what they needed to know, and why they needed to know it.

Reuben's presentation at the SOD meeting was solely focused on information obtained from his vast network of confidential sources.

"I have about 15 different confidential informants working for me at any given time," Reuben said, "but three of these CIs in particular provided information, unknown to each other, that led to seizures of cocaine. In the last three months, we hit 25 kilos in Hawthorne, 47 kilos in East LA, and 58 kilos in Sylmar. Each one of those seizures had the Raging Bull stamp on the kilos of cocaine. At that point, I connected with Tyler and learned about his seizure of cocaine with the same stamp.

"The information provided by my snitches indicates that this character referred to as Toro is not the guy responsible for shipping the dope out. Supposedly, Toro's legend has grown so much in Mexico that El Jefe decided to honor him with stamping 25% of all the cocaine leaving Mexico with a raging bull.

"So, long story short, I have three CIs that are providing information on a drug trafficking crew transporting coke up the 5 freeway from Mexico directly to the Los Angeles area. If the loads of dope do not stop at one of Tyler's targets' houses in San Diego, then it is likely coming to our area of responsibility up in Los Angeles."

Reuben kept his conversation brief. No additional questions were asked, especially about his informants, as he was known to keep their identities and locations concealed from everyone except the CI Coordinator in Los Angeles, who was responsible for securing the paperwork which confirmed the identity of individuals working as confidential informants for the DEA.

* * *

After Reuben's brief presentation, the SOD Coordinator wanted to bring up some of the DEA agents representing their offices in Mexico, so that they could provide the most recent intelligence obtained regarding the movements and whereabouts of El Jefe, as well as the routes controlled by his drug trafficking organization.

SOD Coordinator Winston came up to the front of the room after Reuben stepped away. "After the agents from San Diego and Los Angeles presented, I figured we would hear next from the agents in Mexico City and Juarez. They both have some interesting intelligence that might be helpful to some cases out there, and at the very least they will keep you up to date on some of the expectations for the upcoming operations. In Mexico City, we are attempting to cultivate an informant that might be able to help us infiltrate the highest levels of the CDC, while in Juarez, we have information about this character Toro, as well as informant information about direct observation of El Jefe at a restaurant in the border city there, which is very brazen for him to leave the confines of his home state of Sinaloa and get that close to the United States. It obviously shows that he feels protected there, but without further ado, here is Special Agent Brandon Ledbetter, from DEA Mexico City."

Brandon Ledbetter approached the podium in a nice blue suit. As a DEA agent assigned to an international location, specifically in the hotspot of Mexico City, Brandon felt the constant pressure to always represent his position in the best way possible. He looked the part, he had rehearsed his speech, and he wanted it to be flawless and come across like he knew what he was talking about.

Unlike Reuben Valdez in Los Angeles that could fit into any drug trafficking organization in Southern California, Brandon could not have stood out more in Mexico City. A 6'1" white male, 205 pounds, with light brown hair and blue eyes, it was obvious whenever the gringo was walking around Mexico City. While he wasn't able to incorporate himself into the drug trafficking world as easily as Reuben, his size and stature did have the good fortune of getting him noticed by every attractive female he came across in Mexico City, attention that was not received in such voluminous amounts when he was assigned to the DEA office in Dallas prior to being selected for Mexico City. Despite being married with two kids, the attention Brandon constantly received from attractive women in Mexico boosted his self-esteem in a way that it had never been boosted before, and it instilled in him a confidence that had been lacking for the majority of his youth and young adulthood.

Brandon started with a smile that came easy and greeted the crowd.

"Thank you for inviting me here today. It is always nice to get back to the States whenever possible. As we all know, DEA has been trying to capture El Jefe for many years, and he has always been just out of our grasp. However, we have recently developed a Confidential Informant – a very high-ranking Confidential Informant – that we believe may be able to finally change our fortunes. We have been able to confirm some of the details provided to us by this Confidential Informant through Mr. CI Handler himself, SA Reuben Valdez from Los Angeles.

"Obviously, we have to be very careful with who is allowed to know this information, as there have been at least two occasions recently in which the Mexican Federal Police leaked our plans to apprehend El Jefe when we came across information confirming his location. These were all Federal Police that had passed polygraph tests and everything prior to working with DEA; they were paid off by somebody in between the short amount of time they took the polygraph and starting working for us.

"This informant has even told us that he was going to be attending a meeting being held by El Jefe himself that was scheduled to start today. The informant said that he would report back about the reason for the meeting. As of this time, we are not sure what the purpose of the meeting is, but we expect it to be something big because this is not the sort of thing that normally happens.

"The CI approached us with a willingness to cooperate that was somewhat surprising, but up to this point, everything is working out beautifully. We don't have any seizures directly related to this CI at this time, but what we do have is a treasure trove of intelligence identifying the names and locations of certain individuals working for the Cartel de Culiacan that we previously only knew of by a nickname."

Brandon spent the next 10 minutes going through a who's who of the cartel, providing names and photographs of the traffickers, as well as descriptions of their role within the organization. The DEA had never had access to such intelligence.

"If any of you guys come across information linking your cases to any of these targets, just give me a call. Since we have these individuals identified and know where they live, we might be able to work out a successful extradition with the Mexican government, if the cards fall just right. Thank you."

* * *

As Brandon sat down at the table with Tyler to discuss a few details, Daniel Benson approached the stage. The loudmouth 45-year old male from Philadelphia was a veteran of these types of events. He was born and raised in Philadelphia but spent 15 years in the New York Field Division before being transferred to Juarez where he had worked for the previous three years. Nobody could understand why Daniel had chosen Juarez of all places to go to when he was a veteran agent in one of the biggest field divisions in the country. The initial reason was his blatant disgust for DEA management in the New York Field Division, all brown nose suck-ups that he considered worse than cock roaches. He had been loud and vocal in his disapproval of the top levels of management, and they were more than happy to get him out from under their hair by singing his praises to the supervisor of the office in Juarez, hopeful to be rid of one of their most vocal critics once and for all, even despite his reputation for producing successful cases.

Of all the international offices to choose from, Daniel had picked Juarez for two simple reasons. First, it was in the heart of the beast, located in Mexico and on the border with the United States. He would have more than enough work to do here. Second, and equally important in his mind but not verbalized, was his unquenchable lust of Mexican women. Unlike Brandon in Mexico City, Daniel was very much single, a bachelor his entire life. While he did not boast about his conquests like many others, he lost count after seducing more than 100 Mexican women in his first year in Mexico. Of all the women Daniel had dined and bedded in Philly, he was enamored with Mexican women. Daniel had known that he was going to be a rock star when he went to Juarez, and he was exactly right.

He worked hard, and he played hard. His work efforts had paid off in the cultivation of several informants, many of which had provided information assisting the DEA El Paso case that was scheduled to present after him.

After explaining the level of the informants he was working with, as well as some of the information they had provided which led to seizures of drugs and money in El Paso, Santa Fe, and Phoenix, he turned his attention to what everybody wanted to hear.

"The answer is yes. I have an informant that has seen El Jefe. What a lot of people do not know, is yes, I myself saw El Jefe."

The surprise in the crowd was unmistakable. Daniel was the only living DEA agent that had ever laid eyes on the leader of the Cartel de Culiacan.

"I was meeting a snitch at the Buffalo Wild Wings in Juarez for lunch one day, because she had information about a small private plane that had crashed in West Texas a few weeks earlier. She claimed this plane was transporting cocaine for the Guardianes del Golfo...not the Cartel de Culiacan. Why the GDG was encroaching on territory belonging to the Cartel de Culiacan, I don't know. I do know El Paso DEA confirmed the plane crash and the dope that was inside, although the pilot survived and escaped. I wanted to meet with the snitch and see what other information she could provide. This snitch was about 25 years old, and to be honest, she was smoking hot."

Several laughs went around the room, as those who knew Daniel best knew of his voracious appetite for attractive Mexican women. With all the drug traffickers in Juarez, the vast majority were young to middle age men in varying degrees of health. The percentage of attractive women involved was much lower because the attractive women usually had other areas or ways to get out the drug trafficking world, whether it was through modeling, better opportunities at business, or just marrying an successful businessman, opportunities that weren't available to much of the male population.

Despite the odds, Daniel had managed to find the one "smoking hot" Mexican drug trafficker, and then develop her into an informant.

Daniel continued, "As we were enjoying some good old fashioned fried cheese sticks, I noticed five black SUVs pull up in front of the restaurant like they owned the place. Men carrying rifles got out of the first four vehicles."

Some of the agents shifted uncomfortably, trying to picture the scene and imagine what they would have done if they had been in the same situation.

"At that time, I didn't know if the guys with rifles were coming in to rob somebody or murder somebody, but I discreetly pulled my holster off my hip with the Glock inside, and slid it under my left thigh so that it was concealed to everybody outside the booth where I was sitting. I figured I might be going down, but I wasn't going down like some chump, I was going down fighting."

"Hell yeah, bro," Reuben said from his seat in the audience. He had been involved in several dangerous predicaments during his career in Los Angeles and held the same viewpoint that it was better to go down with a fight than without one.

"Well, I noticed the guys walked in, and they didn't appear to be looking for anybody really. Instead, they all fanned out, like they were sweeping the place. I was sitting in the third booth to the right against the window, and I heard the guy with the rifle nearest to me stop at the first booth and make a demand for cell phones. The people in the booth quickly gave them up and then the guy with the rifle moved to the next booth and made the same request.

"At that point, I realized that all those people weren't there to kill or rob anyone, but I still wasn't sure what was going on, so I moved my gun from under my thigh and lightly placed it on the floor and slid it to the side of the wall against the window. That probably saved my life, because when the bodyguards came to my table next, the bodyguard pointed his rifle at me and told me to get out of the booth and radioed to somebody that he had a gringo.

"While all the bad guys with rifles were running around the restaurant taking everyone's cell phones, I stood there while another man that seemed to be in charge walked up.

"The man looked me up and down and said, 'What the hell are you doing here, gringo?'"

"I told him that I was there meeting with my girl. He turned and looked at the snitch sitting in the booth who was about to pee herself in fear. He had this disgusted look on his face and asked why we were meeting in Juarez and not in El Paso. I told him that too many people in El Paso knew my wife and would've ratted me out, so we always met somewhere in Juarez."

More of the agents shook their heads at Daniel's explanation of infidelity as the reason for his presence in Juarez, which was very believable.

"After all those years of running around on good women, and making excuses for my actions, I was a pro and that was the first thing that came out of my mouth," Daniel said, smiling and laughing.

"Jerk," joked Ana Lucia, the female Hispanic agent from El Paso that knew Daniel well and was scheduled to present with her co-case agent in the next slot.

"I don't deny that," Daniel said laughing and looking at Ann Lucia. "But lucky for me, it saved my bacon that day. The leader looked at me and asked for me to show him my identification to make sure I was not a narc. I pretended like my Spanish was a little off, and that I did not understand what they thought I was doing, but I lifted my hands while they yanked my identification out. Fortunately, every time I went out to meet with an informant, I left all my DEA identification at the office, and just carried a fake identification showing me with a hideous handlebar mustache with a P.O. Box in El Paso.

"The leader then pointed his gun at the snitch, and asked her if she was really screwing me," Daniel said, smiling. "I gave her a wink and a nod, and she begrudgingly said yes and nodded, even though it was NOT TRUE."

Daniel said these last two words loud, as if he were doing so for any hidden microphones in the room that had captured his conversation that might later be given to the DEA's Internal Affairs office known as the Office of Professional Responsibility (OPR). Sleeping with informants was off limits and would be a huge reprimand if discovered. It had led to the downfall of numerous promising careers for young and seasoned DEA agents alike.

"The snitch's confirmation that she was my lover seemed to appease the two guys with rifles, and they didn't even think to check under the table where I had stashed my gun, so I quickly slid back into the booth and finished off my delicious cheese sticks."

"God forbid you let those go to waste," Ana Lucia joked again from her table.

"Well by that point," Daniel said, "everybody in the freaking place was staring at me, but everybody else had already provided their phones, and the guest of honor opened the door of the 5th black SUV out in the parking lot and came in, and it was none other than El Jefe himself, Julian Castro Rodriguez. Now sure I still had my gun, and could have taken him out then and there, and maybe I should have taken one for the team, but I would have definitely been killed, and my snitch would have suffered even worse prior to being murdered, so I just sat back and took in as much as I could without trying to be too obvious."

"Such a gentlemen. You're going to make somebody a lucky lady one day," Ana Lucia said.

"How is your luck these days?" Daniel countered, eliciting more laughs from those in attendance.

Ana Lucia shook her hand and said, "Get back on track and finish so I can go."

"So anyways, El Jefe walked in, and met with a Hispanic man in a booth that had been sitting there by himself prior to our arrival. I did not recognize him and neither did the snitch. They spoke for about 20 minutes and then left, with one of the SUVs taking the man that El Jefe had met with. El Jefe hopped into the last SUV and they took off. Why they felt like they had to meet at a freaking Buffalo Wild Wings, I do not know. What I do know is that before the body-guards left, they returned everybody's phones, and made an announcement that they were going to pick up the tab for everybody eating in the restaurant...everyone except the gringo and his gringo-loving girlfriend."

"Nice!" Tyler said from his seat next to Brandon from Mexico City and Ana Lucia from El Paso.

"So, El Jefe won over everybody in the restaurant that day. Not only did he pay for their meals, but he did not pay for the gringo's meal. I'll get him back for that one day," Daniel promised, finishing up his presentation with a few additional slides related to information obtained regarding Juarez drug trafficking routes and identified stash locations on the Mexican side of the border.

Daniel strolled off the stage with all the confidence in the world, winking and pointing at Ana Lucia as she rolled her eyes in an attempt at disgust but something that came across more as a laugh.

Chapter 5
Los Ángeles (Redondo Beach), California

Tuesday, August 22

The final presenters prior to lunch were Ana Lucia Rodriguez and Roderick Chambers from the DEA's El Paso Field Division. Ana Lucia and Roderick, who everybody called Rod, had worked together for several years. Ana Lucia was small in physical stature, but quick witted with a sharp tongue. Rod's demeanor was the opposite. He was a tall black man that was quiet and reserved. The only time Rod changed was when he was on the basketball court, where he turned into an animal. That aggression on the hardwood had earned him a scholarship to play basketball at UTEP. After a junior season in which he averaged 14.2 points per game, 9.8 rebounds per game, and 4.3 assists per game, and was voted the team's Most Valuable Player, Rod tore his ACL in the first game of his senior season. He had been a borderline NBA player before, but after the injury, the scouts were scared off.

Nevertheless, Rod had been determined to rehabilitate and then tryout for an NBA team. He could have earned an extra year of eligibility but decided he had been in college long enough; he had earned his degree and wanted to start earning money. Unfortunately, fate had other plans for Rod. He was a victim in an alcohol related car crash in which the other driver was three times over the legal limit. While the injury from the crash did not threaten his life, the resulting debris mangled his legs, fracturing his right femur and snapping his tibia and fibula.

Rod once again set forward with dogged determination to become healthy again, but he did so with the resignation that he would no longer be the same basketball player he once was. He decided to pursue a career in law enforcement as soon as he was healed, and eventually made his way to the DEA after taking a job with the New Mexico State Police for a couple years. Part of Rod's humility was his resignation that he had never made his goal of being on an NBA roster, even though he had accomplished more than most in his playing days at a Division 1 school.

Rod smiled as he went up front, and clicked on the Power Point presentation, while Ana Lucia spoke at length regarding their case, and how they had been able to identify dozens of stash locations and couriers, and make several significant seizures of drugs and money, just in the last year and a half since they joined Operation Raging Bull.

When it was finally Rod's time to speak, everybody leaned forward in anticipation. He did not speak often but had a deep voice that caught your attention when he did. Rod's contribution to the presentation was something that everybody present was interested in hearing.

"During one of the seizures of drugs that Ana Lucia was talking about, we were able to flip the guy that was running the stash pad. He agreed to introduce me to one of his contacts from Mexico that was responsible for sending loads of cocaine to certain cells in the El Paso area. At that point, the Mexicans south of the border were only providing dope to the Hispanics in El Paso. They did not do business with other races. The snitch we developed was convinced that I could pull off being the leader of a black gang that wanted a better deal on some product."

"Racist drug dealer," Ana Lucia interjected, to the laughs of most in the audience. "Just because he's a big black guy with a shaved head he must be a gang banger."

"Well, I met with the guy from Mexico nicknamed Gordo one night at a little local bar in El Paso, and we sat and talked for hours while he tried to feel me out to check my story and see if he could trust me. He could not hold his liquor well, and after a few drinks, he started bragging that he had seen the infamous sicario, Toro. Since we had just joined Operation Raging Bull, I asked about Toro.

"Gordo told me that several months earlier he had been at a bar in Juarez when several thug-types walked in, a couple of which had rifles slung on their back. Gordo overheard the bartender telling someone not to mess with the group of guys because they were all sicarios. About 30 minutes after the sicarios showed up, Gordo overheard two guys beside him negotiating payment for one of the guys to have sex with a 12-year-old girl. At the same time those negotiations were going on, another man walked up on the other side of them and asked for a drink from the bartender. The man that had just walked up was one of the sicarios that had come in earlier, but he was not distinguishable as tall or big or anything like that. Gordo swears up and down this was Toro. He said Toro looked at the men negotiating the deal for the 12-year old girl in disgust, and as soon as he got his beer that came in a glass bottle, he broke it on the side of the bar, and then used the jagged end to slit the throat of the child-sex trafficker. Before that guy had even hit the ground, Gordo said Toro had grabbed the guy offering to purchase the 12-year old for sex and used that same jagged bottle to puncture both of his eyes. As the man started screaming, Toro grabbed him and said, 'you have sex with women. Twelve-year-old girls are not yet women.' Whether or not the man that got blinded heard Toro, I don't know. Gordo said Toro whistled to the group that he came in with and made a motion with his hand like it was time to leave. Sitting in a booth behind them was a group of Mexican Federal Policemen, who also had their guns showing. They were staring hard but unmoving as Toro started walking out, and he stopped and asked if they had a problem with what he did. One of the policemen answered, 'No, Toro,' very lightly, but Gordo claims he heard it and immediately knew who the man was.

"He described Toro as normal looking, about 5'10", 180 pounds, short black hair, no tattoos or scars to note, so basically nothing to go on. Gordo's suspicions were further confirmed when this was found the following morning," Rod clicked the pointer to change slides on the presentation, showing a photograph from the local Juarez paper.

The day after the alleged sighting of Toro and his fellow assassins at the bar near Juarez, six federal policemen were found hanging from light poles on a highway leading into the city. Each deceased man had a note pinned to his shirt explaining the reason for his murder. One was a snitch for the Guardianes del Golfo, one had stolen money from a money shipment headed to Chihuahua and then on to Culiacan, and another was a snitch for the feds. I was able to confirm that the man in the picture had indeed been a source of information with one of the agents in the Juarez office, prior to Daniel getting there. I was able to confirm that the man in the picture had indeed been a source of information with one of the agents in the Juarez office, prior to Daniel getting there.

The alleged sighting of Toro was interesting, but law enforcement was no closer to finding him than they were to capturing El Jefe. Regardless, the information would be stored away to be used later.

As they broke for lunch after the presentation, Rod received a phone call from the monitors of their wiretap investigation back in Texas. He nodded at Ana Lucia, who looked at her phone and realized that she had missed a call earlier. The monitors knew to contact Ana Lucia first, and if she did not answer, then to call Rod.

He hung up the phone quickly and looked at Ana Lucia. "Looks like we have to cut our trip short and get back home. We just intercepted a call from Blanco indicating that he is expecting a shipment of 't-shirts' to arrive tomorrow."

T-shirts was a common slang term used by traffickers to refer to cocaine because undershirts were plain white, the same color as cocaine.

"Cool," Ana Lucia said. "I'll change our schedule to get us out of here first thing tomorrow."

Chapter 6
El Paso, Texas

Wednesday, August 23

The following morning, Ana Lucia and Rod turned on their cell phones as soon as their flight landed in El Paso. Both had messages from the wire room asking them to call as soon as possible, so Ana Lucia made the call while Rod grabbed their bags.

As Rod wheeled their bags out of the terminal, he approached his partner who had just ended the call and was looking at him expectantly.

"The load's supposed to land at Blanco's pad in an hour," Ana Lucia told him.

The wiretap interception on an El Paso drug trafficker nicknamed Blanco had only started one week earlier, after he was identified earlier in the month. Ana Lucia and Rod were excited the wiretap on Blanco's phone was already producing results.

"I'll get our team to Blanco's house ASAP," Rod said, calling his boss back at the office, "so surveillance will be set prior to the courier delivering the load of dope. Do we know how much he's bringing?" Rod asked Ana Lucia, as he was fielding the question from his boss, a 45-year old white male named Mitch, a good boss who supported the workers in the group.

"They didn't say," Ana Lucia said, "but most of the loads we've identified have been around 50-55 kilos of coke."

Rod relayed the message to his boss, who indicated he would instruct the remainder of the Group 1 agents from EL Paso DEA to go to Blanco's residence in the suburbs east of El Paso.

Jogging to their vehicles which were left in an airport parking lot designated for law enforcement personnel, they both hurriedly entered their vehicles to get to Blanco's neighborhood in time to observe the delivery of cocaine.

Rod and Ana Lucia met at a CVS Pharmacy a few miles away from Blanco's residence. Rod left his black F-150 in the parking lot and hopped into the back seat of his partner's blue Ford Focus. They had scouted Blanco's neighborhood several weeks earlier and knew there might be several lookouts in the surrounding area. It was common for the traffickers to pay young teenagers or older ladies $20-50 anytime they saw or suspected law enforcement. They had even intercepted a neighbor calling Blanco a few days earlier to warn about a narc, even though it was not anybody from DEA or the local police, just a paranoid kid. For those reasons, they could not park their car on the street and stay in the car, it would be noticed.

The plan was for Ana Lucia to park on the street in view of Blanco's house. She exited the car, sure to be noticed by the young boys that had a radar for attractive women. She walked down the street to a small park that was nothing more than two picnic tables, a community restroom, and a basketball court. The neighborhood lookouts were sure to notice Ana Lucia leave the car and meet up with whom they assumed was her boyfriend, the only Hispanic male in Group 1. Anyone other than Hispanics would have raised suspicions. What the lookouts didn't account for was Rod sitting in the back seat of the Focus, unseen from the outside due to the dark tint on the windows and the sunshade in the windshield.

With so many people walking in the area and down the sidewalk, the car and DEA radio were turned off. Ana Lucia would field any calls from the wire room and relay the messages to Rod by group text messages. It was simply too risky to communicate by radio and risk someone outside the vehicle hearing the transmission.

It did not take long for the wire room to call. Just like clockwork, a courier called and informed Blanco that he was in the McDonald's parking lot, and Blanco acknowledged and indicated he would be on his way.

"Blanco leaving shortly to pick up load car from McDonalds," Ana Lucia texted Rod. "Sounds like a new courier, and B doesn't trust him coming to pad."

"10-4," Rod responded, "who we got at McDonalds?"

"Trevor," Ana Lucia replied, referring to a 28-year-old mixed race agent. Trevor Johnson was young, and because of his skin tone, could fit in well with any race.

Less than two minutes later, Rod observed the garage door open at Blanco's house. He was startled as a bump hit the rear of the Focus. He realized that one of the lookouts was actually sitting on the rear of the car, oblivious that anyone was inside, and obviously watching for anyone coming or going to Blanco's residence.

"B just left in a white Ram," Rod texted.

"Copy," Ana Lucia replied.

"On the lookout for a white Ram," Trevor responded.

Five minutes later, Trevor saw the white Ram arrive and travel to the rear of the McDonalds. Trevor had expected that was where Blanco would meet with the courier, as it offered the most concealment from the street and the windows of the restaurant itself, so he had positioned his vehicle in an advantageous location to see the back-parking lot.

"Eyes on," Trevor texted, then transitioned to his DEA car radio to communicate with the remainder of the surveillance team.

Blanco, whose complexion was very light, thus the nickname, Spanish for white, exited the Ram and met with a short Hispanic male, that shook his hand. Trevor saw Blanco appear to say something, and then hold his hand out as the courier gave him the keys to his car and walked into the restaurant.

"Blanco is entering the driver's seat of a blue Toyota 4-runner," Trevor put out on the radio. It has Mexican license plates...I can't make it out."

"Copy," I'll pick it up when it leaves the lot and call out the tag," said fellow Group 1 member Stanley, a 7-year veteran of DEA.

"Okay," called out Mitch, the supervisor, "but then let the 4-runner go without following it since we know it's going back to Blanco's house. I'll send the message to Rod."

El Paso Group 1 had run smoothly for the previous two years. Everybody knew their role and was good at helping when needed. Mitch knew that not all DEA groups were like that, and he was glad to be in such a good group, and even more glad that he had two case agents like Ana Lucia and Rod that were such go-getters. They were the case-makers for Group 1. Every group needed them, and he had two, so he was lucky that they liked working together.

"4-Runner in garage," Rod texted from the back of the car minutes later. "Lookout is on the back of Ana Lucia's car, FYI."

"We've got eyes on in case you need help," Ana Lucia responded from the park, watching her vehicle closely to make sure Rod was safe inside.

After more than an hour, the wire room contacted Ana Lucia and told her that Blanco had called the courier and indicated he was on the way back to the McDonalds, so Ana Lucia put the message out to her team.

"Out," Rod sent when the 4-Runner left the area, driven by Blanco. Everything was working perfectly so far.

Less than five minutes later, Trevor had the 4-runner in sight back at the McDonalds.

"B out meeting with courier in parking lot," Trevor sent out in the group text.

Since they had already determined the Mexican license plate of the 4-runner delivering the dope, there was no further need to follow the vehicle back into Juarez. They remained in place until Blanco got back in his white Ram and left the area and returned to his residence.

"That was the perfect deal," Mitch put out on the radio. "Not often you see something go so smoothly and at the exact time they say they are going to do it."

Real time and drug dealer time were usually very different, but the fact that this transaction went the way it did proved that Blanco was a professional.

After Blanco returned to his residence, Ana Lucia and her "boyfriend," walked back, and got into his truck which was in the parking lot nearby.

"I'll grab the laptop and work on the search warrant," Ana Lucia texted. "Rod, you okay to stay back there?"

"Can't leave now," Rod sent back. "Sweating my balls off but I'll survive."

The warm Texas August afternoon had cooled slightly with the setting of the sun but being inside the Focus with no air conditioner was not the most comfortable place in the world. Rod considered it his duty to sit back there, as uncomfortable as it may be, while his partner worked on the search warrant. He would not pass that off to anyone else.

Two hours later, Ana Lucia had finished the search warrant, and found the duty judge that was scheduled to be available after hours. Ana Lucia went to a nearby Office Max and printed out the search warrant, and then went to the judge's residence, located in a nice neighborhood 20 minutes north of their location.

As soon as the warrant was signed, Ana Lucia sent the text everyone had been waiting for, "Good to go. Hit the house."

Mitch, Trevor, and the rest of Group 1 had stationed themselves behind a Wal-Mart that was in the same shopping center as the CVS where Rod left his truck. Each person suited up in tactical gear to include a ballistic vest and helmet, along with combat boots. Seven members were dispersed in two different cars that made their way slowly to Blanco's location.

Rod had thought ahead and brought his own vest and helmet to Ana Lucia's car, so he managed to put those on as he saw his co-workers turn down the street approaching Blanco's residence. The lookouts had left the area after Blanco's return, and he did not suspect they were still watching the street at this hour.

As seven DEA agents exited the two SUVs, Rod got out of Ana Lucia's Focus, glad to finally get some fresh air after having sweated off several pounds. Rod got in the back of the entry team as they approached the door.

Two members of the team peeled off to look over the back fence to make sure nobody ran out the back, while Rod stayed where he was. He was also lucky enough to use the ram when called upon. He loved the fact that he was not only allowed, but also paid, to break open doors.

"POLICE! SEARCH WARRANT! OPEN THE DOOR. POLICE! SEARCH WARRANT! OPEN THE DOOR!" came the loud knock and announce which was immediately repeated in Spanish.

When the door was not opened after the second announce, "Breacher up!" was called.

Trevor had the ram, and handed it to Rod, who took it and approached the door with a mindset to get it open on the first try. He aimed directly for the top of the doorknob and hit it with such power that the door flew off one of its hinges and splintered as it hit the wall behind it. As they had trained so many times, Rod moved to the side as the entry team entered the residence. After they entered, Rod came in behind them, bringing the ram with him in case there was another locked door inside that needed to be opened.

As the first two members of the entry team entered the living room, a loud scream rang out, followed up by a young child's crying. Rod entered the room to see a woman sitting on the couch cradling a five-year old girl.

The woman had turned her head, anticipating that she was about to be murdered. Blanco was nowhere in sight.

The woman was immediately placed in handcuffs and detained. After the room was quickly cleared of any threats, Rod approached her and asked in Spanish, "Where is Blanco?"

She looked at him and answered, "In the shower."

The Group 1 leaders looked down the hallway, which consisted of two closed doors on the right and two closed doors on the left. As soon as the entry team began to approach the first door, Blanco exited from the second door on the right, holding a revolver in his right hand. Fortunately for him, the gun was pointed to the ground.

The point man on the entry team leveled his rifle at Blanco while the remainder of the team yelled, "Gun! Gun!" and "Police!"

Fortunately for Blanco, he did not raise his gun. The lead DEA agent on the entry team had his rifle leveled at Blanco's chest, and could easily squeeze the trigger before Blanco raised the gun and gotten a shot off.

Once Blanco saw the police badge on the vests of the intruders in his residence, he knew that it was law enforcement coming to arrest him and not someone else coming to murder him and his family. He almost appeared relieved and lowered his gun to the ground and got on his knees and raised his hands.

The Group 1 entry team went through the remainder of the house without incident. During the team's initial search, they did not find the dope. The house was a modest three-bedroom, two bath residence that was 1500 square feet, with a little area outside and a cellar attached to the rear of the property.

The Group 1 agents split into teams of two to each room, so that two sets of eyes could look at each room and notice any potential hiding spots for drugs or money. Other Group 1 agents quickly went about securing the front door so that none of the neighbors would walk over, who had heard the commotion and the loud knock and announce.

A handcuffed Blanco was at the kitchen table as Rod sat down to speak with him. Ana Lucia came in, having arrived after getting the warrant signed.

"Hello, Blanco," she said. "I'm Ana Lucia, and this is Rod. Is that your wife and daughter in there?"

Blanco nodded.

"Well, once we find the dope, you're probably going to jail for the next 10 years. If you don't want me to charge your wife with conspiracy and call Child Protective Services and get them to take your daughter to some foster home where neither of you ever see her again, don't screw around with me. Tell me where the dope is and how I can get more dope."

Rod loved the way Ana Lucia came out firing. She did not beat around the bush.

"I don't know," Blanco said.

"Don't insult my intelligence by claiming you don't know anything. You think just because I'm a woman I'm stupid?"

"No."

"Then tell me where the dope is. And if you can get some more dope, then I might be willing to speak with the attorney and get a few years shaved off your sentence."

"And your wife will be able to stay with your daughter tonight and every night hereafter," Rod said, trying to give the trafficker another reason to work with law enforcement, "and not get taken by Child Protective Services."

Blanco looked at his wife and daughter from the table. `They had been strategically placed on the couch so that he could see them but were just out of hearing range. Blanco looked defeated.

"Ok," he agreed. Just get them out of here right now."

"Where is the dope, Blanco?" Ana Lucia asked.

He looked at her before speaking. "In the cellar behind a false wall, 50 kilograms."

* * *

"The false wall contains enough space for much more than 50 kilograms," Ana Lucia said. "I know that you have more than one individual that you get dope from. If you want to significantly decrease your jail time, I need you to call one of these people and get more dope."

Blanco shook his head. "There are lookouts all up and down this street. They will know that police were here. They might have called someone from the Cartel de Culiacan. They would know it's a set-up."

"If we let you stay here, what would you tell them?" Ana Lucia asked.

"I would tell them that you didn't find the dope in the false wall. It's believable. Still, I won't be able to make an immediate call for more cocaine. They might even make me come back to Mexico for a while until things cool off."

"Ok, well, I hope you enjoy spending the next 10-15 years behind bars. At least you know your child and wife will be together."

"Wait..." Blanco said. "There might be another possibility."

"What's that?"

"There is a guy I know from childhood. His name is Oscar. He started working for El Jefe's rivals at the GDG. I've heard that he set up a location in Chihuahua and is moving dope into El Paso."

"That'll get him killed if El Jefe finds out," Ana Lucia said.

"Right. Which is why he has to be very careful."

"Why would Oscar set up a GDG stash pad in territory controlled by the Cartel de Culiacan?" Ana Lucia asked.

"They undercut El Jefe's prices, selling it for cheaper than the Cartel de Culiacan. That's what Oscar's bosses at GDG told him to do. So he did it."

"And have you ever got dope from Oscar and the GDG?"

Blanco didn't answer.

"I won't tell. I just need to know if that is something that you could do now. Make an order. Bring them out. We take the dope. You get less jail time."

Blanco nodded. "I'll make the call."

Chapter 7
Mexico City, Mexico

Thursday, August 24

Just before lunch the following day, Brandon Ledbetter's flight from Los Angeles arrived in Mexico City. He had enjoyed the opportunity to spend a few nights in Southern California but had taken an early flight leaving out of Los Angeles International Airport in the morning so that he could arrive shortly before lunch. Brandon was not expected to report to work that day, and his wife was not expecting him home until later in the afternoon. He took advantage of the several hours of free time he was afforded, and coordinated to get picked up by his mistress, Leticia Fernandez.

Brandon had his pick of beautiful Mexican women to choose from when he came to Mexico City, and for no reason, he picked Leticia. Brandon liked the casualness of their relationship and the absence of expectations. Leticia told him that she did not want to get married or have kids, and she had no problem with the fact that he was married. To Brandon, it seemed like everyone he knew in Mexico had an affair, almost like it was a part of the culture. At least that was what he told himself to justify his misdeeds.

He had spoken to Mexican women, both socially and professionally, that readily acknowledged their husband or boyfriend was involved in one or more relationships. The fact that Leticia was okay with carrying on a causal relationship with him and let him continue to enjoy the fruits of his job and personal life as a husband and father seemed too good to be true. Sure, Brandon had heard the horror stories of American diplomats working in foreign countries and was warned of the aggression of foreign women that was not exhibited by women in the United States. Regardless, Brandon was confident that he had found the one woman that was not like the rest. As long as he carefully covered his tracks, he would be able to leave Mexico at his scheduled departure in the next few months and return to the United States with his marriage still intact and his wife none the wiser.

"Hello, handsome," Leticia said as Brandon leaned in to give her a kiss. Leticia was driving a small Mexican sedan that was paid for, using her money instead to pay off some of the student debt she had from her time at the university. Having graduated from college just a year earlier, she was several years Brandon's junior, and still in the area of pinching pennies to make sure that she could pay the bills.

"How was LA?" she asked.

"It was good, first time I've been there." Brandon tried to refrain from talking about work, although Leticia occasionally probed in what seemed like an innocent fashion.

"Did my tall, strong, very handsome American man arrest a bunch of bad drug dealers?" she asked smiling, using her right hand to move down Brandon's inner thigh while she kept her left hand on the steering wheel weaving in and out of the busy Mexico City traffic.

"Just don't crash," Brandon said smiling, liking the forwardness of foreign women compared to women from the US.

Leticia looked over at Brandon and licked her lips. "I'm ready to get you home."

"Me too, but we have to get there first, keep your eyes on the road!"

As Brandon was shifting in his seat, he felt the all too familiar vibration in his pocket indicating that he had a message on his work phone. He pulled it out and froze. It was the message from his informant that was scheduled to report back to him about the meeting at El Jefe's ranch from a couple days earlier.

Brandon clicked on the WhatsApp icon and saw the message directly from the informant. He tried not to noticeably shield his phone from Leticia, but he could not risk her seeing anything on the phone that could potentially jeopardize an exceptional DEA investigation.

Brandon had only met with this informant once, for a brief period, and by himself at a lounge in the Mexico City airport when both men happened to be traveling to different locations. Although Brandon was aware of the DEA rule requiring the presence of two agents during a meeting with an informant, in that instance, the informant's private plane had been scheduled for departure less than an hour later, so Brandon used the opportunity to meet with the individual for the first time in a public area. No information was shared which would result in a seizure of drugs or money, so the content of that meeting need never be discussed in a court of law, and Brandon felt comfortable with carrying out the meeting despite no other law enforcement members being present.

Another reason that Brandon decided to have the meeting with the informant at the airport lounge was because it was an opportunity to have the individual sign the DEA Confidential Informant paperwork, acknowledging that he would provide information to the DEA. Many times the reason for the agreement to work with law enforcement was to reduce criminal charges, or for monetary reward or compensation, but this informant initially made no requests, so the reason behind his sudden decision to provide information to the DEA was suspect, which was another reason that Brandon wanted to check him out in person.

When the necessity of signing DEA Confidential Informant paperwork was discussed, the informant had agreed to sign the documents, but with an alias. He informed Brandon that there was no way he was signing his real name to DEA paperwork in case the secret was ever exposed. Despite Brandon's assurances that would never happen, the informant had refused to budge. Eventually, Brandon agreed to the alias. As long as he knew the true identity of the informant, all other information provided by him would be attributed to an Informant number and not a name, so once again, the DEA agent justified his actions despite them being outside of DEA policy.

Nobody in DEA had cultivated an informant in the previous 20 years that had direct access to the personal residence of the leader of the Cartel de Culiacan. DEA agents always had to be suspicious of unspoken motivations behind informants' desires to work with law enforcement, but at the same time, if their information led to drugs being seized and drug dealers arrested, then Brandon considered that information worthwhile no matter the reason behind the motivation.

Another delicate matter that Brandon and his boss were considering was the likelihood of future criminal charges against the informant, whether in the US or in Mexico. Working with an informant in Mexico that had pending charges in the US was something that would not be looked upon favorably by many in the American media as well as with politicians, especially if the outcome of the relationship with the informant was revealed and produced anything other than a favorable result...and even then there existed the possibility that wouldn't be enough to satisfy public opinion.

Brandon had limited communication with the informant on WhatsApp and had not received a message in well over 10 days. Their communication was limited to Spanish, so Brandon slowly read the informant's message and then carefully thought of a reply.

The fact that he was sending a message to one of the most potentially important informants the DEA had cultivated in a generation, and was doing it while in the car with his Mexican mistress who was feeling him up while driving in and out of traffic made Brandon shake his head in part shame, part excitement.

"We need to meet now. I only have 30 minutes," the informant said in the message.

"Are you in the capital?" Brandon asked, not thinking the informant was currently in Mexico City.

"Yes, and I don't have long to meet. Come to the new coffee shop that opened by the downtown Federal Police station. You know the one?"

Brandon looked up from his phone and at Leticia, not sure what he should do. He was surprised that the informant was in Mexico City again. He wanted to meet with the informant and debrief him about the meeting at El Jefe's ranch, but Brandon knew that he needed to go home and get his government car and then come back to meet the informant. He could not risk having his mistress drop him off.

"I need about an hour," Brandon typed. "I have to get home and get my car and I'll be there."

"Won't work," the informant replied. "You just got back from the airport and will be close to downtown soon...just get dropped off."

Brandon looked away from his phone again, realizing the implication of the message he just read. This informant, working for the cartel, knew he had just got off the plane. How did the informant know that? Was Brandon being followed? Did the informant have the Federal Police watching and reporting? Either way, Brandon felt very uncomfortable about the situation.

"I'm with a civilian. I don't want anybody to know we're meeting," Brandon typed.

"Tell her to drop you off and then leave."

Sheesh, the informant obviously knew who he was with.

"How much time do you have?" Brandon asked.

"I need to leave here in 30 minutes."

Brandon looked at his watch. He could be there in 15.

"And it is something you can't talk about on here?" Brandon asked, seeking a way to avoid having Leticia take him to a meeting with an informant from the Cartel de Culiacan.

"I have a present to give you. DEA will be pleased. If you are not here in 30, then I must leave. I can't risk sending it to you, but it is BIG."

"Ok, but can you give me a minute to find another spot to meet?" Brandon asked. For his own safety, he always liked to pick the meeting spot with an informant.

"No, we meet here. There is a spot in the back. It is the only place I trust. And I can't be seen or else this falls apart."

The look on Brandon's face had changed from pleasure at seeing Leticia and thinking about getting back to her place, to stress at the insistence of meeting with this informant at a time and location of the informant's choosing.

It went against his training and good sense to do this meeting. First, and most obvious, he should not risk his mistress potentially seeing this informant from the Cartel de Culiacan. Second, the meeting time and place was being chosen by the informant. DEA agents often had to be flexible with their time, but he knew they should never compromise on the location. If they could not control the location, they could not control who was there and what might happen there. Third, Brandon was meeting with the informant by himself, without the presence of another law enforcement officer, again. Brandon knew the importance of having somebody with him that could verify the accuracy of his reports, but he did not want to miss out on the "BIG" information that the informant promised to provide. If his actions were ever questioned, surely DEA would approve of him bending the rules in this one instance because it was obviously for the greater good of the agency.

Also, this was not just any informant. This informant personally knew El Jefe and claimed to have a present that DEA would be thankful for. Brandon had never been involved in any kind of a similar situation, but the lack of anything bad ever happening to him at that point in his career convinced him to go through with it. Brandon assured himself that he would be fine, and the DEA would thank him afterwards.

Brandon turned to Leticia and told her that they had a change of plans. He would not be able to go to her apartment but needed her to drop him off somewhere for a meeting.

* * *

He was surprised that Leticia had not been upset about the detour and told her he was grateful for her understanding. When Brandon opened the door of the small coffee shop, he was overwhelmed with the strong and familiar aroma of coffee. He thought silently to himself, "Please don't let this be a setup," because he knew that if it was, he was as good as dead.

The counter was to the left of the entrance, with one barista working and another alternating between taking orders and making drinks. Ahead 20 feet was a series of tables spread out across the room. The interior of the shop was dimly lit, as there were no windows on the sides since there were other businesses on either wall.

Brandon noticed only one other customer sitting in the store at the time. He looked at the barista as he started to approach the customer.

"Senor," the employee said, "please find the door in the rear and a guest is waiting for you in the room back there."

Brandon nodded as he walked slowly past the customer, toward the door on the back wall. His senses were on overdrive trying to determine if he should turn around and leave or enter through the door to see if the informant had information as important as he claimed. He decided that he had to see what was on the other side of the door. If it were as big as the informant claimed, this could not only make his career, but it could be huge for the DEA.

The doorknob did not creak as he turned it and pushed the door open to the inside. The way the door opened did not give Brandon any kind of a view into the room or where he was walking into. All he could see was the wall.

As if expecting Brandon's trepidation that he was walking into a trap, the informant was at the door and opened it wider to greet the DEA agent with a hug, despite only having met once previously.

"Good to see you again," Brandon said in Spanish.

"Likewise," the informant replied.

"What can you tell me about the meeting that El Jefe had in Sinaloa?"

"He called together around 50 men and women employed by the cartel, and tasked them all with one mission, finding the assassin that poisoned and murdered his wife a few weeks ago, as well as finding the individual that paid for the assassination."

"Ok," Brandon said, "so the meeting didn't have to do with any shipment of drugs or drug proceeds?"

The informant noticed that the DEA agent did not appear shocked with the knowledge that El Jefe's wife had been murdered. "No," the informant replied, "but you should know that El Jefe himself promised $10 million to whoever could provide information proving the identity of the murderer, and $10 million to the individual that provides proof of who ordered the murder."

"Ok," Brandon said, "so what is your role in this mission?"

The informant waved off the question as if it were unimportant. "Each individual in attendance was provided with this," the informant said, pulling out a thin Samsung device. "It only has one application on it that can be used to chat with others about any information they have on the murderer."

"But won't these people be in competition with each other? Ten million dollars is at stake."

"El Jefe has promised compensation to anyone that provides any information that leads to the killer, even it is combined with other information that actually reveals the killer."

"Wow, okay," Brandon said, looking around as he just realized he had yet to breath deep after worrying about the possibility of an ambush in the room.

"So, you said you have something big for me? What is that?" Brandon asked.

"Well, each individual in attendance was assigned one of these," the informant said, holding up the phone. "There was a very careful process in determining who got one, and what was assigned to them. One was made for everyone. El Jefe himself does not have one, but he monitors it closely. There was one made for an individual in the capital here that oversees a warehouse where tons of cocaine are stored. An extra phone was produced, but not documented on the books. There is not any evidence that it exists.

Brandon's eyes widened as he looked at the phone. "So, what do you know about it? I assume it is associated with a phone number like WhatsApp?"

"Yes, but it is setup through a contact with a Mexican phone company. There is no point in attempting to contact them, because they are on the cartel payroll, and if they get any request from law enforcement, whoever it is, then they will notify El Jefe of the suspicion and the telephone number requested will simply be terminated and a new number and device will be assigned."

"So, DEA can't track it?" Brandon asked.

"No, and if you try, you will reveal yourself too early."

"So how can we figure out who these people are and where they are?"

"Well, when the decision was made who would get these devices, a list was made. I was able to make a copy of that," the informant said, pulling another sheet of paper out of his pocket.

"This list shows what telephone numbers and identification numbers for each device were assigned to who, and that individual's home city."

Brandon looked at the list quickly and realized the importance of the information provided. It revealed many of El Jefe's high-ranking contacts that would be contributing information to the hunt for the murderer of El Jefe's wife. A few of the names were individuals DEA had previously identified as being associated with the Cartel de Culiacan. There were other names, however, that the DEA had expected of being involved but did not have proof. Now, they would potentially have that proof. As Brandon scanned through the list, he noticed that there were names of a couple of individuals that had the designation, DEA Contact out beside it.

"What does that mean?" Brandon asked, pointing to the designation 'DEA contact' that had the name Vaquero listed beside it.

The informant smiled. "Surely you realize that contacts have been developed within your own organization. Even the DEA isn't immune to corruption."

"These are dirty DEA agents?"

"No, they are simply the contacts for DEA agents. Just like with other individuals employed by the cartel, one central individual is needed for communication, and then to pass that information on to the higher-ranking members. That way, there will never be any direct communication between the corrupt DEA agents and other members of the cartel. These DEA contacts act as buffers. If the corrupt DEA agent is arrested, he or she will not be able to disclose any information to law enforcement other than a phone number and possible description for their contact. The corrupt agent will not be able to provide any information regarding specific members of the Cartel."

"Smart," Brandon said. "They do that in other areas as well so I guess I shouldn't be surprised."

"Yes".

"Well I notice that these DEA contacts are the only ones that don't have a city listed. How can we figure out where they are?"

"The last piece of information I can give you, then I must leave, is that the location of each one of these devices is being monitored. It is at an off-site location somewhere in Sinaloa. I can't get you that information as it comes in, but I might be able to occasionally send some information."

"Okay, so basically we can't track the location of these devices in real time but are able to monitor the communication."

"Yes, and you have that list, which should help you to identify several individuals in the cartel that you likely don't know are working for them."

"Yes, of course, thank you very much for the information. Now, I have to ask because my bosses will want to know but tell me why you are providing this information if you're not getting paid."

"Easy," the informant replied. "If you capture El Jefe, then I will get the $5 million reward being offered by the DEA. Or, if the DEA helps me to identify who murdered his wife, and I provide that information to El Jefe, then I get the $10 million reward."

"I didn't think you needed the money."

"I don't, but once you get a taste of power, all you can think of is how to get more power."

Brandon shook his head at the response. After meeting with the informant again, Brandon believed he knew the reason for the informant's decision to provide information to the DEA, and it wasn't because he wanted more money, but it did have to do with his thirst for power. "Why would DEA want to find out who murdered his wife? It doesn't matter to me."

"It should. Because if you find out who killed her, then El Jefe will personally reward the individual providing that information. If that person is me, then we can draw him somewhere outside Sinaloa, and perhaps you can finally capture him."

The prospect of potentially capturing one of the most wanted criminals in the world was enticing, but so was the possibility of taking down his entire criminal network, which Brandon now had on a list in his hands.

"Excellent," Brandon said as the informant moved to the door to leave. They shook hands as the DEA agent opened the door and walked back into the coffee shop.

As he walked out of the door, Brandon immediately froze in his tracks. Sitting at a table in the coffee shop looking at her phone was Leticia. Brandon immediately turned around to tell the informant to stay in the back room, but he had already crossed the threshold. He grabbed the informant by the shoulders and turned him around and pushed him back through the door.

"What's going on?" the informant asked.

Brandon swore under his breath. "The woman who gave me a ride here is sitting at a table out there."

"Why?"

"I don't know. I just told her to drop me off. I didn't think she was going to wait. I definitely didn't think she was going to come inside."

"This is a huge problem. Do you think she saw me?"

"I don't know, I don't think so but I'm not sure."

"And now she knows about this place."

"I know. I'm sorry."

"I have to leave now, so you need her to get out of here immediately."

"I will."

"And Brandon, I know that is the girl you are having an affair with. I'm not going to black mail you. I'm bringing you this information so you can capture El Jefe and take down his organization. I will get what I want by sticking to the plan and not telling your wife about your girlfriend. If it makes you feel any better, most other agents in the DEA office in Mexico City are having an affair with a Mexican woman as well. If I wanted, I could have blackmailed every one of you, but I don't want that. You just happened to be the lucky guy that picked up the phone the day that I called your office."

"Lucky me," Brandon said sarcastically, turning around to walk out the door.

He walked up to Leticia and grabbed her under the arm. "We have to go right now," he said as seriously as he could muster.

"Okay, but jeez, why are you grabbing my arm so tight? Don't be a jerk, Brandon," Leticia said, wrenching her arm away and turning her back to the rear and heading out the front. "I was just trying to wait for you to give you a ride home."

"I didn't ask you to do that. You know I was meeting somebody here for work," he whispered as he pushed the door open and ushered her outside into the hot Mexican afternoon.

"Where are you parked?" Brandon asked.

"On the street, there," she pointed, as she walked to the car. "But don't get in if you are going to keep acting like a jerk."

Brandon had slid the phone and list given to him by the informant in his right pants pocket. He opened the passenger door and quickly got into the passenger seat.

Leticia looked at her phone as she opened the driver's door. She touched the photos application on her phone. Before getting in the car, she held the phone close to her face to shield the bright sunlight. She smiled to herself. She had gotten a picture of the man walking out behind Brandon. She knew that he must be important if Brandon had decided to meet with him instead of spending a few hours alone with her. Leticia was not sure she would need the photograph or ever use it, but she had some insurance down the road in case things with Brandon did not work out the way she hoped.

Chapter 8
San Diego, California

Thursday, August 24

Tyler debated whether he should answer the incoming call from the wire room to his desk phone. He had just logged off his computer and was hoping to get home before 7:00 p.m., a reasonably early time considering the many late nights he had worked for so many years, but his curiosity got the better of him, and he picked the phone up and greeted Veronica, the lead wiretap monitor on his case. She was fluent in both Spanish and English and listened to the intercepted calls that were in Spanish and translated them so that Tyler knew what the conversations were about. He hoped that she was calling with an update on their newest wiretap target, a money remitter named Chico that was based in Tijuana and collected cash from Cartel members in Southern California.

"You still in the office?" Vero asked, quickly getting to the point like always.

"Yeah, why?" Tyler said.

"We just intercepted a call from Chico. He's on his way to Los Angeles."

"I thought he stayed in the safe confines of Tijuana and had money couriers come to him," Tyler said.

"He does, but he's going to LA to meet with his brother, Tito. They're going to rob somebody tonight with $300,000 because Tito is in debt to some people in Vegas."

"Chico's going to rob one of his own guys?"

"Sounds like it," Vero said. "We missed the earlier calls when Tito and Chico planned it. Chico just called Tito and said that he was almost in Anaheim but left his other phone at home, so he had to use another phone, the one that we are intercepting."

"Yeah, I'm sure he has five or six phones like everyone else, and we are only intercepting one of them."

"Better than nothing," Vero said, and Tyler agreed.

"Chico told Tito to make sure that his gun was not loaded. He said they are not going to hurt anybody, and he does not want to risk anybody getting shot. Tito sounds like an addict, kind of a loose cannon. What are you going to do?"

"Let me make some calls."

* * *

Tyler's first call was not to any of his co-workers in San Diego, but instead to Reuben Valdez in Los Angeles. There was no way Tyler was going to be able to catch Chico before the robbery occurred, but perhaps the LA DEA agent could track him down and make the stop before the robbery took place. After explaining the content of the intercepted call, Tyler and Reuben discussed their best options.

"Since you know the type of vehicle Chico is driving, I could get a California Highway Patrol officer to stop Chico before the robbery occurs. I am up in Palmdale now finishing up a search warrant. I won't be able to make it back to LA before Chico gets here, so the CHP officer would be on his own," Reuben told him.

"I'm not comfortable with that. He might disclose that we are on a wiretap."

"I know," Reuben said. "Hey, if you have an intercepted call in which they said they are not going to harm the guy they are robbing, I say let the robbery take place, and then seize the money when you find Chico. That way you can charge him with possession of drug proceeds and the robbery."

"I was thinking the same thing, but should we really let the robbery take place?"

"What choice do we have?" Reuben said, attempting to justify their decision. "Neither of us can get there in time. Let me know when Chico is on the way back, and I'll have him stopped with the money."

"Okay, but I'll start heading toward LA as well to help you out."

"Sounds like a plan."

* * *

Things did not go according to plan. Chico dropped his car off at a Food 4 Less parking lot in Maywood, California, southeast of downtown Los Angeles, and went with Tito to conduct the robbery. Reuben and Tyler were able to locate Chico's vehicle shortly before midnight and prepared to have him and Tito arrested when Tito dropped Chico off back at his vehicle. Four hours after midnight, a noticeably intoxicated Chico was dropped off by taxi in the Food 4 Less parking lot, with Tito and the money nowhere in sight.

Unwilling to let Chico drive to Tijuana in such an impaired state, Tyler instructed the CHP officer to stop Chico, who was arrested and booked for DUI.

The good part about Chico's intoxication was that he was very open and forthcoming about what had transpired several hours earlier. Chico admitted they had taken Tito's car so that there was no chance the individual getting robbed would recognize his vehicle. The brothers had used ski masks to cover their face, and the robbery took place in the parking lot of a nearby casino, during a transaction Chico had knowledge would happen when a trafficker from Fresno was providing money to a trafficker from Los Angeles. Chico explained that nobody was shot, but they did deliver a few blows to the heads to the guy from Fresno and the guy from LA. They took the money and fled the area, but instead of Tito leaving and taking the money to Vegas, they traveled to the Commerce Casino to win more money, which didn't work, so they cut their losses and Tito left for Vegas, while Chico hailed a taxi. He was able to remember where his vehicle was parked because he had left a sticky note with the name of the grocery store and the intersection. In his stupor, Chico thought that was the most brilliant idea in the history of mankind, and happily slapped Tyler on the back as he told the tale.

The agents preserved a recording of Chico's admission to provide to the Assistant United States Attorney later. However, the AUSA wanted the LA County Sheriff's Department to charge Chico for a DUI while he looked at the evidence and later superseded with a federal charge.

With no money seized, Tyler considered the operation a failure, but the intelligence gained from the operation would later produce fruit. It was fruit that was eventually lifesaving to another DEA agent facing death in a foreign land.

Chapter 9
Chihuahua, Mexico

Saturday, August 26

The dirt of the Chihuahua Desert crunched under the boots of Toro as he walked along a desolate path in the pre-dawn hours. Unable to sleep, Toro got out of bed several hours earlier and started walking to clear his head. Many of the members of his team had not yet returned from their late-night drinking and chasing women. He could sense that some of them were getting anxious, having not had an assignment for almost two weeks. It was the longest they had gone without action in some time.

On this morning though, Toro's mind was occupied for other reasons. Having not thought about it previously, for some reason when he awoke that morning, he was very aware of the date and the impact this day had on the outcome of his life 22 years earlier. He did not reflect on August 26 every year with remorse, or any kind of emotion, because that had to be suppressed for survival reasons. A weak young pre-teenage boy in Mexico without family or friends would not make it long in the world.

His steps led him up a small rise, with a building that he had once known well that was off in the distance approximately 100 yards. It was not the building where Toro was headed, it was a location off to the side near the path he was on, one of the only small patches of grass that had been able to survive in the dry conditions on the outskirts of the Chihuahua Desert. Having not been to the location in almost 22 years, he was glad that it had been maintained properly and approached it respectfully and with a sense of reverence that he hadn't felt or shown anybody in his adult life, even in the presence of El Jefe.

Toro looked down on the grave site of a small plaque that listed the name Aracely Torres Lopez. Three Alamy flowers sat in a clear plastic vase at the top of the marker. Those flowers had been her favorite, and for a brief second, Toro almost allowed himself a smile at a memory from his childhood that came flooding back to him at the sight of the Alamy.

He was able to repress the smile, but not the memories that came rushing back.

One of Toro's only positive childhood memories was of "Madre Aracely" as he referred to her, and his older sister, Alicia. He had never known his biological parents. He did not know if they were good people or bad guys, rich or poor, farmers or businessmen, law enforcement or drug dealers. They were simply gone as early as he could remember as a boy of five years old. What he did remember, was Madre Aracely giving him some fruit one morning, and asking if he would like to accompany her to a home where she had more food, as well as friends that would take care of him. Toro had told the lady that he would only go if his sister Alicia could go with them.

He took Madre Aracely to his sister who was huddled underneath some blankets in the alley behind a small market with multiple shops lining the dusty street. He had been out looking for food, a boy of just five, because his sister had been sick. Unknown to him, her temperature had soared to over 103, and if she had not received care within several hours, she would not have made it.

Toro remembered Madre Aracely had picked up Alicia with surprising strength for an older lady and carried her and placed her in the old vehicle that she had driven to the shopping area. She drove the two siblings to the home of a doctor, where fluids were given, and antibiotics provided. What medications, Toro could not remember. All he could recall, was that Alicia got better, and with her recovery came his undying gratitude and loyalty toward Madre Aracely, something that he promised himself he would never, ever, betray.

While he kneeled at the gravesite and touched the plaque that had her name engraved on it, he shook his head. The woman had been the only mother he had ever known. She had protected him and Alicia as if they were her own children and taken them back to the small cottage outside the church where her husband was the Pastor of a small congregation of between 50 and 100 people. That cottage and church was the building that stood over Toro's shoulder to the left.

Toro tried to shake himself out of the slumber that had come over him, the fog that had seemed to ensnare his thoughts. Why had he come here? On this of all days. He had never allowed himself to feel anything after...

Once again, as on the day 22 years earlier, the same rage and anger built up inside Toro as he recalled the events that led to him losing two of the only people that he had ever cared about, his adopted mother and sister. It was not right. There was nothing he could do about it now, but the truth was, if he had been there, maybe he could have stopped what had happened. Toro realized that was likely the reason he had left the area, leaving Madre Aracely's grieving spouse, Padre Miguel, all alone.

He had been with Padre Miguel when it happened. The shock of what he saw when the two returned from their morning-prayer time was seared into his memory for as long as he lived. Madre Aracely's lifeless eyes looking up from the floor, having been stabbed multiple times as she had fought to protect Alicia from the three men that had come onto the property to snatch her away.

It was at that exact moment when the young boy died, and Toro rose. As the three men dragged Alicia's semi-conscious body to the vehicle that was just outside the small cottage, Toro had flown into an uncontrollable rage. He did not remember what he did or how he did it, but at the end, when he regained his senses, two of the three men were lying dead on the ground outside the cottage. Unfortunately, the third man had been able to escape with Alicia. Padre Miguel never spoke any more about the incident. Perhaps because he had been scared about the violence that seemed to come so naturally from the young boy, perhaps because he didn't want to incite any more violent tendencies or cause any more mental anguish from such a traumatic event.

Where the third man had taken Alicia, Toro did not know. He had attempted to track the man down, but with limited resources as a young boy, had not had any success. The two men that he killed had no identification on them, but he had noticed a small tattoo on the inside of their wrist, that he later came to find out was common to a group of sex-traffickers that sold young girls into sexual servitude to wealthy clients. The knowledge that Alicia was likely being raped and assaulted over and over, and that Madre Aracely had died trying to protect her while he had been off praying to God had left Toro inconsolable. How could God have allowed this to happen? Why would He allow it to happen? What good could possibly come from this? The young Toro rejected Padre Miguel's comments about God's will, and His plans always having a purpose.

It was in that moment the switch flipped. He would never allow himself to be hurt like that again. To suffer that kind of loss. To grieve like that. To show any form of weakness. He rejected God and left Padre Miguel and this area behind and set out to make his own way.

"It has been a long time, my son."

The voice that interrupted Toro's thoughts and memories was as familiar today as the day it had been when he left so many years earlier.

Without turning around, Toro simply said, "Yes, I came to pay my respects to your wife."

Padre Miguel walked up and placed a wrinkled and soft hand on Toro's left shoulder, and placed his forehead on Toro's back, as he wept softly, still grieving the loss of his beloved wife 22 years after her death.

* * *

78

Toro's body stiffened uncomfortably at the expression of emotion from the older man, who he calculated had to be in his early 80s at that time. He did not return the man's affection, but he did not pull away from it either. Honestly, he could not remember the last time he had been embraced by anyone.

The old man was the only person on the earth that knew of Toro's youth. He was the only person with knowledge of the spark that lit the fire to his eventual career path. He was also the only person that could share in the despair of losing Madre Aracely, a woman that had been much too loving and kind-hearted for the end that she suffered.

"My son, would you please honor me by coming to my breakfast table this morning?" the old man asked as he still clung to Toro's shoulder.

"No. I need to be going."

"Ever since the day you left shortly after Aracely's funeral, I have prayed for your protection and wondered about your location and if you were safe."

Toro smirked at Padre Miguel's mention of prayer. "I'm still alive." He turned around and looked at the old man, "but it has nothing to do with your prayers to God."

He practically spat the word God as he walked back the way he had come, freeing himself from the old man's embrace.

"Saul," the old man called, stopping Toro in his tracks. It was the first time anybody had used his given name in a very long time.

"It has been 22 years since the day my beloved was taken from this earth, and the day that your sister's innocence was stolen away, and I am still no closer to understanding why the Lord would have allowed something that horrible to happen to such a godly woman and beautiful and smart young girl. But—"

"But nothing. Nothing can justify the atrocity that was allowed to happen that day, especially since you and I, who should have been protecting them, were away and praying to the very God that betrayed us."

For the first time in a very long time, Toro had allowed his voice to rise, for his words to express the anguish he felt at the loss of Aracely and Alicia.

"We were not betrayed, Saul. Only the peace of the One True God has been able to comfort me all these years and get me through to the next day. I sense that you have not experienced that same peace."

The emotionless and cold-blooded mindset that had overtaken him for so long urged him to walk away from this man without another word, but something else inside him goaded a response.

"Are you serious?"

Padre Miguel nodded.

"No, I have not found peace, at least not from this," Toro said, nodding his head. "I don't know how anybody could after that day. I take it you have not heard what I've become."

"For a few years I heard rumors. I looked for you everywhere I could for five years, until I finally gave up and resolved that when you wanted to be found, you would be. I guess today is that day."

"I didn't want to be found. I was actually just leaving."

"Saul, please do not run away any longer."

"I'm not running away from anything."

"You are running away from the Lord. It is written all over your face."

"I don't believe in your God," Toro said. "I am impressed that you have maintained your faith all these years. Madre would be very proud, I am sure, but I do not waste my time on such things."

"God loved Aracely, just as He loves you now," Padre Miguel said, sensing the opportunity to speak to this man he had known as a young boy and treated as a son so many years earlier.

"God has a funny way of showing that. If that is how He cares for us, then I want nothing to do with it. Leave me in peace."

"You will never be in peace until you come to rest in the Lord," Padre Miguel told him.

"Look," Toro said, starting to get aggravated at the old man's insistence in the Lord's protection and love, "even if I was weak-minded enough to continue to believe in a fake God's love for people He allows to be murdered and raped, I have far surpassed even the crimes of those people that committed the heinous atrocities that day."

"Oh Saul, did you join the very men that caused you this pain?" the old man asked with a hint of betrayal in his eyes.

"The people that did this," he said pointing to Aracely's grave, "came for Alicia, to sell her for sex. Madre Aracely sacrificed her life trying to protect Alicia. I have nothing to do with these sex traffickers, but I am employed in the business of justice. I bring justice to criminals."

"Well since I don't see a police badge, or sense that you have followed into that field, I must question the morality of bringing criminals to justice at the behest of other criminals."

"You always were a very insightful man," Toro responded, realizing that Padre Miguel had picked up on Toro's profession rather quickly. "Too bad you couldn't use that insight to realize the pointlessness of following a God that does not exist."

"He does exist, my son," the old man said. "He always has, and He always will. I only hope that you will realize that before it is too late."

"Padre, it is too late for me. I have taken more lives than I can count. I am too far gone." With that, Toro turned around to walk back down the path.

"Saul, NOBODY is ever too far gone to receive God's love."

Toro made no motion to stop. Padre Miguel made one last plea to him.

"Do you know the history of your name? Of its significance?"

Once again, the deep darkness that had enveloped Toro's soul told him to leave, but what man without a past does not question where he came from?

"Do you know where my name came from? Or is this another attempt to get me to stay and have breakfast with you?"

"I would love for you to have breakfast with me, but if you are insistent on leaving, and I am not sure if I will ever see you again, then this is something I must tell you."

"Ok, but that's it," Toro allowed.

"Why your name was chosen by your mother, I don't know. Saul was the name of the first king of Israel, God's chosen people. Before that, God's people were ruled by a series of judges. It is written in the Old Testament of the Bible. Perhaps your mother named you that because she wanted you to be the first of your people to turn from the life that had previously defined you, and to be something new. Saul also has another important reference in the bible, perhaps one that applies more to you today. The Saul of the New Testament of the Bible was a horrible persecutor of Christians, responsible for the deaths of many people. He was as bad or worse than anything you have done, killing God's own people. But the Lord spoke to him on the road to Damascus and revealed Himself to Saul. He was blind for three days, and after that time, his vision came back, and he committed himself to following the Lord wholeheartedly and telling anyone who would listen of the One True God. Saul changed his name to Paul and wrote many books of the bible, proclaiming God's greatness and that Jesus Christ is the Son of God!"

Toro listened to the story of the two biblical figures and nodded.

"That Saul was not too far gone to be redeemed by God...and neither are you."

Chapter 10
San Diego, California

Sunday, August 27

Tyler's Sunday morning started like almost every other, with a call from the wire room. Miriam, the morning shift supervisor, said she had an important message that had to be relayed. "Tito's girlfriend just left a message for Chico and said Tito was in Vegas and hit a pedestrian and was arrested for DUI!"

"Was the pedestrian killed?"

"Tito's girlfriend said he was messed up really bad."

Tyler shook his head. He should have arrested Tito and Chico before they even got to Los Angeles. This was not going to be good if someone found out.

"Okay, thanks Miriam, let me know if Tito's girlfriend calls back with any new information."

Tyler ended the phone call with the wire room, and immediately placed a call to Reuben in Los Angeles. He knew that Reuben had developed and worked with many informants that had connections between LA and Vegas, and during the course of his investigations, he had established relationships with many of the local law enforcement officers there. He hated to call Reuben on a Sunday but figured that Reuben might be able to find out information about Tito faster than he could.

Reuben answered the phone on the first ring.

"Sorry to bother you on a Sunday," Tyler said.

"Don't be. I'm working. We just hit $200,000 that landed here last night. My informant came to this stash pad this morning and confirmed the money was there, so we are just wrapping things up."

Since Reuben was already working on a Sunday, Tyler did not feel so bad calling his law enforcement brethren. He quickly explained the situation and asked if Reuben had a contact in Vegas that might be able to shed light on the situation with Tito.

"Of course. Give me 10 minutes and I'll have your answer."

10 minutes later, Reuben called as promised.

"Your boy Tito is screwed. Hit a 52-year-old man that is in ICU. Police were on the scene immediately and said he was slurring his words and stumbling all over the place. He won't be getting out anytime soon."

"Jeez, I feel really bad. We should have tried to arrest Tito and Chico before the robbery."

"We don't have the benefit of hindsight like anybody else that makes judgment for our decisions. We did the right thing at the time based on the circumstances. We planned to arrest Tito and Chico, but it didn't work out. Not the first time a law enforcement operation didn't go as planned."

* * *

Los Ángeles, California
Monday, August 28

The East Los Angeles Sherriff's station did not have many visitors early Monday morning as Tyler and Reuben sat in a room waiting on the prisoner to arrive. The laptop beside Tyler was partially opened as Chico was led into the small, windowless room. Having spent the last three days in jail for his DUI charge, Chico's memory was still hazy, and he did not recall much from his admission to Tyler. Chico kept his head down, for if anyone found out he was there when he was supposed to be in Tijuana, it wouldn't take much to realize that Chico had been in Los Angeles on the exact night when a robbery had taken place of money provided by one trafficker to another...a transaction that was known by only a limited amount of people, one of which was Chico.

84

When he walked into the room, Chico first saw Reuben. He then looked to the left of the small table and saw Tyler with his laptop open.

"Chico," Reuben said, speaking in Spanish, sensing his apprehension, "It is your lucky day. You are getting bonded out of jail from your DUI charge."

Although Tyler could not speak Spanish fluently, he could understand it. He sat there as Reuben continued speaking.

"The only difference from normal, is you don't have a normal bond company. The DEA is your bond agent," he said, pulling out his badge and flopping it on the table dramatically in front of Chico.

Still not remembering everything he had revealed about the robbery prior to going to jail, and not wanting to disclose anything that he hadn't previously disclosed, Chico simply responded, "Why?"

"We know about your role as a money collector and money remitter for the Cartel de Culiacan. We know that you are based in Tijuana, and that you regularly receive shipments of money from cartel employees in the Southern California area. We know that you collect the money, count the money in Tijuana, and then have it transported to the bosses of the organization further south in Mexico."

Chico started to make a feeble attempt at denial, but Reuben cut him off before the denial could be verbalized.

"I'm going to stop you before you make some lame and stupid claim that you aren't doing those things. You do them. I know it. You know it, and Tyler knows it and has the calls on this laptop to prove that we have evidence of you discussing your role in the organization."

Tyler nodded his head in agreement.

"What do you want?" Chico asked.

"You have an opportunity to do the right thing and avoid a lengthy prison sentence if you help us out and give us information we need to make additional arrests and seize drugs and drug proceeds."

"I'm not a snitch," Chico said, looking back and forth between Reuben and Tyler sitting at the table across from him. "I'm definitely not going to snitch to the DEA. That'll get me killed."

Tyler shook his head in disapproval and Reuben leaned forward over the table. "It's actually the opposite. Do not work with us, and you will probably be killed in prison. And not just you, but also your brother, Tito."

Chico flashed a brief look of confusion and then disbelief, shaking his head.

Reuben continued, "Tito is in jail right now in Vegas. Seems like being an idiot and driving drunk runs in the family. Tito had the misfortune of hitting a pedestrian that is in ICU."

Tyler had Tito's booking photo on his laptop and turned it around so that Chico could see. He pointed to the date to prove that it was current, so that Chico would realize Tito had been arrested the day after Chico was arrested for DUI.

Chico had done so much to help Tito, but his brother just could not help himself. He was doomed to failure and was now going to take down other people with him.

"He's in jail for a long time. This is California though. Eventually, I will get out."

"Maybe," Reuben said, "but here's the thing. We know that you love and care about your brother. That is the whole reason you came up to Los Angeles to commit a robbery of a money transaction that you knew about. Don't think about denying that either, because I'll get my partner to play the call with you and Tito discussing exactly that."

Chico breathed deeply and sat back in his seat.

"There is nothing we can do for Tito. He is going to be in jail for a while...but he is going to be alive. However," Reuben let this hang in the air for almost five seconds.

"...If anybody were to hear this phone call that you and Tito had planned and committed this robbery, how long do you think it would be before the cartel contracted with somebody in the prison to have

Tito killed? I'm guessing less than 48 hours." Reuben shrugged, looking at Tyler.

Tyler nodded, making his first statement in Spanish, "Yes, I think so. 48 hours...maybe."

Reuben stared intently at Chico. "Not to mention, you are in here now. If you refuse us, and ANYBODY were to find out you are here, they will figure out that you were arrested the same night this robbery occurred. You wouldn't make it too long either."

"The US government wouldn't do that. You'd be killing me and my brother."

"No, MORON!" Reuben pounded the table with his hands. "You can't pass off the blame for something like that. You are in OUR country, breaking OUR laws. You are the MORON that decided to help his crackhead brother try and rob somebody of drug trafficking proceeds that were supposed to go to the Cartel in Mexico. The DEA has not done a thing to contribute to the situation you are in now. However, we sure will take advantage of this situation and help us accomplish what we need to accomplish to do our jobs successfully. Now you decide, right here and right now. If you work with us, then we will give you a phone and you will walk right out. We will give you some bus money to get back to Tijuana. You will have the phone turned on all the time. You will let us know anytime you get information about a shipment of drugs or money. Tyler's number is programmed into the phone already."

Chico softly said, "I don't touch product, just money. Someone different moves the product."

Tyler smiled because he knew Reuben had him.

"Don't say product," Reuben yelled. "It's drugs! Call it what it is. You use that word to make yourself not feel so bad that it is DRUGS!"

"Ok," Tyler said softly in English where only Reuben could hear, gently patting him on the leg. "I think we got him."

He did not want Reuben's bad cop persona to go too far and lose the ground they had gained.

"Ok, I'll do it."

"And if for some reason you lose your moral compass and decide that you don't care about your brother, and try and disappear after you walk out of this jail, we still know the right people to send this recorded telephone conversation. I don't have to tell you what they will do to your brother in Vegas."

"I understand. Give me the phone and let me out of here, I'll be on my way."

"Before we leave, tell us how this operation works," Reuben said.

Chico took a deep breath before beginning. "Normally, the money is collected at several different locations in California. We have houses in Sylmar, Huntington Park, Torrance, and Montebello, one in Riverside, one in San Bernardino, and another in Ontario and Perris. There are others in the San Diego area in El Cajon, Escondido, Chula Vista, and Imperial Beach, by the Mexican border."

Tyler and Reuben were pleased to have learned information about the existence of multiple stash houses used by the Cartel de Culiacan to collect, count, and remit drug trafficking proceeds.

"Have you been to any of these locations?"

"A couple. I am put into contact with the people at the locations and wouldn't know them otherwise."

"Which locations do you know?" Tyler asked.

Chico appeared deep in thought. "I've been to the location in Perris once, Imperial Beach once, and Montebello once."

"Montebello is close by where we are now. Can you show us how to get there?" Reuben asked, reading Tyler's mind.

"No, it has been over eight months since I was there, and I don't remember how to get there. I put the address in the GPS of one of my other phones that is at my residence in Tijuana. I have all the addresses in a folder in a safe in my apartment."

Reuben leaned away from the table so he could speak with Tyler in English without Chico hearing. "That sounds really good." Reuben said. "Do you think he is telling the truth, or just saying what we want to hear so that we will let him go?"

"I know he wants to get out of here, and it's obvious that he doesn't want his brother to get shanked in prison, but yeah, I have evidence which suggested that was true, I just didn't know the locations. Can you see if he can provide names and phone numbers for those locations?"

Reuben nodded and leaned back to the table near Chico. Tyler was content with allowing Reuben to control the interview, even though Chico was his target. Because Reuben was in command of the interview, did not mean he would be the main contact after Chico left. Tyler's presence in the interview room, and his willingness to communicate in Spanish, and his ability to understand and comprehend Spanish, was earning Chico's respect, and was the reason they continued the interview the way they did.

"We need phone numbers for these guys," Reuben told Chico.

Chico shook his head. "It doesn't work like that. I don't have them. Each phone number is sent to me by Tio. He tells me the phone number and who it is for. As soon as the transaction is complete, the guys in those locations get rid of those phones and they are not used anymore."

"Okay," Reuben said, familiar with the practice of traffickers and money remitters for the Cartel using burner phones and frequently discontinuing use of their cell phones to avoid detection from law enforcement. "So, when Tio contacts you, what other information does he provide?"

"How much money they have and when it will be ready to be picked up."

"Do you pick the money up in these different locations?"

Chico shook his head vigorously. "No. I have somebody that works for me in TJ. He drives to California and picks up the money."

"Okay," Reuben said, rubbing his eyes. "So is Tio your real uncle, or do you just call him that?"

"Yes, he is my uncle, and lives in Culiacan."

"How does he get the phone numbers of these people in California that have the drug proceeds?" Reuben asked.

"I don't know, and I don't ask. That's not my business."

"Last question," Reuben asked. "How often do these different locations provide money?"

"Each place usually provides money twice a month, but not at the same time. Tio does not know the amount for sure, just an estimate. I decide when to pick up the money. I send my guy and instruct him where to go so that he doesn't even have to contact the people in each place, that way if he ever gets stopped, he doesn't even have a phone number for the people with the money."

"Provide us with some information that leads to a couple of million -dollar seizures, and that recording of you and Tito speaking about robbing another member of Cartel will be destroyed and you won't have to worry about it again."

Chico felt sick at his stomach at the thought of anybody from the cartel realizing where he was at that moment and what he had told the DEA agents sitting in front of him. Chico had always felt the responsibility of looking out for Tito and carried the weight of that responsibility with him. He refused to let Tito be killed in some Vegas prison. He didn't believe that the DEA agents would release the call which would undoubtedly result in Tito being murdered in his Vegas jail cell, but he couldn't be sure, especially about the Hispanic agent, so he decided to answer their questions until he could get back to Mexico and figure things out.

As the conversation concluded, Chico agreed to contact by text as soon as he got to Tijuana. Chico stood up and shook hands with Reuben and Tyler. Reuben provided some cash so that Chico could find his way down to Tijuana without having to risk being seen in the presence of law enforcement officers.

"Think we'll ever see him again?" Reuben asked after Chico had left the area.

"If we can make a couple of good money seizures off his information, I don't care if we never see him again."

Chapter 11
El, Paso, Texas

Monday, August 28

Around 7:00 p.m., the sun was about to make its descent behind the horizon in the El Paso skyline. Rod knew that they had about half an hour until sunset, and an hour before darkness. He knew how difficult the job became in darkness, but before his worries could start to build, Blanco's phone dinged with a WhatsApp message.

The sender of the message identified himself as Oscar's courier, Pablo.

"I have the 50 t-shirts on sale and am five minutes away from the Home Depot," the message stated. Rod looked on as Blanco, the new DEA informant, received the message.

"Meet me in the parking lot on row 13 near the street, as far away from the store as possible. I'll take your vehicle and be back in 30," Blanco replied in Spanish after getting approval from Rod to send the message

"Ok," Pablo replied.

Blanco nervously shifted in his seat. He wanted to get out of the car but did not want to risk being seen by someone he knew.

"It's going to work out," Rod tried assuring him. We're professionals, and have done operations like this hundreds of times. If you knew how many drug traffickers in El Paso had been informants for DEA, you would not believe me. The reason you did not know they were informants is because we are good at what we do. If they provide enough information, then they work off their charge and never have to spend a night in jail. It works out great for them and us."

"All these informants you speak of, did they all have families here in Texas?" Blanco asked.

"Most of them," Rod said, not divulging too much information. "Everybody has leverage that causes them to work for us. Everybody. We find that leverage and use it so that we can take drugs off the street."

"Maybe most of them had families, but how many were getting dope from the Guardianes del Golfo instead of from El Jefe and the Cartel de Culiacan?" Blanco asked, wiping the sweat form his forehead.

"I'll admit," Rod said, "This is the first."

* * *

A mile and a half away, Ana Lucia noticed a Chevrolet Tahoe with Mexican license plates pull into the parking lot of Home Depot. The driver was a short Hispanic male that looked around nervously.

"I think I've got him in sight," Ana Lucia put out over the DEA car to car radio. "This guy is about to pee his pants."

As soon as her transmission ended, Rod came over the radio.

"CI confirms that he just received a message from the courier telling him he arrived. CI texted that he will be there in two minutes."

"That's got to be the courier," Ana Lucia responded. "Nobody else has pulled onto that row in the last few minutes. Trevor and I will approach the courier and see if we can get consent to search the vehicle."

"Okay," Mitch, the supervisor said. "Be careful, and make sure he doesn't get a chance to get that phone and send a message to anybody back in Mexico."

"Yes sir," Ana Lucia said confidently, as she hopped out of the vehicle, and met up with Trevor, the young mixed-race agent that had impressed on surveillance during the operation the week before.

"Let's seize some dope," Ana Lucia said as they started walking toward the frightened looking drug courier.

* * *

Pablo Torres was a chubby 20-year old male from a small farm in Central Mexico. He decided early in life that he wasn't exceptionally talented at anything that would be able to provide him with a comfortable living, so when the members of the Guardianes del Golfo approached his family one day several years earlier requesting their "permission" to use the land to store shipments of what everyone knew to be cocaine, Pablo realized that he was going to be involved in the drug world like so many other young men in the Mexican culture.

His decision to not resist the requests of the Guardianes del Golfo or GDG, employees boiled down to two reasons. First, Pablo was assured that his entire family would be murdered gruesomely if he refused to work with them. Second, and a nice benefit, was that he was going to be compensated with much more cash than he could earn as a farmer.

Weighing the benefits and consequences of a life as a drug trafficker from the comforts of your family farm deep in Mexico still did not prepare Pablo for the request made to him by his contacts at the GDG. It was one thing to operate in your own country, and hope that if you were stopped, it would be by one of the corrupt law enforcement officers that would take a bribe to ensure your release. It was different to be requested to move into rival cartel territory, living in a residence in Cartel de Culiacan controlled Chihuahua, and then driving GDG shipments of cocaine through Mexico and into the United States.

It was only the second time he had made the run from Chihuahua to El Paso. The previous time he was informed that he was going to be followed by a Mexican Police Officer. Pablo had noticed the black SUV following behind him as he made the four-hour journey from Chihuahua into Juarez and then El Paso, and it had given him a sense of comfort. Yet he was on his own once he reached Texas. Pablo's predetermined meet location had been within a 10-minute drive of the border, and he made it back to Mexico safely, but that was just the first trip. He had not yet mastered the necessity of playing it cool. His nerves still got the best of him, and sweat slowly dripped down the side of his head as he exited his ten year old

Chevrolet Tahoe and looked for the contact that he was supposed to meet at the Home Depot off the 10 freeway in El Paso.

Looking to the right and left, and then behind him, Pablo did not see any signs of the man that he was supposed to be meeting. Pablo cursed under his breath as he began pacing back and forth, regretting the decision he made back at the farm several months earlier, but inwardly knowing that there had been no other choice.

The one previous delivery had gone without a hitch. The customer had been present as soon as he arrived at the parking lot of a nearby movie theatre, and he had relaxed in the air conditioning of the theatre while the customer had taken the car back to another location to unload the dope. But here Pablo was going to have to hang around the Home Depot for at least an hour, trying to not be suspicious while being equally anxious to get out of there as soon as possible and return to Mexico. He thought about which would be worse, prison in an American cell, or confrontation with a Mexican trafficker from the Cartel de Culiacan and decided he would rather be in an American prison. At least he would be alive. But he still valued his freedom and did not want to go to jail. He had too much to look forward to. Heck, he had not even been with a woman yet, one thing he was planning to check off his list very soon upon returning to Chihuahua.

The sweat continued to pour down Pablo's face as he looked for his contact. The panic began to build up in his chest, so much so that he was having a hard time breathing. He knew that the Cartel guys would be sickened at how soft and scared he looked at that moment, but they were not the ones putting their lives and freedom at risk. Pablo rubbed the small Jesus Malverde figurine in his pocket, the patron saint of drug trafficking. Pablo asked for safe guidance and return to Mexico. As soon as Pablo opened his eyes, his gaze fell on a man and a woman approaching him. The female looked Hispanic, and possible the guy with her, but one thing was certain. They were not Blanco, the person he was supposed to meet, which could only mean one thing.

The cops had found him. Fear gripped Pablo so strongly he let out a little stream of urine as he considered whether he should run for freedom.

* * *

"Hey," Ana Lucia attempted to say casually as she and Trevor strolled up to Pablo.

"No habla inglés," he immediately said, as he had been instructed to do.

"No problem," Ana Lucia countered, switching to Spanish, "we can do this in Spanish if you'd prefer."

The young courier slowly raised his gaze from the ground and met the eyes of the two DEA agents. The fear they saw in Pablo's eyes was not something they were accustomed to seeing. It almost elicited sympathy from Ana Lucia.

Pablo stuck his hands up in the air and backed against the car. Sensing the trafficker in front of them was not a danger, and not wanting to make a scene, Trevor motioned for the young man to put his hands down. Trevor did not know much Spanish, so the extent of his involvement would be limited to motions and backing up the more experienced Ana Lucia.

"How did you know we are police?" Ana Lucia quietly asked.

Pablo's gaze had returned to the ground, and he just shrugged. Trevor gave a confused look to Ana Lucia. In his encounters and interviews with drug dealers during the first few years of his career, he had never come across one that seemed so scared. He was used to denials of knowledge of the drugs, denials of ownership of the drug laden vehicle, and a tough exterior that indicated the trafficker was not going to become a snitch.

One thing he had never noticed, which he did in this instance, was the small dark spot against the crotch of the khaki pants of the courier, an indication that the courier had peed in his pants.

Ana Lucia adjusted flawlessly. She put her hand on Pablo's left shoulder. "Do you have any weapons?"

Pablo shook his head, still refusing to look up.

"Since you won't look up at me, then I assume you know why we are here?"

Pablo made no motion to indicate he was going to say anything.

"We know that there is cocaine in this vehicle."

Pablo's shoulders dropped. He started breathing heavily.

"We are going to drive your car to another location where there won't be as many people. While Trevor is driving us over there, you are going to tell me how to open the hidden compartment. Okay?"

"Okay."

Ana Lucia smiled. Too easy.

* * *

Trevor pulled in the back of a parking lot of an abandoned Best Buy.

Rod sent Blanco home, instructing the informant that they would call him if anything further was needed, but assuring Blanco that he had upheld his end of the deal that had been made to prevent Blanco's daughter from being taken by Child Protective Services and separating her from her mother. That had seemed to momentarily appease the trafficker.

As Rod arrived in the parking lot, he thanked Trevor for providing backup for Ana Lucia, but as Ana Lucia's partner, Rod took Trevor's place and spoke with Ana Lucia and the young, scared, drug courier.

"What do we know?" Rod asked.

"So far," Ana Lucia began, "Pablo has revealed how to open the hidden compartment. There is a switch and a button in the glove compartment. If the switch is turned to the left, and the button is pressed twice, it opens this trap underneath the rear passenger seat. Give it a try."

Rod looked at the young courier nervously shifting side to side outside the vehicle. "Looks like it didn't take much for you to get that out of him."

"No, he's terrified. He said this is only the second time he has made a delivery. I think he's too scared to lie."

A sound came from below the rear passenger seat, as a small opening appeared. Ana Lucia pushed it down, revealing an opening underneath the car where the drug traffickers had managed to conceal 50 kilograms of cocaine, spreading across the bottom side of the rear passenger seat, and stacked on top of each other in rows of two kilograms.

As she pulled the kilograms out, Rod placed the young trafficker in handcuffs, something that would have normally been done at the onset of the encounter, but had not been carried out due to the unique circumstances of Pablo looking like he might literally suffer a heart attack on the street in front of them.

Rod, always the one to look for avenues to seize more dope or more money, looked over at Pablo and shook his head in disappointment. There was no way this guy would ever cut it as a DEA informant. He had peed his pants for God's sake. But to his surprise, Pablo approached Rod and Ana Lucia, and offered to be an informant before the question was even raised.

Usually the informants that DEA utilized had to be thoroughly convinced to carry out their betrayal, and that was only successful with a significant amount of leverage or motivation, much like they had with Blanco and threatening to orphan his child and take the girl away from her mother if he hadn't worked with them.

Rod leaned over to Ana Lucia and said with noticeable doubt, "Not sure we want him or need him."

"I'll have to let him down easy," Ana Lucia said.

By that point, Pablo was in full self-preservation mode. He decided he was not going to an American jail. He would not make it longer than a year. He would not go to jail for something that he had been forced to do.

"I know things that can help you," Pablo said.

"Like what?"

He looked around nervously. "This vehicle is not from the Cartel de Culiacan. It is from the Guardianes del Golfo."

Ana Lucia and Rod both nodded, acknowledging that Pablo was being truthful.

"What can you provide for us?" Ana Lucia asked.

"The next time I come back to the US, I will let you know. Next time you just arrest the guy I deliver the vehicle to."

"We can't let you back into Mexico. We have nothing to ensure that you would ever come back," Ana Lucia said.

"But I would, I promise!"

"Sorry, but we can't take promises from drug dealers."

"I should have never done this," Pablo said, starting to cry. "They are stupid for using me. If their airplane would not have crashed a few weeks ago, then I would never be here. Now I'm going to die in jail."

At the mention on the airplane, the two DEA agents looked at each other.

If this group from the GDG had an airplane, then they likely had access to much more dope than originally thought. Maybe the GDG was moving large shipments of cocaine through this area instead of the smaller portions the DEA suspected. The interesting light bulb seemed to pop up for both Rod and Ana Lucia at the same moment. If this group from the GDG had a plane before, then there was only a matter of time before they got one again. Poor Pablo was probably being used until the Cartel got access to another plane, and he was just a casualty of war in the meantime, a pawn that could be used and quickly forgotten and cast aside.

Maybe this is something that we can exploit further, both agents seemed to think as they looked at each other, and then back at Pablo.

* * *

After the tears dried up, Pablo mustered all the resolve he could and gave the DEA agents the very leverage and reason they needed to justify allowing him to return to Mexico and operate as a DEA informant in Mexico.

"This is only 50 kilograms, but I can guarantee there will be hundreds and hundreds of kilograms of cocaine coming through soon, especially once we get another airplane."

"When will that be?" Ana Lucia asked.

"Two months maximum."

"Are you a pilot?"

"No."

"Then why will they need you or keep you around?"

"I'll stay at the stash location in Chihuahua and watch the house, which is what they told me I was going to be doing at the beginning."

"Our bosses won't approve you going back to Mexico, especially if there is no reason for you to return to the US," Ana Lucia said, trying to bait Pablo to provide them with the reason that they could use to justify to her supervisor for releasing Pablo.

"My family on the farm," Pablo said. "If you can get all the hundreds of kilos coming, can you get my family out of Mexico and bring them to the US?"

"No, probably not," Ana Lucia admitted honestly. "But if you can get us...say... a hundred kilograms of cocaine, whether it is one seizure of five seizures, then I will talk with the prosecutor about dropping all charges against you. Anything else you provide in addition to that once the charges are dropped, you will be rewarded financially. You could use that money to pay for your family to come to the United States. Obviously, we would try and make a seizure, so it wasn't obvious that you were involved."

Pablo considered the proposal.

"I'll do it, whatever it takes," Pablo said. "I hate the drug dealers. I never wanted to even do this, but I was afraid my family would be murdered, so if by working with you I can protect them, then that is what I will do."

Ana Lucia and Rod knew that was a common sentiment felt by many drug traffickers forced to work with the drug cartels.

"While you are in Chihuahua, you have to maintain contact with one of our DEA counterparts working in Juarez," Ana Lucia told Pablo.

"Why not you?" Pablo asked

"Because he is closer and will help you much quicker if you need it."

"I don't trust the Mexican Police, and he shouldn't either...especially in Juarez."

"I know, Pablo," Ana Lucia said, "but this guy has been there a few years. He is a gringo but speaks Spanish fluently. If you need anything while you are in Chihuahua, let him know and he will arrange to meet you, okay?"

The young man nodded. "Okay. If you trust him then I will too."

Rod admired how much trust and rapport Ana Lucia had built with Pablo in such a short amount of time. Pablo looked at her as his savior for keeping him out of jail and would have likely worshipped the ground she walked on had she let him. Plus, it did not hurt that Pablo was attracted to her but at the same time knew she was way out of his league.

Rod made the phone calls with Daniel, the DEA agent in Juarez that they had met at the SOD Conference the week earlier. In his typical brash and borderline vulgar approach, Daniel had jokingly insinuated that he knew it was only a matter of time before Ana Lucia came crawling to him asking for help. Stroking the veteran agent's ego, Rod mockingly replied that the reason he made the call to Daniel instead of Ana Lucia, was because he could not trust her to keep everything professional. That elicited the response Rod knew would come, and they quickly talked the rules of the business.

Allowing Pablo to go into Mexico was not something that was allowed for most informants, especially since they already had evidence to arrest Pablo, and there was no assurance that he would return to the US. It was possible that Pablo would go to Mexico and never be heard from again, but Pablo wanted out of the game, and knew this was the only way to do it without going to jail or being killed for refusal to work with the GDG. In the meantime, Ana Lucia and Rod would consider Pablo as a source of information, and they would document paperwork which confirmed DEA had seized 50 kilograms of cocaine from an abandoned vehicle in the parking lot of a Home Depot in El Paso, instead of in a car driven by Pablo.

It would not be easy...or exactly within DEA rules, but Ana Lucia and Rod decided to let Pablo return to Chihuahua with hopes he would update them on shipments of GDG cocaine to El Paso. The Special Operations Division back in Washington, DC was very interested in finding out as much information as possible about how and why the GDG had decided to start using routes and destinations within territory known to be controlled by their rivals at the Cartel de Culiacan, especially after previously coming to an agreement.

For Ana Lucia and Rod, the reasoning behind allowing Pablo to return to Mexico was simple, get more dope and arrest more drug dealers. If it did not work out, then there would be one more fugitive, a low-level drug courier. If it did work out, then DEA could potentially seize hundreds more kilograms of cocaine and arrest dozens more traffickers. It was a potential reward they considered worth the risks. Had they known the far-reaching consequences of the actions that would result from this decision, then the operation would have been shut down instantly and without question.

* * *

"Felipe turned his vehicle around at the border in Juarez as soon as he had safely escorted Pablo through El Jefe controlled territory in Chihuahua and Juarez and into El Paso. Making sure the drug courier's vehicle made it through without being stopped by Mexican law enforcement was the easiest $1,000 Felipe ever made. Working for the Mexican Federal Police, the Cartel de Culiacan, and the GDG, all at the same time, was a different matter. Even for a man that prided himself on his ability to be organized, this was getting to be too much, and before the recent trip to Sinaloa called by El Jefe, Felipe had decided that he was going to disclose the information about the GDG stash pad in Chihuahua. He just wasn't going to disclose that he knew about the stash location because he had been paid to escort the narcotics laden vehicle into Texas. That part would be left out because it would get him killed.

Felipe drove to a local bar and waited for his contact to show up. The woman, who had been his love interest for several months, but was now one of the myriads of informants Felipe used to acquire intelligence, was an American CPB officer based in El Paso. She was a 50-year old divorcee that craved the attention of a younger good-looking law enforcement officer like Felipe. When he called, she answered. She knew that Felipe would provide her with a night of passion as payment for her time and information, and she was perfectly okay with that. Plus, she thought Felipe was a loyal law enforcement officer. She had no way of knowing his true intentions, or that he was working at the behest of the Cartel de Culiacan.

A couple days earlier, Felipe interviewed the management and staff of the restaurant in Durango where El Jefe's wife had been poisoned. The waiter had been identified as Jose Padilla, but he had immediately disappeared. Felipe had gone to Padilla's apartment in Durango, only to find it cleaned out.

Mostly cleaned out. There was one thing Felipe found that the law enforcement officers that previously searched Padilla's apartment did not find. Moving the refrigerator from the wall, Felipe found a piece of paper that had at one time been attached with a magnet. The piece of paper had managed to slid off and fall in the crack between the wall and the refrigerator. The phone number had a Juarez area code, with the name Maria written on it.

Felipe had used his contacts at the Mexican telephone company, Tel Cel, to determine the user of the phone number, and learned that it was registered to Maria Lopez out of Juarez. A quick search of social media revealed Maria was a pretty young Mexican woman that usually posted on social media multiple times per day. However, there had not been any posts since the death of El Jefe's wife.

The Mexican Police Officer provided the name of Maria Lopez and Jose Padilla to his CBP contact, and occasional lover, and asked her to check on border crossings. If she could provide the information instantaneously, then Felipe assured her that they could go get a motel and spend the rest of the night together. The woman looked longingly at the good looking younger Mexican Federal Police officer, and made a phone call.

She returned moments later. No records of border crossings for Jose Padilla. However, Lupe Lopez had crossed the border the day after El Jefe's wife was killed. She had provided a contact address for her grandmother living in Los Angeles.

Felipe smiled. Jose Padilla had been safe when he fled Mexico after poisoning El Jefe's wife, leaving no trace of where he was going. His girlfriend, however, had. Felipe fulfilled his end of the bargain that night, and then booked a plane ticket to Los Angeles."

Chapter 12
Chihuahua, Mexico

Thursday, August 31

Toro dug the grit from underneath his fingernails as he lay on the ground in the woods watching the stash location being used by GDG associates. The information about this specific residence was provided by Felipe, an individual that El Jefe himself personally introduced after the communication devices were passed out at his ranch several days earlier. The way the man moved and spoke, Toro knew that he was a cop. If he was at El Jefe's house, then Felipe had obviously been providing valuable law enforcement information for a considerable length of time. Toro hid the disgust he felt of dealing with a corrupt police officer, and accepted Felipe's number as directed by El Jefe. Felipe indicated that he had come across information that would need to be handled by someone with Toro's capabilities and resources.

Shortly after his meeting with Padre Miguel, Felipe contacted Toro by phone, and explained that he was aware of a stash location in a remote area of Chihuahua that was being used by members of the Guardianes del Golfo to transport shipments of cocaine through Cartel de Culiacan controlled territory and into West Texas, an area designated unofficially as belonging to customers of El Jefe, an offense that warranted death for those involved.

Based on the circumstances described by Felipe, Toro decided that this would be a different operation from normal. The mission was not to go in and kill everybody. There would likely be some casualties, depending on how many people Toro's team came across, but Toro had stressed the importance of making sure that at the very least, two people were taken alive. Toro wanted the opportunity to personally speak with Oscar, the individual Felipe indicated was responsible for coordinating the drug trafficking activities for the GDG in Cartel de Culiacan controlled territory. Doing so would award them the option of getting to question someone from the rival cartel about any possible involvement from the GDG in the murder of El Jefe's wife.

The other individual they would leave alive, at least temporarily, was the young courier, Pablo. There would likely be other individuals there, but those two had the most important roles. How Felipe came across this information and knew the names and jobs of each person, Toro did not know and did not ask.

Toro explained to his team that it was their duty to find out where the cocaine was going, and what trafficker in the US had betrayed the Cartel de Culiacan by using the GDG for their shipment. El Jefe had already authorized the execution of such a traitor.

Toro's group consisted of 10 men, each with their own talents and vices. Leon was the unquestioned second in charge of the group, not just due to his physical presence but also his personality. Leon was by far the largest of the group, standing at 6'5" and weighing 255 pounds of solid muscle. He had a natural thirst for blood despite a privileged upbringing that included a private school education as a kid that led to an academic scholarship at the University of Guadalajara. Eventually however, the dark nature inside him won out, and he became enthralled in the underground world of street fighting, where Leon had maintained an unbeaten record despite more than 30 fights. When the opportunity came to join Toro's group as an assassin, and get paid even better to hurt people, Leon had given up any college aspirations and joined. His aggressive personality sometimes put him at odds with the more reserved leader in Toro, but when the time came for an operation, they worked together flawlessly. Although Toro was physically smaller, Leon was impressed with the speed and viciousness of his strikes in hand to hand combat. Still, Leon did not think that Toro could take him one on one if it ever came to that, which he felt like at some point would happen. Until it did, Leon did his job to the best of his ability, with a healthy appetite for death and destruction.

* * *

Each man of the 10-member team used ear buds with attached, small microphones, so they could communicate instantly with each other. Several members, to include Toro, were positioned in front of the residence from different locations in the woods close to 50 meters away from the front door. The other half of the team, led by the bloodthirsty Leon, were in the woods behind the residence. They had found a lone dirt path with tire tracks on it that looked to be a couple of days old. Leon assumed that this would be the path of the vehicle that would deliver the dope to the location.

Toro's instructions were to wait until the cocaine arrived at the residence before initiating the attack. Only then would Toro and his team have the evidence needed to prove Oscar and the people with him were moving drugs that did not belong to the Cartel de Culiacan.

Felipe had his own reasons for wanting Toro's team to wipe out everybody in the stash location being used by the GDG. Mainly, Felipe wanted to erase any trace of evidence that proved he had provided safe passage through Mexico and into Texas for the GDG courier transporting the cocaine. Felipe, driving his black SUV, had provided "security" for the courier, Pablo, on his first delivery into Texas a week earlier.

Felipe had considered that Toro and his group of hit men might look at Oscar's contacts on his phone and discover the phone number that Oscar had used to communicate with Felipe to inquire about providing security, but the Federal Policeman was very careful. The phone Felipe used to communicate with Oscar only had one number in it, and Felipe was careful to not use it to communicate with anyone else. Prior to contacting Toro and providing the information about the GDG stash location, Felipe broke the phone used to communicate with Oscar, and discarded the remnants out the window on the side of the street, so that there would not be anything further connecting him with the GDG workers about to be killed.

Toro replayed the conversation with Felipe in his head as he laid on the ground in the woods in the early morning hours. Felipe's reluctance to provide any actual evidence troubled him, but since El Jefe had personally vouched for Felipe, Toro was going to do as he was told.

The silence of the morning was finally disturbed as Leon came across the radio. "I have a Land Rover coming down the dirt path. It is about 1 kilometer from the residence."

"Very good. If the vehicle goes to the rear of the residence, we will wait for your signal until we go in. Remember the plan," Toro said, urging his team members to leave Pablo and Oscar alive if possible.

"10-4," Leon said, preparing his AK-47.

* * *

"I see two people moving in the front of the residence," Toro said to his team. "Leon, how many do you see back there with you?"

"I see two as well, the guy pulling up will make three."

"Okay, so we have five. Give us a heads up and we can take care of the two in front so that they won't run to the back," Toro said.

Toro moved into a crouched position and gave a hand signal to the guy beside him to slowly start approaching the residence. They did not suspect the occupants in the front would be on the lookout, especially since the load car was arriving in the rear, but you could never be careful enough.

Toro stopped 20 feet from the residence, concealed behind the last tree before the front door. To his left, through a window with open blinds, Toro could see the back of someone's head. It appeared the individual was sitting on a couch or chair and watching television on the opposite wall. Toro saw a second person walk from the area near the television, toward the other side of the residence. The blinds on the side of the house to Toro's right were closed though, so he would not know where the man was when they decided to enter the residence.

As Toro scanned the front of the property and mentally noted where his other team members were, Leon began speaking over the radio. "The guy that drove to the rear of the property is out of the Land Rover and meeting with one of the two guys standing in the back. One guy looks like he is the boss. The other guy from the residence is just standing around while the other two talk."

"Let's assume the guy that looks like the boss is Oscar," Toro said quickly.

"Copy," Leon responded. He was more than ready to challenge the leader at some point down the road, but during the midst of an operation, he kept all communication at a respectful level. These team members might be taking orders from him one day soon.

"The driver is back to the Land Rover," Leon called out.

This is it, Toro thought. If he comes out with something, Leon is going to pounce immediately.

"Duffel bag being brought out. We will leave the boss in the back and take out the driver and the other guy on my command. Ready up front?"

"Ready."

"Okay," Leon said, "we will attack from the side, so we will be shooting out to the woods. You guys up front make sure your bullets don't come back towards us."

"Copy that," Toro said. "We will enter the residence before we engage."

A brief pause, as Leon slowly moved forward, trying to not make any sounds in the woods. Then, "Go."

The early morning calm exploded with a burst of gunfire. Leon's burst from his AK-47 raked the man that had driven up in the Land Rover. The other sicarios in the back jumped up at the same time and were firing shots. The courier from the Land Rover, and the individual from the residence standing to the side were both shot more than 20 times each before their bodies hit the ground.

A stray bullet had grazed Oscar's left arm, and another hit directly in his left shin, but he was alive. Oscar thought it was a miracle he had survived, not realizing he was intentionally left alive. Oscar turned to hobble back to the residence, until he crashed to the ground with what seemed like a mountain of a man on top of his back. Before he knew what was going on, Oscar was rolled over, looking up at Leon. Grasping Oscar by the throat with his left hand, Leon delivered a punishing blow to the man's face, instantly breaking his nose and cracking several teeth. Oscar's world turned black with Leon on top of him.

* * *

As soon as Leon gave the signal from the back, Toro shot through the front door and entered, immediately looking to his right for the man that had recently gone out of sight. As soon as Toro went through the door, another member was on his heels, looking to the left.

Toro encountered a tall, slender man, who had only recently arrived at the location a few days earlier, to officially run the location so that Oscar could take off. He was not expecting the welcoming that Toro and his crew provided. The man instantly fell to the ground as Toro quickly fired two well-placed rifle shots into the man's right knee. As the man fell forward, Toro used the butt of his rifle to uppercut the man, sending his head jerking against the back of the wall. Toro slung his rifle to his back and removed zip ties from his tactical belt, and immediately bound the man's hands and legs.

While Toro was taking care of the man to the right, another member of the team named Miguel immediately went to clear the left side of the room, where Pablo had been sitting on the couch eating a bowl of cereal. Seeing the guns and hearing the gunfire left Pablo terrified, certain of his impending death. The fight or flight instinct did not kick in. He would not fight, and he could not run away. Both were pointless. So, he did the first thing that came to mind, he fell on the ground face first with his hands up, begging the intruders to spare his life. Perhaps the tears rolling down his face, and the small pool of urine collecting on the floor where he peed himself, caused Miguel to briefly pause before inflicting too much pain. He quickly pulled out his zip ties and bound Pablo's hands and feet, while the other three men on the team stormed through the remaining two bedrooms, looking for any additional occupants, but finding none.

Less than 30 seconds after the first shot was fired, two men were dead, and three others subdued. Toro and his team hadn't suffered any casualties, but he gave the customary instruction for everybody to check themselves regardless, for sometimes in the heat of the moment, the adrenaline coursing through the veins could lead a man to not realize he had suffered a potentially mortal wound. Everybody checked in and confirmed that they were okay.

Toro went to his microphone to provide further instructions. "Miguel and I will bring our two captives outside with you Leon. The remainder of the team needs to split up. Burn the two dead bodies and search the house for evidence. Report to me outside when you are done. I will see what information we can pull out of these three."
* * *

Toro and Miguel dragged their two captives outside and let them sit against a tree outside the residence. Leon dragged a still unconscious Oscar to the same spot. Pablo looked over at his blood-spattered boss's face and closed his eyes in sheer terror at the pain he was sure he was going to experience. Toro and Leon both noted Pablo's reaction, and kept him to the side while they spoke to the tall man that Toro had encountered in the residence.

"Miguel, go get one of the kilograms out of that duffel bag, and bring it over," Toro said, as Leon towered over the scared and detained men, staring at them without speaking.

Miguel quickly returned with a kilogram and handed it to Toro. The leader of the group inspected it closely, looking at the G stamp in the middle of the kilogram. From his experience, Toro knew all

110

the symbols that were used by the Cartel de Culiacan to claim ownership of their dope, and the G symbol was not one of them.

Toro held the kilogram in his left hand and looked at Leon beside him. "Correct me if I'm wrong, Leon, but I don't believe this symbol is one that El Jefe uses on his kilograms."

"It definitely is NOT," Leon spat as he looked back at the men disgustingly.

The tall man tried to appear calm despite the circumstances, while Pablo made no such effort to hide his fears, and was openly weeping and shaking, believing the worst was about to come. Oscar was still unconscious on the ground.

"Then that means you," Toro said pointing at three men, "do not work for El Jefe or the Cartel de Culiacan. Yet here you are, moving product in his territory."

Toro said nothing else, and simply stared, waiting for a response. When none came, Toro spoke up again, "Tell me why you are here."

The tall man did not say anything and shook his head and shrugged his shoulders.

"What is your role?" Toro asked.

The man stuttered as he tried to find the words to say, finally responding, "I came here to relieve Oscar."

"And this is Oscar?" Toro asked, nodding at the man Leon had knocked out during the assault.

The tall man nodded his head.

"And when did you get to this residence?" Toro asked.

"Two days ago. I promise, I had nothing to do with anything else that went on previously."

"Okay," Toro said calmly, looking at Leon with the knowledge that this man was not going to be able to provide much useful information on the past drug shipments out of the location. "Now I am going to ask this question one time, and one time only. You are not with El Jefe and the Cartel de Culiacan. What cartel are you working for?"

"I was sent over. By...by..."

"By the Guardianes del Golfo!" Leon shouted at the man, finishing his sentence for him. The man looked up at Leon, and slowly nodded his head, knowing that his fate was sealed, and accepting the reality of the situation.

"One more question," Toro said. "What do you know about the murder of El Jefe's wife?"

The man looked from Leon over to Toro as he leaned back on the tree behind him. Once again, he did not seem sure how to answer. A straight denial would result in either torture or death. An admission would be equally bad, but he gave up hope that he was going to live through the day. Since he was going to die either way, he decided to die with loyalty to the GDG. "I don't know anything."

Toro looked over at Leon and shrugged his shoulders. He then turned his gaze upon Pablo, who was looking down at the ground, scared to even look in the direction of the two hit men. "Are you sure that is your answer?" Toro asked, giving the man one final opportunity. The man did not respond.

With a simple nod of his head, Toro gave Leon permission to execute the man. Smiling, Leon put away his weapon. He had no intention of shooting this man. Instead, he delivered a sudden and vicious kick. The man's head jerked back so hard that Toro would not have doubted if his neck were broken. As the man fell to the ground on his side, Leon walked over him, and stomped on his head for almost a minute, until the man was no longer recognizable, his skull caving in and blood soaking the ground around him.

The blood had also spurted onto Leon's boots, as well as Pablo sitting nearby. Toro looked at the chubby 20-year old. "Now it's your turn," Toro said.

* * *

Pablo's fears had betrayed him, and somehow, on only his second trip into the US to deliver cocaine, he had been arrested by the DEA. His agreement with Special Agent Ana Lucia Rodriguez to become a DEA informant and provide her with information that led to many more seizures of drugs was the only thing that kept him out of jail.

More scared of spending a lifetime in prison than he was of death, Pablo agreed to update the DEA agent in Juarez of his next shipment of cocaine, even telling SA Daniel Benson that he would let him know the exact route he would use to drive the dope through Juarez into El Paso, and the time that he would going down that route.

Not knowing that Toro had no intention of killing him in that moment, Leon's brutal murder of the other man had the desired effect of getting Pablo to tell them exactly what they wanted to hear.

"What is your name?" Toro asked.

"Pablo."

"What do you do for this organization, Pablo?"

"I drive the product from here to El Paso, and meet with somebody there."

"Very good. I'm glad you decided to be honest with us."

"Please don't kill me," Pablo begged the two men. "I will tell you whatever you want, I swear."

"Good, so tell me, are you supposed to drive this dope to El Paso today?" Toro asked.

Pablo nodded.

"Who do you meet with in Texas?" Toro asked.

Thinking quickly, Pablo replied, "I just leave my car in the Home Depot parking lot, and a man comes to get it and then brings it back to me about an hour or two later. I don't know who he is or what he looks like." The cracking of his voice gave the feeling of authenticity.

"You will still make that delivery today. El Jefe wants to know who has betrayed his trust."

Immediately realizing the precarious situation he was in, since he was supposed be followed into Texas by the DEA agent from Juarez, Pablo froze, unsure what to do. He didn't want to meet his end at the end of Leon's boot, so he simply nodded his head.

"Pablo," Toro asked, "what can you tell me about the murder of El Jefe's wife?"

Sensing an opportunity to provide information that he had overheard, he looked at Toro. "Around the same time that El Jefe's wife was killed, I saw Oscar looking at his phone at a message that came in, and he shook his head and muttered something about having to send money to a waiter! I didn't think anything about it at the time, but after the information came out about El Jefe's wife being poisoned at a restaurant, I wondered if the waiter that Oscar mentioned having to pay was the waiter that poisoned El Jefe's wife. You have to ask Oscar."

Leon's brow furrowed as he processed Pablo's statement.

Toro and Leon then looked over at Oscar, who had finally woken up.

"We intend to ask Oscar," Toro said.

* * *

Toro instructed Miguel to take Pablo away so that Oscar could be questioned alone. The leader of the stash location was now sitting up and leaning against one of the many trees in the area. He was moaning due to the pain he felt in his face, and his vision was blurry. The front of his brown t-shirt was stained with blood.

"I'm going to ask you questions, and you are going to give me answers. Understood?" Toro asked. Oscar leaned his head back against the tree and looked up at the sky.

"Answer!"

"Yes, okay," Oscar said.

Toro pulled out his cell phone to record the man's admission. "What city are we in?"

"Chihuahua."

"And who controls that territory?"

Oscar paused before answering. "El Jefe."

"Yet you are not working with El Jefe or anybody from Cartel de Culiacan, are you?"

"No."

"You admit that you are trespassing on Cartel de Culiacan controlled territory."

"I do what I'm told, just like you. I didn't decide to come here," Oscar said, starting to regain some of his vigor. "I was sent here."

"Who sent you here?" Toro asked.

"He's nobody. Just my contact. I'm sure he gets instructions from someone else, but I don't know that person."

"I think you know more than you think you do."

"I'm telling you that's all I know," Oscar said defiantly.

"Oscar," Toro said, standing up, "you will die one of two ways. Quick and painless, or messy, and at the hands of this man," Toro said, nodding his head over at Leon who smiled at the thought. "You see what he did to the guy that came to replace you? Can you see what's left of his head?"

Oscar stared at the blood and skull remnants left on the ground from the man's brutal death. He tried not to show fear, but in that moment, it was impossible. "What do you want to know?" Oscar asked.

"What do you know about the waiter that killed El Jefe's wife?" Toro asked.

Oscar closed his eyes and tried to breathe deeply as he considered how to respond.

"I know that the waiter's girlfriend lived in Juarez, but she is not there anymore."

"And how would you know that?" Toro asked, leaning over, and placing his hands on his knees. Oscar looked over again at what was left of the other man's head and convinced himself that nothing was worth that kind of death.

"I was instructed to pay the waiter enough money to get out of Mexico."

"So, you came to Chihuahua to move product in our territory and murder El Jefe's wife?"

"No, I didn't murder El Jefe's wife. And the GDG didn't murder her either." Oscar stopped what he was saying at that point.

"You work for the GDG, idiot," Leon broke in, unable to keep his silence any longer. "If you paid the killer, then of course it was your bosses that ordered the hit. Now tell us which one or else I will feed your brain and your heart to the fish in the Rio Conchos."

"No, look! My contact from the GDG, it is not the same guy that I spoke with regarding payment to the waiter. It was two separate guys."

Leon and Toro looked at each other. "Who was this other guy?" Toro asked.

"I don't know, he never gave me a name. He did not even give me a nickname. We just communicated through text."

"So, he could've been from the GDG, just a different contact?" Toro said.

"Well, yes, I suppose he could have been, but I don't believe he was, for one big reason."

"What reason is that?" Toro asked.

"Well we only communicated by text. I never met the guy face to face. But...well...I do not think he was a native Spanish speaker. Sometimes I would abbreviate certain words, and he would not understand it and respond incorrectly. It just gave me the sense that it wasn't somebody from the GDG, maybe somebody from another country, like a gringo or something."

"DEA, FBI, CIA? What do you think?" Toro asked.

"I have no clue. I just know that somehow, they knew I was here. They knew my phone number. They agreed not to tell anybody about my presence if I paid the waiter and flew him to Juarez."

Toro breathed deeply and stood up, looking at Leon.

"Tell me," Leon said, "how did this guy that contacted you get your number?"

"I have no clue, I swear."

"Did you communicate by telephone?" Toro asked.

"By WhatsApp," Oscar replied.

"Whoever it was, knew your contact phone number. The same number used to contact your bosses in the GDG?"

"Yes," Oscar said.

"Then it was probably the GDG," Leon said, looking at the two men.

"Or somebody that had identified that number already," Toro said. "Like the American government."

A long silence followed, as Toro and Leon considered the ramifications of the possibility that the Americans had somehow been involved in the murder of El Jefe's wife. Reason taught that the simplest explanation was also the most likely: The GDG put the hit out on El Jefe's wife. But the Americans would have thought that exact thing. What if they set it up to look like it was the GDG? Toro wondered what their motive would have been, other than once again interfering in the affairs of a foreign country.

"Where is the phone that you used to contact this person?" Leon asked.

"I got rid of it immediately," Oscar said. "I told my contact I had to get a new phone, so that there wouldn't be any question in case the waiter was caught."

Toro ended the recording on his phone and nodded at Leon. "I think we have the information we need."

"Do you mind if I take care of Oscar?" Leon asked.

Toro looked at the man whose eyes were defeated, in full acceptance of his impending fate. Toro nodded as he got up and went inside the residence.

* * *

"Who is supposed to receive this dope?" Leon asked, as Oscar sat there in his final moments of life.

Not wanting to betray Blanco, his old friend in El Paso that was receiving the dope, Oscar claimed that it was just some unknown contact in El Paso. Leon grabbed Oscar's hand and sliced off his right thumb, then asked the question again. After Oscar again refused to answer the question, Leon bent down and pulled the cell phone out of his pants pocket.

For a brief second, Oscar's eyes went wide as he realized that Blanco's number was stored on the phone that Leon held in his hands. "It's in there," Oscar admitted through gritted teeth. "The only number with an El Paso area code."

A quick search history confirmed the El Paso number that Oscar had been in contact with several times the previous week.

Leon now had all the information he needed and turned around to Oscar. The man had upheld his end of the bargain by providing information they needed, so Leon decided to allow him the decency of a quick death. Leon removed his handgun and placed one bullet directly between Oscar's eyes.

Chapter 13
Juarez, Mexico

Thursday, August 31

"I don't know what's going on. I haven't heard from him," Daniel said. The DEA agent from Juarez sat in his car, which was parked at a gas station just outside the city limits of the border city.

On the other end of the phone, Ana Lucia sighed with exasperation. "Pablo knew to call you as soon as he got in the car to drive the dope from Chihuahua to El Paso?"

"Yes," Daniel told her. "I spoke to him on the phone last night and confirmed the details."

"It doesn't make sense," Ana Lucia said. "About two hours ago Oscar sent a text to our informant, Blanco, and confirmed that Pablo had already left with the dope. Pablo should have sent a message at some point over the last two hours since he left."

"True, but Pablo doesn't know that you flipped the guy in El Paso and are getting all the messages sent to him. Maybe Pablo just decided he doesn't want to work with DEA and is going to take his chances with the Cartel."

"If that's the case, then we are going to hammer him," Ana Lucia said, pacing back and forth in the DEA El Paso office."

"It's weird, I just didn't get the vibe that Pablo was going to blow us off. He called me last night to give me the information. I still think he's coming, maybe something is wrong with his phone."

"If I've learned anything from this job, it's that there could be any number of reason things happen, and it might be something we haven't even considered."

"Well hey, I don't have anything on my calendar today," Daniel said. "I'm going to sit in my car for a couple more hours and watch the road for Pablo's vehicle. If he left Chihuahua a couple hours ago, as Oscar indicated on the text to Blanco, then Pablo should get here in the next hour or two. If I don't hear something after three hours, I'll take off."

"Okay," Ana Lucia said. "I'm going to talk to Blanco and have him confirm an ETA for Pablo, maybe that will give you a window to expect to see Pablo arrive in Juarez with the dope. If we find that guy, then we might just have the Border Patrol stop him before he gets into the US. Rod and I would love to talk to him and find out why the big crybaby didn't do what he said he was going to do."

"Sounds good, speak to you soon." Daniel ended the call and continued monitoring the traffic driving north into Juarez, which is the route that Pablo would take if he were delivering a shipment of dope through Juarez and into El Paso.

"Where are you Pablo?" Daniel said to himself, "and why haven't you sent me a message?"

* * *

Ana Lucia immediately called Blanco, the DEA informant in El Paso expecting to receive the shipment of dope later that day, and asked Blanco if he had heard anything else from Oscar, his friend in Chihuahua that was responsible for coordinating the shipment of dope. Everything had gone so smoothly on the first operation when Oscar sent Pablo to El Paso with 50 kilograms of cocaine, she should have known the second operation would hit a snag.

During their conversation, Blanco confirmed that during his most recent communication with Oscar, he had received confirmation that the courier had left two hours earlier.

"Can you send him another message and ask what time to expect the courier?" Ana Lucia asked.

"At this point I would be expected to communicate with the courier. Anything I sent to Oscar might seem suspicious," the DEA informant told Ana Lucia.

"Just humor me," she told Blanco. "We have our reasons. We just need to find out this information."

Blanco agreed, and told Ana Lucia he would call her back after speaking with Oscar.

About five minutes later, Ana Lucia answered her telephone as soon as the DEA informant's number popped up on the caller ID. "What's the word?" she asked.

"Well, it was kind of weird," Blanco said.

"How so?" the DEA agent asked, having placed the call on speaker phone so her partner Rod could overhear the conversation.

"I called Oscar and there was no answer, so then I sent him a WhatsApp message, asking what time the driver was going to get here with the product. Oscar immediately responded with the time the driver should get here."

"What's weird about that?" Ana Lucia asked, shrugging her shoulders at Rod in confusion.

"Well, Oscar didn't answer the call, but answered the text immediately, before he even had time to call the driver or send him a message. Something could have happened in the two hours since the driver left, a flat tire or a road-block, so Oscar would normally at least check with the driver to confirm everything was okay and he was still expecting to arrive at the same time. Oscar didn't do that though, which I thought was strange."

Ana Lucia thought about the reason for Oscar's failure to check with the driver. "We know that Oscar sent a security car with the driver, so maybe he thinks he would have heard something from the security guy if something had gone wrong."

"Maybe," Blanco said, sounding unconvinced.

"What time did Oscar say that the driver would get to your location?" Ana Lucia asked.

"3:30 p.m."

"That's less than two hours," Ana Lucia said, looking at her watch. "He must be on the way."

"Yes," Blanco said, wanting to end this transaction so that his interaction with the DEA would be over.

"Let me know if you hear anything else."

"Of course."

Ana Lucia looked at Rod. "We should head down to the border and wait for Pablo to show up. We will go with the plan to have Pablo stopped at the Border, but make it clear that we do the questioning," Rod told his partner.

Ana Lucia nodded her head in agreement. "Okay," she said, "but..."

"What's up?" Rod asked her.

"Something just doesn't feel right."

* * *

Daniel kept his eyes on the road leading into Juarez. He knew that this was the route that Pablo had told him that he would take, as it led toward the international border with the US. He also knew that Pablo should be coming by his location at any moment if he was supposed to get to El Paso when he was scheduled to deliver the narcotics laden vehicle to Blanco. Daniel scanned the radio to pick up a station that was worth listening to but could not find anything. He realized that it was not because there were not good music choices, but rather because he was restless. Like Ana Lucia in El Paso, he also had an uneasy feeling about the situation, and was concerned why Pablo had not made contact. The easiest and most likely scenario was that the young man just decided he did not want to work with DEA and had decided to stop contacting him. It would not be the first time an informant got cold feet and it would not be the last. Daniel told himself the worst-case scenario was that the guy had simply made the decision to stay loyal to the cartel.

As Daniel shifted in the seat of his gray Ford Explorer, his eyes suddenly narrowed. He saw a vehicle approaching that he recognized as the same make and model of the vehicle that he knew Pablo was driving. Years of surveillance and calling out vehicle types had made Daniel a pro at determining what kind of vehicle he was looking at.

He slowly put his Ford Explorer into drive and edged forward in the gas station parking lot toward the road, so that he could get a good look at the driver of the vehicle as it went by. Daniel had not met with Pablo, but Ana Lucia had provided a good enough description that he was certain he would be able to confirm the young man if he saw him in a vehicle.

As the Tahoe passed up the location, Daniel got a good look at the front seat of the vehicle. He picked up his binoculars which had been resting in the passenger seat of the Explorer, and quickly confirmed that the vehicle that had just passed by him had the license plate of the vehicle known to be driven by Pablo.

Daniel immediately phoned Ana Lucia.

"Hey, where are you?" Daniel asked.

"Rod and I are here at the Border, waiting at one of the offices off to the side. Any word from Pablo?"

"No, that little punk hasn't sent me any messages. However, I did just see his vehicle drive by me heading into Juarez. He should be at the border in the next 15 minutes."

"Okay, great. Well thanks for sitting there and confirming. We will be here and be ready to interview him after he is stopped."

Daniel continued to speak on the phone with the El Paso DEA agent as he followed behind Pablo's vehicle approximately 100 yards.

"Listen, the last time Pablo came, did he have anybody in the vehicle with him?" Daniel asked.

"No, it was just him," Ana Lucia confirmed, pacing back and forth in the small room with an interview table, while Rod stood outside talking to the contact from the Border Patrol that had granted them access to that specific room that was outfitted with recording devices so that all conversations would be monitored and recorded.

"Well, this time he has some company," Daniel said. "And the guy in the passenger seat looks like a freaking giant."

"Crap," Ana Lucia responded. "Well I guess that's why he didn't send you a message to let you know that he was on the way. He couldn't send a message because there was someone else in the car with him."

"Yeah, I suppose. But something else I noticed..." Daniel said, looking in his rearview mirror at all the vehicles coming up behind him, as well as those around him.

"Yeah?" Ana Lucia asked.

"Remember how Pablo said that he had a safety vehicle follow him? He told me that it was a black SUV."

"Yeah, I remember."

"Well I don't see a black SUV anywhere. There is no vehicle following him today. Why would that be?"

"I don't know. Maybe since he has taken two loads already, the crew he is working for thinks he will be safe."

"Maybe...but he is still a courier working for the GDG driving through territory controlled by the Cartel de Culiacan. That has not changed, nor the need for security. If he were to get stopped, he would be arrested and then instantly killed, and this whole entire operation would be compromised. If the GDG has gone to this much effort to move dope through Chihuahua and Juarez and into west Texas, they wouldn't get lazy and send a courier without security on just the third shipment."

Ana Lucia listened to Daniel's reasoning, and had to admit that he had a good point. She still felt that sense in the pit of her stomach that something was not as it seemed. Something was off.

"All good points. I'll be sure to ask Pablo after we arrest him and whoever is with him," Ana Lucia said.

"I'll follow behind until we get to the line for the check point," Daniel said. "I'll let you know what lane he is in and how far back he is so the BP agent can be ready.

"Sounds good," Ana Lucia said. "Thanks Daniel, I appreciate your help. Be careful."

"Will do," he responded, wondering who was in the passenger seat beside Pablo, and moving closer so that he might be able to get a good look at the man.

* * *

The Chevrolet Tahoe slowly moved forward as it approached the Ysleta Port of Entry, allowing vehicles into El Paso. During the several hour drive from Chihuahua to Juarez, Pablo had decided that he was most likely not going to live to see the sun rise the next morning, and that scared him so much that his brain almost shut down and he couldn't think. But the survival instinct inside his mind brought up the different scenarios that might possibly result in a non-fatal ending.

Pablo made sure to stay in the first of three lanes. On his previous entries into El Paso, he had been assured safe passage into Texas if he entered the second lane. If he went to lanes 1 or 3, then there was no assurance that he would be able to make it through, which was why Pablo wanted to take his chances. Better arrested by CPB going through Lane 1 than murdered by Leon somewhere in El Paso.

With the monstrous hit-man Leon sitting beside him, Pablo knew that once they made it into Texas, people were going to die, including him. If the DEA intercepted their vehicle once they got into El Paso, then there was no doubt in Pablo's mind that Leon would instantly kill him, and attempt to kill the DEA agents. The man beside him just had a scary desire for violence.

Of all the scenarios, Pablo was not sure if any of them would work, but it was likely the only chance he had. Perhaps a stop at the border by the Border Patrol might keep him alive, as well as the DEA agents in El Paso.

As his vehicle continued to wait in line, and slowly moved forward again, a horn honking to his right caused Pablo and Leon to both look over at the cause. That was when he saw it. It was unmistakable, and he froze, hoping against hope that Leon had not seen the gringo in the gray Explorer that was in the middle lane about one car length behind them. Someone attempting to get over from the #3 lane and in front of the gringo had honked his horn trying to get the man's attention to allow him to get in front.

It wasn't the fact that it was any gringo that was there that caused Pablo's heart to skip a beat, it was the fact that the gringo had been looking directly at him, and even made direct eye contact with him when he turned around suddenly. The fact that the gringo quickly averted his gaze made it even more obvious that he had been watching Pablo and Leon in the Tahoe. Pablo knew that it could only be one person, it had to be the DEA agent from Juarez that he had spoken to the night before.

Please, thought Pablo, *please do not let Leon become suspicious. We are almost to the border. Let us just get there and see what happens.*

But Leon did see the gringo in the car one lane over and behind looking at them. Leon's gaze stayed on the gringo in the Ford Explorer even after the man had stopped looking at them. The hit man then turned and looked at Pablo, and noticed sweat was starting to come down his right temple.

"Why are you sweating?" Leon asked.

"I just always get nervous when I come through here, it's only the third time I've done it. I'm not a pro." Pablo counted and saw 12 cars between him and the checkpoint. *If only I can make it up there.* But as he was looking ahead, once again, his heart skipped a beat.

Peering out from one of the checkpoints, several hundred feet in front of them, was the recognizable face of the large black DEA agent, Rod, from El Paso. Standing beside him was the female agent, Ana Lucia. They were waiting for him to come through the border. They must have thought he had decided to make a run for it when he had been trying to save their lives.

Pablo closed his eyes, unable to avoid contemplating the pending disaster, for he was certain that Leon had seen the same thing. He could sense Leon pulling his pistol out from under his thigh, "What is going on?" Leon growled through clinched teeth.

Another bead of sweat fell down Pablo's head, and he knew better than to look at the fearful hit man, or else his face would betray his thoughts.

The final bead of sweat was all Leon needed to know. He kept his gaze on the two Americans at the border entry that were watching their vehicle. They were not CBP. That much was obvious. Leon then turned to look at the gringo in the gray Explorer that was in the lane beside them and one car length back. He was not CBP. Leon knew better than to believe this was coincidence. He had agreed to ride with Pablo as the passenger so that Pablo would drive him directly to meet with the customer in El Paso, because that individual's betrayal had to be handled. But now it was clear, there would be no customer in El Paso. Was this all an elaborate setup? Was the young fat kid working for the DEA, the FBI, or the CIA? Why else would all these gringos be here as they approached the border?

The gringo in the gray Explorer refused to look at Leon despite the man's intimidating stare, again confirming that he was trying his best to not be recognized, but it had been too late. Leon knew the gringos were going to come after him, and he was not going to sit idly by and allow himself to go to jail, not as long as he was on the Mexican side of the border.

Before he had the time to turn back around, Leon heard the driver's door open. He turned quickly to look and was surprised to see that Pablo was making a run for it, leaving the car parked in the middle of the lane, with the driver's door wide open.

In Leon's mind, Pablo's flight confirmed his guilt. It was up to him to inflict Pablo's punishment, and then handle whatever the gringos decided to do.

* * *

Daniel was on the phone with Ana Lucia when Pablo and the other man in the passenger seat turned and looked directly at him. The veteran agent had been on enough surveillance operations to know when he had been burned. The problem was now that he was stuck in the line of vehicles trying to enter the United States, and he could not exactly pull out and turn around.

He felt the stare of the passenger of the vehicle as he turned around to look at him again. For one of the only times in his long career, Daniel was not quite sure what to do. Trying to determine the best course of action for the predicament he found himself in, he was caught completely unaware when he noticed movement out of the corner of his eye.

Looking up, Daniel noticed that Pablo had exited the vehicle, and was running toward the border on foot!

Ana Lucia and Daniel both spoke over each other with surprise on the phone call as they witnessed Pablo running away from the vehicle. They watched in shock as the passenger of the vehicle exited as well, and ran toward the front of the vehicle, apparently in chase of Pablo.

Pablo tripped as he moved away from the vehicle. As he regained his balance and ran toward the border checkpoint, he looked ahead at Ana Lucia in desperation, the panic in his eyes evident despite the distance of ten car lengths between them.

Pablo made it no farther than one car in front of him when three shots rang out, immediately followed by an intense and searing pain in his back that caused him to collapse against the station wagon that was in the lane beside him. With his vision blurry and consciousness escaping, Pablo looked down and saw his shirt soaked with blood, the same blood that was smeared on the station wagon he had fallen against.

* * *

As soon as Leon shot Pablo in the back three times, Daniel drew his DEA issued Glock from his holster, opened the door of the gray Explorer, and stood between the door and the base of the vehicle, using the bulletproof exterior as cover while he yelled at Leon to drop his weapon.

Leon had no intension of dropping his weapon, even if it was an American federal agent telling him to do so. After three well placed bullets into the back of Pablo, Leon turned around with his weapon aimed directly at the grey Explorer that was now two car lengths behind him and to his left. Leon fired four more shots at the vehicle, with all the bullets lodging themselves in the protective door frame and window of the bulletproof Ford Explorer. Meanwhile, Daniel was able to get off one shot before ducking for cover behind the opened door. The bullet pierced Leon's left shoulder and knocked him off balance. Although nothing more than a flesh wound, Leon realized he had never suffered any type of gun shot or serious wound during his career as a street fighter and assassin. The fact that a gringo of all people had managed to get him, albeit just a graze, infuriated him. The gringo would pay, Leon promised himself as he regained his balance and moved forward.

* * *

The shock of seeing her DEA informant gunned down in front of her trying to run to her for safety was quickly replaced with one of the two natural tendencies. The ingrained tendency of fight or flight arose, and there was no question of flight. The fighting tendency prevailed, and despite her best judgment, and not thinking of the legal ramifications of an American federal law enforcement agent charging into sovereign Mexican territory to shoot a Mexican citizen, albeit a murderer, Ana Lucia darted into the first lane of the oncoming traffic of vehicles awaiting entry into El Paso.

Her partner was left standing at the checkpoint as she charged past the checkpoint and into Mexican territory. While Ana Lucia had charged forward on instinct, not considering the consequences of her actions, Rod immediately grasped what his partner had done. He also thought that he could not leave her by herself in a gunfight. When he saw the assassin turn around and fire several shots toward Daniel's vehicle, Rod knew he could stand by no longer. He jumped onto the road and sprinted to catch up to Ana Lucia and try and stop the giant of a man that had killed Pablo and shot at Daniel.

* * *

Two vehicles behind the Tahoe that Pablo was driving was a large utility van, occupied by Toro and the remainder of the hit team. Their plan had been to enter the United States. Although Pablo had not been aware, Toro knew that CBP guard in lane 1 was also on the payroll of the Cartel de Culiacan and would have allowed the van through despite the people and weapons on board.

Every team member in the van had the same communication from earlier and had been able to hear the conversation between Leon and Pablo. When the gringo shot at Leon from the gray Explorer, Toro knew he had to spring into action.

As another member opened the sliding door of the van, Toro leveled his weapon at the gringo in the gray Explorer.

Focused on the threat in front of him in Leon, Daniel had again rose up and fired several rounds at Leon, who jumped to the other side of the Tahoe that he was now using as cover.

Standing and firing and using the driver's side door as cover against the threat from in front of him, Daniel failed to see the threat emerging from the van behind him one car length and to his left. Having put on his vest minutes earlier while sitting in line waiting to cross over the border, the DEA agent was trying to avoid suffering a head shot from the man in front of him. He was not prepared for a threat from behind. He instantly felt searing pain under his left armpit, as two well placed rifle shots from Toro, who was behind him, hit Daniel in the only vulnerable spot in his upper body.

The two shots threw Daniel against the open car door, and he turned his head to see the threat behind him.

Instead of moving towards Daniel, Toro saw the threat ahead in Ana Lucia and Rod. Toro went to his left, ordering two other team members with him, and instructed the rest to go right to finish off the gringo in the Ford Explorer.

Gurgling blood and trying to use his right arm to pick himself up, Daniel used the last remaining ounces of his strength to enter the safety of the bulletproof Ford Explorer and close and lock the door behind him. However, Daniel looked out the rearview window and was stunned as he saw more and more men exiting the van that was behind him. He noticed that two men were moving to their right, trying to outflank him and approach from the passenger side. The other men were moving forward, and even past him on the left...but why?

130

As the blood outside Daniel's body soaked the shirt and pooled inside his body, he started choking up blood. He turned his head toward the front windshield to see where the other gunmen were heading. It was then that he noticed Ana Lucia and Rod, heading towards his direction in the #2 and 3 lanes, and directly toward the gunmen advancing in the far left #1 lane. Understanding that he was opening himself up to the threat by opening his door again, Daniel moved over to the passenger seat and opened the door in an attempt to warn Ana Lucia and Rod of the gunmen to their right. He was unable to get the warning out, as he momentarily felt the burst of rounds from an AK-47 used by one of the men that had moved to outflank him. Most of the bullets impacted with his vest, but several fatal bullets hit his neck and head above the vest. Daniel's lifeless body slid against the passenger door, then fell to the ground.

* * *

Ana Lucia ran up the lane between the cars in the #1 and #2 lanes as fast as her legs could take her, while Rod ran between the #2 and #3 lanes. As soon as she passed the fourth car, she could see Pablo laying on the ground against a vehicle just ahead of her. As she realized what she was seeing, she heard an AK-47 blast in the direction of Daniel's vehicle. Running as fast as she could, she was stunned when she ran into the open door of a Dodge Ram truck. The driver of the vehicle had opened the door and peered behind him to see what was going on, not aware of the DEA agent running past his car.

The force of the collision with the door knocked Ana Lucia off balance, falling to the ground on her right side and landing with a loud grunt. Most urgently, she lost the grip on the Glock she had held in her right hand but dropped as she opened her right hand to brace herself for the fall. The gun landed on the ground and skidded off several feet away from her, underneath the car in the #1 lane to her right.

Struggling to get up and grab her gun, she failed to see Toro as he came around from behind the same vehicle. She looked up at him just in time to see the butt of his gun come down on her head, instantly knocking her out.

* * *

Not expecting a gun battle on the Mexican side of the border when he went to the international check point that afternoon, Rod, like Ana Lucia, had only carried with him his DEA issued Glock .23 handgun. He was very aware of how outgunned they were at that moment, with multiple gunmen with AK-47's against three agents armed with handguns. As bad as those odds were, he couldn't exactly leave Daniel to die out there, so he set off running in between cars in the #2 and #3 lanes, to the left of Ana Lucia, and used his athleticism and long legs to try and get to his fellow DEA agent. He had already passed Ana Lucia when she collided into the truck door and fell to the ground losing her gun.

Rod was only four vehicles away from getting to Daniel when he saw the passenger side door of the grey Explorer open. Suddenly, a vicious burst of gunfire from an AK-47 came from in front of him. While most of the bullets hit either Daniel or the bulletproof door, several whizzed by Rod. He could hear the bullets as they raced through the air, leaving him lucky to be alive.

Instinctively, Rod dove for cover, using the front of the vehicle he was standing beside as cover between him and the gunmen. He knew the gunmen had to be close. He also knew that there was no way that Daniel had survived.

Peering out to his left, he immediately saw two men attempting to move out further to his left and outflank him from that position. Rod's vision went back to the Explorer, where he saw a giant of a man walk in front of the car, toward where Daniel's lifeless body was propped against the still open passenger door.

Leon closed the door of the Explorer and stepped over the fallen DEA agent, intending to deliver a final shot to the head of a man already deceased, for no other reason than this man was the first person to ever injure Leon. Even though the bullet had only grazed him, Leon had no mercy. The hatred and anger raged, and he did not want the man's family to be able to recognize Daniel when they claimed the body. Leon smiled to himself at the thought as he pulled out his handgun and pointed it down at Daniel's head.

Before Leon could deliver the final shot, Rod raised up and fired two shots at the hitman, both of which hit Leon directly in the back, causing him to stumble and fall against the car.

Leon sucked in as much air as he could muster, thankful that the vest he was wearing had stopped the potentially fatal bullets, but incredulous that he had now been shot three times in one day after going his entire career up to that point clean.

As soon as Rod placed the two shots toward Leon, the two other team members of the hit team that had outflanked him to his left laid down suppressing fire in his direction with their AK-47s. Rod got as low to the ground as his 6"6 inch frame could get him, and then moved to his left, with only one vehicle in between him and one of the hitmen. Rod had never taken a life and had prayed at the DEA Academy that he would never have to do so, but in that moment, he knew, it was either kill or be killed.

* * *

Of all the cars separating the tall DEA agent from two murderous hitmen, fate had it that he was hiding his long frame behind a lime green Chevrolet Matiz, one of the smallest cars in production, and of course the smallest in the long line of cars waiting to enter the border.

Rod looked and saw two young teenage girls cowering in fear in the vehicle, the passenger screaming and the driver crying. Rod opened the door of the car and urged the girls to get out of the car and run to the border, knowing that the car was moments away from being riddled with bullets. The girls took Rod's advice, and both occupants climbed out of the driver's seat and ran toward the border.

Almost instantly, a burst of fire from one of the AK47s sprayed the small compact car, with the rounds piercing from side to side. Rod laid completely down on the ground, trying to make himself as small as possible. As soon as one spray of rounds was complete, the second hitman started spraying rounds through the car as well. Miraculously, all the rounds went over him.

As Rod laid still, underneath the car he could see the boots of both men approach the vehicle, certain that they had killed their prey. Knowing this was his only chance, Rod rolled to his side and shot underneath the small vehicle, placing two bullets each in the boots of the hitmen. Rod's training on the DEA range and come in handy, as all four bullets found their mark.

While the goal had not been to kill the hitmen with the shots at their feet, it did have the intended effect of momentarily stunning them. The hitman standing outside the passenger side front seat of the vehicle fell to his knee in pain, and then delivered a long string of fire underneath the car. By that point, Rod had already made his move, once again using his athleticism to his advantage. As soon as Rod fired the four rounds below the car and into the feet of the hitmen, he got to his feet, and jumped on top of the hood of the small Matiz, leveling his Glock at the hitmen shooting underneath the car.

Two well placed head shots immediately dropped the closest threat. Rod then quickly moved his barrel toward the second hitman that had been assessing his wounded feet, shocked at his partner's death. The second hitman, standing behind the rear passenger side of the vehicle, raised his AK-47 at Rod just as the DEA agent placed two more rounds directly into the target's head.

In all his training at the DEA Academy, and then all the quarterly training sessions that followed graduation, Rod had never been able to place most shots in the head region. His group and the Firearms instructors had put together several shooting courses that culminated with having to make several head shots on paper targets, and Rod had never won any of those competitions. Yet when it mattered the most, all the training he had been through had helped him deliver four shots that saved his life in that instant. However, there was one more threat Rod would have to survive before the ordeal was over.
***

"Cholo and Negro just went down!" Leon said into his microphone, slowly moving out from behind the vehicle he had been crouched behind after being shot in the back of the bulletproof vest he was wearing, shielding himself when all the rounds of the AK-47 burst through the small car and headed in his direction. With a Dodge Durango and the shot-up Chevy Matiz between him and the DEA agent, Leon did not want to leave any loose ends, especially since Rod had shot him in the back minutes earlier. Leon had taken off the vest that had saved his life and wanted nothing more than vengeance.

"Leon," Toro responded in the microphone, "we are back in the van. We have to leave in the next 30 seconds, or we might not be able to avoid the authorities."

Leon fired one shot through the small Matiz toward Rod, who raised up and fired two rounds at Leon, but then his Glock jammed. Rod made sure the magazine was firmly in place, and he racked the slide back three times to make sure the gun was operational, and again attempted to fire a shot at Leon as he strolled confidently toward him, but once again, the gun failed to fire.

"If this gringo can last 20 seconds with me, then he deserves to live," Leon said while Rod was trying to get his gun working again. Leon cast aside his weapon and wanted nothing more than to go hand to hand with the federal agent, to see which one was the better man.

When Rod saw Leon put away his weapon, he knew what that meant. He dropped his gun and straightened to meet the man. It was the first time Leon could remember somebody that was not scared of him. While Rod was just slightly taller, the former basketball player was outweighed by the hitman by more than 30 pounds.

Leon feigned a blow with his right hand, which had the desired effect of causing Rod to dip his shoulders and head away from the blow. At that time, Leon used his street fighter experience and then jumped up, delivering a punishing blow with his left knee directly to the stomach of his opponent. Rod had been able to get his right hand in front of the knee at the last second, but still the force of the blow stunned him and knocked his breath out.

With Rod doubled over, Leon lifted his left arm and drove it down on Rod's back. The bullet wound Leon had suffered when Daniel shot him earlier in the fight left Leon without as much power in his left elbow strike as normal, but it was still strong enough to drive Rod to his chest on the ground.

Leon kneeled down to roll Rod over with his left hand, and deliver a potentially fatal punch to the face with his right hand, however as soon as Rod rolled over he lunged forward and punched Leon in the jaw with all his might, and then punched him again and again.

After being temporarily stunned at the DEA agent's ability to respond to the beating, Leon steadied himself and bear hugged Rod, then ran with him and crashed into the bullet ridden Matiz. Rod refused to let the man go and took a bite out of Leon's left ear. Rod jerked his head to the side, ripping the ear in half, and causing the heavier man to buck back in pain.

With unbridled rage, Leon broke free from the bear hold the two men had on each other, and then pulled back with all his strength and delivered a punch, but Rod was too fast, and had moved to the side. The punch made a huge dent in the small vehicle. Rod then delivered a side kick, with all his might, directly at an angle and into the lower leg of Leon. The strength of the larger man's bones was the only reason it did not snap in two, but the kick was powerful enough to deeply bruise the bone and leave the hit man temporarily wobbly.

With Leon off the attack mode, Rod looked up to see another armed man coming at them. Weaponless, Rod dashed toward the border and took concealment behind another vehicle, trying to get away from the man.

The other hitman grabbed Leon and told him they were leaving. Leon looked back at where the federal agent had disappeared, enraged that he had not been able to finish the deal by hand, but Leon wanted to live to see another day, preferably from outside a jail cell, so he took the advice of his teammates and went to the waiting van, pain searing through his leg from the deep bruise in his leg.

The remaining hit men, led by Toro, had ordered all the passenger vehicles behind their van to move immediately or face certain death. Each vehicle had promptly moved out of the way, so that the van that Toro and his team had been in could make their exit, driving back south into Juarez.

As Leon got in the van, he leaned against the wall, suffering from more wounds and scraps in this one instance than he had experienced in his entire career combined. The van raced south into Juarez, away from the border. Leon's eyes narrowed, as he looked beside Toro. Sitting against the other side of the van's walls was Ana Lucia, still unconscious, but bound and gagged.

Toro looked at Leon. "She's DEA."

Leon smiled, "Good."

Chapter 14
Juarez, Mexico

Thursday, August 31

There was no time to brood on the loss of two team members. They did not live by the same mantra as the American Special Forces of "Leave No Man Behind." It was known that there might be situations when they would have to leave a fallen comrade, and this was one such occasion. Despite the realization, it did not sting any less. Toro pushed the thoughts from his mind as he looked ahead and focused, instructing the driver of the specific location to take the van.

Toro looked intently out the windshield as he provided directions, trying to remember the exact route to get to the location he was looking for. It had been a few years since he had been there, but his memory served faithfully as he instructed the driver of the different turns needed to get to the location.

The van pulled off the main street and moved down a dusty path. The wail of sirens screaming toward the border were noticeable. Shortly before the shootout, Toro had the foresight to contact Felipe and tell him to make sure that law enforcement was not deployed for five minutes if there was a report of gunfire. Felipe initially claimed that he would not be able to hold back the cavalry for five minutes, but whatever he did must have worked, for Toro's team left the area less than five minutes after the first shot.

The ranch ahead finally came in sight. The dusty path led to a small gravel driveway that ended at a 2000 square foot single level residence.

Signs near the residence indicated the property belonged to Lopez' Horse Farms. A large horse stable sat approximately 100 meters away from the residence.

Once the vehicle stopped, Toro instructed the remainder of his team to stay inside while he exited and knocked on the front door. Toro instinctively kept his head down, weary of any American satellites overhead. The veteran assassin knew the Americans were going to spare no expense at finding the group responsible for kidnapping one of their agents. He also figured that the gringo that had been killed was likely a DEA agent, causing further concern about their ability to escape apprehension.

The occupant of the house quickly came to the door. It was the same man that had been there the only previous time Toro visited. Lopez of Lopez' horse farms, was paid handsomely by the cartel to maintain the property as a front for the real reason it had been constructed several years earlier, the passageway to a secret tunnel that connected Juarez to El Paso.

Both men standing in the doorway knew that El Jefe had used a considerable amount of resources to construct tunnels from Mexican border cities to American border cities, to include locations from Juarez to El Paso, Nogales (Mexico) to Nogales (Arizona), Mexicali to Calexico, and Tijuana to San Diego. Each Mexican town had several different locations to access the tunnel. While the cartel still used the tried and true fashion of shipment of drugs and money with vehicles on public roads, use of the tunnels was reserved for only the most important of items that needed to cross the border back and forth safely.

El Jefe knew the importance of protecting this investment, and the necessity of hiding the location by masking it as some type of a residence or business. Toro knew that a strip club in Nogales, Mexico, contained one pedestrian entrance to the tunnel there, while another entrance in Tijuana was outside a homeless shelter.

Each location had a pedestrian entrance in one location, and a vehicular entrance in another. Toro's only knowledge of any of the exits in Juarez was this pedestrian entrance. He had never needed to use the vehicle entrance and was grateful that he had at least been to this location.

When Lopez recognized who he was speaking with, he lowered his head in respect and nodded, assuring Toro that he would make sure everything was fine.

Toro returned to the van while Lopez walked off toward the horse barn, unlocking the padlock and opening the side double gates, creating a wide enough area for the van to pull inside.

Once inside the barn and protected from the overhead surveillance of drones or satellites, Toro instructed his team to exit the vehicle. Leon pulled Ana Lucia out of the van. She had regained consciousness but was still weary. Looking at the female DEA agent, Toro was confident that she would never remember this location if she were released or freed.

"Men," Toro said, "there is a tunnel here constructed by El Jefe that leads directly into El Paso. All but one of us will take the tunnel and cross into Texas."

Not wanting to disrespect and question their leader, some of the remaining men were nonetheless unclear on why Toro had given those directions. Sensing their uneasiness, Toro spoke up. "The Americans will likely have a satellite or drone overhead, and they will know that our van came to this location. They will know later today or early tomorrow. Either way, this van must leave so the Americans will continue to look for it. Somebody must take that responsibility. You will be arrested, yes, but your legal defense will be provided by the best of El Jefe's attorneys, and your family will be compensated with one million dollars, I will make sure of that myself."

"I'll do it," said Jorge, one of the young sicarios.

"Very well," Toro said, looking at the man. "Leave quickly, and drive south toward Chihuahua, giving us as much time as possible before they stop you and realize the rest of the team is not with you."

"Won't the police question why we came here?" asked another.

"Yes," Lopez said, speaking up. "But I will tell them that you came here and threatened to kill me if I did not give you any gas, which I have several reserves of in containers here. Fill the van up quickly before you leave, so it will be a truthful statement."

Jorge obeyed the instruction and picked up two containers and started pouring the gas in the van.

"After you leave, I will then leave in the white van," Lopez said, motioning to a large white van that was also backed into the horse barn, which looked similar to the one that Toro and his team had taken. "I will leave the van somewhere and get a ride back here, telling the authorities your men took the vehicle."

"Very good," Toro said, impressed at how prepared Lopez was for this exact situation.

"Okay, but aren't we risking the police finding the tunnel?" one of the other men asked.

"It's a risk, yes, but it is very well hidden, yet in common sight," Lopez answered.

"Let me guess, it is down in the big cellar," Leon said, looking at another big set of double doors in the middle section of the horse barn, in between Lopez' van and the van used by Toro's team, in the area separating the horse stalls.

"Somebody might think so," Lopez said, "but no." He opened one of the 16 horse stalls in the barn, each of which had a number painted on the wood above it. Of the 16 stalls, only the first 12 stalls had horses, the remaining stalls 13-16 were empty.

Lopez took the horses from stalls #5 -6 and walked them into one of the four remaining empty stalls. He returned to stall #5 and brushed away straw, and then dirt, until a small knob was revealed that looked like a grade school lock. The man rotated the knob back and forth until getting the correct combination, and heard an unlocking sound, coming from stall #6 beside it. The entire length of the ground beneath stall #6 disappeared.

The surviving cartel hit men peered into stall #6 to see what had happened. What appeared to be a service elevator was revealed. It was 10 feet from the floor of the horse stall to the floor of the elevator, with a small ladder on the side for those that needed assistance getting down. The sides and the floor were made of steel, with the lone exception being a numeric panel located on the wall closest to the ladder.

"Ok, everyone must quickly get into this elevator," Lopez told them. "I have given Toro the code to input the panel once everybody is ready. When he enters the code, the elevator will descend, and the floor of the horse stall above you will close. After the elevator descends, it will not return for 30 minutes, by design, in case law enforcement were to ever discover it and try to follow somebody down there."

The eyes of the sicarios grew wide in amazement. The doubt of Toro's reasoning had temporarily been replaced by wonder at the ingenuity and revelation of this multi-million-dollar tunnel.

"Once everyone is gone," Lopez continued, "I will smooth everything out and return the horse to this stall, before I leave in the white truck, but you must please hurry." As he said that, Jorge cranked up the van, and without speaking, left the barn, trying to lead law enforcement as far away as possible before being obtained.

"With all due respect, Toro,' another team member said, "If the Americans are going to be looking for us, then why are we going to America of all places? El Jefe can't protect us there."

Leon smiled, "Let me take this one for you," he said looking over at Toro. "The Federal Police, and all the Americans are going to be searching every square inch in Juarez over the next couple hours and days, especially looking for this lady. What better place to hide out than El Paso? They will never suspect us to go there, they will surely believe we will hide with friends or family here in Mexico." Leon looked at Toro with a newfound respect at the intelligence of the plan.

"Now I am curious," Leon said, looking at Toro, what are we going to do when we get to El Paso? Is there anybody there to receive us?"

Toro looked up from his phone. "I just made the arrangements. Somebody will be at our exit location in two hours." Toro had used the phone provided by El Jefe at the mansion the week earlier. His message had been simple. "I have an asset that will be leveraged to find out who ordered the murder of El Jefe's wife, but I need assistance at the pedestrian tunnel in El Paso in exactly two hours."

In less than a minute, a response came that assistance would be provided. The man responding was a defense attorney from El Paso that was on the cartel payroll to represent any member of the cartel working in Texas that was arrested by law enforcement. The defense attorney had known that being in El Paso, he would be expected to carry out this duty for Toro, or else face certain death, so his response had been immediate.

Toro quickly sent another message. "Have somebody experienced in social media at the safe location when we arrive."

The defense attorney from El Paso quickly replied, "Ok."

The team members started going into the service elevator one by one, until finally Toro lowered Ana Lucia down, and then went down himself.

"And why did we bring a DEA agent with us?" one of the team members asked, the obvious question that no one had wanted to ask out of fear of invoking their leader's anger, or looking stupid in the process, but the veteran sicario answered without any hint of frustration.

"If the Americans want her back, then they are going to have to reveal who ordered the hit on El Jefe's wife," Toro told his guys once they were inside the elevator, "because if they didn't order the murder, then I bet they know who did. And if they do not know who killed her, then they will find out, and we will be rich."

The realization of the importance of the DEA agent flashed in each person's eyes, as the ground above their head returned to place and the elevator descended into the depths below.

Chapter 15
El Paso, Texas

Friday, September 1

The investigators of DEA's Office of Professional Responsibility continued questioning Rod into the early morning hours following the shootout at the border. Rod was mentally tired as he went over every single moment from the day before that ultimately led to the death of DEA SA Daniel Benson and the kidnapping of SA Ana Lucia Rodriguez. He was frustrated that his and Ana Lucia's decision making was being critically questioned, especially since Rod knew one of the two investigator's reputation for being lazy and never able to put together a significant investigation when he had been in the field. Although he had been unsuccessful in the field, he still somehow got promoted, and was now expressing disbelief at the poor decisions made by Ana Lucia and Rod.

As the sun was coming up in the early morning hours of the first day of September, the interview was momentarily interrupted as someone came in to speak with the OPR investigators. Rod took the moment as a reprieve from the constant barrage of questioning he had been under for the previous several hours. However, when the OPR investigators came back in 20 minutes later, their tone was even more somber.

According to media reports coming out of Mexico, two young female teenagers had been caught in the crossfire of the shootout. Preliminary reports, according to the media, indicated that the two young teenagers were shot by .40 caliber ammunition. The sicario team used AK47s, which do not use .40 caliber ammunition; the two teenage girls had been shot by Rod at some point during the melee.

Rod denied ever shooting toward the teenage girls but acknowledged that he did usher them out of the vehicle they were in prior to the vehicle getting shot by the assassins. The investigators did not seem to believe Rod. They were convinced that he did not remember correctly due to the fog of battle.

More delays resulted after the latest revelation, during which time the OPR investigators were on the phone with the DEA Administrator in D.C. The OPR investigator Rod knew eventually walked back into the room and gave him the grim news. Rod was being suspended without pay indefinitely, while his actions in Juarez, and the allegations that he irresponsibly shot two innocent teenage girls was investigated.

* * *

The safe house chosen by Defense Attorney George Danielson had two bedrooms, two baths, and was a 1600 square foot residence in a small residential El Paso neighborhood on Cayman Lane, less than two miles from where Toro's team had exited the tunnel. Shortly after arrival, Ana Lucia's hands remained zip-tied and she was placed on the ground against a wall in a room at the front of the residence, within eyesight of the front door.

In the pre-dawn morning, a social media expert working for the Cartel arrived at the residence, and took a quick video made by Toro, who concealed his lower face with a mask. In the video, Toro kneeled beside the captive DEA agent, and explained that she would not be harmed if the US government revealed who was responsible for ordering the murder of El Jefe's wife. A deadline of midnight Saturday night was provided. Toro was clear and menacing in the message. If the Americans did not disclose the message by the required deadline, Ana Lucia would be killed.

* * *

The late morning and early afternoon hours ticked slowly by in the small safe house, with the different members of the team taking turns watching Ana Lucia. Meanwhile, the other members of the team slept in one of the two bedrooms or watched television in the living room.

All the blinds in the house were closed tightly to prevent anyone from seeing inside the residence. Despite the safety the residence offered, it quickly became apparent that this was not going to be a long-term option for Toro's team. They were like caged animals that needed to be released. Sitting around and watching television all day was not what they were made to do. They were killing machines, and if they were not killing, at the very least they needed the freedom to move around and enjoy life in whatever way possible.

The monotony of the day was broken up at lunchtime when George returned to the house with a dozen pepperoni and cheese pizzas from Domino's. The men ravaged the pizza, having not eaten in almost 24 hours. Toro also offered some to Ana Lucia, who accepted the pizza with a silent and barely noticeable nod of her head. Her zip ties were removed for a brief period so she could feed herself, but upon completing the meal, her hands were secured again. Even the male assassins were weary of the capabilities of the DEA agent, knowing that she had been highly trained.

While spending the entirety of the day with her hands tied behind her back and sitting against the wall, Ana Luca had used the time to assess the weak points of the residence and the team, and determine whether or not she would have an opportunity to escape. Despite being relatively close to the front door, she did not think she would be able to get to the door and get outside prior to being stopped, especially without the use of her hands. Worse, she had no idea what the outside of the residence looked like, or even where she was. She had not been able to see when they arrived the night before. She realized they had used a tunnel, and perhaps had possibly returned to Texas, which she realized would likely mean that her law enforcement brethren were looking for her in the wrong country. Even if she was in El Paso, she was not sure what part. Nevertheless, Ana Lucia realized that if the time came, she might have to take the chance regardless and go from there. She was not sure if she was going to have the opportunity to do that with this team. Each member of Toro's team had an advantage over her. They were all bigger and stronger, and they were all armed, while she was not only without a weapon, but restricted from using her hands because of the zip-ties. So far, she had not been harmed, but she realized that was only because of the commands of Toro. Ana Lucia didn't want to do anything to make him upset, so she continued to bide her time, hoping that something would come up along the way that would give her the opportunity to attempt an escape.

As Ana Lucia thought about her situation, Toro concluded that his team could not stay in that location another night. He was not sure he would be able to control them from either assaulting Ana Lucia, or leaving the residence on foot, which would dramatically increase the likelihood of their capture. During the early afternoon hours, Toro came to Leon with a proposition.

"I don't think that our team can or should stay here another night, but somebody must stay with the DEA agent. The place is too small, and I am worried somebody might do something stupid that will result in the rest of us getting arrested, so I have requested George to bring us another van. He will have it here in the evening. Once it gets dark, I would like you to lead the team, and get them out of here and back to Mexico. Obviously, the police are all over Juarez, and likely Chihuahua. You cannot risk returning there, so I would suggest you take the team to Nogales, Arizona. It is a five hour or more drive west. There is another tunnel there you could use to get back into Mexico. Once back in Mexico, hang out for a few days and reassess the situation, and I will be in touch. If I do not make it, then it will be your responsibility to lead this team. I know you have been wanting the opportunity to lead a team of your own, and this is your chance to show that you can do it successfully, first with getting them out of El Paso and to Nogales, and then later, depending on what happens here, you might be called upon further. Do you have any questions?"

"Will I get the phone number for the contact in Nogales before I leave?" Leon asked, satisfied for the opportunity to finally lead.

"Yes. I will make sure that George gives it to you. I have turned my phone off, and do not plan to use it again unless absolutely necessary, so we must wait on him to get the number of the guy that will meet you."

"Okay, I will get our team to Nogales safely."

Toro nodded his head and walked back into the living room. He still considered Leon at fault for causing the shootout that led them to the situation that they were in, but he also knew that the other guys on the team would obey Leon's instruction if Toro was not present. Nobody else would come close to demanding that same respect, or fear, so the decision was made and Toro called a quick meeting in the back bedroom, out of earshot of Ana Lucia, so that he could meet with the remaining members of the team while Leon watched the DEA agent.

Shortly after the meeting, George returned to the residence with a black Mercedes van. The vehicle did not have any windows on the side, completely concealing the inside from view. Without much talking, each man took the weapons they had brought and got into the van which had pulled into the garage. Leon made sure to get the number of the contact in Nogales from George, who instructed him to find the 10 freeway and head west until he came to the 19 freeway in Tucson, Arizona, where he would go south. At that point, the contact from Nogales would be able to direct him further.

As soon as darkness fell, the vehicle exited the garage and departed the area. Toro wondered if he would ever see his crew again, and he went and sat down on the wall opposite of Ana Lucia.

* * *

George looked noticeably relieved not to be responsible for a houseful of professional killers, even if this was not his own personal residence. He had picked up some burgers from McDonald's and brought them to the kitchen, always speaking with Toro in Spanish and being careful not to let Ana Lucia get a good look at him. He didn't know how this situation with Ana Lucia was going to play out, and he honestly didn't want her to die, but he also didn't want any kind of a follow-up investigation to uncover that he had been responsible for providing safe harbor for the individuals that kidnapped a federal agent. The pay he received from his Cartel contact was more than enough to make up for his concerns.

The veteran defense attorney had been on the job in El Paso for 34 years, the last 13 of which he had been on retainer for the Cartel, making an extra $10,000 monthly just for being available to help when called upon, which admittedly was becoming more and more frequent and did take up an extended portion of his time. But George had managed to save a large portion of the pay provided to him by the Cartel, not to mention the other payments that he received if actual legal services were provided, services which often required much more compensation. As a result, George had saved well in excess of $2 million, and had every intention of taking those savings and riding off into the sunset in the near future, preferably to spend the remainder of his days on the coast of some south Pacific island, far away from West Texas.

George was standing in the kitchen as Toro approached him, keeping a watchful eye on Ana Lucia in the front room. He had warned her that he was watching the door and the window, and if she tried to escape, he would place a shot to the back of her head that would kill her before her body hit the ground. George heard the exchange, and a chill ran through his body. Despite all his years in this line of work, he had never gotten used to some things. Physical threats of torture and beatings were one of those things, especially when the person being threatened was a DEA Special Agent.

"Senor," Toro began, careful not to use George's real name so that Ana Lucia would not overhear it. "I'm hopeful that we will be out of here by Sunday at the latest. If you can provide food for us tomorrow, that should be all that is necessary. I hope this situation will get resolved soon. Have you heard anything regarding any type of answer to our demand?"

"No, I haven't, although I'm sure the government is working non-stop to get an answer, if they don't have one already. If, somehow, the US government was responsible for the murder of El Jefe's wife, then I would assume they are also in the process of developing a cover-up story, presumably one that will place the blame for the murder on someone else."

"What are the chances we get the truth?" Toro asked.

"I'd say 50/50. Maybe they find out who did it and let you know. Nothing this government does anymore would surprise me."

"Let's hope for her sake they come up with something," Toro said.

"I assume you have this situation well thought out, but I would request that you give me a heads up regarding what you decide to do, just so I can make plans accordingly as well."

"Yes, of course," Toro said. "I am going to keep my phone turned off so that there won't be any distractions. Please show up here tomorrow around 9:00 a.m."

"Will do," George said, and walked out of the house and into his van to leave the area.

* * *

After several hours of sitting against the wall looking at each other in silence, Ana Lucia decided to try and initiate a conversation with the infamous assassin. "So, are you the real Toro?"

Somewhat tired, Toro had only been able to sleep a couple hours earlier that day. The normal tough exterior remained, but he did feel mentally fatigued from the events of the previous two days. Perhaps because none of his team members were there, and perhaps because he respected the DEA agent, he responded.

"Why would anybody claim to be Toro?"

"Because Toro is well known. DEA knows about Toro. Heck, El Jefe was even putting Toro stamps on kilos of cocaine that were coming to the US. Did you know that?"

"No, I didn't. It doesn't matter."

"What's your real name?"

"It doesn't matter."

"Sure, it does. I cannot sit here all night without losing my mind. I'm not asking for your life story, just something to pass the time."

"My name is Saul."

"Interesting. I won't ask any questions."

"I couldn't give you any answers because I don't have them. I never knew either of my parents."

Ana Lucia was surprised that she had gotten this infamous hitman to reveal to her that minimal amount of information. She continued to press on. "That's too bad. I knew both of my parents. Great people. They were from Durango and immigrated here to El Paso. I was the first from my family to be born in the United States. Great example of a loving couple. I'm sorry you did not have that in your life. So, is that what led you to this line of work?"

"The absence of parents?"

Ana Lucia nodded.

"No."

"Was there somebody else?"

"You ask too many questions."

"What does it matter? The way I see it, one of two things is going to play out here in the next 48 hours. One, my friends are going to find me, and when they do, they will shoot and kill you. Or two, my friends do not find me, you either kill me or let me go, and then return safely to Mexico, and disappear. Either way, your conversation with me here right now will not have any impact on your future, other than keeping you from being bored for the next few minutes."

Toro's respect for the DEA agent continued to rise. Her lack of fear was impressive, as was her calmness, and her logic.

"My sister and I were raised by two people. They were the best people I have ever met, much like your parents." Toro stopped as he considered what to say next.

"You know," Ana Lucia said, "the people of Mexico get a bad reputation. The outside world thinks all Mexicans are drug dealers and murderers, but that could not be further from the truth. Most of the Mexican population is beautiful and kind people, like the two people that raised you."

Toro realized that he had never mentioned his two adoptive parents to anybody in the world. He could not believe that he had just revealed it to the DEA agent. Perhaps in a different environment when he was not mentally tired, he would have been smarter.

Ana Lucia could tell that Toro was struggling to decide whether he should say something. She could sense that he wanted to, but he was weighing what to say and how. "You mentioned you have a sister? I didn't know that."

The cold-blooded look then returned to Toro's eyes. "That's because she was taken when I was young."

"Taken by who?"

"The scum of the earth, child sex traffickers. I was never able to find out which one. The woman that raised me, the woman I think of as my mother, died trying to protect my sister when she was taken."

Ana Lucia's eyes widened in shock. Every person had a history that led them to the point where they were in life, and she knew that Toro had just revealed what led him into the infamous hitmen that he was today.

"No wonder you—"

"Went crazy?"

"No, you went into the business you did. You've probably unattached yourself from all physical relationships and emotions, right?"

Toro remained silent, looking at her expressionless. "You don't have to answer," Ana Lucia said. "I know. I studied to be a Psychologist, but I could not stand sitting inside all day. Kind of ironic since I've been inside all day today, and this might be one of my last days on earth."

Toro did not make any facial reaction to indicate which way he was leaning regarding Ana Lucia's fate. "What about the man that raised you? Is he still alive?"

Why Toro continued answering her questions, he did not know. The truth was that nobody had ever taken the time to ask them.

"He is still alive. He is a good man, still."

"Do you ever see him anymore?"

"Rarely. Although I did see him just a few days ago, before all this happened."

"What does he do for a living?"

Toro smirked. "He's a priest, with a small congregation outside Chihuahua."

Ana Lucia was caught off guard with that revelation. "And he maintained his faithfulness to God after what happened with his wife, and your sister?"

"He is a good man. As good as I am bad."

The two did not speak for the next minute, with Ana Lucia processing the information, and Toro trying to push away the thoughts of the fate his sister endured, as well as Madre Aracely's last moments.

Finally, the prevailing question on her mind was verbalized.

"Are you really going to kill me at midnight tomorrow if you don't hear anything? Because, selfishly, I don't want to die. I'm not afraid to die, but I don't want to."

"The threat has been made. It can't be retracted."

"Why do you even care who murdered El Jefe's wife?"

"Because he will give $10 million to the person that finds that information." Toro leaned forward. "And the majority of people in Mexico suspect that there was involvement from the American government, so if they know, then they will tell us."

"Even if some branch of the American government was responsible, which I don't believe is the case, then they would never disclose that information and put themselves at risk. You should be suspicious of any kind of information you get. You gave them 48 hours to come up with a story. It will likely be false, that's what I think."

"Yes, it's possible," Toro said. "But I will look at the evidence provided. If it withstands scrutiny, and is accepted by El Jefe, then that is sufficient for me."

"Even if it implicates the wrong person? Someone innocent like Madre Aracely."

Hearing her name on the lips of somebody else sounded strange to Toro and invoked in him the same anger that he felt on the day that she was killed so many years ago. Toro ended the conversation, and got up and walked away, staying close by to maintain a proximity with the DEA agent just out of sight.

Ana Lucia did not know if she had made the situation any better or any worse. One thing was clear, while Toro was a vicious killer, he still held the reason for his transformation close to his heart. She sensed that it weighed heavily on his mind, especially in quiet moments like this.

"Saul," Ana Lucia said leaning her head against the wall, refusing to call him by the nickname given to him as a hitman, "you can get out of this situation. I'm sure that you justify killing people in Mexico by thinking about the harm that they have done in their role as drug dealers or corrupted politicians or police officers, but I'm none of those things. I'm just somebody trying to make the world a better place, because those are the values instilled in me by my father and mother, the couple raised in Durango, just south from where you were raised by your adoptive parents."

Toro stood in the kitchen, out of view of Ana Lucia, but close enough that he could hear her breathing, not to mention her words. He did not respond

"I don't know what I'm trying to say," she said. "I guess...I just want you to know that you are not too far gone to stop this and fix this situation."

The same words also spoken to him by Padre Miguel during their last visit rang in his ears, as he called to mind their most recent conversation. Toro resolved to not carry on any further dialogue with Ana Lucia for the remainder of the night.

Chapter 16
El Paso, Texas

Friday, September 1

Leon sat in the passenger seat of the van as it exited the safe location. The directions given by the attorney to get to the nearby 10 freeway were easy. They took the 10 freeway west, just as directed by George and Toro. However, about traveling west for 15 miles, Leon told the driver to take the exit on S. Resler Drive. The 23-year old driver, Nestor, had only been working in this group for less than a year, and he knew better than to verbally question Leon. Nevertheless, he questioned their actions internally, knowing that if their vehicle was stopped, then they were either all going to jail, or a police officer was going to die.

All talking in the back of the van stopped as the other six members of the team realized they had exited the interstate. They were waiting and watching, anxious to see where Leon was taking them.

A mile off the exit Leon told Nestor to make a left turn onto El Cajon Dr. into what appeared to be a nice residential neighborhood.

"Leon, you care to tell us what we are doing here?" one of the men in the back finally asked. "Don't we want to get to Nogales as soon as possible?"

"We will, but first, we have some unfinished business."

"Do you know somebody over here?" Nestor asked, looking over at the passenger.

"Yes, there's an address I want to check out. It might be where Blanco lives, the guy we were initially coming to visit. The betrayer that was using the GDG to receive his dope."

All the occupants looked at Leon in surprise. "How did you get this address?" one of them asked, remembering that they had all been ready to follow Pablo to see him meet with Blanco.

"If you knew where Blanco lived, then why did we even have to follow Pablo over there?" Nestor asked. "Couldn't we have just gone straight there?"

Leon gave him a piercing look, warning him that he almost considered the man's tone disrespectful and crossing a line that could not be uncrossed. Still, Leon answered. "I'm not sure this is Blanco's house. I just want to check it out."

"What makes you think it is, Leon?" somebody asked.

Leon smiled. "Pull up on the curb here, in front of the house there with a truck in the driveway." Nestor pulled the black Mercedes van on the curb right in front of the house, with Leon looking to see if it looked like anybody was home. A light was shining from inside the residence.

"After we assaulted the GDG stash location in Chihuahua, I took possession of Oscar's phone, and looked at his text messages. There was one number with an El Paso area code. I kept the phone with me, and as we drove, I noticed that Oscar had Blanco on Find my Friends. Apparently, they have been communicating for years, although they have kept their professional dealings separate until recently. I found that Oscar's friend Blanco was located at this residence," Leon said. "As of this morning, Blanco's phone stopped giving off a location, so Blanco likely dumped the phone. I just want to see if he is still at home."

Nestor looked nervously at Leon. Someone from behind spoke up for what everyone else was thinking, "I think we are going to get the information we need about the killer of El Jefe's wife from the US government. We don't need Blanco anymore. He probably doesn't know anything anyways."

"Maybe not," Leon said, "but nobody escapes justice. Not cartel justice at least." Leon exited the vehicle and walked with purpose toward the front door.

* * *

Blanco walked out the front door with a duffel bag draped over his right shoulder. His eyes were focused on the old Chevrolet Malibu that was stopped in the road with the lights on, facing the neighborhood exit, positioned in the opposite direction of the unseen van from which Leon had just exited. Blanco temporarily made eye contact with the driver of the Malibu, his wife who had not returned to their house since the DEA had made Blanco an informant. His gaze shifted to the back seat of the Malibu, where his five-year-old heart and soul sat in the back in a booster seat, waving at her father who she had not seen in several days.

After hearing the news of Ana Lucia's kidnapping, Blanco was instantly worried about what that meant for him and his family. Would they be given extra money to leave El Paso? Would he go to jail as expected but then get out early after the deal with the prosecutor, based on the help he provided which led to the seizure of additional cocaine from the GDG group led by Oscar? Whatever the answer, things needed to be decided quickly, because Blanco knew that people were going to be looking to him for payment for drugs that he never sold, drugs that were seized by the DEA. When nobody from the El Paso group answered the phone the day after Ana Lucia's kidnapping, Blanco quickly assumed that he had been forgotten and was going to be left for dead. Refusing to sit around and accept that fate, Blanco and his wife spoke and agreed they would no longer trust the DEA, who had gone silent during the time when Blanco needed them the most. Blanco decided they must pack up their little girl and flee not just from the DEA, but also whoever was going to be coming and looking for the cartel's money. They agreed to live out their remaining days somewhere in New Mexico, with Blanco picking up odd jobs where he could, to help make ends meet. He had saved $10,000 just in case he ever needed it, and he figured if ever he needed the money, it was now. He left the bag containing the money just inside the front door as he walked out to place his bag of clothes, all that he would take with him, inside the car driven by his wife.

So focused was Blanco on the imminent reunion with his wife and little girl, he failed to notice the black Mercedes van sitting on the street in front of his house, but Blanco's longing gaze at his family was quickly broken by the man who walked up from the sidewalk.

Blanco's skin complexion had always been very light, and many people were often surprised when they met him for the first time, and he spoke fluent Spanish. On this day, it confirmed his identity to Leon, sealing his fate.

"You are Blanco, I take it," Leon said, striding straight toward him. As Blanco's gaze went from his wife and child to the man approaching him, his first reaction was not one of self-preservation, he was only focused on the safety of his family. Once again, he looked directly into the eyes of his wife who had rolled the window down of her car, just 50 feet away, and with a shake of his head and a look in his eyes, Blanco gave a clear instruction for her to not get out of the car. It was at that moment that his eyes bulged out, and changed from warning to pain, for the blade that Leon had plunged into his lower left abdomen had caused such pain that he lost his voice in the pain and shock.

Leon then grabbed Blanco by the shirt and pulled him close, taking out the blade, and leaned over, whispering in his ear, "El Jefe sends his regards."

While Leon made that statement, Blanco could see the tears and despair in his wife's eyes. In a moment of clarity, Blanco saw movement from the van sitting on the street. He saw the side door closest to the house open, and then the driver's side of the van closest to his wife's vehicle open as well. Realizing what was happening, Blanco knew there was only one thing he could do at that point to protect them.

"GO! NOW!" He yelled in Spanish, mustering all the energy he had.

Leon turned around to see what was going on and immediately went to grab the pistol at his side, and Blanco used that opportunity, and every reserve of strength he could find, to jump up and attempt to put the larger man in a headlock, from behind.

To her credit, his wife sped away as quickly as she could. The driver of the black van, Nestor, was able to shove his left hand in the open window and grab the steering wheel as the car accelerated forward. He was dragged by the vehicle as he hung onto the steering wheel with his left hand and grabbed at the back of the woman's head with his right hand. The jerking back and forth of the steering wheel caused the vehicle to veer wildly to the right. Nestor's superior strength then caused the Malibu to swerve back to the left, directly into the front of a passing truck.

Nestor's body suffered the direct impact with the front of the truck, instantly breaking his back and damaging his spine, leaving him bloodied and paralyzed.

The door to the Malibu was caved in, and Blanco's wife had been stunned in the impact with the truck, but fortunately she had on her seatbelt, and her survival and motherly instincts kicked in. She immediately backed the vehicle up and fled the area, not waiting to see what the driver of the truck said or did, leaving Nestor's crumpled body lying on the ground.

Back at the house, Leon flung himself backwards with all his might, crushing Blanco against the brick of the house. With Blanco's grip weakened, Leon was able to turn around and dig his hand directly into the area where he had stabbed Blanco moments earlier.

A scream erupted out of Blanco's mouth as he held on as tightly as he could, knowing that his efforts would ultimately prove futile. Nevertheless, the injured man put up the best fight he could and took a huge chunk out of Leon's damaged left ear, which had been bitten by Rod.

The tenderness of the damaged ear being bitten, again, caused one of the most intense pains Leon had ever felt. The rage that boiled up inside Leon in that moment was unfiltered, and he began delivering punishing blows, first a right hook, then a left, then right and left, again and again, directly into the stomach of the injured Blanco.

Those blows took a toll, and Blanco fell against the wall outside the house. Leon picked him up and threw him like a rag doll through the partially opened front door.

Leon walked to the duffel bag against the wall near the front door and opened it up to see the $10,000 that Blanco had intended to use to start a new life with his family.

"Where is the rest of the money?" Leon demanded to know.

Trying to regain his breath, while still clutching his side, Blanco told him that was all he had.

"I'll just see for myself," Leon said, and started to walk through the house, kicking Blanco in the side as he walked away, cracking some of the man's ribs, and then grabbing the man by his shoes, and using his blade to slice Blanco's Achilles tendon, assuring himself that the man wouldn't be able to flee.

Blanco did manage to find his telephone. He had stashed it in his duffle bag with the money. Blanco immediately called 911, whispering his address and informing the operator that someone had come to his house to rob and kill him. The 911 operator said they were sending a law enforcement unit to the house as soon as possible.

Blanco quickly ended the telephone call, and one last time, attempted to call Rod. Blanco had no way of knowing that Rod had been suspended from the DEA earlier that day, and that his phone had been taken from him by DEA management and was sitting on the desk of an administrative support specialist at that time. The call rang and rang, and with no answer, Blanco realized that his wife and child would likely never get the help or protection they needed from the vindictive Cartel de Culiacan.

Leon's quick search showed that Blanco had left little to search through. Leon strolled back into the foyer, looked at Blanco, and then at his phone, and realized that the man had most recently called 911.

Leon pulled out his handgun and placed it against Blanco's head, pulling the trigger without even saying another word. He picked up the duffel bag and walked outside to the van. When he was informed that Nestor was on the street outside and was not moving, Leon told them that they could not afford to wait because the police were on the way.

"We're leaving him," Leon said, blood trickling down his face from his now twice bitten ear. "Somebody else get behind the wheel and drive."

Chapter 17
San Diego, California

Saturday, September 2

"You have to get to LA," Vero relayed to Tyler, while the intercepted conversation continued playing in the background. The lead wiretap monitor for Tyler's case knew the importance of the call. "Tonio is picking up Felipe from the Tijuana airport right now, and they are on their way to Los Angeles. Felipe said he found out who killed El Jefe's wife, some guy named Jose Padilla. The guy is living in Los Angeles. He's going there to kill Padilla and then collect the $10 million reward from El Jefe."

Tyler had been hoping to spend his day at home, saddened and grieving over the death of a fellow DEA agent in Juarez days earlier. He instructed Vero to update him immediately with any new call and started contacting everyone he knew that might be able to help him find Tonio's vehicle and follow it to Los Angeles.

* * *

Reuben Valdez was the only person in the DEA office when his phone rang.

"You're the only person that will answer the phone!" Tyler raged.

"It's Saturday morning. You know DEA hours are 9-5 Monday thru Friday. What's going on?"

Tyler explained the information exactly as it was relayed to him from the wire room.

"Do you have any idea how to find Tonio's vehicle?" Reuben asked.

"I know what kind of vehicle he drives. A Chevy Cobalt. We can set up south of LA and hope to find him when he is traveling north."

"That'll be tough," Reuben said, "but it might be our best shot."

The two men agreed that Tyler would travel up the 5 freeway in San Clemente and find a location with a good vantage point of the vehicles traveling northbound. Reuben would find a location on the 5 freeway south of downtown Los Angeles in case Tyler missed the vehicle as it traveled north.

"The question," Reuben said, "is if we should stop the car or let it get all the way to its destination. If we let the vehicle get there, we can identify the guy that killed El Jefe's wife and find out who paid him to kill her. That's what this guy wants that kidnapped Ana Lucia. Maybe we could save her life."

"I was thinking the same thing," Tyler said. "But can we really let a vehicle go when we know the occupants are intending to kill somebody in Los Angeles?"

"Normally I would say no. But in this case, with the life of a DEA agent on the line, I would say we would be derelict of duty if we didn't do it this way."

"I agree, but the bosses will never allow it."

"Did any of those guys answer their phone?"

"No."

"Then you say you tried. It might be the only chance we have to rescue Ana Lucia."

"Ok, let's do it."

* * *

Two hours later, Tyler saw Tonio's vehicle as it traveled up the 5 freeway. Debating whether or not he should end the surveillance and stop the car, he continued to allow the vehicle to travel north, convincing himself that he would be able to stop the pending execution once the residence was identified in Los Angeles.

Once the car got in the Los Angeles area, Tonio began performing counter-surveillance measures, exiting freeways, and getting back on immediately. Stopping at green lights. Speeding through yellow lights that were about to turn red. Pulling to the side of the road. Entering a neighborhood and making multiple left turns in a row, all the while, Felipe watched the mirrors to make sure they were not being followed.

Reuben was able to catch up with Tyler, but knowing what they were doing, both of the veteran agents were careful to avoid being compromised, but also did not want to risk losing the vehicle, knowing that Jose Padilla was as good as dead if that happened.

The two veteran DEA agents were able to maintain a reasonable distance from the Cobalt without being seen, until disaster struck. An 18-wheeler turning left on a highway somewhere off the 110 Freeway turned too fast, and fell over, spilling its contents on the road, blocking all motorists from continuing. Unfortunately for Tyler and Reuben, the Cobalt was already passed the area where the accident occurred, and they were two car lengths behind.

Both agents frantically looked for a way to catch back up with the Cobalt, with Tyler even driving on the sidewalk, but it was too late. The Cobalt got on the 110 freeway, and within moments, was out of sight.

* * *

"There it is. Pull in front of the mailbox and I'll get out," Felipe instructed Tonio once the Cobalt arrived in the South Los Angeles neighborhood on 92nd Street. A white Tacoma, driven by Tonio's friend Chuy, had already arrived, and stopped on the street one house over. The entire front yard of the property was surrounded by a waist high black metal gate. The sliding gate had to be pulled back for vehicles to enter or leave the driveway, which was to the right of the house from where Felipe was facing the residence. An old burgundy Chrysler Sebring was parked in the driveway.

Felipe tugged on the gate, but it was locked. With ease, he put one hand on the gate and jumped over it, landing on the side of the yard near the residence. Felipe motioned at Tonio to continue driving around the neighborhood, watching for any signs of law enforcement so that it could be relayed to Felipe in time for him to get out of the house. Meanwhile, Chuy would stay in the Tacoma and watch to see if any vehicles came directly to the residence while Felipe was inside. Satisfied that Tonio was watching the entrance to the neighborhood and surrounding streets, and Chuy was watching the house, Felipe walked to the front door with all the confidence in the world.

The door was answered by a Hispanic female that appeared to be in her 70s. Guessing that it was the grandmother of the waiter's girlfriend, Felipe gave his biggest smile and asked if Maria was there, claiming to be an old friend from Juarez that had recently relocated to Southern California.

The older woman, despite her age, had not lost her mental sharpness, and immediately narrowed her eyes, realizing that nobody was supposed to know the location of her granddaughter. At the first sign of denial, Felipe used his shoulder to bust open the door, knocking the older lady onto the floor of the living room. Felipe quickly entered the house and shut the door behind him. A quick scan confirmed the layout of the house. The front door opened into a living room, which had a television against the wall to his left closest to the street, with a couch ahead and a recliner on the left side. The kitchen was straight ahead, with the open floor plan allowing the individual to see both living room and kitchen. On both sides of the living room were hallways, which Felipe deducted could have no more than two small bedrooms on each side, perhaps a closet or a bathroom in place of the bedroom. Having made the assessment, Felipe withdrew his gun from his back waist and kneeled, with the barrel inches from the face of the elderly occupant.

The commotion from the living room of the residence brought Maria down the hallway to Felipe's right side. Seeing her, Felipe smiled big. Seeing her pregnant belly, he knew he had the leverage to bring out Jose Padilla from whatever rock he was hiding under.

* * *

Maria called out to her grandmother, but the older woman told the pregnant Maria to run and not look back. Felipe pushed the barrel of the gun into the grandmother's head. "I'm not here to kill your grandmother," Felipe said. "I'm not even here to kill you, or your baby, but I will without hesitation if you do not tell me where Jose is...right now."

The panicked look Maria gave to her grandmother confirmed her consideration of the demand. She obviously knew that telling Felipe where Jose was would result in his death, but not doing so would result in the death of her grandmother, and likely her own unborn child, who she would do anything to protect, as would Jose. It was the main reason that they had fled the violence of Juarez and come to the United States.

"Now!" Felipe yelled after several seconds of silence, "or I start with your grandmother here and then will shoot your stomach. And do not think about running, I will chase you down in the street and cut that child right out of you."

"Okay, please just don't hurt my grandmother or my child," Maria said, rationalizing that Jose would give his life for this unborn child, something he had confirmed to her daily.

"Jose is not here."

"Not good enough! Now she dies!"

"NO! NO! He's close by. I can call him."

"No, Maria, they will kill the poor boy. You will bring him to his grave if you call," the grandmother said.

"He would do anything to save this child," Maria told her. "It's what he would want."

"Where is he?" Felipe demanded to know.

"He's about two blocks over, helping lay sod and plant flowers at a house."

"Get your phone and bring it to me. I'll watch you send him a text to come home immediately because you are bleeding."

Jose responded within a minute, telling his girlfriend he would be there shortly to take her to the hospital.

During the two minutes that it took Jose to go from his location to the residence on 92nd street, Felipe took out two zip ties from a cargo pocket and tied the hands of both women behind them. He then led them to the bedroom on the hallway to the right where Maria had come from. The bedroom had a small window facing out to the front yard. Felipe left the blinds open slightly so that he could see out. He instructed the two women to lay down on the ground and found some rags and clothing to tie around their heads and put in their mouth to keep them from speaking. Felipe told them that if they tried to escape, then he would instruct the guy sitting in the white truck outside to shoot them both immediately.

Felipe informed Chuy, who was still sitting outside the residence in the Tacoma, that young Jose Padilla should be showing up any minute.

True to his word, a small Ford work truck pulled on the street in front of the black metal gate. Not waiting to unlock the gate, he jumped over it just the same as Felipe. Jose raced into the residence calling the name of his beloved, only to be met by Felipe standing to the side of the front door with a gun leveled at his head.

"Hello, Jose. Follow me to the bedroom, where you will see your young pregnant girlfriend. If you want her to survive and your baby to be born, you will tell me what I want to know."

Jose's eyes widened with despair and grief as he saw Maria bound and gagged on the floor of the bedroom lying next to her grandmother. Jose held a special place in his heart for the woman that had welcomed them into her home in their time of need and provided them food and shelter. He resolved to sacrifice himself to ensure their survival.

Felipe motioned for the young man to sit down in a desk chair that he pulled to the middle of the room. Jose sat in the chair facing Felipe, who pulled out his telephone to record the confession of the killer.

"Do you know why I'm here?" Felipe asked.

The young man turned and looked into Maria's eyes, and his own eyes teared up with the realization that he was never going to marry her or see the birth of their child. He tried to compose himself and looked at Felipe.

"I will tell you what you want to know, as long as you swear to me that you won't harm them," Jose said to Felipe.

"You are in no place to make demands, young man. But I am not a soulless human being. I do not take pleasure in killing old ladies with nothing to do with what you have done, or young ladies that are pregnant. When I press the record button on this phone, if you answer the questions honestly, then you have my word that I will not harm them. If you do not answer truthfully, then you have my word that I will inflict more suffering and pain on them than your brain can imagine. Do you understand?"

Even as a Federal Police Officer that had initially dedicated his life to the protection of others from criminals, the overwhelming influence and power of the drug trafficking world in his life had calloused Felipe's hearts to the point where he was able to say the things he had just said without so much of an inward look at himself and his moral compass.

Jose nodded his head, and Felipe hit record.

"State your name," Felipe started.

"Jose Padilla."

"Where are you from Jose Padilla?"

"Juarez initially. Then I moved to Durango."

"Where did you work while in Durango?"

"At a restaurant, Javier's steakhouse."

"And were you working at that restaurant on the night that El Jefe's wife was dining there when she was poisoned and killed?"

A pause, and then "Yes."

"Did you poison El Jefe's wife?"

Another pause, and another affirmative answer, "Yes."

"With what poison?"

"I don't even know. It was given to me by somebody else."

"So, you did this at the request of another person. How much did you get paid to murder an innocent woman?

Jose shook his head and looked down at the floor in front of him. "$50,000 US dollars. Half was given in cash before, and the other half was given in a wire transfer after."

"Where is the cash?" Felipe asked, intending to take the money back.

"I put most of it in the bank, but I still have $10,000."

"What were you going to do with this blood money that was given to you to murder another man's wife?"

"I was going to use it to build a house in Ontario or somewhere in San Bernardino, after Maria gave birth to the baby. There is a doctor here in LA that her grandmother trusted, which is why we stayed here."

With that disclosure, Felipe turned the camera on the pregnant Maria, bound and gagged on the floor. "That is the Maria you are talking about?"

"Yes, it is. Now please, let her go."

"We're not finished yet, Jose. Tell me, where is the cash that you still have? That way I won't have to destroy your girlfriend's grandmother's house looking for it."

Resigned, Jose admitted that the money was in the closet behind Maria. Felipe strolled over and slid open the closet door. Pulling the black duffel bag off the top shelf, Felipe looked inside and saw the $10,000.

"Now that one piece of the puzzle has been solved regarding the killer, let's find the other piece. Who paid you to do this? Who ordered El Jefe's wife to be killed?"

Jose thought about his answer, and then slowly shrugged his shoulders. "I don't know the man's name, or where he was from, but he was Mexican named Oscar."

"Was he from law enforcement, or a political figure?"

"No, I don't believe so, but I have no proof that he wasn't."

"What can you tell me about him?"

"Well, I can tell you that I don't believe he was the person responsible for ordering the..."

"Murder?" Felipe added, finishing the sentence.

Jose nodded. "And why do you say that?" Felipe asked.

"Because, when Oscar was paying me the last time and I met him, he got a text message that he was having a hard time reading...because it was in English."

"So, the Mexican contact received a text message from an American?"

"I believe so, but I don't know. All I know is that the text was in English."

"What did the text say?"

Another pause. "It said to make sure the daughter was not killed. El Jefe's daughter."

Felipe had enough information. He sat the phone in a position so that it would continue to record. He would need to get Wi-Fi before he would be able to send the video on the Group chat, but he was confident the video would earn him the reward for identifying the killer. Now he had to finish it.

He walked behind Jose and grabbed his forehead with his left arm, intending to cut his throat with the blade in his right arm. Instinctively, Jose struggled, bringing his arms to his throat to protect himself. Felipe quickly brought the blade down into Jose's right stomach, pulling it out just as quickly.

Reflexes caused Jose's protection of his throat to momentarily drop as he moved his hands to his stomach to the site of the stabbing. That was all Felipe needed, as he quickly brought the blade up and opened the man's throat, from left to right, for all to see in the video.

Despite the gag in her mouth, Maria's screaming and sobbing could be heard, but Felipe refused to feel sorry for her, although he did intend to keep his word to Jose that he would not harm the woman. Walking back over to table, Felipe ended the recording, confident that he had earned $10 million, as soon as he could get WIFI to send the video to the Group Chat.

Felipe's attention then returned to Maria, who had stopped screaming. He looked at her and noticed that her gaze was out the window. Turning to see what she was looking at Felipe noticed the form of a man running by the window and toward the front door. Felipe kicked both women in the head, knocking them unconscious. He pulled his gun out to greet the intruder as he stepped over the dead body of Jose Padilla.

* * *

Just prior to getting to the location, Felipe had called Chuy, the individual acting as a lookout, and provided him with the address on 92nd Street and told him to wait in front of the residence in order to provide security. That call was intercepted by Veronica and the wiretap monitors in San Diego, and relayed to Tyler and Reuben in Los Angeles, but it came almost 10 minutes after the two agents had lost sight of the Cobalt.

Tyler and Reuben had split up, traveling in different directions attempting to find the Cobalt. When Vero called Tyler with the address, he passed it on to Reuben, but he realized he was at least five minutes closer, so he raced to the location as quickly as possible.

The white Tacoma was immediately in sight upon making the left turn onto 92nd street, parked in an area on the street in front of a residence with a waist high black metal gate five to six houses east of the intersection with San Pedro. Approaching from behind, Tyler found an open spot on the curb three car lengths behind the white Tacoma. He quickly jumped into the back seat of his Official Government Vehicle and slid on his DEA vest. There was no time to put in the metal plates that would protect him from more high-powered rounds, but what he had on would at least offer protection against most handguns.

Trying to conceal his presence, he exited the rear passenger door of the Silverado and approached the white Tacoma from the rear passenger side. The driver of the Tacoma, Chuy, was staring up and down the street, and looking in his driver's side mirror, intently watching for the presence of a law enforcement vehicle. The Silverado that parked behind him did not even get his attention when it parked, and he was surprised when the door opened, and he was met with Tyler's Glock pointing at him. Fortunately for the DEA agent, the door had been unlocked, which he had surmised it would be in the event that this was a get-away vehicle.

Just prior to opening the door, Tyler removed his handcuffs. Keeping the gun trained on the driver, the DEA agent handcuffed Chuy's right hand, and placed the other cuff on the steering wheel, ensuring that Chuy would not be able to leave. He also noticed a Smith & Wesson revolver under the man's right leg. Keeping his Glock on Chuy, Tyler grabbed the gun and emptied it, throwing it in under the car and out of reach. He then grabbed the keys out of the ignition and slid them in his pocket.

Fate had Tyler pass by the window of the bedroom where Felipe had Jose, Maria, and Maria's grandmother just after Felipe murdered Jose. In his haste, he hadn't seen Felipe or even Jose, but because of his speed and the randomness of where his glance went inside the window, he made direct eye contact with Maria, and noticed her lying on the floor with her mouth gagged. It was at that moment that she stopped struggling and screaming, the moment when Felipe realized he had company. Also, a horn started blaring from the street. Chuy was doing whatever he could to warn whoever was inside of Tyler's presence. Tyler did not wait a moment longer and ran toward the nearby front door.

Both men entered the living room of the residence from different points at the same time, with Tyler charging in from the front door, and Felipe moving from the hallway to Tyler's right. Both men's guns were out and fired wildly at the other as they moved instinctively towards any cover or concealment they could find.

The shots were wildly inaccurate, lodging in different sections of wall and floor. Felipe's momentum took him to his right where he found concealment behind a bar in the middle of the kitchen. Meanwhile, Tyler lunged for the hallway to his left to keep a wall separating him from the gun fire coming from the kitchen.

Felipe threw his arm out, wildly shooting towards the hallway, but coming nowhere close to hitting the DEA agent who was low to the ground. After five rounds slammed into the wall above his head there was a momentary lull, and Tyler moved out slightly and fired three rounds directly into the bar in the middle of the kitchen where Felipe was hiding behind. With return fire moments later, Tyler realized that Felipe was still alive and well, and this time his shots were getting closer, going through the wall all around Tyler.

At that exact moment, Tonio burst through the front door. Tonio ran through the living room into the kitchen to get with Felipe, but in doing so went directly past Tyler's line of sight, meaning that neither man would have concealment during the brief moment when Tonio went through the living room. Both Tonio and Tyler fired at each other in desperation. Of the five shots that Tyler fired at Tonio as he ran through the living room towards the concealment of the kitchen, one found its mark, lodging itself directly in the man's left hip, causing him to stumble and fall into the kitchen. In the heat of the moment, Tonio was able to get up and return fire, as did Felipe. The wall was now tearing away above and around him, and with twice as many shots coming in as before, Tyler moved as far back down the hallway as possible, realizing that he was going in the opposite direction from the woman that was bound and gagged, but backwards was the only area available to him where he could safely go.

Tyler knew when he moved back, Felipe was going to move directly toward him with Tonio providing covering fire. Realizing how dire the situation was, Tyler moved towards the rearmost door on the hallway, and opened it to realize that it was not a bedroom that had a window leading outside, but rather a closet. Turning back to face the oncoming threat, a round slammed into his vest, with the impact knocking out his breath and slamming him against the rear wall.

At what he thought was his last moment, Tyler heard the unmistakable sound of a rifle firing. As he gasped for breath and tried to raise his gun and steady for a shot, Reuben came into sight, firing his rifle towards the kitchen. He stopped at the hallway and looked down to see Tyler slumped against the back wall. Firing two more shots into the kitchen area, Tyler saw the large man run toward him, and grab him by the vest and drag him out as if he were a small child.

Being dragged out the front door, Tyler saw flames leaping from the kitchen, having been caused by Felipe and Tonio knocking over a candle in their attempt to flee.

Once they reached the safety of the street outside, Reuben claimed he had hit one of the two shooters, but that they fled through the back yard. Tyler assured Reuben that he was fine and just had the breath knocked out of him.

Tyler looked back and realized the woman that he saw through the window was still in the house, and that she would be killed in the fire. Not thinking twice, Tyler ran back into the house, even as the flames leaped all around, already spreading from room to room. Not knowing what his friend and counterpart from San Diego was doing, Reuben went in behind him.

* * *

As the first responders arrived on scene from the Los Angeles Police and Fire Department, the two women that had been saved by the DEA agents rested on the tailgate of Tyler's Silverado, as the elder woman, having regained consciousness, wept while watching her home burn to the ground.

Before they arrived, Reuben looked anxiously at his watch, and then looked up at Tyler.

"I've got to go," Reuben said.

Tyler shook his head. "We were just in a shooting. We have to stay here until the bosses arrive."

Reuben looked conflicted. "No, I mean I'm going after the guys that did this. I saw both guys. They cannot be too far away. They probably stole a car on the next street over. I'll find them." Before Tyler could respond, Reuben ran to his Ford F-150, throwing his rifle into the rear of the truck, and then racing off down the street just as the first fire trucks were arriving on scene.

Tyler had seen the body of Jose Padilla lying in the floor when he went into the room to rescue Maria and her grandmother. He was upset that the man had been killed, but he also closed his eyes and prayed that the woman before him would be able to provide the least bit of information that might be useful in saving Ana Lucia's life.

Tyler could have used Reuben's fluency in Spanish to speak to Maria, but he asked her if she understood English, and she nodded. The firemen were getting out of the trucks at that same time to put out the blaze and make sure it did not spread to another residence.

"I'm very sorry for what happened in there. Whatever he did in Mexico to cause this retaliation, I am sure he had his reasons," Tyler said, pointing at Maria's stomach. "I am a father too and would have done anything to get my child out of a violent situation. I do not judge him for that, but what I need to know, and lives depend on your answer, is who paid your boyfriend to do what he did?"

Having interviewed hundreds of people over the course of his career, Tyler tried the common law enforcement approach of interviewing in which he justified the guilty person's actions, in this instance using Jose's desire to raise a family away from violence and death as justification for getting paid to murder the wife of the leader of the Cartel de Culiacan. He was also careful to avoid the specific word of murder. Drug dealers often disguised words such as cocaine for product, drug trafficking proceeds for paper, or even used the less harsh word deed to refer to a cartel paid assassination. For that reason, Tyler was careful to not use the word murder when he described what the woman's boyfriend had done in Mexico.

Still, Maria seemed reluctant to speak, so Tyler had to quickly adjust his approach. "If you are worried about being sent back to Mexico, then don't be. I will make sure you are not deported, so you can have your baby here in the US, because we both know what will happen if you go back to Mexico. But first, tell me who ordered him to do the deed?" Tyler looked up and made direct eye contact with a

LAPD officer that had arrived on scene and was approaching him from about 50 feet away.

Maria, still with no clue who Tyler was, asked if he was a police officer. Tyler pulled out his DEA badge and showed her. Her eyes got wide as she saw the badge.

"All I know is what Jose said just before that awful man killed him. Jose told the man that he was paid by a man named Oscar, but that Oscar was receiving instruction from somebody that sent a message to him in English. It had to be an American."

At that moment, the LAPD officer forcefully grabbed Tyler's shoulder and demanded his identification. Tyler showed him his badge, and within moments, the LAPD officer was requesting more information about the shootout that occurred. Tyler made all the necessary calls to DEA management, who were immediately informed of the necessity to report to the scene of a shooting involving a DEA agent. Tyler knew that the DEA management from the Los Angeles Field Division were not going to be happy about a shooting in their area of responsibility without being notified, because Tyler was certain that Reuben had not informed them of his presence.

Tyler followed DEA procedure, waiting to provide his gun to DEA management. He also refused to make a statement about the shooting until their arrival, much to the frustration of the LAPD officers.

While on the scene, Tyler considered the information he had just been given. If an American was truly responsible for paying for the murder of El Jefe's wife, then it was most likely an American working for one of the main branches of law enforcement. A private American citizen would not have had the knowledge or resources to carry out the mission, which meant there were only a few agencies that possessed that kind of capability. But who? Would his own agency have ordered the murder of an innocent woman? Or perhaps the FBI, HSI, or CIA? And why?

Chapter 18
Mexico City, Mexico

Saturday, September 2

Most of Saturday passed by without word from anybody in DEA regarding Ana Lucia's kidnapping and the search to find her, or any information that would save her life. The death of a fellow agent in Juarez was heavy on the minds of everyone in the agency, but Brandon really felt like his co-workers should be doing everything possible to make sure that a second agent was not added to that list. Brandon had tried to put away his worry and enjoy a nice meal with his wife and kids at a local eatery in the neighborhood surrounding his government living quarters. He wanted to be close to his residence, and his Official Government Vehicle, in case something came up requiring his attention. That telephone call came in two hours before Toro's deadline, well after Brandon and his family had returned from their family meal.

Brandon was deleting texts sent by his mistress, Leticia, which included photos of her in various stages of undress, when the call came. He hadn't spoken to Leticia much since learning the news about Ana Lucia, and what was left of his conscious was seeming to convict him of his transgressions and urged him to break off the relationship with the younger woman and confess his misdeeds to his wife. As those thoughts were rumbling through his mind, Brandon's phone showed an incoming call from SOD Coordinator Michael Winston.

"Hey, Mike," Brandon answered, "You have anything?"

"Yes, two things. First and most urgent, contact the informant you have there in the Cartel. Something happened in LA, it's a long story, but Tyler Jameson and Reuben Valdez were involved in a shootout earlier today in South Los Angeles. Both are okay, but somebody from Mexico figured out that the waiter that poisoned El Jefe's wife had fled to LA, and someone drove to LA to kill the waiter and collect one of El Jefe's two $10 million rewards. Tyler intercepted some of the conversation on his wiretap down in San Diego. The waiter was killed during the shootout, but Tyler was able to rescue the waiter's pregnant girlfriend, and she told him that her boyfriend didn't know specifically who had paid him to kill El Jefe's wife, but he suspected it was an American because the individual that provided him payment for the murder received a text at the last minute which was in English."

"Meaning that an American was responsible for ordering the murder?" Brandon asked.

"It appears so."

"Do we have any idea who?"

"Not yet, but it's more than we had a few hours ago. Can you provide that information to the informant and tell him to give it to El Jefe? Assure him that we are working tirelessly to find out who did this, but he cannot kill Ana Lucia. If he does, then he will never find the information El Jefe wants."

"I'll call and see, but we are basically saying we know it's somebody that speaks English, but we're not sure who. I don't know if that's going to work."

"Just call the informant and see," the SOD Coordinator pleaded. "It's the least we can do."

"Okay," Brandon said. "Was there something else you wanted to tell me?"

"Yes, regarding the situation with El Paso DEA, the SAC there has steadfastly maintained that Rod is suspended despite the situation. They even demoted the group supervisor, so I have not been able to get a contact for anybody in that group until just now. I was given the name and number for Trevor Johnson. He worked with Ana Lucia and Rod in El Paso. If you find out any information about Ana Lucia, call Trevor."

"Okay, thanks. Let me make some calls."

* * *

"**Before** Brandon could place a call to the informant, he received an incoming call from a restricted number.

"My name is Toby Phillips. I work in the embassy. I've seen you around some. We talked about the Pats winning another Super Bowl a couple months back during the July 4th celebration."

Brandon remembered. Toby was a black male under six feet tall with wide, stocky shoulders, and a thick lower body. He remembered Toby's fluency in Spanish and the ease with which he spoke Spanish with the Mexican nationals working in the cafeteria. Hailing from Boston, Toby was obsessed with all things sports related, and passionately discussed the Patriots, Celtics, Red Sox, Bruins, and even the Revolution of Major League Soccer. Toby had said he worked in the Agricultural Section in the State Department...which Brandon knew probably meant he was a Case Officer with the CIA. Even other federal agencies weren't clued in on the identity of the CIA case officers, but it wasn't that difficult to figure out if you hung around the Embassy. They were usually very smart, very easy to talk to, and very unassuming in their interaction with others. They didn't look like the straight laced, super-serious feds running around the FBI or DEA.

"Right, Toby, from the Ag section of the State Department," Brandon said.

"That's right. By now I'm sure you realize my employer."

"Yeah, I figured it out."

"Well you should know that we have some aerial surveillance that has been deployed to assist in finding your co-worker that was kidnapped."

"Really?"

"Yes, and we were able to determine that the vehicle that left the border with your co-worker traveled to a near by horse farm. It stayed there for a few minutes and then left with another vehicle, driving further south. We were able to arrange for a stop of one of the vehicles. There was only one person inside. He was obviously a member of the team that kidnapped your co-worker earlier in the day. A considerable amount of leverage was used on this individual to try and find the location where Special Agent Rodriguez was taken, but the man did not know."

"Okay," Brandon said, wondering why the CIA Case officer called him if he didn't have any active information to pass on.

"But while the man didn't know where Toro's group went, he was able to tell us with certainty where they did *not* go."

"Where is that?"

"They did not stay in Juarez, nor did they go to Durango or Chihuahua."

Brandon knew those were the main locations law enforcement was looking for Ana Lucia. If she wasn't there, then where was she?

"How confident are you that the man was being truthful?"

"Very. If I am able to assist with any more aerial surveillance, I will let you know."

"Thanks," Brandon said, ending the call and looking at the map of Mexico to determine where Ana Lucia had been taken."

* * *

"Brandon, that doesn't tell me anything I don't already know," the informant said after the information from the SOD Coordinator was relayed. "We always knew the Americans were involved, but we don't even know which of your agencies was responsible for the hit. El Jefe wants somebody held accountable for the death of an innocent civilian. While it's appreciated that you are attempting to find the requested information, what you have now is simply not enough. Out of respect for your efforts, I will take this information to El Jefe, but I do not anticipate it will be sufficient to meet his demands."

The informant returned his call less than ten minutes later. Obviously, he had direct contact with the big boss, whether it was in person or by phone, confirming his high-ranking status in the organization. Just like he suspected, the informant told Brandon that El Jefe said the information cultivated in Los Angeles was not sufficient to call off the execution of Ana Lucia, nor would he instruct Toro to push back his pending deadline. Further, even El Jefe himself did not know Toro's exact location, as the veteran hitman had gone radio silent, refusing to disclose his whereabouts to anyone not involved.

"There is one thing that I can provide you," the informant said.

"It needs to be something good."

"I have received the first batch of coordinates for the location of all the cell phones I gave you the last time we met. I am going to send an encrypted email to the email address you provided me during our first meeting. There might be something that interests you."

The line went dead. Brandon quickly ran over to his laptop and accessed his work email address. An incoming email had just been received.

Looking at the longitude and latitude, he saw many that he knew were in Mexico. But then he saw a coordinate that was from Texas, which he knew from previously working in Dallas. Brandon looked up the coordinates. It was in El Paso. He looked at the list of names that had been provided by the informant during their recent meeting. The individual in El Paso was a defense attorney.

Brandon's earlier conversation with the CIA case officer played in his head, with Toby telling him the CIA was certain that Ana Lucia was not in Juarez, Durango, or Chihuahua. He didn't say anything about El Paso. Brandon quickly placed a call Trevor Johnson in El Paso."

* * *

El Paso, Texas

Trevor Johnson had a previously scheduled date for Saturday night with a very attractive Hispanic woman that he met at a local Starbucks the week earlier. He just had not felt right about going out and enjoying himself on a date knowing Ana Lucia might be killed. Like everyone else in El Paso, he suspected that Ana Lucia was in Juarez, if not somewhere else deeper in Mexico. He didn't think there was anything that he could do that would contribute to finding the kidnapped DEA agent, but nevertheless, he had asked to move the date to the following week because he knew that his mind would not be in the right place. His date, Catherine, a marketing director at a local accounting firm, had seen the news about the shootout involving DEA agents at the border separating Juarez and El Paso, and although she didn't know much about the situation, correctly assumed that Trevor's cancellation of their date didn't have to do with her, as much as it did with what was on the news.

Yet when Trevor's phone rang at 10:30 p.m. Saturday night, he quickly answered, hoping for good news that Ana Lucia had been found and rescued. With Rod suspended and his boss demoted, Trevor knew that if a lead came to the group, he was going to have to be the one to track it down, so when Brandon called from Mexico City and informed him that a defense attorney with known links directly to the Cartel de Culiacan had been identified in El Paso, Trevor agreed to track down the defense attorney and follow him around to see what he could find out. Brandon stressed that it was unknown whether this individual had knowledge of Ana Lucia's whereabouts.

The GPS location showed pings as close as 10 meters in the Castner Heights neighborhood, located in northeast El Paso. Brandon assured Trevor that he would have the SOD Coordinator contact the ASAC in El Paso to inform him of Trevor's assignment. Trevor hadn't been sure who he was supposed to report to, especially since he had never even spoken directly to the ASAC, so Brandon decided to take that responsibility off his plate so that Trevor could get to Castner Heights to see if by some chance, this defense attorney did in fact have something to do with Ana Lucia's kidnapping.

* * *

Ana Lucia's mind was slowly starting to focus on her surroundings, but her thoughts remained sluggish and unable to concentrate on anything specific. The dose of morphine that had been injected into her earlier that day had been administered so that Toro could rest himself and not worry about the DEA agent escaping. The morphine had been provided to Toro by George, the defense attorney, who had delivered four doses earlier that morning, with instruction that providing it once every 12 hours would have the desired effect of rendering Ana Lucia in a dazed state that would prevent her from leaving or fighting back.

The defense attorney had also picked up a cheap pre-paid telephone from Wal-Mart, and provided it to Toro, because he refused to turn on his Mexican cell phone while in the United States. His paranoia regarding American law enforcement capabilities was the reason behind his decision, and his instincts had always served him well, so he followed them again in this instance.

Toro used the prepaid cell phone only when he needed to contact the defense attorney a couple times on Saturday, and once in the afternoon to speak with Leon, who confirmed that the group had made it to Nogales, Arizona, and then into Nogales, Mexico. Leon failed to inform Toro about the group's detour the night before and killing of Blanco, an incident that also cost the team Nestor, the third member of the group that had been lost since the mission started in Chihuahua days before.

Toro had rested on the wall opposite Ana Lucia for a couple hours earlier while she was feeling the effects of the Morphine, but now, as the hour approached midnight, Toro and Ana Lucia both sat against opposite walls looking at each other.

"What time is it?" Ana Lucia asked.

"11:45, 15 minutes until midnight. It doesn't seem like your government is as concerned about your safety as I thought they would be," Toro told her.

"My government does not deal with terrorists."

"I'm not a terrorist. Not in the American sense at least."

"You've kidnapped an innocent person and are threatening to kill me unless certain information is released. Sounds like a terrorist to me. Might not be what you were, but it's what you've become."

"You haven't been harmed. In fact, nobody has touched a hair on your head. I made sure of that. That would not have happened in a terrorist camp."

"Other than smashing me in the face with your gun at the border and injecting me with whatever crap you did earlier to make me feel tired and sluggish, no you haven't hurt me, but that's little consolation since I only have 15 minutes to live before you kill me and post the video online."

"Nothing else will be posted online," Toro assured her.

"Why do you even care who killed El Jefe's wife?"

"She was an innocent woman," Toro said.

"No, she was a woman who was married to one of the biggest criminals in the world, someone that has been responsible for ordering the murder of thousands of people. He is pushing drugs into the United States that is destroying our society and causing deaths here. Sure, the consumers are here, I get it, but it does not make it right. People are dying because of drug overdoses. Families are being broken because of addictions.

"Surely El Jefe's wife knew what he was doing. She enjoyed a luxurious life because of the income he earned in drug trafficking, a business which necessitates the murder of who knows how many people every day. I honestly have no idea who was responsible for ordering the woman's murder, but I do think that it's very ironic that after all the people El Jefe has ordered to be killed, he is now willing to do anything when his not really innocent wife is killed."

Silence hung in the air for several moments as Toro considered whether to respond. Before he said anything else, Ana Lucia continued, "I'm sure you convince yourself that you are justified in your actions because you are killing guilty people, but by doing so you are making yourself a judge of that person's guilt, whether it is for the crime of corruption, stealing, murder, rape, or whatever. What have you convinced yourself is the crime I have committed that will satisfy your conscious when you kill me in a few minutes? Because the way I look at it, I'm on the right side. I stand against corruption, stealing, murder, and rape. While you might kill those people, I arrest them so that they receive judgement by a jury of their peers. That's the main difference between you and me. But you agree to work for a murderous drug cartel. Even if you are killing bad people, it does not make it right to work for a bad guy. You're just killing off his enemies."

"I don't need to be a good guy. I'm fine with what I am, a bad guy, a killer."

"Yeah, and you became that way after your adoptive mother was killed and your sister was taken, but if you were that committed to making bad guys pay for their crimes, then why didn't you join law enforcement?"

"Because they are corrupt. I would not have had as much access as I do now. Once I started with El Jefe, the first 10 people on my list were all police officers that were corrupt, stealing money or drugs, or raping girlfriends or wives of Cartel employees. And you know who provided that information to the Cartel? Other police officers. It was obvious that corruption was everywhere."

"Well, now you have a decision to make, because this will be the first time you have to kill somebody that isn't guilty."

"Just so you know," Toro told her, "the person that poisoned El Jefe's wife was found today in Los Angeles. He was killed, but before he was killed, he admitted that he received payment for the murder from another Mexican, but that person was receiving instruction from an American. He knew that because of a text in English that instructed the waiter to not kill El Jefe's daughter, just his wife. So yes, the Americans are involved, and they are guilty. They just conceal their identity and involvement well."

The defense attorney had contacted Toro and updated him on the situation in Los Angeles just after Felipe had uploaded the recorded confession from Jose Padilla.

"Maybe the Americans did do it. Maybe the DEA even did it, but that was not me. I had nothing to do with it. I should not be blamed for the crimes of my countrymen. Should you?"

Toro looked at his watch. It was three minutes until midnight. He had hoped, and thought, that the Americans would provide information that would justify his not having to harm the DEA agent. He was worried about her knowledge of the tunnel from Juarez to El Paso, but she did not know the specific location of the tunnel.

Toro hadn't considered it a forgone conclusion that she was going to be murdered when he initially took Ana Lucia, but now he had painted himself into a corner, and could not go back on his word after posting the video online. It appeared his gamble had backfired, and he was going to have to kill an American DEA agent, even though he secretly agreed with her recent arguments that she should not be held responsible for the actions of her countrymen.

Toro continued to stare intently at Ana Lucia when his thoughts were interrupted by the ringing of the prepaid phone.

"Yes?" Toro answered.

It was George. "A message just came across the group chat from Vaquero in Los Angeles."

"Who is that?" Toro asked. He had not taken the time to learn names of any of the other people at the meeting at El Jefe's mansion.

"He's the cartel contact in Los Angeles for a DEA agent that is on the cartel payroll," George explained. "The DEA agent only goes through Vaquero, so he doesn't have to speak to multiple cartel members in Mexico."

"So, there is a corrupt DEA agent in Los Angeles?" Toro asked, loud enough so that Ana Lucia overheard as well.

"Yes, and apparently he contacted Vaquero with evidence about who ordered the hit on El Jefe's wife."

"So, it was DEA that ordered the hit?" Toro asked, again loud enough so Ana Lucia could hear.

"It must be, that it is the only way that a DEA agent would have evidence of who ordered the hit."

"What's the evidence?" Toro asked, "And how do we confirm its accuracy?"

"Juan Montoya just sent a message, and he wants you to go to Tijuana to meet with the DEA agent and verify the authenticity of the evidence he provides. I am working on arranging you a private flight to TJ in the morning. I'll be over about 7:00 a.m. with the details."

Toro ended the call without another word and continued to stare at Ana Lucia.

"It looks like you have a reprieve," he told her, "at least temporarily."

Chapter 19
Los Angeles (Van Nuys), California

Sunday, September 3

Vaquero's message to the group chat of the Cartel had the desired effect, earning a response from Juan Montoya himself. Montoya wanted the entire process to appear legitimate and did not want to appear to accept any evidence without intense scrutiny. For that reason, he instructed Vaquero to have the DEA agent bring the information himself, in person, to Tijuana, and show it to Toro, the only person with a reputation that carried with it the assurance of completing a job without any prejudice. If Toro sensed the evidence was fake, he would sooner kill the DEA agent than accept the evidence and let it slide. Another main reason Toro was chosen for this role, was his ability to take care of himself in case there was any trouble with the DEA agent or law enforcement.

Reuben wasn't surprised when he looked at his phone in the early morning hours and saw a message from Vaquero informing him that he was requested to travel to Tijuana to meet with Toro and show him the evidence he had implicating the individual that had been responsible for ordering the murder of El Jefe's wife.

After telling Tyler that he was going to try and track down the two shooters, Reuben had every intention to flee the area. He suspected he would be required to travel to Mexico the following day after Vaquero sent out the message to the Cartel, and he had been worried that the questioning by the DEA's Office of Professional Responsibility might possibly last well into the hours of the following morning. He gathered his wits about him and realized that he had to return, if at the very least for Tyler's sake, and discuss what happened.

At 10:00 p.m. in Los Angeles, within the Central Standard Time midnight deadline for Toro's request for information, Reuben was still sitting in an interview room answering questions about the shootout. He had informed Vaquero about the shootout, and his requirement to answer questions from their internal affairs investigators. Vaquero, the go-between for the DEA agent and the Cartel, assured Reuben that he would take care of everything if he promised to be at the Van Nuys Airport the following morning. Fortunately, after a lengthy series of questions about what led to the shooting, as well as a step by step explanation of what happened and when it happened, Reuben was released from the interview with the OPR shortly after midnight in Los Angeles. At that time, Tyler was still answering questions.

After waiting until almost 1:00 a.m., Tyler finally exited the interview room, and Reuben was there waiting for him. The two agents and friends walked out of the Federal Building and went to the nearest Denny's so they could eat and discuss between each other what happened during the operation, and more importantly, what they said to the OPR agents. They knew that if their stories differed in any way, then the OPR investigators would recognize it and become suspicious that they were hiding something.

The two men's conversation continued deep into the night as they discussed the likelihood that they would be disciplined for another operation that had ultimately not been successful. Meanwhile, each man continued to check his phone to see if there was any update on Ana Lucia. Not only was there nothing reported about her being murdered; there were not any reports about the information that Reuben knew had been reported to the Cartel by Vaquero. Reuben genuinely liked and respected Tyler as a fellow DEA agent, and despite the length of time he had been working with Vaquero at the Cartel and providing and accepting information from them, Reuben's conscious still weighed him down at times, especially like this when Tyler was completely unsuspecting that Reuben was about to travel to Tijuana to meet with the very individual who had kidnapped

Ana Lucia, and provide evidence which Reuben knew to be fake, to implicate another DEA agent in the murder of El Jefe's wife, even though Reuben knew that DEA agent had nothing to do with the murder. But it was required by the Cartel. Reuben had to do it or face the consequences. He had been the Cartel's informant for too long, sometimes receiving information, other times providing it.

Eventually, Tyler left Denny's and made the three-hour trip back south to San Diego, hoping to arrive before his children woke up. Reuben, meanwhile, went to his apartment in Reseda, where he slept fitfully for a couple hours, before waking up and going to the airport.

During the meeting with Vaquero in their customary location in the parking lot of the Van Nuys Airport, Reuben's thoughts continued to go over the events from the day before as he followed Vaquero to a single engine Cessna. Reuben boarded the plane, armed with just a satchel containing the documents he was supposed to show Toro.

Vaquero told Reuben that he would not be going to Tijuana with them. He instructed Reuben to go to a newly constructed bar on Avenida Revolucion called La Guarida de los Cerdos. He assured Reuben that transportation would be provided from the airport to the bar, so that he would be in time for his scheduled meeting at noon with the infamous Toro.

* * *

El Paso

A light knock on the garage door leading into the kitchen indicated that the defense attorney had arrived. He had several questions and wanted to go over a few things prior to Toro's departure for Tijuana. The highly paid defense attorney, despite his status in the cartel, and his reputation for defending the most hardened criminals, had never himself taken any kind of classes in self-defense. He had not even shot a gun in over 10 years, instead relying on those around him to provide security. For those reasons, George had been very concerned about the responsibility that had been passed down to him of detaining Ana Lucia once Toro was gone. He planned on continuing to administer morphine to keep her wits dimmed down and her actions sluggish, all the while maintaining the zip-ties that kept her hands behind her back.

Toro opened the door and allowed the defense attorney to enter. The defense attorney spoke in a hushed but urgent voice. "I understand that Montoya is ordering you to go to Tijuana, but me being responsible for this DEA agent was never part of the deal. This is not what I do, and when you start giving people responsibilities for something in which they are not proficient, that is when you start having problems."

Toro looked at the man, expressionless. "If you have a problem with watching a sleeping woman, then why didn't you bring that up to Montoya when he told you I was going to be sent to Tijuana?"

The defense attorney shook his head. "You know I can't do that. And I'm not blaming you, I'm just saying this situation is getting out of hand. What am I supposed to do with her? She can't see me, if she does then she can't live, but I'm not a killer."

"Calm down. I gave her Morphine shortly after midnight. There are two more doses here. Give her one prior to noon here in El Paso and you should not need the other one. My meeting is at noon in Tijuana, which is 10:00 a.m. here in El Paso. Give me three hours. If you have not heard from me by 1:00 p.m. here in El Paso, then assume I have been set up, and she must die. If you hear from me before then and I have what I need, then she can be released."

"How am I going to do that?" George whispered, trying to keep Ana Lucia from overhearing his voice.

"That's not my problem," Toro said, starting to get irritated. "But if it were up to me, then I would probably leave her in the desert somewhere, or maybe in some campground that is far away from the road. That would give you time to get out of there and allow her to walk to find someone. Survival is on her at that point."

"Ok, well what if something happens to you, and I don't hear back from you? Like I said, I'm not a killer."

"Again, not my problem. That's something you will have to figure out yourself." Toro turned his back and walked to pick up Ana Lucia, who was slumped against the wall. She was awake, but her senses were dull, and she put up no resistance at all. He led her to the back of another large black Mercedes van that George had driven to the residence and parked in the garage. Putting Ana Lucia in the back, Toro slid his pocketknife into the sock underneath her right boot. She could not take advantage of it now, but when she regained her senses, he guessed she would be able to use it effectively. He looked at the two remaining syringes that had previously contained morphine that were brought by the defense attorney. Having emptied the syringes and refilling it with water, Toro knew that the time was coming, once he had left, when Ana Lucia would no longer be suffering the effects of the morphine. Toro would at least provide her with a chance.

He knew that if he had not administered the morphine, then there would have likely been some kind of an altercation between the two of them, and he would have had to kill her, which he didn't want to do. But her chances against the defense attorney were much improved. Toro realized that he respected Ana Lucia. He was not attracted to her in a romantic way even though she was attractive, but she was the only victim he had ever been around that refused to be afraid. She had constantly looked him in his eyes even in the face of death.

But Toro had seen men like George before. He saw the fear in the man's eyes, and knew that as soon as he was gone, George was going to enlist the help of some thug that owed him for his legal services, a thug that was not reliable to control himself, someone that would likely assault a sharp tongued attractive Hispanic female DEA agent. Plus, he just did not trust that George was not going to have the DEA agent killed, even if Toro got the information he needed. The man was too worried about his identity being discovered. Perhaps Ana Lucia did need to die to protect the secrets of the Cartel, but she did not deserve to die. Toro decided he would leave it up to fate, not that he believed in the existence of God anymore, but he would at least give Ana Lucia the chance to fight for her life against George, and whoever he got to help him do his misdeeds.

Toro got into the back seat of the van, directly across from Ana Lucia, while George entered the driver's seat. The vehicle backed out of the garage, and then left the street heading toward the Fabens Airport, a private airport 20 miles southeast on the 10 freeway, away from the city.

"What do you know about the plane in El Paso?" Toro asked George.

"It's a small jet that is being used by some famous Mexican band that happens to be in El Paso at the time."

"Enough for eight people?" Toro asked.

"Yes, it should be," George answered. "Why?"

Toro did not answer. He used the remaining time to contact Leon.

"It's Toro. Are you and the team still in Nogales?"

"Yes, Toro, we are waiting here until we hear from you. We have not heard anything today. Did you kill the girl?"

"No, a message was sent out that a DEA agent from Los Angeles has evidence of the man responsible for setting up the murder of El Jefe's wife. I am flying to meet with him in Tijuana and inspect the evidence."

"Do you have any idea what the evidence is?" Leon asked.

"No, I don't."

"Do you think it might be a setup?"

"It's possible, but I don't think so."

"Why do you say that?"

"Just my gut. But, just in case, I would like to have you guys there with me in Tijuana."

"Okay, we can get on the road now."

"No, you won't make it there in time. The meeting is at noon in Tijuana. I am about to get in a small jet from El Paso. I will instruct the pilot to stop at the airport in Nogales. Go there now, and I will contact you when we land. You will have to board quickly so we can be on the way soon after. Be ready."

"We will. And Toro...there is a rumor around here that some-body found the waiter that poisoned El Jefe's wife and that he was killed in Los Angeles. Is that true?"

"Yes, somebody from the Federal Police found him."

"Do you know who from the Federal Police?" Leon asked.

"Some guy named Felipe. I have met with him once. He is actual-ly the one that provided us with the information about the residence in Chihuahua that was being used by the GDG, so this all kind of started with him."

"Okay," Leon said. "I will make sure we are at the airport and ready within the hour."

Toro ended the call and continued to sit in silence as the vehicle traveled east on the 10 freeway toward the airport. Upon arrival, George pulled the van directly on the tarmac to a 12-person jet, used by a popular Mexican band named Los Pajaros de Chihuahua that was currently in El Paso on tour. The pilot was already in the jet, waiting on Toro.

Toro climbed up to the front passenger seat to have one last word with George. "It is almost 7:00 a.m. here. I will be in Tijuana by 10:00 a.m., Central Standard Time, and meet with the DEA agent, which will be noon there. Do not do anything with her until at least 1:00 p.m. Central time. That means you are only responsible for her for six hours. Do not, and I repeat, do NOT, let any thug you get to help you lay a hand on her. Everybody keeps their pants up. If she dies, then she dies, but she does not get raped or assaulted prior to that point. Understood?"

The defense attorney nodded, looking back at Ana Lucia lying in the van. Without another word, Toro exited the passenger side of the van and walked up to the private plane.

Sitting in the parking lot of the small airport, DEA Special Agent Trevor Johnson had been able to find a spot where he could main-tain visual of the black van being driven by the defense attorney that

194

he had been following around since the previous night. Trevor was absolutely sure when the van drove by him earlier there had not been anybody in the passenger seat, but he was equally sure somebody had just exited from the passenger seat, and it wasn't the defense attorney, meaning that somebody had been sitting in the back of the van when he could have been sitting in the passenger seat, which struck Trevor as strange. Having not attended the SOD meeting in California almost two weeks earlier, Trevor did not have a picture of Toro. If he had, perhaps he would have been able to confirm it was the man getting out of the defense attorney's van and onto the plane. Regardless, Trevor suspected the defense attorney was up to something, and he sat there trying to put the pieces of the puzzle together in his head. He watched as the plane went down the runway to takeoff, and the black van driven by the defense attorney pulled back out towards his location in the parking lot, leaving the area before the plane was even off the ground.

* * *

Tijuana, Mexico

Felipe walked out the exit of the emergency room at Hospital Mexico, located just a kilometer south of the international border with Mexico and the United States. The cash he had provided to the nurses at the triage had been sufficient to expedite his visit.

He was in extreme pain, and needed medical attention, and had fortunately made it into Mexico without being apprehended in California after the events of the day before. One of the rifle rounds from the DEA agent that arrived at the residence on 92nd street in Los Angeles had hit his upper left arm, just below his shoulder. The round had shattered the bone, leaving him in excruciating pain.

When Felipe had advanced to the hallway during the firefight the day before, he had been able to get one shot off at the DEA agent trapped in the hallway, before feeling his left arm explode in pain from the rifle round. Felipe had been able to use the gun in his right hand to get a couple of shots off at the man with the rifle to prevent him from immediately coming through the doorway. Had he advanced in unmolested, Felipe knew Reuben would have easily taken him down, but the veteran Federal Policeman had used that brief delay in entry to leave the man in the hallway, and instead dash for the back yard through the kitchen, and in his haste grabbing Tonio who had also been shot in the hip by one of the rounds from Tyler's Glock. Rushing out with rifle rounds landing around them, Felipe and Tonio hadn't intentionally knocked over the candle that started the fire, but it had provided them with what they needed to escape the area.

Felipe and Tonio had grabbed the first person they saw with a car, and held him at gun point, explaining that they only needed to be taken to Mexico immediately, and that they wouldn't hurt the man, but they could not allow him to leave and possibly alert law enforcement that they had stolen his vehicle. Despite the pain in his left arm, Felipe had driven the vehicle, while Tonio sat in the backseat with the owner of the vehicle, trying to maintain his gun on him while dealing with pain from the gunshot wound he had suffered to his left hip. The trio made it to the international border, and let the man take his vehicle back north to Los Angeles.

Tonio and Felipe both went to the Hospital Mexico, seeking medical treatment for their gunshot wounds, but first and foremost, now that Felipe was back in Mexican territory and could use his cell phone, he sent the Cartel Group Chat the recorded confession of Jose Padilla, which also included the man's last moments when he was killed by Felipe. Despite his pain, he smiled with the realization that he was going to be $10 million richer very soon.

As he walked out of the ER early on Sunday morning, Felipe looked at the Cartel Group Chat, and realized that Toro was going to be coming to Tijuana a few hours later to obtain the evidence of who ordered the hit on El Jefe's wife. Thinking that he had to tie up loose ends, and that by doing so, he might also acquire the evidence provided to El Jefe, the prospect of getting $20 million instead of $10 million was very appealing. He had a plan. This time, he was going to call on his law enforcement brethren.

Due to his injury sustained in Los Angeles, Felipe was unable to use his left arm, so he knew that he would need assistance to carry out the mission, but it was a mission that he considered had to be carried out, for survival and monetary reasons.

Felipe pulled out his work telephone, and contacted the Mexican Federal Police in Tijuana, informing them that he would be at the office within the hour, but that he needed all hands on deck for a pending operation, and the arrest of two high value targets, alive if necessary, but preferably dead.

Chapter 20
Tijuana, Mexico

Sunday, September 3

Reuben arrived at La Guarida de Los Cerdos precisely at noon. The entrance to the bar was off the sidewalk of the busy Avenida Revolucion, with tattoo parlors, restaurants, and many other small businesses in the congested area. Even in the middle of the day, the area had numerous pedestrians walking back and forth, but Reuben was surprised at the number of people that were already in the bar area at noon on a Sunday.

Reuben took assessment of his surroundings upon entering the building. Inside was much more spacious than it appeared from the outside. The entrance was a rustic wooden door wide enough for one person to enter through at a time. The door was in the middle of the room on the lower level in an area he estimated to be about 2000 square feet. He thought the bar looked more like a dance club, with the middle of the room opened on a slightly raised platform, with booths and high tables lining the walls in each direction. On both sides of the walls were televisions, some playing replays of an old Liga MX professional soccer game in Mexico between Club Tijuana and Club America.

The location had an upstairs balcony that completely encircled the perimeter of the large room.

Upon entry, the bar and servers were to the far left. Approximately fifty stools sat in front of the bar, and only a few were empty. Reuben walked over to the far side of the wall away from the entrance and plopped down at the bar next to the last stool, laying his satchel on the stool nearest the wall, which is where he guessed Toro would sit when they met.

He continued to assess the location, noting there was an open doorway on the wall on the side where Toro would sit, leading to a hall that went toward what he guessed was a rear exit. On the other side of the bar closest to Avenida Revolucion was the men and women's bathroom. Comfortable with the layout, he sat down on the stool and ordered a coke with rum. He kept the satchel close by, with a hand on it.

* * *

Welcoming the members of his team on board the private jet as he picked them up in Nogales, Mexico, Toro noticed that Nestor was not present. Toro initially thought to wait to let Leon explain what happened to the member of their team that was no longer with them. They lost two at the shootout in Juarez, and another sacrificed himself by driving the van away from Juarez to help the remaining members avoid capture by law enforcement.

Toro looked at Leon, noticing that for the first time in his memory, the larger man seemed in pain. The second thing Toro noticed was the fact that Leon was missing his left ear. It was a tangled and red mess, with puss starting to ooze out of the wound. It was obvious that an infection had set in.

Finally, Toro brought up his observations as the two men sat in the jet traveling toward Tijuana. "When are you planning to tell what happened to Nestor and to your ear?"

Leon tried to push away the pain, but his body temperature seemed to have risen, and he could not stop the sweat that was coming down his head. He grimaced ever so slightly.

"I knew where Blanco was living, so we paid him a visit before we left El Paso on Friday night. We took care of him, but lost Nestor in the process."

Toro took the information in without showing his frustration at Leon. "Did you lose your ear in the process as well?"

Leon smirked. "Yes, what was left of it, but I made sure Blanco paid for it."

Nothing more was said about the situation as the jet continued toward Tijuana.

Having not accounted for the stop in Nogales, Mexico, to pick up Leon and the remaining four members of the hit team, Bruno, Cesar, Jose, and Jesus, the jet was late arriving at the airport in Tijuana. Refusing to go into a situation blind, Toro sent Leon and the other four members of the team into the bar to provide him with a layout of the building, as well as look for any possible signs of law enforcement. Toro found a small taco shop two blocks away to wait to get an all clear from Leon. He was slightly worried about the man's attention to detail, and that he would not be as sharp as he needed to be due to the infection. Toro also noticed that Leon had been massaging his left shoulder that had been grazed when shot at the border in Juarez.

While Toro sat in the taco shop, he continued to watch Avenida Revolucion. He noticed a few men sitting around in cars, a few couples standing and talking on the street, dog walkers that seemed to linger on the busy sidewalk, but he wasn't sure if they were who they appeared to be, or something more. He continued watching for several minutes, until receiving a call from Leon, notifying him that the inside of the bar appeared to be free from law enforcement. The bathrooms, bar floor, and upstairs area had all been checked, and there was no suspected law enforcement present. Leon provided a layout of the bar and told him that he thought the DEA agent was sitting at the bar against the far wall, opposite the entrance. There was a satchel on the stool beside him that he was keeping a hand on, which he assumed was the evidence that was going to be provided. Toro told Leon that he would be there within five minutes.

* * *

Felipe sat in a chair by the upstairs window of a small apartment above a tool shop on Avenida Revolucion, located across the street from the bar. Having amassed a formidable team of Mexican Federal Policeman, they all waited downstairs inside the tool shop, taking over for the time being and flipping the sign on the front window to show that it was closed. He knew better than to send his guys in to the bar prior to the arrival of Toro and his crew. Toro's men would have undoubtedly seen any Federal Police, so Felipe waited by the window holding the binoculars in his right hand, because his left arm was immobilized after being shot by Reuben the day before in Los Angeles. Watching the entrance closely from the upstairs window across the street, Felipe confirmed when Toro entered the bar. Having seen Toro at El Jefe's mansion, Felipe remembered enough details to recognize the man when he saw him again.

Felipe informed his most trusted man to enter the bar. Twenty-five-year-old Manuel Diaz was the hardest working, and most loyal officer on the Mexican Federal Police force. Felipe knew for a fact that the man had refused multiple overtures by the Cartel to get on their payroll. While it was obvious that he could only refuse the Cartel for a certain period until he either agreed to work with them or was killed, Felipe decided to use the man while he could. Felipe's instructions to the subordinate were to enter the bar after receiving confirmation that Toro was inside, and then attempt to order a drink and do whatever necessary to confirm that the DEA agent had brought the evidence he claimed to have and provided it to Toro. Then, and only then, once Manuel provided the confirmation from inside, would Felipe approve his team to initiate an assault on the bar, with instructions to shoot to kill both the corrupt DEA agent, and the infamous Toro, as well as anybody else they might encounter on the inside.

Worried that his inability to use his left arm might result in getting killed in the upcoming shootout, Felipe decided to stay in his position, watching the entrance from the upstairs apartment across the street, and coordinating the operation. He pressed his earpiece firmly into his ear as Manuel entered the bar and assured the young Federal Policeman that he could hear him.

* * *

Toro took survey as he walked into the bar. He noted Leon standing at a high table on a bar against the opposite wall, directly opposite the door. He acknowledged Leon as he walked toward the bar, looking for the other four members of his team, as well as any possible signs of law enforcement. Not seeing either, Toro slowed his approach to the bar, and looked behind him, noticing Cesar and Bruno on the balcony above him. Jose was in the hallway between the restrooms, and Jesus was all the way on the far side of the room, to the far right from the front door.

Toro made eye contact with the DEA agent as he approached the stool. Reuben gave a head nod as he turned toward the open stool next to the wall. Toro made no motion to acknowledge other than continuing to walk towards the stool, sitting down with his back against the wall, enabling him to look out along the entire room.

"So, you're Toro," Reuben said. Toro nodded his head. "Is Ana Lucia safe?"

Toro looked at the DEA agent, expressionless. "She is. Whether she stays safe depends on what you have in that satchel."

Reuben pulled out the contents and explained what they were. He was facing Toro and the wall, careful so that nobody else would be able to see the documents.

"This," he said, holding up a file with a brown cover and a sticker with the designation CI, followed by several numbers, "is a Confidential Informant File that the DEA uses to document Confidential Informants that work for them. Each informant is signed up by a DEA Special Agent, and the agent is responsible for completing the necessary paperwork required to officially establish the individual as a DEA informant. The prospective informant is told that his or her identity will be maintained a secret unless the disclosure is necessary during a court proceeding. The informant has to sign a contract agreeing to work with us, like in any other job. He has to sign in two different places. For those that become informants after being arrested, they sign different paperwork, but that doesn't apply here."

Reuben opened the informant file. He turned to the last page of the form. "Here, you see the name signed by the informant, Jose

Padilla, written in cursive, but legible nonetheless." Reuben looked up at Toro who gave a slight head nod for him to continue.

Reuben turned to a different page in the informant agreement, showing the same signature of Jose Padilla, the name of the waiter from Durango that was identified as being responsible for poisoning El Jefe's wife.

"These documents show that Jose Padilla was a DEA Confidential Informant. You might be wondering how somebody that was living in Juarez for most of his life ended up becoming an informant with the DEA's Los Angeles Field Division. Well, this next document shows that Jose was signed up with the DEA office in Juarez. Juarez signed him up first, and then Los Angeles completed the paperwork to use him as an informant as well. This is the paperwork, showing that Jose Padilla was also working with DEA in Juarez and Los Angeles."

With that revelation, Toro's eyebrows raised. Reuben continued, "Padilla signed up at the same time with Los Angeles because his intent was to come to Los Angeles so that he could live in LA. Now, here are the records you need to prove who was responsible for ordering Padilla to murder El Jefe's wife."

Reuben breathed deeply as he prepared to present the next pieces of information. He was not sure why Vaquero instructed him to present it this way, but he hoped it was sufficient to save Ana Lucia's life, and allow him to walk out alive.

"This is a report that DEA Special Agents have to complete after debriefing an informant. You will notice it references another case file. I don't have access to that case file, but the information contained herein is sufficient to explain what happened." In actuality, the name of the case agent, and the case number on the file, were both made up by Reuben the day before, as he produced a fictional account of what happened with Jose Padilla, but did so on official DEA paperwork, to give it the look of authenticity.

"Now, obviously, a government report won't say we paid an informant to go murder the wife of the leader of the Cartel de Culiacan; it will instead document that some type of intelligence was obtained during the course of a meeting. But look at the dates of the two reports. One is from two days prior to the murder of El Jefe's wife, and it is signed by an agent in Juarez." Reuben had made sure to falsely designate the office code for the Juarez DEA office, which was also listed following the fake name of the agent writing the report.

"The second report," Reuben showed him, "was signed by an agent from Los Angeles, two days after the murder. The first report signed by the Juarez agent indicates that Padilla was going to try to obtain information from a Cartel member. The second report signed by the LA agent indicates that the desired information was obtained during a meeting in Durango, Mexico. As a result of the value of the information provided, the DEA provided entry into the United States for Padilla and his girlfriend. We knew Padilla was in Los Angeles two days after the murder of El Jefe's wife because the DEA Special Agent documented meeting with him."

Toro did not speak but continued to look at the documentation to confirm its authenticity. The documents appeared to be legitimate, and he had no way to know that Reuben had made up the entire story.

"The last thing," Reuben said, flipping to the last report in the file, the kicker to put it over the top. "The last file shows that Jose Padilla was paid $50,000 upon arrival in Los Angeles. From my experience, no information ever provided by any informant in the history of DEA has resulted in a payment of that much money if only intelligence is provided. Only if the informant helps with a seizure of money, and he gets a certain percentage of the seizure, will anybody be paid that much or more, but this case file makes no mention of a money seizure, so why did Jose Padilla get so much money, two days after El Jefe's wife was poisoned?"

"Who authorized the payment of that money?" Toro asked.

This was the point where Reuben had known the conversation would eventually lead. It was the one and only real name that Reuben had been instructed to provide on the otherwise completely fabricated documents. He was not sure why this specific name was requested and had to be included.

"All payments of that much money have to be approved up the highest chain of command in that Field Division, but the interesting thing about this is that the Special Agent in Charge of the Los Angeles Field Division didn't sign off on this document. It was signed off by the Deputy Administrator of the DEA, Allen Peterson."

"And where is this Deputy Administrator now?" Toro asked.

"He's at Headquarters in Washington D.C. He used to be the SAC of Los Angeles, but he was promoted to Deputy Administrator. He is the highest-ranking individual in DEA that started as a DEA agent. The actual DEA Administrator was appointed by the president from another position and leads the DEA despite never doing the job of a DEA agent."

Toro inspected the final document showing the payment amount provided to Jose Padilla. From everything explained by Reuben, it appeared that everything was accurate and official. Toro closed the file, and looked briefly at Leon, who was watching from the table in the middle of the room. Toro gave a quick nod of his head and took his phone out and sent a quick message on the Cartel Group Chat, confirming that he was in receipt of the evidence provided by the DEA agent. At that moment, screams broke through the air and the Federal Police made their move.

* * *

Toro, Leon, and the remaining four members of the hit squad had forgone carrying rifles in an attempt to blend in to the surroundings inside the bar, but each man had two handguns concealed, either in a side holster or tucked into the back of their pants. Each man promptly sprang into action as soon as the threat surfaced.

Standing in the middle of the room directly across from the entrance, Leon was close by Manuel Diaz, the loyal young Federal Policeman working with Felipe who had given the go ahead to the team. Diaz was standing closer to Leon, when the Federal Police officer pulled his gun and started approaching Toro and the DEA Agent. Leon quickly responded from behind with a head shot that instantly dropped the young officer. He then swung to his left as the doors to the room burst open, and was the first to see the Federal Police clothed in all black enter the large room, one by one through the narrow door.

Immediately upon entering, the first two men turned to their left, towards the bar where Toro and Reuben sat. The other bar patrons concealed Leon's presence, but he quickly knew that he and his team members were outgunned, and he would have to act quickly and decisively to make sure they got out alive. Realizing the direness of the situation, Leon pulled out both guns, and holding one gun in each hand, ran forward toward the two Policemen firing away. The two Federal Policemen, who had been advised about the location of Toro and Reuben inside the bar by the now deceased Manuel Diaz, did not know about Leon's presence, or the rest of the hit team members, and failed to account for them as they entered. The mistake was fatal, as the first two members through the door immediately fell to the ground, suffering gun-shot wounds to the side and head.

Moving quickly ahead, Leon continued firing toward the entrance. Since the door was only wide enough for one person to enter at a time, the third individual on the team was attempting to get through by the time Leon turned his dual guns in that direction, mowing the man down. The Federal Policeman attempted to return fire as he fell but was unable to tell where the shooter was. Instead, the third Federal Policeman sprayed his rifle toward the bar, with most landing harmlessly in the wall or underside of the wooden bar. One bullet, however, struck Reuben directly in his right rib cage.

Having worked together many times before, the remaining members of the hit squad moved like a fine oiled machine. On the balcony overlooking the street on the outside, Cesar and Bruno both turned and found a window, and from overhead proceeded to rain bullets down on the Federal Policemen that were now trapped behind their co-worker that had fallen in the doorway entrance on the sidewalk by Avenida Revolucion.

Of the remaining four members of the seven-man Federal Police team that set out to assault the bar from the front entrance, all four were struck by the cascade of bullets from the two sicarios overhead. The four policemen never knew where the shots came from before being hit, and never had a chance to return fire, before falling to the ground.

* * *

When Leon's first shot rang out, Toro immediately put the confidential informant file into the satchel and put the strap over his chest, so that the satchel pressed against his back. However, the phone that he had used to send the message to the Cartel Group Chat fell to the ground, where it was left.

Toro instinctively drew his own weapon to identify the threat. He turned to fire on Reuben because he believed the DEA agent had set them up, when he heard the sound of the rear door being blown off of its hinges in the rear hallway closest to him. Like Leon dealing with the threat coming from the front entrance, Toro knew that if the police entered through the rear entrance, then his crew would quickly be overwhelmed.

The second seven-man team of Mexican Federal Policemen had been assigned to assault the rear entrance to the location at the same time as the front was being breached. The first man of the seven-person team had entered the hallway when Toro entered the same hallway from beside the bar.

Once the Policemen entered the rear entrance, they were only able to go left, towards Toro and the bar, as a wall to the right prevented movement in that direction. Toro turned in the hallway quickly and fired twice. The well-placed head shots dropped the first Federal Policeman immediately. He had been able to squeeze off a couple rounds from his rifle, but they went harmlessly into the side wall.

As the lead policeman on the entry team fell in the hallway, the second man entered as quickly as possible, firing anywhere and everywhere. Toro slid down like a baseball player stealing a base, with his left leg out and his right leg tucked underneath him, hoping that the return fire would sail over his head, which it did by mere inches. Toro's return shots, in contrast, found their mark, dropping the second police officer just inside the doorway.

Quick as a cat, Toro maintained firing rounds toward the door, while he crouched ahead and stripped the first police officer of his rifle. Having seen the first two men of their team fall immediately upon entering the rear of the property, the remaining five members of the team momentarily delayed their own entry. That delay was all the time Toro needed. Now armed with a rifle, Toro holstered his handgun and began firing towards the door, still standing in the hallway waiting for somebody to be brave enough to enter, but the other police officers were now leaning against the side of the building outside the entrance, with no concealment in the rear of the property.

Meanwhile, on the other side of the room, Leon tossed a rifle from the deceased policeman up to Bruno who was on the balcony overlooking Avenida Revolucion at the front. Bruno raced down the balcony until it turned and then went along the far side of the room, above Toro. A window over the rear of the property provided a perfect view of the five Federal Policemen that were stacked against the brick wall attempting to avoid Toro's fire. None of the five men looked up before they were all taken down by the rifle rounds that came from Bruno shooting out of the window above. Just like that, two different seven-man teams of Mexican Federal Policemen had been eliminated, while nobody from Toro's team had suffered a single wound.

Toro maintained his rifle at the doorway, while he used his mic to ask what Bruno could see overhead. He reported that all was clear. Just as Toro was about to breathe a sigh of relief, a report came in from Cesar, still on the balcony overlooking Avenida Revolucion. Two additional police vans were coming down the street toward the front entrance. Toro's instructions to Leon were urgent. Before the policemen could get out of the van, Leon, Jose and Jesus, the sicarios that remained on the ground level, started instructing all the bar patrons to immediately exit the facility while the gunfire had stopped. The civilians that had been caught in the vicious shootout were quick to use the first moment available to escape to the outside, some stumbling over the corpses of the deceased police officers.

The momentary diversion worked, as dozens and dozens of the remaining bar patrons exited the front door, just as the doors of the vans containing the policemen were sliding open so the backup units could storm the bar.

Perched from his upstairs location in the apartment across the street, Felipe knew that he could not order the responding policemen to shoot all the innocent civilians, so he yelled into his police radio for the policemen to push past the civilians and enter the bar.

Once the armed policemen were in view, the complete chaos of the situation only seemed to intensify, with some people deciding to take cover inside the bar, although most decided to flee even faster, while they still could. Reuben made his way against the wall leading to the front door, but the wound to his right side prevented him from exiting at full speed. He tried to maintain the bleeding by holding a cloth napkin he had picked up against the bullet wound, but the blood had now turned the white cloth a deep red. Reuben tried to maintain his balance by using his left hand to compress the wound, and his right hand to steady himself against the wall. He realized he wasn't going to make it out the door prior to the policemen entering, so he did the only thing he could do since he wasn't armed, he found what little concealment there was, turning over one of the high tables and cowering behind it.

While the civilians fled, Toro barked out additional instructions on the radio, telling Leon and Cesar to come assist him and Bruno in the rear, instructing Jose and Jesus to drop their rifles and exit the facility pretending to be the fleeing civilians. Upon getting outside, they were instructed to steal the first vehicle available, and meet Toro and the other members of the team on the side street running north and south where they would ultimately come out from the rear exit. Toro knew that Leon's size would likely be a giveaway that he was a member of the sicarios, thus preventing him from exiting the facility pretending to be a civilian. The other two Sicarios however, Jose and Jesus, would be able to successfully blend in and get out, which they did, just as the policemen came through the entrance, wildly going in all directions looking for any of the shooters that had taken out their co-workers. Pushing past one of the policemen as he exited, Jose pointed to the balcony overhead, and instructed the police to clear the area overhead before moving on, giving his team on the backside of the property extra time.

* * *

Toro led the group of Leon, Cesar, and Bruno out the rear of the bar, which led to a gated parking lot with dozens of cars parked in the lot. Quickly stripping all the deceased policemen of their rifles and handguns, the four men moved out through the parking lot and exited the gate, leading to the side street of Calle Miguel Hidalgo. Toro and his team turned left to walk back towards Avenida Revolucion, where he expected to be met by a vehicle driven by Jose or Jesus, however, at that exact moment, a black police van skidded to a stop at the intersection less than 100 meters away. Not knowing if they had been spotted, or if the Federal Policemen were just trying to block off all possible exits, Toro and the team turned around, and headed in the opposite direction, toward Avenida Constitucion, with Toro instructing Jose and Jesus to meet them at that street instead.

Toro kept his eyes ahead and jogged forward, while Leon looked back over his shoulder at the Police van blocking the intersection, noticing that each man had exited and gotten behind vehicles parked on the street as concealment, with rifles and guns facing toward them. Before Leon was able to blurt out his warning, another black Police van rushed to a stop at the intersection with Avenida Constitucion, blocking their path that direction. With minimal concealment, it was obvious the only option they had was to return where they came from, through the gate and back into the bar. However, as Toro looked back in that direction, he noticed the federal policemen coming out the rear entrance of the bar and into the parking lot. Toro looked at Leon, and realized they were trapped.

* * *

Toro and Bruno crouched in an attack position, with their rifles facing forward to Avenida Constitucion, while Leon had his sights on the Federal Policemen coming out of the parking lot, and Cesar held the Federal Policemen stopped behind them at the intersection of Avenida Revolucion. The four men, hopelessly outgunned, were determined to not be taken alive, but none of the policemen advanced from their positions. Toro assumed it was only a matter of time before the assault began. He did not think about his pending death on the small street in Tijuana. His life did not flash before his eyes. He was only focused on the men standing before him that had guns pointed at him. For some reason, those men did not fire when they had the chance. He did not understand why they did not end it then and there, but a few moments turned into seconds, and soon, a minute had passed by with both parties still aiming their guns at the other. It was a true Mexican stand-off, with neither backing down.

After a minute and a half of eerie silence following the shootout, the policemen that had exited the van on Avenida Constitucion in front of them got back in the van, which left. Toro and Leon glanced at each other, unsure what the Federal Police were doing, and if it were a trick to draw them out so that they could then be killed. If so, then why hadn't the Federal Police just killed them when they had the opportunity? Toro was trying to figure out what was going on when another vehicle pulled up.

Raising his rifle yet again, Toro noticed that the vehicle was a black Mercedes sedan with tinted windows. It did not look like a law enforcement vehicle. The rear passenger door opened, and a well-dressed man exited. He held his hands up to show that he was unarmed, and then approached the four cornered sicarios.

"Toro," the man yelled as he approached, "it is good to see you again."

Leon took his eyes off his target to look at the man. "Who is that?" he asked Toro.

Toro lowered his weapon, realizing the man walking up to them was Juan Montoya, the second in command of the Cartel de Culiacan. He informed the others of the man's identity.

"Senor Montoya," Toro acknowledged, refusing to say more.

"I do have to apologize for what happened here," Montoya said. "It appears the Federal Police were acting on information provided to them by the DEA agent you were meeting with, in an attempt to arrest you."

Although it was not true, Montoya knew that it was the most likely scenario to be believed. Leon's face contorted in disgust and he gripped his rifle tight as he vowed to hunt down and kill the DEA agent.

Continuing, Montoya said, "One of the men you know was in charge of the police operation, but thankfully for all involved, I was able to instruct him to withdraw before there was any more bloodshed."

"Who ordered this?"

"The DEA agent set it up, but the lead Federal Policemen was Felipe, who was at El Jefe's residence the last time you were there. Felipe has assured me that he didn't know you were the main target, or that you were receiving information identifying the individual that killed El Jefe's wife."

"You expect us to believe that?" Toro asked. "Do you believe that? With $10 million dollars on the line?"

"What I believe isn't important. The only thing that is important is that you were not killed, and that you have the evidence with you still. You do still have the evidence, right?"

Toro nodded.

"And you believe it is legitimate?"

Toro nodded again.

"That is likely why the DEA tried to set you up, so the information couldn't be relayed to El Jefe."

Toro still did not believe that, and he still did not trust Felipe or his motives. "Come with me now," Montoya said, waving his hand toward the Mercedes. "Felipe, come out so that they can see you are with me."

The rear driver's side door slowly opened, as Felipe exited the vehicle, his left arm still in a sling from the gunshot wound suffered in Los Angeles the day before.

Montoya had called Felipe just as Toro and his crew were leaving the back of the bar. If the call had come in moments later, his men would have killed Toro and he would have retrieved the satchel, earning him $20 million instead of the $10 million he was already set to receive.

"I instructed Felipe of the necessity to call off the operation or forsake his opportunity to be rewarded for finding the person that killed El Jefe's wife. It is only right. He found the killer. You found the person that paid for the killer. You should both be rewarded, and you will be. I will take you to collect the reward now. So, come."

Toro walked toward the Mercedes, and then turned back toward his team. "I will be back, and we will share the money, just as I promised." He got in the car without another word.

"And one last thing," Montoya said to Leon, walking back toward the car. "You will get assistance from the Federal Police, Felipe has assured me, but please find the DEA agent before he gets back to the United States. Find him. And kill him."

Chapter 21
El Paso, Texas

Sunday, September 3

"The Lord is the Everlasting God, the Creator of the ends of the Earth! His understanding no one can fathom! He gives strength to the weary! He gives power to the weak! His book tells us this so that we will be comforted in our time of need. Times like we have right now!" Pastor Jeremiah Banker of Mt. Zion Baptist Church in Horizon City, a small town east of El Paso, yelled these words out as he looked over his congregation. While they were meant for all, he was trying to give support to one member in particular, Monique Chambers, wife of DEA Special Agent Rod Chambers. Monique confided in him earlier in the morning that Rod had been suspended from his job with the DEA and had been restricted from working the investigation to locate his kidnapped partner, Ana Lucia. As a result, Rod was extremely upset, and had forgone church that morning in favor of the comforts of a local bar.

DEA Special Agent Trevor Johnson entered the sanctuary just as Pastor Banker was making his remarks. Having been invited by Rod to visit the church when he first arrived in El Paso and joined Group 1, Trevor knew the location of the church, and expected to see the veteran DEA agent. Looking out over the crowd of people, Trevor realized Rod wasn't in the audience, but he did spot Rod's wife, Monique, a very composed and articulate professional business-woman that Trevor knew was very successful, and whose salary matched that of her husband. Trevor had met Monique on two previous occasions when the Chambers' family hosted all the members from El Paso Group 1 for a cookout. Those days seemed long in the past, although it had been just over a year.

Trevor lowered his head in reverence and apologized as he went down the aisle, and quickly ducked in beside Monique, while Pastor Banker continued his sermon. He leaned in to whisper to Monique. "I'm sorry to interrupt you during the service, but I have to speak to Rod immediately. It's about Ana Lucia. It could literally be a matter of life and death. I called and even went by your house, but nobody was home. This was the only other place I could think of to look."

Monique looked at Pastor Banker and nodded her head to indicate that she was okay, and mouthed a silent apology, as she leaned back and said, "Hello, Trevor, it's great to see you again. Can we step outside?"

Trevor immediately got up and walked quickly into the foyer of the church. He knew every second mattered and was afraid that he was going to be too late. He also realized that he needed the help of another person he could trust. Being such a new agent, others in the group, other than Ana Lucia and Rod, might not trust his judgement yet. They would be afraid to help knowing Rod had been suspended. Trevor knew that Rod was the only person who might be willing, and able, to help.

"Trevor, I'm sure you've heard about Rod's suspension," Monique said as she walked out the main doors and into the foyer of the church.

"Yes, I have...I'm not sure what I have right now, but it's something I need to run by somebody I trust, and right now there is not anybody I trust more than your husband."

Monique sized up the young agent and noted the urgency in his voice and in his eyes. She remembered that Rod had spoken glowingly of the young agent and admitted that Trevor had made a very favorable impression when he first arrived in the office.

"Rod isn't in a very good place, emotionally. After what happened the other day in Juarez, and then getting suspended by the DEA, he kind of took a turn for the worse. I smelled alcohol on his breath this morning, and he left the house before I came here."

"Do you have any idea where he went?" Trevor asked.

"Yes, I do. When our daughter left home six months ago and then got arrested, Rod started frequenting a bar close to our residence called The Watering Hole. I suspect he is there now."

Unable to move past Monique's mention of her daughter, Trevor followed up. "Wait, you mean Keisha?" He had met the young lady both times he had visited the Chambers' house.

"Yes, she started dating that guy that is every parent's worst nightmare, and soon she moved out. Rod was called less than two weeks later and informed she had been arrested for drug possession. She had track marks on her arm and everything, it was awful. We really need your prayers."

"My god," Trevor said. "Rod never mentioned any of that. I had no idea. I'm so sorry."

"Thank you for your concern. I know some people like to keep personal things like that to themselves, but my viewpoint is the more people that will pray for you, the better chances you have. The Lord says the prayer of a righteous man is powerful and effective. So, will you keep her in your prayers?"

"Yes, of course I will," Trevor said, looking down at the ground, ashamed of the fact that he hadn't been to the inside of a church since he moved out of his childhood home and had the independence to make his own choices about where he did and didn't spend his time.

"Thank you, I appreciate it very much. I have been praying for Ana Lucia's safe return. Is there anything you have heard that you can share?" Monique asked.

"No, the deadline for information was last night at midnight, but nobody has heard anything since then. The guy that took her hasn't sent out any messages."

"Well then I take that as a good sign that the Lord is protecting her. I will believe that until I hear otherwise. Just like I believe that He will redeem Keisha and protect her during this journey through the wilderness."

Trevor wished he had the same faith as the woman in front of him.

"Now, you go to The Watering Hole. I am sure you can find it on GPS, but it is just a mile away from our home. Good luck, Trevor," she said.

Trevor could not help but be impressed with how composed the woman was despite the difficult circumstances in her life. Trevor wondered if he should even bother with trying to track down Rod, or if he should just go back and follow the defense attorney some more. He decided that he needed to speak to someone, to make sure he was not reading too much into the situation. Trevor thanked Monique and hurried out of the church and to his car that was waiting in the parking lot.

* * *

Ana Lucia was slowly starting to regain her senses, enough so that she could realize that she was in the back of a large van, and that her hands were still restrained behind her with zip ties. She rolled on her side to look ahead and could see the form of an older white male in the driver's seat. The vehicle came to a stop, and the driver exited the vehicle, closing the door behind him. She could hear footsteps as the driver walked toward the rear of the van. Thinking that this might be the last opportunity that she had to escape, Ana Lucia attacked as soon as the van's rear double doors opened, kicking out hard with her right leg. Her right heel connected directly with the man's stomach.

George had suspected that Ana Lucia was not going to be able to fight back, having been assured by Toro prior to his departure, that she had been administered one of the remaining syringes of morphine. George had no way to know that Toro had replaced the morphine with water.

The defense attorney doubled over after Ana Lucia's kick knocked the breath out of him. Ana Lucia then rolled onto her back and delivered the hardest possible kick directly to the man's face. Although not a direct hit, the blow did hit the side of George's face, breaking his cheek bone, and causing him to fall backwards and onto the ground.

Realizing that this was her opportunity to escape, Ana Lucia wiggled as best she could until her feet hung down over the rear of the van, finally finding the hard surface of the ground underneath her. It had been several days since she had stood and walked, and in the initial shock of the moment, her legs collapsed underneath her, delaying her from fleeing immediately. She urgently set her feet underneath her, willing herself to get up and run away, not even taking the time to look at her surroundings to see where she was.

As she stood up, she looked directly into the eyes of George, who was still lying on the ground. Instead of fleeing as she knew she should do, hate and fury got the best of her, and she picked up her right leg, intending to stomp on the defense attorney's head and inflict as much pain as possible. Seeking to preserve himself, George did the only thing he could do. He grabbed Ana Lucia's left leg that was still on the ground, and yanked it toward his body as hard as he could, causing the DEA Agent to lose her balance and fall backwards, striking her head on the rear bumper of the van, knocking her unconscious.

George got up from the ground and looked around. He had pulled the black van to the back yard behind his residence, intending to leave Ana Lucia in the basement downstairs until he heard from Toro. He frantically tried to figure out what the next step should be. There was no way he could take her into his home at this point. The more he thought about it, George wondered why he considered it an option in the first place. He reminded himself there was no way law enforcement would ever get in his home, so he had figured that it would buy him the extra hours that he needed. But now, he had an even bigger problem. The DEA agent had seen his face. She had looked directly into his eyes, which meant only one thing: she had to die.

* * *

Trevor walked into the dimly lit bar located in the Mission Hills neighborhood of El Paso, squinting his eyes to adjust to the change in light. Rod was one of only two men sitting at the bar. He only looked up from the glass in front of him when Trevor slid onto the stool beside him.

"What are you doing here?" Rod asked, looking back at his drink.

"I need to run something by you, but I need to make sure you are thinking in your right mind. How many of these have you had?" Trevor asked, picking up the glass that was sitting on the bar in front of Rod.

"I've been suspended from the job, Trevor. Whatever information you think you have, take it to one of the agents in the El Paso Field Division. Don't put a stain on your career by coming to me with something when you should be going to somebody else."

"I don't care that those morons at the Field Division or Headquarters decided to suspend you. I trust you more than anybody else back there. You are the best chance I have at finding Ana Lucia."

Rod cocked his head and turned to look at Trevor.

"It's noon, Trevor. It has been 12 hours since the deadline, and as far as I know, nobody gave Toro the information he demanded. Ana Lucia's probably been killed. There's nothing we can do about it."

"No, I don't believe that. Nothing has been posted online or sent to the media about it. I believe she's still alive."

"Even if she is," said Rod, "there's nothing we can do. We can't go down into Mexico to rescue her, that's what got me in this situation in the first place."

"What if she's not in Mexico? What if she's right here in El Paso?"

Rod looked at Trevor like he had grown another head.

"That's crazy. Why would she be here? And how?"

Trevor shrugged his shoulders. "It's smart. This is the last place you would think of to look for her. Who knows how she got here?

You know they have smugglers all over the border, there are private airplanes. We have heard about tunnels. There are all kinds of ways."

Considering the young agent's words, Rod nodded his head and turned to face him.

"It's still very unlikely, but I guess it would be smart...and possible, but El Paso is a big place, even if she was here, then how would we find her?"

"That's what I wanted to speak with you about, to get your opinion on some information that was provided to me." Rod looked at Trevor, and saw the same spark in his eyes that he used to have the first few years in the DEA when he was hell bent on changing the world by helping to stop the flow of illegal drugs into the West Texas corridor. He grabbed Trevor and pulled him into a booth near the back of the room.

"Tell me what you have," Rod said once they had sat.

"I got a call from Brandon Ledbetter, the DEA agent based in Mexico City. He said that he met with you and Ana Lucia at the SOD Conference in Los Angeles a couple weeks earlier."

"Yeah, I know Brandon. He's a good agent."

"He said that during the SOD meeting, he mentioned a high-level informant that he had established, somebody that was a high-ranking member of the Cartel de Culiacan."

"Yeah, I remember," Rod again confirmed.

"After Brandon left the SOD Conference in Los Angeles, this informant met with Brandon in Mexico City and provided a lot of phone numbers being used by drug traffickers or other people working for the Cartel throughout the US and Mexico. Brandon started tracking the phone numbers, and one of the numbers they are tracking belongs to a criminal defense attorney here in El Paso."

"Okay," Rod said. "He's probably just paid by the cartel to defend their workers that get arrested. His job is to find out how much information the government has on other members of the Cartel.

They have done it that way for years. They do it here and everywhere else. That doesn't prove Ana Lucia is here."

"No, it doesn't, but get this, I went and sat on the defense attorney's house last night in Castner Heights. He did not leave but the lights were on until about 2:00 a.m., well after the midnight deadline. Early this morning he gets up and leaves his residence driving a large black Mercedes van, and travels south to a small residential neighborhood just a couple miles north of the border. Nobody is in the vehicle, and he pulls into the garage of this residence. Garage door closes. A few minutes later, the garage door opens, and the van leaves the residence. Nobody is in the passenger seat, just the defense attorney driving. I follow the van to a small airport east of El Paso. The van pulled directly onto the tarmac and a Hispanic male exits the passenger seat. I am certain that he was not in the passenger seat of the van when it left George's house, or the second location."

"Okay," Rod said, "that is suspicious. What happened to the guy that got out of the vehicle?"

"He went directly to a small jet that was waiting on the tarmac for him. I got the tail number of the jet, and it is owned by a Mexican band out of Chihuahua. The manager of the band was arrested in El Paso last year for money laundering for the Cartel de Culiacan."

"Wow," Rod said. "You did all that on a Sunday?"

"Yes, I used my laptop to look it up. But that's not it. The black Mercedes van was rented by a white guy named Tommy Stetson on Thursday afternoon, an hour after Ana Lucia was kidnapped. This guy, Tommy Stetson, is a 33-year-old convict that just got out of jail on some technicality when his defense attorney, the one we are tracking, found some evidence that he was able to use to get the conviction overturned. That was two months ago. One month ago, Stetson got arrested for domestic assault, beating the crap out of some crackhead girlfriend, so I'm sure George is the defense attorney again."

"And Stetson can't pay for his legal defense and is instead doing whatever asked of him by the defense attorney," Rod said, connecting the dots.

"Yes. Also, I checked the utilities on the house where the van went to that is close to the border. Utility information shows that the bills are being paid by a guy named Salvador Martinez. We arrested his brother six months ago when we stopped him driving 125 kilograms of cocaine to New Mexico. He worked for the Cartel too."

"I remember that guy," Rod said. "You were able to gather all that information just today?"

"Yes, so what do you think?"

"It is suspicious, but basically the only link with Ana Lucia is that she was kidnapped by somebody from the Cartel de Culiacan and this defense attorney has several links to the Cartel."

"Right, but we should check it out, right?" Trevor asked.

"Yeah, so why did you leave the defense attorney if you thought that he had something to do with Ana Lucia?"

"I didn't know what to do. If I tell anybody from DEA, it will take too long to get all the people necessary to conduct a surveillance and then enforcement operation. Plus, I do not trust the DEA management to even let us conduct an operation. They'll probably shoot us down because they don't want the possibility of any additional bad press coming out."

"You're right about that. It might be worth checking out."

"Oh, and the last thing," Trevor said. "Late Friday night El Paso police found Blanco dead in his home, shot in the head. Whoever it was, the Cartel sent somebody into El Paso. They've shown they can get people here."

Rod sat back in the booth, deflated. First Pablo, the courier, had been killed in the shootout, and now the original informant, Blanco, had been killed in his own home. Both men had been DEA informants, and now both men were dead. He did not want Ana Lucia to suffer the same fate if she had not already.

Nodding his head, Rod said, "We have to do it. What do you suggest?" giving preference to the young agent who had done a great job obtaining leads and information.

"Brandon is sending me the GPS location of the defense attorney. The coordinates come in every 5 minutes, so it is not continuous, but it is better than nothing. Let me go track him down. You go check out the location for this Tommy Stetson that rented the van. Stetson lives west of Castner Heights around the 375 Loop and 54. It is kind of a desert and mountainous area. It would be the perfect place to hide out if he had a kidnapped DEA agent."

"I'll check Stetson's house," Rod said. "Find the defense attorney, and then hit me up and we'll figure out what to do from there."

* * *

Rod followed his GPS as he drove his personal vehicle, a Jeep Patriot, off the main highway and down the dusty path toward Stetson's residence. Once his GPS showed that he was a quarter- mile away from the dirt road where Stetson lived, Rod pulled to the side of the road. Normally, he would drive by the residence and get a look at it before he decided where to park his vehicle, but in this situation, the area was clearly desolate, and any vehicle pulling down the dirt road where Stetson lived would be noticed. Rod was worried that his vehicle was too close as it was, so he popped the hood of the Patriot to give the appearance that engine problems had caused the vehicle to be stopped and abandoned. Meanwhile, he set out on foot towards the residence.

The dirt road he was on led to another smaller dirt road about a quarter mile toward the west. A rise in the terrain to his right blocked the view of Stetson's residence. He would not have suspected there was a residence back there if he did not have the information from Trevor.

Instead of walking down the dirt road, Rod moved off the road and up the hill, which rose about 30 feet before sloping back down. At the top of the hill, Rod peeked over to observe the property. He saw that the ground sloped down and leveled out for about 50 feet before rising again to another hill about 20 feet high. In his line of sight just above the second hill, was the top of what appeared to be a residence. Not seeing any sign of life, Rod moved to the second hill, and laid down flat on the ground, looking out at what was an old trailer mobile home that had trash strewn around the front yard. Rod thought it looked like the house of a meth user. Rod stayed there for five minutes to see if he could detect anyone in the residence but did not see any movement. He thought he could hear something but was not sure if that was simply sounds of the passing traffic on the nearby 375 Loop north of El Paso.

Deciding not to wait any longer and knowing that he was once again violating the law by trespassing, Rod moved toward the trailer. He pulled out his personal handgun, a baby Glock, a slightly smaller version of the government issued firearm that had been taken from him a couple days earlier when he was suspended. Rod put his left hand to the front doorknob of the trailer, and slowly turned the knob to check if it was locked. It was open. Pushing the door open with his left hand, Rod held the gun with his right hand, and walked into the trailer.

He did not see anything. There were no sounds inside the trailer. Rod slowly and quietly closed the door behind him, and walked through the two-bedroom trailer, clearing it of any threats. Stetson nor Ana Lucia was there. Rod continued to walk through the trailer, picking up any notes, bills, or anything that might have information. He continued to look around, until he came to a small window just over the sink in the tiny kitchen of the trailer. The window looked over the rear of the property, to an area backed up 200 feet away by the freeway, which was raised up above the ground and out of sight by the motorists overhead on the 375 Loop. Rod's eyes focused on a figure at the edge of the property and tried to figure out what he was seeing.

Rod was able to tell it was a white male, but the man's back was to the trailer. Rod assumed that it was Stetson, but he stayed silent while he tried to figure out what was going on. When he finally realized it, Rod immediately contacted Trevor.

"I think your hunch was right," Rod told him. "I've found Stetson on the back of his property, and I think he's involved."

"What's he doing?" Trevor asked.

"Digging a grave."

* * *

Trevor had been following around the black Mercedes van for close to an hour, as it wandered aimlessly. Had Trevor arrived at the Castner Heights residence three minutes earlier, he would have been there as the van exited the back gate of the defense attorney's residence, but he was able to ultimately locate the vehicle at a nearby gas station as George filled the vehicle up with gas. The following hour had been confusing, with the defense attorney identified as the driver, and clearly seeming to drive around without any purpose, apparently wasting time. For what reason, Trevor did not know, but he was convinced the defense attorney was involved somehow. He wondered if there was some chance that Ana Lucia was in the back of the vehicle. Why else was George driving around this big vehicle with no purpose? The van was carefully obeying all traffic laws, especially those normally used by law enforcement to stop vehicles suspected of containing narcotics or narcotics proceeds. The defense attorney had seen many reports of his clients being stopped for different reasons and was making sure not to make any of those same mistakes. Blinkers indicated change of lane or a turn, speed limit was followed exactly, appropriate distance was maintained between vehicles, and the vehicle was careful to stop at all red lights and stop signs, and not roll through them as so often happened. The fact that Trevor had followed the man for an hour and had not noticed one single traffic violation was perhaps the biggest clue that something was amiss, and perhaps there was something in the vehicle that he didn't want found by law enforcement.

But why drive around if there was something in there? Why not park it at his house or somewhere safe, instead of driving around and taking the risk of getting stopped by the police? It was the very same question that was causing George to sweat on the inside, refusing to take the DEA agent back to his residence out of fear of being caught by his neighbors, but being instructed by Stetson to not come to his property for an hour so that he could dig the grave that would be used to bury the DEA agent's body. Stetson's explanation was that if Ana Lucia were unconscious, they would dump her body into the grave, and then kill her there. That way, the police would never be able to find any sign that she had been killed in a vehicle, or a residence. There would be no sign of a murder unless they found her body in the grave, at which time Stetson would be long gone and using the $50,000 George had planned to give him for his help.

George looked in the back of the van to make sure that she was still out. The woman had taken a significant blow to the head, and George was hopeful that she would be out for a while. There had not been any stirrings or mumblings to indicate that she was regaining consciousness, so he thought there would be time to get her to the grave and let Stetson take care of the rest.

Trevor notified Rod as the black Mercedes finally started approaching Stetson's property. It was arriving from the same direction which Rod had traveled earlier, so he knew that he needed to move his vehicle. It was simply too risky to leave it there. Rod rushed back to his vehicle and drove it down the road and past the dirt road leading to Stetson's house. As the road snaked around about half a mile away and was out of sight, Rod pulled over and parked again. He exited, running ran as fast as he could back to the property. Rod noticed the dust of George's vehicle just after it had pulled down the dirt driveway. He called Trevor, who told him that he was also approaching. Rod agreed to wait for Trevor's arrival, and that he would park at the entrance of the property, where they would both approach it together, regardless of the fact they did not have a search warrant.

* * *

Ana Lucia had again regained consciousness, and this time she was smart enough to lay still while she tried to figure out the best way to get out of the situation. Lying on her left side, she felt the press of what felt like a switchblade concealed within the inside of her boot. How had that got there? And who put it there?

In what seemed like deja vu, the vehicle came to a stop, and the driver exited the vehicle and approached the rear. Ana Lucia readied herself for the door to open, prepared to see the man again, but this time, there was a delay, and he did not come to open the door. Instead, she heard two voices on the outside. She tried to use the delay in time to slide the blade out of her boot, and was finally able to pull her back legs back far enough to grasp the blade in her right hand which was still constricted behind her, just as the door to the van opened.

Instead of being faced with the same man as earlier that she was confident she could overtake, this time Ana Lucia saw Stetson, a white male wearing a wife beater t-shirt with a shaved head and a sleeve of tattoos on both arms. The man grabbed her under the armpit and pulled her out of the van.

Ana Lucia looked ahead and noticed the grave. Stetson did not seem to mind that she was awake. He seemed fully confident that he would be able to take care of any fight put up by a woman. Ten feet away from the grave, Ana Lucia stuck her right foot in front of Stetson, and twisted her hips violently as she swung her left foot around, tripping the man and causing him to fall forward toward the grave. Falling on her back side, she pressed the button to bring the blade out, and used it to slice free from the zip ties that had kept her hands behind her for the previous two and a half days.

Stetson used his hands to brace his fall, releasing his grip on the gun that had been in his right hand. The gun fell on the side of the six-foot deep grave, teetering near the edge.

With her hands finally freed and the blade in hand, Ana Lucia lunged on top of Stetson in an attempt to stab him in the back of the head, but he rolled over at the last instant and moved his head, as the blade went harmlessly into the dirt.

Stetson grabbed Ana Lucia by the shoulders and rolled so that he was on top of her, but she slammed her knees into his crotch. She then used her ground fighting training learned at the DEA Academy in Quantico, and placed both her legs on the outside of Stetson, with her feet firmly planted in the ground, and exploded up with her hips, rolling to her left to get him off of her. As Ana Lucia regained position on top, she saw the gun on the edge of the grave, and went to grab it, only to feel herself yanked back at the last instant as Stetson grabbed her leg and pulled her back. Ana Lucia lost grip on the gun as it slid down the recently dug grave.

With her legs pinned to the ground by Stetson, Ana Lucia turned to punch him in the face, but he lunged at her, tackling her as she fell back onto the ground. Knowing she could not afford to let the man stay on top of her, she used all her strength to roll yet again, but the roll took both over the side and down into the grave. Several moments later, two shots rang out.

* * *

After driving the black Mercedes van up to Stetson's trailer, George had quickly walked away, finding a small shed a hundred feet from the trailer. The shed looked old and unusable, and it probably was, but just behind the shed was another rental car, a Ford Taurus that had been left there so that George could quickly escape. He hopped into the car and peeled off down the dusty driveway, looking in his rearview mirror to see Stetson leading Ana Lucia out of the van.

George was fed up with this life and had decided that he was going to book a one-way ticket to a small island in the South Pacific as soon has he was able to book a flight.

George looked in his rearview mirror again one more time as he came near the exit to the dirt road leading from Stetson's house, but noticed that he no longer saw either Stetson or Ana Lucia. He didn't see the two DEA agents blocking the exit until the last moment, slamming on the brakes just before it crashed into Trevor's OGV.

The defense attorney attempted to feign outrage as he demanded to know why he was being detained and Trevor had a gun leveled at him. No longer caring, Trevor opened the driver's side door and pulled George out, throwing him on the ground and keeping his gun carefully on him. Both Trevor and Rod had noticed the defense attorney's attention on his rearview mirror as he approached, looking directly back towards the grave Rod had seen dug earlier.

"Do you guys know who I am? I am going to have your badges by this afternoon! This is an unreasonable search and unlawful detainment! If you don't let me go—"

"Shut-up!" Trevor yelled, dropkicking the man in his side. "I know who you are! You're a piece of crap defense attorney that makes a living defending drug dealers and murderers." Trevor leaned down and spat on the man in disgust.

"Please make a move so that I can justify putting a bullet in your head."

George froze, knowing Trevor meant every word he said.

At that moment, the two shots rang out. Trevor and Rod looked at each other in shock, and then at the defense attorney, whose face had drained of color.

Without a word, Rod sprinted toward the grave.

* * *

Rod approached the grave, having already convinced himself that he was going to have to shoot and kill another bad guy. He was also convinced that he was going to see Ana Lucia lying at the bottom of the grave. As he closed in, he didn't see Stetson anywhere; he bounded up to the grave to see if that was where the shots had come from.

Looking down, Rod saw Ana Lucia. She was leaning against the side of the grave exhausted from the previous few days. A gun laid on the ground by her side. On the other side of the grave was Stetson, with two bullet holes in his chest, his eyes still open even in death.

A look of relief flooded Rod's face. Ana Lucia smiled for what seemed like the first time in decades. "Thank god you're here, but about five minutes earlier would have been great!" she said, trying to crack a joke despite the circumstances.

Rod quickly pulled Ana Lucia out of the grave and told her that they had the defense attorney detained at the exit to the dirt road. She wanted to go with him to confront the man.

As they came back, George was still in the same position on the ground, with Trevor standing over him with a gun pointed at him. Once Trevor saw Ana Lucia alive and well, he looked up in the sky and thanked God.

Realizing what that meant for him, George tried to get up to run away. Trevor leveled his gun for the kill shot, but Rod stopped him, and instead ran down the older man and tackled him to the ground. He delivered a couple of punishing body blows to the side, in what he hoped would be a painful kidney shot. Rod then stood over the man and kicked him several more times in the side. Leaning down, Rod asked him, "Where is Toro?"

George rolled onto his back, trying to catch his breath, and looking up at the sky. "He's gone, he's back in Mexico!"

Trevor placed George in handcuffs, and then went over to Ana Lucia and Rod as the three embraced each other, grateful that this nightmare was over, and that Ana Lucia was alive. They knew the media storm this story was going to generate, and they gathered to go over the story that they were going to tell the world. Deciding that the truth was the best way to go, if for nothing else then Trevor's future career, he pulled his cell phone out and called 911.

Chapter 22
Mexico City, Mexico

Sunday, September 3

The vibration of the cell phone in Brandon's pocket produced an exasperated eye roll. He had received 42 text messages, 13 telephone calls, and seven voice mails from Leticia since the previous day when he told her that their relationship was over. After all of Leticia's assurances that she did not want a serious relationship and was perfectly happy being his mistress and nothing more, Brandon did not expect the outflowing of emotion and grief that she was showing. He told his wife that he was dealing with work issues, and snaked away from the living room of his government living quarters and into the bedroom as he pulled the phone out, and saw that instead of another message from Leticia, it was a call from the informant.

Hoping that it was information that might be used to find Ana Lucia, Brandon answered. While not the information he was hoping for, the intelligence provided by the informant was equally impactful.

"What do you know?" Brandon asked after his greeting.

"About your DEA agent, nothing, I'm afraid. But what I do know I believe will make you happy. El Jefe is traveling away from Sinaloa, where he is protected, and will be visiting La Paz, in Baja, California. He will still be protected, but not as much."

"I'll need answers for two questions. How do you know this and what is El Jefe doing there?" Brandon asked, anticipating the questions he would be asked by DEA management when he told them the intelligence.

"I know because he left the ranch in Sinaloa earlier today. One of my tasks has been to coordinate with the Mexican phone companies to jam all the cell phone signals coming in and out of the location, so nobody can make a call or send an email if they see El Jefe. I know he is going there for two purposes. First, he is meeting with somebody from Vancouver, Canada, a representative of the drug trafficking gang in Canada. They meet once a year at the same time to go over contract details for drug shipments coming from Mexico and going to Canada. They have done it every year for the last ten years. That meeting is tomorrow. The meeting today, where you have the best chance to get El Jefe, is when he is going to pay the reward for the two men who found out who was responsible for killing, and ordering the killing, of his wife."

"Somebody found that out? Does that mean that Ana Lucia is safe?"

"I would assume the answer to that question is yes, because I know for a fact Toro is one of the two people traveling to Baja to collect a $10 million reward."

"Well, if he is traveling to Baja, then where is Ana Lucia?" Brandon asked.

"I'm not sure, but I will let you know when I know."

"Okay, so where and when is this meeting taking place? I need specifics if I am going to get a team out there to apprehend El Jefe."

"I understand, Brandon. There is a wonderful restaurant on Balandra Beach in La Paz, Baja California, directly west of Sinaloa. It is where El Jefe takes all his important business ventures when he is trying to impress or thank people. He will be there, I'm sure."

"When?" Brandon asked.

"He is scheduled to meet with Toro, who is getting one $10 million reward, and Felipe, who is getting the other reward, in a few hours at 5:00 p.m."

"On a scale of 1 to 10, how sure are you that El Jefe will be there?"

"10, 100% sure, Brandon."

"What will his security look like?"

"It will be heavy, as always. That is part of the reason he chooses this location. The restaurant is on the beach and is protected on that side by the water. The owner of the restaurant closes it down, and has his own security team watching the perimeter of the location, in addition to the 15-man crew that El Jefe will bring with him that will be watching the streets at least a mile away from the restaurant. If you want to get him, you are going to have to go through at least 20-30 men. People will die, I just want to warn you."

"Okay," Brandon said. "Thanks for the intelligence. Keep your phone on," he said, ending the conversation, and immediately started placing other calls to formulate the plans of a potential operation to arrest the most wanted fugitive in the western hemisphere.

* * *

Tijuana, Mexico

The Mercedes pulled into the small private airport that did not even have a name, nothing more than a landing strip and a small building for pilots and passengers to take a bathroom break if delayed. Felipe quickly exited the vehicle, eager to remove himself from the tension that existed inside the vehicle, sitting across from Montoya and Toro. Felipe suspected that Montoya likely knew that he had set up the Federal Police to find and kill Toro in Tijuana, but Felipe had done his best to claim that he hadn't known Toro was going to be there. The man did not say anything, and his calmness and refusal to show his cards was slightly unnerving. Felipe was so close to finally being rewarded with millions of dollars he did not want anything to get in the way.

As he walked to the private jet, different from the one that brought in Toro hours earlier, Felipe placed a phone call to Tonio to check on the man that was in the shootout at the house in LA with him the day before.

"How are you?" Felipe asked.

"I just got out of the hospital thirty minutes ago. My hip is killing me from where that bastard DEA agent shot me. What are you doing?"

"I'm going to collect the reward. I will be $10 million richer tonight. I will reward your loyalty for being with me yesterday."

"One million?" Tonio asked.

"Yes, you will get your million, just like I said." The fact that they had been friends since childhood was the only reason Felipe would not go back on his word. "There is something else you should know. The Hispanic DEA agent that showed up at the house in LA last night with the rifle, the same guy that shot me in the shoulder... he is the one that showed up at the bar and met with Toro. He was dirty the whole time, working for the Cartel! Vaquero was his contact in Los Angeles."

"If he is working with the Cartel, then why did he show up and start shooting at us?" Tonio asked.

"Not sure, but he will be punished. He was able to escape the bar, but it was reported that he was shot and is injured. One of Toro's assassins, Leon, was instructed by Montoya himself to hunt down the DEA agent and kill him. I have instructed my buddies at the Federal Police to assist Leon with the search for the DEA agent as well. Leon makes Toro look like a nice guy. The DEA agent will be dead by nightfall. If Leon does not find him, then my men will."

* * *

La Paz, Baja California, Mexico

After the jet landed on a small strip in La Paz, Montoya put Felipe and Toro in a bulletproof Land Rover and told them that he would not accompany them to the meeting with El Jefe, as he had other business to attend. From the landing strip to the restaurant was no more than one mile; Toro counted 25 security personnel that he knew worked on behalf of El Jefe. Once the Land Rover pulled off the main street and onto the private drive leading to the restaurant,

Toro noted an additional 15 security personnel that appeared to be employed by the owner of the facility.

The doors of the Land Rover were opened for them as they pulled in the circular driveway of the beachside restaurant, where valet drivers normally waited to take the visitors' vehicles to a nearby parking lot. Toro and Felipe were led into the empty restaurant and then out the back and seated at an oak table on the rear patio overlooking the beautiful Gulf of California that separated Baja California, Mexico from the mainland coast of Mexico. It was the only table outside the restaurant, with the water just 100 feet away.

Rising at the head of the table to greet the two men was none other than El Jefe himself, smiling and opening his arms to embrace the two men that had discovered the individuals responsible for murdering his wife. El Jefe hugged Felipe and turned to do the same with Toro, who did not return the embrace.

Not taking offense, El Jefe motioned for Felipe and Toro to sit down so they would have a view of the water. Already at the table was a variety of alcoholic drinks and ice water, along with grilled shrimp, lobster tails, crab claws, and oyster shells.

"Gentlemen, whatever you would like to eat or drink, feel free to take for yourself," El Jefe told them. "While we eat, if each of you would explain to me how you came to find this information, I would greatly appreciate it." El Jefe motioned to a nearby security guard. Four men, each carrying a duffle bag, walked from the side of the back patio and placed each bag on the end of the table.

"But first, to put any concerns you may have at ease, I want you to know your reward is here. I am a man of my word. Two of those bags are for you Felipe, and two are for Toro. Each bag contains $5 million. This is the reward for the information you have provided, $10 million to each," El Jefe said.

"So, Toro, would you show me the information provided to you at the meeting earlier today in Tijuana? I understand from Senor Montoya that the information was provided by a DEA agent from California."

"That's correct," Toro answered. He removed the documents from the satchel and placed them on the table in front of the leader of the Cartel de Culiacan. El Jefe spent the next couple minutes going through each document carefully, before putting them back in the satchel and handing it to one of his bodyguards. Toro and Felipe meanwhile sat silently. Toro did not touch the food or drinks, but Felipe consumed both eagerly.

El Jefe leaned back in his seat at the head of the table, contemplating the information provided by Toro. Noticeably fighting the urge to explode in rage, El Jefe then asked Felipe to explain how he determined Jose Padilla was the man that poisoned his wife, and then how he tracked Jose Padilla to the house in Los Angeles.

As Felipe began to explain the investigative measures taken to identify Padilla as the murderer, Toro's attention was broken as he noticed a disturbance in the water. So entranced was El Jefe in Felipe's story, he did not notice the water breaking, and the ten men that suddenly and simultaneously emerged from the water.

The Mexican Special Forces Unit, which worked closely with US Special Forces, came out of the water, carrying black ballistic shields in front of them that were over five feet in height and provided protection from hand guns and rifle rounds. The shields had a clear section at the top that allowed the user to look out and see what they were approaching, while still protected. In addition to being five feet high, the shields were three feet wide. Each man that came out of the water had the top edge of the shield just at the crown of their head. They crouched as low as they could while still moving quickly, to provide the most cover for their legs that were only minimally exposed below the knees. Each man carried the shield with his left hand by holding a horizontal bar connecting the two sides. With the right hand, they maintained a rifle that pointed out from the right side of the shield. Upon emergence from the water, each man quickly hooked their arms through horizontal bar of the shield and used their left hand to rip away the waterproof bag that had protected their rifles during submersion under water. All this was accomplished while continuously moving forward.

El Jefe's bodyguards standing on the rear porch noticed the men at the same time as Toro, and five men rushed to the front of the table shooting fast and furious at the men who had just come out of the water intending to apprehend El Jefe. Toro was also standing and firing at the invading men in black as they moved out of the water and onto the sand, quickly approaching the rear patio of the restaurant.

The madness of the ensuing scene created mass chaos among everyone inside the restaurant whose job had been to protect El Jefe. The defenders of the Cartel leader had not considered the possibility of an attack from the water, and many rushed around in confusion trying to determine what was going on. While hundreds of rounds burst forth from the AK 47s used by security personnel from the restaurant itself, none of the Special Forces were deterred, protected by the shields, and they continued moving toward the rear patio.

By the time the nearest Special Forces member had crossed half the distance between the water and the rear patio, only 50 feet away, one of El Jefe's bodyguards grabbed him and pulled him away, toward the inside of the restaurant, but before he could get inside, the bodyguard fell with a head shot, and then, the unthinkable, El Jefe was shot in the back. The bullet traveled through him out the right side and ultimately lodged somewhere inside the restaurant.

El Jefe fell against the wall, stunned, and clutched at the wall in attempt to stay up.

The bodyguards continued to drop like flies as they rushed outside the rear patio to take on the invading Special Forces, casualties of the deadly accurate shooting from the highly trained Mexican Military Special Forces.

Realizing that he was outgunned for the second time in the same day, Toro could see that they were quickly going to be overtaken. He noticed when El Jefe was shot and rushed to his side to grab him and keep him from falling to the ground. Holding El Jefe with his left hand, Toro used the gun in his right hand to shoot at the only exposed part of the nearest Special Forces member.

The bullet found its mark in the right shin of the man now 30 feet away, who was shooting at two bodyguards that had rushed to the table to return fire. Fortunately for Toro, the man stumbled and fell to the ground, for just several seconds. During that time, Toro put El Jefe's arm around his neck and started moving him inside the restaurant, but at the last moment, something caught his eye. It was Felipe. The corrupt Mexican Federal Policemen had grabbed all four of the black duffle bags in the chaos, and had run toward the beach around the side of the restaurant away from the Special Forces, where a boat awaited for El Jefe in case he needed a quick escape. The Special Forces mission was to capture El Jefe, and the soldiers did not pay Felipe any attention as he had rushed off to the side.

Toro realized that Felipe was going to use the boat to escape with all $20 million. In one motion, even as he carried El Jefe inside, Toro leveled his handgun and fired two shots, hitting Felipe from 100 feet away. The policeman fell to the ground at the edge of the water, with the blood coming from him turning the water a dark red. The four bags, totaling $20 million, fell to the ground and into the water. Within moments, several hundred thousand dollars that fell out of the top of the bags of money were floating in the water, stained red from Felipe's blood.

Toro moved as quickly as he could through the empty restaurant. One of El Jefe's bodyguards breathlessly relayed that the guards a mile out in the front of the restaurant were under assault as well from the Mexican Police. The bodyguard took El Jefe and carried him toward the bulletproof Land Rover.

As Toro turned around to stand his ground, he heard something hit the ground behind him. Leveling his gun while turning, Toro did not see a Special Forces soldier inside the restaurant, but instead the concussion grenade that detonated nearby.

The effects of the concussion grenade left Toro on the ground, his vision blurry and without a sense of what was going on around him. The last thing he realized was that he was not going to escape.

Chapter 23
San Diego, California

Sunday, September 3

A relaxing Sunday afternoon shooting basketball outside with his son Conner, and followed up by an hour in the recliner with his daughter Bella watching Mickey Mouse, was much needed for Tyler Jameson after the day before that almost resulted in his death in the shootout in Los Angeles, and the resulting interrogation from the DEA's OPR investigators.

When Tyler's phone rang in the early afternoon hours while he sat in the living room of his residence in Tierra Santa, California, his wife looked at him pleadingly, asking for him to not answer the call and instead spend time with their children. Tyler agreed to let the call go to voicemail, but stated he at least had to check the message. The fact that it came in on a Sunday afternoon was an indicator of importance because the wire room monitors and other co-workers at DEA considered that a time for the agents to spend with their families.

The message was from Veronica, the lead Spanish speaking monitor on the wiretap Tyler was leading out of DEA's San Diego office. The urgency in her voice requesting an immediate call back was all Tyler needed to know that whatever information she needed to pass on was not something that could been delayed, so he snuck back to the bedroom to return her call to see what was going on.

"Thank God you called back Tyler, there is a big problem!" Veronica started.

"What's going on, Vero?" Tyler asked, trying not to let his tiredness reflect in his response. He had started the day informing Vero about the shootout the day before involving Tonio and Felipe, and

240

how they ultimately escaped. He wanted updates about their locations if Tonio continued to use the phone but suspected that he would get a new phone after the shootout the day before. To his surprise, Tonio continued to use his phone, and a call between Felipe and Tonio, both who were in Tijuana, was intercepted and listened to by Vero at the DEA wire room.

"Tonio went to a hospital in TJ to get treated for a shot in the hip," Vero said. "As he was leaving the hospital, Felipe called and told him that a DEA agent showed up to provide evidence about who paid for the waiter to poison El Jefe's wife."

"What?" Tyler asked doubtfully. "How would a DEA agent know who ordered the murder of El Jefe's wife? Are you sure?"

"Yes, I'm sure. And Tyler...Felipe confirmed it was Reuben that showed up."

The revelation left Tyler silent as he tried to process the meaning on what he just heard.

"That doesn't make sense," Tyler finally said. "Reuben was with me until early this morning. If Reuben was in Tijuana this afternoon....wait...how did Reuben know who to communicate with at the Cartel to arrange the meeting in the first place? That would mean..."

"That he was dirty," Vero said, finishing his thought.

"No way, not Reuben," Tyler said.

"He saved my life yesterday, literally. I would be dead if Reuben didn't arrive when he did."

"True," Vero acknowledged, "but it also doesn't mean he's not dirty."

Tyler sat down on the edge of the bed and rubbed his head, contemplating the significance of the call and what it meant for his coworker from Los Angeles.

"That's not all," Vero said.

"Dear god, what else?" Tyler asked, not wanting to know.

"There was a shootout at the bar in Tijuana where Reuben went to provide the information to Toro, the same guy that kidnapped Ana Lucia. Felipe didn't say what happened to her, but he did say

Reuben was shot in the shooting and was injured, but Felipe said that one of Toro's assassins, some guy named Leon, was instructed to track down Reuben and kill him. Felipe also said he was going to instruct his subordinates at the Mexican Federal Police to join the hunt. They have orders to kill Reuben before he gets back to the US side of the border."

"Oh my god" Tyler said. He was conflicted. The thoughts that Reuben might actually be corrupt were a huge betrayal to Tyler and his law enforcement brethren, but how else would Reuben have known who to contact to provide evidence of the person that ordered the murder of El Jefe's wife? And what evidence did he provide?

Tyler pushed those thoughts from his head. At the end of the day, Reuben Valdez was his friend, corrupt or not. Reuben Valdez saved his life the day before, corrupt, or not. His mind was made up.

"What are you going to do?" Vero asked Tyler.

"I can't leave Reuben down there to be murdered. I must help him. I cannot trust the Federal Police, so I am going there by myself. I'm going to Tijuana."

"I thought you would say that. You can't go alone though. You are a white boy going to a war zone in Tijuana. I have a sister that lives in TJ, let me at least drive you down there, you can do your investigative stuff and find him, and we can get him back."

"Absolutely not!" Tyler said. "I can't take you down there. I won't put you in harm's way."

"I know Tijuana. You will not find Reuben if you go by yourself, and you might not make it out alive. If you go with me, then at least nobody will question you. I will cover for you if anyone asks questions."

"I won't risk it."

"Reuben's life is in danger. If you go down there, your life will be in danger too. The best way to help you will be with somebody that blends in and can fluently speak the language."

"I can speak enough to get by."

"No, you can understand Spanish and speak enough to get your-self in trouble, but the locals will be suspicious of a gringo down there asking questions after everything that's been happening. No-body will answer your questions or help you."

Tyler considered her proposal. He knew she was right, but also knew that he should not put her life at risk for the purpose of saving the life of a DEA agent that might be corrupt and working for the Cartel de Culiacan.

"My shift is over at 3:00 p.m.," Vero said, "It's 2:00 now. I'm leav-ing an hour early. I'm going to TJ myself."

Vero's passion about justice and standing up for what was right, along with her intelligence and street savvy were several qualities that Tyler had admired ever since they started working together a couple years earlier.

"Ok, I'll be at the office in 20 minutes. Be ready to leave immedi-ately."

* * *

The duo decided to take Vero's car, an eight-year old Honda Civic. They figured that would be less flashy than Tyler's personal vehicle, a shiny new SUV used to drive around his family. He would not risk driving his official government vehicle into Mexico.

The next big decision was what to do with his gun. Taking his DEA issued firearm with him might give the appearance that he was on an official DEA mission, especially if he was stopped by the Mex-ican Federal Police. After everything that transpired in Juarez with Ana Lucia and Rod, that was something he did not want to risk. He left his Glock behind. However, Tyler was also worried about what might happen if they encountered the assassin from Toro's group.

As they drove into Mexico, both Vero and Tyler noticed dozens of armed Mexican Federal Policemen stopped half a mile from the border checkpoint line. Each policeman was inspecting outgoing ve-hicles thoroughly. Tyler didn't know what they were telling the pub-lic, but it was clear that the Federal Police was looking for Reuben, and had positioned themselves at the Border thinking that would be the quickest way he would attempt to get back into the United States. Clearly, that would not be an option to get back safely.

They drove into Tijuana as close as they could get to the location of the shootout at the bar. Wearing a Padres hat low on his head, Tyler walked down the street with Vero at his side. Despite the hours that had passed since the shooting, dozens of onlookers stood watching the law enforcement presence assembled that went in and out, collecting as much evidence as possible for the event that had resulted in the death of many of their comrades.

They were looking for any kind of sign that might tell them where Reuben had fled after leaving the bar, or any sign as to where the assassin was at that time. Vero spoke with a few of the spectators, but nobody offered any information they could use to find Reuben. Tyler's eyes continued to scan the area, until they landed on a teenage boy nearby cooking small sausages and other meats and vegetables on a small portable grill. Tyler nudged Vero with his elbow and nodded at the boy as she took the hint and approached while Tyler stayed back.

Tyler watched as Vero spoke with him and then took out her wallet and handed him some US dollars. The teenager looked around and put a sausage with some onions on a paper plate and handed it to Vero, who thanked the teenager and walked back to where Tyler was standing.

Vero smiled. "The kid was here and saw everybody fleeing the bar, including the one guy that was bleeding from his side. He ran down the street east and then turned north. It had to be Reuben."

"Did he say if anybody had spoken to him about Reuben?"

"Nobody asked him anything," Vero said, as they followed the direction the teenager claimed to last see Reuben.

Tyler stopped and kneeled as they made the northbound turn. Droplets of blood were on the sidewalk and leading down the street away from Avenida Revolucion.

Tyler looked up at Vero with worry. "If we see this blood, then you can bet the Sicario found it as well," Tyler said.

244

"Let's see if we can follow it," Vero suggested. "It's like tracking a wounded animal."

"That's not too far off from the truth right now."

A couple blocks away, they stopped at the corner of an intersection that had a black metal gate surrounding a small church building. The gate remained open from its earlier Sunday afternoon service. At the head of the gate was a barely noticeable bloody handprint.

"He would've been smart to come here," Tyler said. "There were probably still people here from church, and they wouldn't turn away someone in need."

Vero nodded and walked into the building. It was a small house that had been converted into a church. The double doors out front led to a foyer, and then the living room area that had been converted into a worship center, with eight rows of pews in the middle of the room facing the front. Tyler hung back as Vero moved forward and met with an older female. The two women spoke for several minutes before Vero returned.

"We're getting closer," Vero said. "That was the church secretary. She described Reuben and said that he did have a gunshot wound in the side, and that he seemed to be doing okay but had lost a lot of blood. Reuben told them that he had been shot in the shootout with the Cartel and the Federal Police, but that he was afraid to go to the hospital because he was an American and they would think he was involved with the shooting. One of the church members happened to be married to a doctor, so she took Reuben to her residence, which is actually back south."

"Great, let's get there!" Tyler said.

"No – wait. He's not there anymore."

"What? Why not?"

"As the lady left the church with Reuben, a big, strong, Mexican man pulled up outside the church. He must have written down the license plate of the woman that left with Reuben, and checked the registration, because he showed up at the residence where she took Reuben about ten minutes after they got there. The woman called back to the church and said that the doctor had been able to get the bleeding to stop but urged Reuben to get to a hospital for medical treatment. Then they got a knock on the door from the big guy who identified himself as Leon, and by that time, Reuben had disappeared, slipping out the bedroom window."

"So, we don't know where Reuben is now?"

Vero shook her head, "But we know where he was. And my sister lives close by there in an apartment tower."

"How high is it?" Tyler asked.

"At least 20 stories."

Tyler nodded his head. "We need to get to the top of that building and look out. Reuben can't be far, especially if the assassin is on his trail."

* * *

Even though Vero's sister was on vacation and out of town, Vero was able to access the Green Tower apartment building with a key that her sister had given her. They made their way to the top of the building and looked out over Tijuana from 24 floors up. Not sure where to go after finding out that Reuben had left the doctor's home, Tyler thought that perhaps what they needed was a bird's eye view. He was sure that Reuben was aware that he was being tracked by the assassin, and as a result he was likely in hiding. Tyler suspected that Reuben was hiding in plain sight, and he wanted a better vantage point to try and determine where that hiding spot might be.

Once they made it to the top, Vero and Tyler split up and walked around the top of the building, looking out all around Tijuana and the streets that led toward the US border. Tyler found the physician's residence, and then spent a few minutes intensely looking up and down the nearby streets in all the directions. Looking northeast from the building, Tyler noticed a small park that sat down below a larger highway. The park had several trees in the area, but also a congregation of what appeared to be homeless people gathered in a grassy area. Even with binoculars, Tyler could not confirm or deny if Reuben was one of the people there. But Tyler liked the location, and the fact there were other people there that Reuben might be able to conceal himself amongst. He pointed the spot out to Vero and asked if she had seen anything which might be a possibility. When she had not, they both decided to act on Tyler's hunch.

* * *

Ten minutes later the Civic was parked a couple streets away from the park and Tyler and Vero approached on foot. Not noticing any federal policemen or sicarios in the area, Tyler counted 12 people sitting on blankets or a makeshift tent in the grassy area. One person had started a small fire that he was trying to warm food over. Each homeless person looked at the duo suspiciously. Veronica made no delay in getting to the point, asking if a large Hispanic man had come to their park in need of medical care, or was even perhaps resting in one of the two tents.

The men and women looked at each other, deciding whether to trust Vero. Once she saw that they did not immediately say no, Vero suspected Reuben was there. She pulled out her wallet, again attempting to earn the truth with money. After assuring them that she was a friend, and not with the police, the last question they asked was if she was with the man that had stopped by earlier. The way he was described was clear they were referring to Leon. Tyler's heart sank as he began to think that the assassin had already checked in the location, and he turned back and tuned out the individual that began speaking with Vero, until she suddenly grabbed him by the shirt, and started running with another homeless man toward an overpass on Alfonso Bustamante Labastida, nearby the park. Standing in the area between the park and the overpass, was an older male that almost gave the appearance of being a lookout. The man that brought Vero and Tyler over gave a nod of approval, and the lookout moved down to the sleeping bag and said something. Moments later, Reuben Valdez poked his head out of the bag, and started weeping tears of relief to see the familiar face of his friend Tyler.

* * *

"Man am I glad to see you!" Reuben said with a slight grimace as he attempted to pull himself out of the sleeping bag. "I was planning to stay here until dark, and then try to sneak past all the policemen at the border. Do you guys have a vehicle?" he asked, looking at Veronica.

"Yes, this is Vero, she is one of the wiretap monitors for my case. She drove us here. She if familiar with TJ so she offered to come along and help us look for you."

"Thanks Vero, but how did you guys know I was here?"

"We intercepted a conversation about the assassin looking for you," Tyler said.

Reuben blushed with embarrassment. "I can explain what happened," he started.

"I'm sure you can, and you will whenever we get back to the US, but for now we need to make sure this sicario doesn't catch us."

Tyler turned to Vero. "Can you go get the car and drive it back over here?"

"Sure, but there are still dozens of policemen at the border. How are we going to get by them?" Vero asked.

"We might have to travel east and enter the US from Mexicali instead of Tijuana."

"Okay, that might work." Vero said. Without another word, she turned to run to the car. As soon as she ran off, Reuben sat up from the sleeping bag.

"You look rough, buddy," Tyler said attempting a joke.

"I feel worse than I look. This doctor got the bleeding to stop, but I really didn't know how I was going to be able to walk anymore. It's a miracle you are here."

"We're not out of the woods yet."

Before the words came out of his mouth, the lookout that was standing by the overpass let out a grunt. By the time Tyler turned around, the elderly man was already unconscious on the ground, with Leon standing over him and staring at Tyler and Reuben.

* * *

The gun on Leon's hip remained there as he stared at the two men. "So, if you're the dirty DEA agent," Leon said speaking in fluent English and pointing at Reuben, "then I guess that would make you another dirty DEA agent, gringo. Is that right?"

Tyler looked at him. "Yes, I'm a DEA agent. No, I'm not dirty. Whatever you think this man has done, you would be well advised to let him go, or else the full weight of the US government will come down on you."

"Is that why you are in Tijuana in a Honda Civic driven by a civilian from San Diego?" Leon asked, laughing. "Is that the full weight of the US government? If so, I am not worried about it. The Federal Police will have your Civic before you even get back on the freeway. Tell me, gringo, what is your name?"

"Tyler," he said, moving between Leon and Reuben.

"Well, Tyler, do you know that the Mexican Federal Police is under orders to arrest this man?"

"Actually, the orders are to kill him. That's why I am here. I know because I'm listening to a wiretap in San Diego that intercepted all you guys talking about it, so you are done. The US government knows who you are and what you are trying to do, so if you kill Reuben, then they will find you."

"Do I look worried about your government, gringo?" Leon said, spitting out these last words. Moving forward quickly, Leon swatted at Tyler as if he were a fly. The man towered over Tyler by eight inches, and outweighed him by at least 80 or 90 pounds, and used his strength to easily push Tyler to the side.

Knowing he was physically outmatched, and needed to incapacitate the bigger man to have any hope of escaping, Tyler kicked his left leg at a downward angle as hard as he could, in the same manner that Rod had done during their fight at the border in Juarez. At the last moment, sensing the attack, Leon pulled up his left leg, and took the blow harmless in the side of his calf, although it did cause him to slightly lose balance. Tyler used that moment to spring, punching as hard as he could, but Leon deflected the blows with the ease of an experienced street fighter, and then countered with a devastating punch that struck Tyler's chest so hard, he was sure that the blow cracked his sternum. It sent him flailing backwards, where he landed on his back, stunned and unable to breath.

Reuben looked on with dread as Leon approached him and pulled out his gun. "Now, where were we?" Leon said, speaking now in Spanish. Before Leon lifted the gun, Reuben heard a loud thump, and Leon's eyes bugged out of his head for a moment, and then went blank, as he fell to the ground in a slump. Standing behind Leon, was Veronica, armed with a tire iron from her car. She had crept behind the killer silently, and struck upward with such a blow, that she had to yank downward with all her strength to get the tire iron out of his skull. Vero lifted Reuben and walked with him to the Civic that she had parked just 50 feet away. She did the same with Tyler and got in the car, intent on getting out of Tijuana as quickly as possible.

* * *

Before Vero had driven one block south, Tyler was able to catch his breath to warn her that Leon had noticed their vehicle and put a warning out to the Mexican Federal Policemen assisting with the search for Reuben to be on the lookout for the Civic. As he was saying that the siren of a police vehicle wailed. Tyler looked up to see the police vehicle was traveling in the opposite direction in the other lane, but had observed their vehicle and swung across traffic in a brazen attempt to get behind the Civic and make the stop. Fortunately for the trio fleeing from the police, a public transportation bus was changing lanes when the police vehicle made its move. The big bus was unable to stop in time to avoid crashing into the passenger side of the police vehicle, stopping the vehicle, and knocking the driver unconscious.

"We have to abandon the vehicle," Tyler realized, looking at Vero. She looked back at him with worry in her eyes. "You've done enough," Tyler said, "we found Reuben, now drive back, without us. We'll figure it out from here."

"No, I'm not leaving you," Vero said. "If they find you then they'll kill you!"

"It won't matter, Tyler," Reuben said. "Even if they find her with the car and she is by herself, they will still arrest her, and God only knows what else. She'll probably be safer staying with you."

Vero nodded her head in agreement. "We're all in this together. We have to get out of it together."

All three exited the car, Reuben much more slowly. Putting Reuben's arm around his neck, Tyler and Vero moved through back alleys and across small streets, trying to put as much distance as possible between them and the Civic, until Reuben finally couldn't go any longer, and they sat down on a bench at a bus stop while they reassessed the situation.

"I'm sure you already thought about this," Reuben said, struggling for words, "but can you not just call the US Consulate in Tijuana? We need to take a taxi there and they'll give us safe passage."

"What if they don't let you back in the US?" Vero asked.

"Then we'll cross that bridge when we get there. At least you two will be safe."

Tyler nodded his head. "I didn't think about that," he admitted. "Sometimes the most obvious decision isn't always the clearest in the thick of battle."

The taxi ride to the US Consulate in Tijuana took 10 minutes. The American flag blowing in the wind was a welcome sight as the taxi driver pulled up to the sidewalk in front of the pedestrian gate. The armed guards standing behind the Consulate gates watched the taxi carefully waiting to see who exited. But it was the two cars parked on the street, both in front and behind the taxi, that worried Tyler. It could easily be a trap set by the sicarios to shoot them as they exited the vehicle and walked to what they assumed was the safety of the Consulate. Tyler asked the taxi driver to move forward slowly, meanwhile, he instructed Vero and Reuben to lay down in the back seat so they would not be seen. As the vehicle moved slowly by the pickup truck parked 100 feet up from the gate of the Consulate, Tyler looked into the vehicle, and noticed a Hispanic male on the phone, looking in the mirror and appearing to communicate with someone behind him, likely the man in the other vehicle Tyler had noticed. On side of the passenger seat of the truck was an AK-47.

"Yep," Tyler said. "They would have mowed us down before we got into the Consulate."

"Why are the guards just letting those guys sit there?" Vero asked.

"I'm not sure, but outside those gates is Mexican territory, where they have no jurisdiction. We cannot risk it. There's only one other place I can think to go," Tyler said, giving the cab driver directions and pulling out his telephone to make a call.

Ten minutes later the taxi pulled into a driveway of a middle-class residence and entered a two-car garage. The garage door closed behind them as Tyler exited the vehicle. Waiting for them inside the garage was Chico, the informant that Tyler and Reuben had developed in Los Angeles a week earlier.

* * *

"What are we doing here?" Reuben asked through clinched teeth as the doors of the taxi opened.

Tyler tossed cash toward the cab driver and stepped out of the vehicle to meet with Chico, who gazed longingly at Vero, and then suspiciously at Reuben.

"What's wrong with him?" Chico asked.

"Let's go inside to talk," Tyler said.

Once inside, Reuben insisted on sitting at the round table in the kitchen with Tyler, Vero, and the recently developed DEA informant, Chico.

"You told me you had company with you, but you failed to mention who it was," Chico said, looking at Reuben. "I know who he is, who are you?" he asked Veronica.

"I'm Vero, and I work with Tyler."

"You don't look like an agent," Chico said.

"I'm not. Tyler needed somebody to guide him through TJ, and that's why I'm here."

"It doesn't matter why she's here," Tyler said. "We wouldn't be here if we didn't have to be."

"And I would not have given you this address, which is my cousin's house by the way, if you hadn't told me that you would make this meeting worth my while. What do you have to offer me?" Chico asked Tyler.

"We need safe transportation back to California. If you provide that, then you have my word that nobody at the prison in Nevada will ever find out about you or your brother's role in the robbery. I will personally shred your DEA Informant file. You will never be obligated to work with DEA or provide DEA information. I suspect that is something you would like."

"Yes, it is," Chico said, nodding his head and looking back and forth at Reuben and Vero. "But something doesn't add up here. You guys are the DEA. Why don't you just drive back yourselves, or at least get your own people to help you?"

"A corrupt section of the Mexican Federal Police is assisting a few sicarios looking for us. We have seen them around the city in different places, as well as sitting outside the US Consulate, and waiting at the border to go back to the US. They put a lookout on the vehicle that we were driving, so we cannot use it anymore. We need you to drive us to Mexicali so that we can enter the US border there and go into Calexico."

Chico raised his eyebrows and sat back in his seat, taking in the information. Reuben closed his eyes as he felt sweat drip down his pounding head. Vero leaned forward, worried that Chico could not be trusted and that he would betray them to the very people that were hunting them. Reading her thoughts, Chico asked, "And why do you think I won't just turn you over to the Federal Police right now? Or the sicarios?"

"Because you're not a killer," Tyler said. "You handle the money for the cartel, we know that. You don't handle drugs, you don't even like drugs, and you have never been violent toward anyone, other than the one out-of-character time you robbed somebody in order to help your brother. Plus, if you make a call that you have found us, then questions will arise as to how you found us. Eventually, someone from the Cartel will connect the dots, especially since you just went to California, your man got robbed of his money, and your brother went to jail in Vegas, all at the same time. I am honestly surprised nobody has figured it out already, but that's probably because so much other stuff has been going on.

"There is always the option that you could kill us and dispose of our bodies somewhere, but the DEA would eventually determine it was you. They would track our movements back to this location based on the location of our phones. The way I look at it, there really is not an option. You must help us. You don't trust us, and we don't trust you, but we can both help each other this one time, and never have to communicate again. Do we have a deal?"

Chico considered the scenarios Tyler had laid out before him and knew that the DEA agent was correct in each one of his assessments. "We do. But there is only one problem."

"What's that?" Reuben piped up, untrusting of the cartel's money remitter turned DEA informant.

"I can't take you to Mexicali today."

"We have to get back to the US today," Tyler said, knowing that Reuben needed a hospital and might not survive another 24 hours without it. "Why can't you take us?"

Chico shrugged his shoulders and gave a devilish smile, struggling to find the words. Reuben smirked at him and shook his head. "It's because he has a job today, and I'm guessing this DEA informant didn't advise his DEA Informant handler about the incoming shipment of drug proceeds."

Tyler looked at Chico and the informant nodded his head. "Have you received any other money shipments since you became a DEA informant?" Tyler asked.

Chico again nodded. "This is the second one. I got $2.4 million on Tuesday."

"Unbelievable," Reuben said. "We can't trust this guy."

"What did you do with the money?" Tyler asked.

"I drove it down to Loreto, a small town in Baja on the Gulf just north of La Paz. I made a day of it and stayed the night, enjoying the beach, and then came back the next day. For what it is worth, I'm supposed to be doing the same thing this time."

"So, you're receiving money today?"

"Yes, in a couple of hours."

"How much?"

$3.6 million."

"And you're going to drive it down to Loreto again?"

"I will tomorrow. I will count it tonight and confirm the amount. That is why I cannot take you to Mexicali today. I'm very much interested in you destroying this informant file you speak of, but I just can't go today."

Each person sat back in their chairs, trying to consider where they should go from that point, until finally, Vero came up with the solution. Having listened to him discuss his money remitting activities on the DEA wiretap many times in the past, she knew that he utilized a series of hidden tunnels connecting locations in Tijuana to San Diego. While those locations were unknown to law enforcement, she remembered that Chico knew exactly where they were.

"The guy bringing the money is coming out of the tunnel?" she asked.

Chico looked at her surprised. "And who are you again?" he asked.

Without responding to that question, Vero continued, "The solution is simple. You put us in your load vehicle that goes into the tunnel, and we will come out on the US side."

Chico shook his head and waved his finger. "No, there is no way that I can disclose the location of the tunnel. The feds will be swarming everywhere within hours, and I will be blamed."

"No," Vero said, "these two guys will wear blindfolds when we go, so they will not know where the entrance is to the tunnel."

"What about when they get back to California? They will know where the entrance or exit to the tunnel is on that side," Chico said.

Tyler spoke up. "All I'm worried about is getting Reuben to the hospital. I don't care about the tunnel. You have my word that I will not return to that location, as long as you can safely get us there."

Chico sat silent for a moment, trying to determine if he could trust the gringo in front of him. Knowing his thought process, Reuben spoke up once again, vouching for Tyler. "Tyler is a great guy, especially for a gringo."

Vero nodded in agreement. "If Tyler gives you his word, then he keeps it. Whatever the promise," she said, smiling and looking at him.

Sensing the shift in the balance of power in the relationship between DEA agent and informant, Chico felt uplifted. He locked eyes with Vero, and nodded, and stood. "We leave in 15 minutes."

* * *

The Lincoln Navigator pulled into the rear of the small auto-mechanic shop in downtown Tijuana, just three blocks south of where Reuben had been involved in a shootout at the bar earlier in the day. An employee working late closed the gate behind Chico, and then immediately left the area, as he had been instructed. The 12-foot high gate was covered with black tarp and surrounded the property to the rear of the mechanic shop, blocking views out as well as in, unless it was from overhead.

Chico turned to Reuben and Tyler in the back and told them that they could take off their blindfolds, as they had reached their destination. He was confident that in the darkness, they would not be able to make out any distinguishable characteristics of the mechanic shop to lead law enforcement back later. Chico had mostly been worried that they would memorize the location, or the streets surrounding the shop, which was why he had only agreed to take them through the tunnel if they consented to wearing a blindfold on the drive.

Vero sat in the passenger seat, unsure why she also hadn't been requested to put on a blindfold, but she guessed it was because Chico could tell that she wasn't an agent, and he presumptively assumed that she did not have the same level of awareness of her surroundings as trained federal agents. Regardless, Vero sat silent, content with watching the road in front of her, making sure that Chico was not leading them into a trap.

"We're here," Vero told Tyler and Reuben. Tyler slid off his blindfold, while Reuben remained still in the back seat.

"Come on buddy," Tyler said, taking off the blindfold for Reuben as worry crept in. The older, bigger Hispanic agent mumbled something in Spanish as his eyes rolled in the back of his head.

"He's lost consciousness," Tyler said.

"Should we just take him to the hospital in Tijuana, and forget all this?" Vero asked.

"I would normally say yes, but I'm sure the police and the sicarios are still waiting for us at the hospital. It has not even been a full day since Montoya gave the order to kill him, they will not have given up this soon. We have no weapons to fight back. I just don't think he'd make it, or us."

"Yeah, but do you think he's going to make it through here?" Vero asked.

Tyler opened the door of the vehicle and walked on the dirt in the rear of the mechanic shop, approaching Chico, who had opened a large set of double doors that appeared to lead to the building behind it, but instead led to a paved road that declined and went underneath the street.

"How long will we be in this tunnel?" Tyler asked. "Reuben's not doing well. We need to get him to a hospital immediately."

"It will take 20 minutes once you start," Chico responded.

"How long until we get started?" Tyler asked.

"Just a few minutes," Chico assured him, looking into the tunnel, as a light from inside slowly became brighter and brighter. Within moments, a Toyota Sienna van emerged from the tunnel, and drove up the slope, which lead to the area where they stood.

The driver of the van exited and spoke briefly with Chico. Tyler stood nearby to rush along the conversation. Chico and the van driver communicated in Spanish as Tyler waited impatiently.

"Any problems?" Chico asked.

"No, it was as smooth as always," the driver responded. "There are a lot of small bills though, so the money is in three different bags."

"Okay, not a problem," Chico said. "It fit in the compartment?"

"Yes. Perfectly." The van driver looked uncomfortably at the gringo, wanting to ask his boss, Chico, why he was standing there, but showing respect for Chico by not doing so.

"Don't worry about him," Chico said. "He's got something he needs to get across, and I'm going to do it for him. That's all. We are going to go in the tunnel in my vehicle, so close the doors to the tunnel behind us. Take the Sienna back to the garage at my house, leave it there, and then come back here in 45 minutes with your truck to let me back in when I return. Then, we will go back, and do what we always do, take the money out, count it, and then put it back in and drive it to its destination tomorrow. Understand?"

"Yes, sir," the driver responded respectfully.

Having understood everything they said in Spanish, but feigning confusion and urgency, Tyler lifted his hands up in the air and asked, "Can we get going now?"

Chico looked at Tyler with contempt. He was pleased at how the tables had turned, and briefly thought about just turning him into the Federal Police and being done with the situation, but again he realized that doing so would prompt more questions than he was willing to answer.

The driver looked at Reuben and then back at Tyler. "I have some Advil in the glove compartment of the van," he said. "It might not be much, but maybe it would help."

The driver's unexpected offer of medication took everyone by surprise. Vero, who was standing outside the vehicle, nodded to the driver. "Yes, please, anything would help. Thank you very much."

"I'll grab it," Tyler offered. "And yes, thank you very much."

Tyler went around to the passenger side of the van and opened the door and the glove compartment, finding a small bottle with an Advil label on it. He quickly unscrewed the opening and poured out a couple of tablets. Looking back at Chico and the driver, he noticed they had quickly returned to their conversation.

Knowing the van was going to be used to transport the $3.6 million to another location that might have even more money, Tyler removed his I-phone, turned it on silent, and placed it behind several old dusty papers that were in the passenger side door pocket, intending to track his phone and pass on the location to his DEA counterparts in Mexico the following day. Tyler quickly closed the door and walked over to Vero and Reuben, forcing the Advil down the man's throat.

By the time they were done, Chico was back in the driver's seat of the Navigator. "And now, I take you guys to safety, and you forget that I ever existed."

"That's the deal," Tyler said.

The Navigator drove down the incline into the tunnel underneath the streets of Tijuana. Vero looked behind her to see the driver closing the doors behind them.

Tyler had always suspected the existence of the tunnels, and Vero had heard them mentioned in the course of her duties of listening to intercepted calls for DEA investigations. It was surreal to be in one of the tunnels, but not for law enforcement purposes. Tyler was conflicted that he had allowed over 3 million dollars of drug trafficking proceeds to pass by him unmolested, but he consoled his conscious with the promise that it was possible that the vehicle might be able to be tracked down the following day with the help of tracking the I-phone he had placed in the passenger door side pocket.

Tyler was impressed with the craftsmanship of the tunnel. Much like the tunnel connecting Juarez to El Paso that Ana Lucia had passed through days earlier, this tunnel was wide enough for two vehicles to pass through simultaneously. It also had a separate area for a pedestrian to walk through. True to Chico's word, after about 20 minutes, Chico's Navigator finally came to the area where it would exit the tunnel. Chico insisted that even Vero put on a blindfold this time, as where they exited would surely be noticeable to her as a California resident.

The Navigator exited the tunnel, and then picked up speed, indicating it was on the freeway. Finally, Chico told them to take off the blindfolds, and found a location to stop off the 5 freeway in Chula Vista, close to the San Diego Bay.

"This is as far as I take you," he said. "I got you back to the US, now you uphold your end of the deal. Make sure that informant file is destroyed."

"I will," Tyler assured him. He looked at Vero, "Call 911, and give them our location and tell them we need an ambulance immediately." Tyler and Vero pulled Reuben out of the Navigator and sat him down on a park bench. Without another word, Chico drove away, while Vero called 911, and Tyler sat holding his buddy, hoping he would hang on.

Chapter 24
La Paz, Baja California

Monday, September 4

Toro sat silently on the twin size cot with his back against the wall of the small holding cell. The only interaction he had with anyone since awaking was when a man brought him a breakfast burrito several hours earlier and slid it inside the cell on a paper plate.

There were three other empty cells inside the room, and a large steel door stood between the room and whatever else was outside. There were no windows, so Toro had no way of knowing where he was or the time of day.

He had always sworn he would never be taken alive by law enforcement or the enemy. As he sat there waiting for someone to walk through the door, Toro resolved to be strong until the end. There was no leverage that could be used against him. The only punishment that could be used against him was imprisonment or torture, and neither would have the desired effect of causing him to lose his honor in the final moments of his life.

When the steel door slowly started to open, Toro looked down at his feet, refusing to give the individual walking in the satisfaction of believing that he was awaiting that person's arrival. When the person spoke his name, Toro's memory recognized the voice, and his mind flashed in confusion as he looked up at the man standing before him.

Toro stood up from the cot and walked to the bars confining him inside the cell. The two men stared intently at each other before Toro finally spoke. "Senor Montoya."

* * *

"You are alive, so things could be worse," Montoya said.

"Spoken by someone on the other side of these bars," Toro replied to the second in command of the Cartel de Culiacan.

"That's true," he said, nodding his head. "I'll see what I can do about that."

"Did El Jefe escape? Or is he dead?"

"He was shot, but survived, and was able to escape. There was a small house a block away from the restaurant where an old couple lived. Underneath their house is a tunnel that went in both directions to the water. His bodyguards were able to get him to the water and in a boat that took him back to Sinaloa. Now, he is in hiding. His whereabouts, even I don't know."

"Is that because he doesn't trust you anymore?"

"After what happened last night, El Jefe will not trust anybody for a while. He has a security team of 10 people at most."

"That was not local police at the restaurant," Toro said, changing the subject to the group that had captured him and wounded El Jefe. "It was either the Americans or Mexican Special Forces, helped by the Americans. They were too specialized and well trained."

"You're right, it was the Mexican Special Forces."

"If the Mexican Special Forces aren't on El Jefe's payroll, then how are you able to walk in here with your freedom?" Toro narrowed his eyes at Montoya, who only smiled in return.

"Everyone has a price, Toro. If not a price, then they have a reason to live, and I'm sure you've come across many offers in exchange for life in your line of work."

"I have. I am curious what you could have offered them that El Jefe could not. Also, I'm curious why you didn't make this offer prior to the Special Forces attacking the restaurant."

"I have my reasons," Montoya said. "Once you hear the information I have learned, I believe your outlook will change drastically."

"What information, Senor Montoya?"

"Toro, what do you know about El Jefe's wife? The woman poisoned by the waiter in Durango?"

The sudden shift in the conversation caught Toro somewhat off guard. He looked at Montoya on the other side of the bars. "I know nothing about her. I don't make it my business to know information about married women."

"If only everybody in our society had that same outlook, perhaps the moral fabric of our culture would not be eroding at the rate that it is, but alas, that is not the case. As for me, I do happen to know information about El Jefe's late wife, but only because I learned that through the course of my business dealings. It just so happens that El Jefe asked me to handle the legal matters upon her death, as well as coordinating her funeral and things of that nature. What I did not realize at the time of her death, was that she had a will. It was my responsibility to make sure the desires contained within that will were carried out."

Growing impatient with the fact that he remained behind bars while the storyteller had the luxury of telling the story from the other side, Toro wished to rush it along to get to the connection that it had with him.

"With all due respect to El Jefe's wife, and to you, please get to the part of the story that will result in you providing me with some kind of a scenario that I will have to consider as a condition of my release from this jail cell. We both know that is where this is heading."

Montoya smiled as he looked at the infamous assassin. "I've never doubted your intelligence, Toro. You see ahead to things others cannot see and comprehend the reasons present circumstances are the way they are. That, in addition to your other talents, are why you have survived for as long as you have in your line of work. Even now, you understand there is a reason I'm still on this side of the cell while you are on the inside, and I won't delay any longer in telling you the information you wish to know."

Toro sat down on the cot, anticipating an offer that if accepted, would result in his release from the small jail cell.

"An attorney from Culiacan contacted me upon notification of the death of Mrs. Rodriguez and advised me about her will. Mrs. Rodriguez accumulated a sizable portion of money through legitimate business ventures during her marriage to El Jefe. She opened a jewelry shop and sold perfume online, things like that. She became very successful and made over half a million US dollars. She kept that money in a secret business account that even El Jefe didn't know about."

"What does any of this have to do with me?"

"Mrs. Rodriguez wanted her money to go to her 11-year old daughter, Esmerelda, but as a minor, she had to entrust the money to an adult. The individual she chose to control the money was not El Jefe, her husband, but instead a priest...from Chihuahua, named Padre Miguel.

Toro was genuinely surprised at the mention of Padre Miguel, the man who raised him as an adoptive father, sparing him from a childhood as a homeless kid searching for food and shelter.

Montoya recognized the look on Toro's face at the mention of Padre Miguel and continued.

"I traveled to Chihuahua and met with Padre Miguel. He lived in a small cabin, outside a little church on the outskirts of Chihuahua. Mrs. Rodriguez left a note for the priest, revealing herself to be Padre Miguel's long-lost adoptive daughter."

The staggering revelation struck Toro so suddenly that for a moment he thought he was suffering a heart attack. He remained silent, but his eyes showed an emotion that Montoya, nor many other people in this world, had ever seen in Toro, grief.

His sister? El Jefe's wife had been Toro's sister? She had been alive this whole time? Living and married to El Jefe? The spouse of the leader of the largest drug cartel? The last time he saw her was when three men, later known to be sex traffickers, kidnapped her, killing their mother in the process.

"El Jefe's wife was the daughter of Padre Miguel of Chihuahua? You are sure?"

"I am. She revealed that in her letter, which I have here." Montoya reached through the cell and handed the letter to Toro so that he could read it for himself. After he was satisfied in its authenticity, he looked back at Montoya.

Toro brewed silently as his mind processed the revelation that his sister had been alive this entire time, married to such a man as El Jefe.

"Padre Miguel expressed his love for Mrs. Rodriguez and agreed that he would abide by her wishes in the will. Padre Miguel explained how Alicia was kidnapped by sex traffickers when she was a young girl, and that his wife was murdered when she was taken."

The mention of the incident lifted the lid of the hate hidden deep inside Toro's heart. The hate, and the hurt, had driven him all these years, even now decades later.

"Padre Miguel also expressed his affection for his son, a young, wayward boy named Saul, a young person who lost his way after his sister was kidnapped and his mother murdered. He told me that he did not know where Saul was any longer, but that he had unfortunately heard rumors that the man started working for the Cartel and had become proficient as an assassin.

"Now, admittedly, Toro, I do not know much about your background, although over the years, what little I have learned is that you were originally from Chihuahua. It didn't take long to make the connection."

Toro looked up at Montoya. "Why did El Jefe marry this woman, out of all the women he could have? And why would she have stayed with him?"

"El Jefe is a man of insatiable lusts. He has been with hundreds, if not thousands, of women. He has an agreement with several people involved in the trafficking of women and pays them handsomely to let him be with those women for nights at a time. It is through these contacts he met Alicia. Of all the women El Jefe had been with during his lifetime, Alicia charmed him more than any other. He even spoke to me of his affection and love for her, and it was not long be-

265

fore he made her his wife, despite she had only turned 15 shortly before.

"Of course, he continued to be with other women during their relationship. He fathered 34 children total, 23 boys and 11 girls, and he has seen that each one is provided for financially and received the best education available in Mexico. El Jefe had a son, Victor, from his first marriage. As you may or may not know, Victor was not a good man. He was 20-years old when he raped my daughter. When my son Carlos witnessed it, he killed Victor. El Jefe allowed my son to live but ordered that he turn himself into American authorities to spend the rest of his life in jail.

"Although Victor was not a good person, Esmerelda is a beautiful young woman with a kind heart that her father delights in. On the night that Alicia gave birth to Esmerelda, I asked El Jefe how he got Alicia to stay with him all those years. It was more of a joke, a question that I did not expect the honest answer I received. El Jefe said that Alicia attempted to escape several times. She was not content with the luxurious life that El Jefe provided for her, but ultimately he told her that if she attempted to escape again, then he would send men back to Chihuahua, where she was found all those years earlier, and decimate the entire village, starting with her father and brother. El Jefe had several drinks in him at that time, but I have no reason to doubt the accuracy of the story he told."

"What you're telling me," Toro said, "is that sex traffickers killed my mother, took my sister, and provided her to El Jefe so that he could have sex with her, and that El Jefe eventually fell in love with my sister and married her? She gave birth to a daughter. She tried to escape, but he threatened to kill me and Padre Miguel." The rage inside Toro's chest was barely containable as he paced the cell.

"That is correct, Toro. For what it's worth, the few times I met your sister Alicia before her death, she was always a lovely and beautiful woman."

"That doesn't make me feel any better," Toro said through clinched teeth.

"I didn't expect that it would. If I know you, then you likely have revenge on your mind, right now, even if it is against El Jefe."

"What are your thoughts, Senor Montoya?"

"I am going to offer you the opportunity to get the revenge you seek, but not just against El Jefe. For all his faults, he was not directly responsible for Alicia's death. You saw for yourself the proof that the current Deputy Administrator of the DEA signed off on paperwork authorizing payment to the man that poisoned Alicia."

"I saw it," Toro confirmed. "Why would that man care about Alicia? Why involve her?"

"To hurt El Jefe, nothing more. I am sure he simply wanted to get El Jefe upset so that he would ultimately make a mistake that would result in the Americans finally catching him. Your sister was a pawn in the plan of the imperialist American agenda."

"So, two people need to die," Toro said, "but one of them is an American high ranking federal agent that will never come to Mexico. The other is the leader of the Cartel that at this time doesn't even trust you, his number two in command and life-long friend."

"Both true statements. Julian is a wounded animal that is paranoid everyone is out to get him. While he is in hiding, there might be ways to find him.

"Leave finding El Jefe to me."

"Okay," Montoya nodded. "In the meantime, focus your efforts on the American."

Toro paced back and forth inside the cell. "It is one thing to kill an American federal agent that is in Mexico. It is another to do it on American soil. Are you telling me that is an option?"

"I am," Montoya said.

"Do you know where I can find this DEA agent?"

"I do."

Chapter 25
Mazatlán, Mexico

Thursday, September 7

In a safe house north of the Los Pinos neighborhood in the beach side town of Mazatlán, DEA Special Agent Brandon Ledbetter stood next to Marcello and the remainder of the Foreign Investigations Unit (FIU) assigned to work with him. Marcello was the unquestioned leader of the FIU team composed of ten other Mexican Federal law enforcement officers, all of which were required to pass lie-detector tests and withstand a vigorous and thorough background examination prior to working with the DEA. Brandon had been lucky to be assigned Marcello's team during the first year in Mexico City, and during that time, he had been very impressed with the professionalism and integrity of each man. Their dedication and hard work had shown in the amount of successful seizures of drugs and arrests of drug dealers. Nevertheless, when Brandon was approached by none other than Carlos Montoya asking to become an informant, with Montoya offering the head of the current leader of the Cartel de Culiacan, the DEA agent was reluctant to include his FIU team, for no other reason than he didn't want to leave them vulnerable in case something broke bad with Montoya and El Jefe. It was not because he did not trust them. He trusted them as much as anybody, and wanted to protect them and their families.

Marcelo opened the door and welcomed another group of men into the safe house. The group of seven men that walked in were the same Mexican Special Forces that had been responsible for attempting to arrest El Jefe several days earlier in La Paz. Brandon had also been impressed with the Special Forces. No one had been killed, and only one suffered an injury when he was shot in the lower part of

268

the leg below the shield that he had used coming out of the water. He was the only one that was not with the Special Forces team at this time.

Each man from the FIU and Special Forces had been vetted thoroughly, and Brandon trusted each man, which was not a common occurrence with law enforcement and military in Mexico. Despite his trust, Brandon was slightly concerned with the reactions that would result from the operation that he had planned. If what the informant told them was true, they would be surrounded by more money than any of them had ever seen, possibly combined, in all the years they had been involved in law enforcement.

Brandon allowed Marcelo to begin the briefing.

"Thank you for coming. We appreciate your courageous efforts in attempting to apprehend El Jefe in La Paz. It was the closest he has ever come to being captured. While finding El Jefe is not one of the goals of the mission, I believe it will have the greatest impact on his illegal drug trafficking activities as any seizure in the history of Mexican or American law enforcement."

The men of the Mexican Special Forces did not appear impressed with Marcelo's claim of the importance of the mission, but they also did not seem disinterested.

"Quick background," Marcelo said. "We are a law enforcement team working in conjunction with the DEA Mexico City Office. This is DEA Special Agent Brandon Ledbetter. A few days ago, Brandon got a tip from another DEA Special Agent from San Diego about a vehicle bringing drug trafficking proceeds from San Diego into Tijuana. Brandon was able to track the money vehicle to a residence in Tijuana, and the following day, the vehicle left the residence. Brandon coordinated with the DEA office in Tijuana to arrange a trusted Mexican law enforcement team to follow the vehicle that left the residence, and it traveled all the way to near La Paz, where the surveillance team saw the driver of the vehicle remove a large bag and place it in the bottom deck of a large yacht. From the information provided by the DEA agent in San Diego, there was at least $3.5 million in the bag that left from Tijuana. While the team was sitting on the yacht in La Paz, they saw another three individuals deliver bags which were also taken below deck on the yacht, meaning there could possibly be $10 million on the yacht, if not more, but Brandon wanted to see where the money went, just in case the money went to a stash pad that had even more money. It was the right call.

"By that point, the CIA helped track the yacht with a drone as it crossed the Gulf of California and landed in Mazatlán. Our team was waiting for them upon arrival. We saw 10 bags come off the yacht and into a box truck that left the area and traveled to the target residence near Palos Prietos on Rio Panuco."

Brandon passed out aerial photographs of the residence identified from the drone provided by the CIA Case Officer, a bilingual black male from Boston named Toby.

The target residence was inside a gated compound on an area of land two acres large that was at the top of a small hill. Even on the aerial photo, the armed guards surrounding the outside of the gates, and the inside the gates were visible. The guards inside the gate were stationed at the four corners of the residence.

"We've seen eight guards on the outside, and at least four inside the gates. We wanted to gain more intelligence about what was inside the house, so we stopped one individual that dropped off a bag of suspected drug proceeds. The stop was made 20 miles north of Mazatlán, toward Culiacan. It took a little convincing, but we finally got the man to talk. He's here with us now and is willing to tell you for yourselves what is being guarded so carefully inside the residence."

Brandon opened the door to the rear bedroom and motioned for one of the other members of the FIU team to walk out to the living room and bring the informant with him. "This is Javier," Brandon told the Special Forces. "Javier, tell them what you know."

Javier looked at Brandon and Marcello before he began speaking. Brandon gave a reassuring nod urging the man to tell them what he knew. The man instinctively rubbed the bruise under his left eye, the remnants of the persuasion method used by the FIU team when they finally convinced Javier to become an informant.

"I delivered a bag of $4.1 million earlier today. I took it into one of the bedrooms of the residence." He paused while he considered how to deliver the next part of the story to the audience in front of him. "The residence has three bedrooms. I walked past two bedrooms, and each was filled with money, from floor to the ceiling, wall to wall. The third bedroom was almost full too. I could only walk in about a step before I started stacking the money up. By the time I was finished, the room was almost full."

"Tell them what the men inside said," Marcelo told Javier.

"I asked them what was going on, and one of the men inside said they haven't heard from El Jefe since the attempt to capture him in La Paz, however, they've continued receiving multiple shipments of money each day. They haven't been told what to do with the money, so they're stockpiling it until they hear something."

Brandon looked at the Special Forces. "We're looking at one of the largest seizures of money in the history of the Cartel de Culiacan. It could potentially cripple El Jefe and his efforts to lead the cartel."

One of the men looked back and forth from Marcelo to Brandon. "Are you sure you can trust this guy?"

"I believe so," Marcelo said. "If he is lying, then there will be consequences that he doesn't want to happen."

"How many men are watching the residence now?"

"We have four men that are still watching the house," Marcelo told them. "Any further questions?"

The leader of the Special Forces turned toward Javier. "How many men were in the house, and were they armed?"

Javier nodded. "I remember seeing three people inside the house. One had an AK-47. The other men were either outside the house or outside the gate."

"That's all we need to know," Ramon, the Special Forces captain said. "We need to get to the location and scout it. We'll be inside within two hours." He turned to the rest of his team. "Go ahead and gear up."

* * *

The FIU team and Brandon were instructed to position their vehicles at different locations approximately a half mile away from the target location. Their job was to control the perimeter and make sure nobody entered the area until they received an all clear from Ramon's Special Forces Group.

It was a tense five minutes once the assault begun. Brandon could not see the residence or the outside of the gate from his position, but he was closely listening to the radio for the confirmation that the Special Forces had safely secured the site. He heard gun shots and concussion grenades. The one other thing he saw was a helicopter swooping down and hovering over the target residence.

When an all clear came, Marcelo and Brandon, who had been paired together, drove directly to the residence in Marcelo's truck. One of the Special Forces members stood guard outside the opened gate and directed the FIU team's vehicles as they pulled into the driveway and past the gate. From the passenger seat of the vehicle, Brandon noticed blood smeared on parts of the wall that surrounded the property. What he did not see were any bodies or anybody detained. Brandon wondered where they were until he saw the huge swat vehicle that had gone in ahead. Marcelo pointed to it and told the DEA agent that all the Cartel guardsmen were in the back of the vehicle.

As Marcelo and Brandon exited the truck, they were approached by Ramon, who was instructing his men to extend the perimeter out further since the FIU team was no longer in position. He did not want any cartel reinforcements to show up while they were there. Brandon could not help but be impressed with the precision and efficiency with which the Special Forces team operated. It made him realize that many of the Mexican law enforcement and military officials were honorable men that would sacrifice their lives for that of the greater good and the safety of their teammates. Corruption was a problem, but it did not mean everybody was corrupt. He was lucky to have found guys he could trust.

Ramon looked at the two men and gave a rare smile. "Your informant was truthful. You should see this." They followed the leader of the Special Forces and were amazed to see the first bedroom of the residence. Stacked floor to ceiling, and wall to wall just as Javier had told them, was more money than Brandon had ever seen. He walked to the second room and saw the same. He walked to the third room and saw a replica of the first two rooms.

He looked at Marcelo, who was impressed at what he was seeing. "How are we going to transport this?" Brandon asked.

"I don't know."

"Not a problem," Ramon told them. "We have five large box trucks we use to transport equipment at a facility in Mazatlán about 20 minutes away. I have already notified them, and they are in route and should be here shortly. I have instructed the drivers to transport the money where you tell them. Also, we detained seven guards. There were 11 men total. Four were killed in the exchange of gunfire. We can send the seven prisoners to whatever prison you prefer," he told Marcelo.

Marcelo and Brandon looked at each other. Never in their wildest dreams had they imagined a seizure of this magnitude. This would make the $20 million seizure of the reward money from the attempted arrest of El Jefe in La Paz look like breadcrumbs.

The DEA agent coordinated with members of the State Department at the embassy in Mexico City, as well as his DEA supervisor, and Toby from the CIA, to determine the safest location to transport the currency.

The money count lasted long into the night. Rays of sunshine from dawn were visible by the time the count was finally concluded. Contained within two separate holding cells of the most secure bank in Mazatlán was over $302 million. It was the largest seizure of drug trafficking proceeds in the history of the DEA or Mexican law enforcement

Chapter 26
Los Angeles, California

Thursday, September 7

Lorena Jimenez watched as employees of the Westin Bonaventure Hotel unrolled a large banner welcoming the International Association of Police Chiefs Conference. The hotel's location in downtown Los Angeles made it a desirable venue for the attendees. Whether they wanted to enjoy the bright lights of LA Live that included the Staples Center, Lucky Strike Bowling, and a host of restaurants, bars, and clubs, or a more low key night in Little Tokyo, Chinatown, or see the famous sights in Hollywood, or Beverly Hills, everything was within a 30 minute drive.

Although the DEA was not a police department, they were still involved in the event. Through the work DEA had with LAPD, as well as other police departments around the state and country, the feds presence at the event was expected. While they didn't have a leading role, the powers that be at DEA liked to be involved nonetheless, for nothing other than making contacts with people around the country that might be able to one day advance their own employment opportunities after retirement from DEA.

As the secretary for the DEA Special Agent in Charge of the Los Angeles Field Division, Lorena had been tasked by her boss with coordinating the travel and accommodations of several high-ranking DEA management officials that were flying in from other parts of the country to attend the conference. Lorena made sure several of the agents new to the Division would be at the airport and pick up the different guests as their planes arrived at the Los Angeles International Airport, and then made sure those agents safely got the guests to the Westin Bonaventure Hotel, at which point she met with them to provide them with their itinerary for the next few days.

Four DEA officials from across the country were attending the event, with hundreds of representatives from police departments. Of the four DEA officials, the one that most DEA agents were anxious to meet was Deputy Administrator Allen Peterson, the current second in command of the entire DEA. Peterson had recently been the SAC of the Los Angeles Field Division and had risen through the ranks from a Special Agent, just as they hoped to do.

Lorena had a more personal relationship with Peterson. When she had been assigned as his secretary, the 45-year-old single mother had been involved in a steamy year-long affair with the married SAC. With shame, she recalled all the different locations they carried on the relationship, like they were teenagers that couldn't control their urges, from the DEA office itself, to a corner booth of a Mongolian restaurant in South Bay, to the back seats of cars parked in Chinatown. It was all for nothing, as Peterson did not keep his promise that he would divorce his wife and marry Lorena, and instead ended their affair shortly after learning that he had been chosen as the Deputy Administrator. Lorena tried to work like normal, especially in the office where rumors of their relationship ran rampant. She silently endured the inner hurt of being rejected after Peterson left Los Angeles and began his assignment in Washington D.C.

She was not sure how she was going to react when she saw Peterson again for the first time since his return, but she convinced herself that she was going to appear professional. She could not betray her feelings, or the agreement that she had recently made with the mysterious individual who referred to himself as Vaquero. How the man in the giant cowboy hat had identified her, she did not know. She also did not know who he worked for or why he was interested in Peterson, but she did like his offer of $10,000 for notification of Peterson's dinner location on Thursday night after his arrival.

Maybe the man needed to speak with Peterson. She hoped the guy would beat up Peterson but knew the likelihood of that was low since Peterson knew how to take care of himself and would be surrounded by at least four other law enforcement officials. For those reasons, Lorena was not worried about whether any harm would come to Peterson.

When Peterson walked through the doors into the lobby of the Bonaventure, followed by one of the newest DEA agents recently assigned to the Division, Lorena pushed those thoughts from her mind.

"Hello, Deputy Administrator," Lorena said professionally.

Smirking at the professional demeanor despite their history, and believing it was for the young agent standing beside him, Peterson turned and looked at the young man and thanked him for the drive and wished him luck in his future career endeavors. Once the agent left, Peterson looked at Lorena, who handed him his room key.

"You'll be on the sixth floor. I hope that will be to your satisfaction," she told her former lover.

"I would be satisfied if you would join me on the sixth floor tonight for old time's sake," he said, squeezing Lorena's butt as they got on the elevator.

"I don't think so," she said after the doors of the elevator closed. "You made your choice, and I wasn't it."

"Don't be like that. What we had was great. I enjoyed every minute. Give me 15 minutes and I will blow your mind like I used to."

The doors to the elevator opened, and Lorena walked to his room and opened the door for him, handing him the room key.

"Two other guests will be arriving soon, and I have to be there to welcome them. Would you like me to make arrangements at the Dragon's Lair restaurant in Chinatown for dinner?"

The Dragon's Lair had always been Peterson's favorite local restaurant. The combination of delicious Chinese food and the cool ambiance had drawn Peterson to the place and kept him coming back. "You know me so well, sweetheart. My brother will be there as well, along with a few other people, so could you get us a table for five?"

Peterson's brother was the Chief of Police in Albuquerque, New Mexico. Lorena had thought about seducing the younger Peterson for no other reason than to make Allen jealous. Maybe that was for later on, but for now, she would collect her $10,000 from Vaquero and see where that led.

"Sure, I'll tell them that you will be there at 6:30 p.m.," Lorena said, as she closed the door and walked back to the elevator. Once she returned to the foyer of the hotel, she took out her phone and placed a call to Vaquero and spoke quickly and quietly in Spanish.

"It's confirmed. He will be at the Dragon's Lair in Chinatown at 6:30 p.m."

"Great work, Lorena," Vaquero told her on the other end of the phone. "I'll have the money sent to your account immediately."

"Ok, thank you. Can I ask... whatever you're doing, please don't hurt Allen too bad."

The line was quiet for a moment before Vaquero spoke. "I assure you Lorena, I will not hurt Mr. Peterson at all."

Vaquero ended the call, smiling to himself, "I will not hurt Mr. Peterson. Toro on the other hand, is another matter."

* * *

Toro found a booth in the Dragon's Lair at 6:15 p.m. and gave the waitress a $100 bill after he ordered his food and asked for her patience in allowing him to stay there longer. The waitress took the bill and told Toro he could stay there until they closed.

There were six booths along both walls, with several tables in the middle of the room. Toro did not care for all the dragon paraphernalia on the walls and hanging from the ceiling. He sat in the fourth booth along the right wall, facing the front of the restaurant. 15 minutes after arrival, Toro had a perfect view of Allen Peterson, his brother, and the other three members of their party seated at the main table in the middle of the restaurant.

The men laughed and smiled as they enjoyed the night. Toro fought the urge to put an end to the fun immediately. If Toro shot Peterson, then he would have to shoot the other four as well. It would be very unlikely for him to escape at that point, although not impossible. Toro could not be apprehended, because he had unfinished business with El Jefe, so he decided to wait, hoping Peterson would make his way to the bathroom, so he could handle the situation without anyone noticing.

Almost an hour after his group arrived at the Dragon's Lair, Peterson did head to the bathroom in the rear of the restaurant, a small room at the end of a hallway about 50 feet long. Toro counted to ten before he got out of the booth. He glanced at the table where Peterson's brother and friends remained, all deep in drink and talk. They did not give Toro a second look as he followed Peterson to the bathroom.

The wooden door pushed open. To the left was a sink and mirror, and on the same wall Peterson was standing at a urinal, in between the sink to his left and the stall with a toilet to his right.

He slid the wire out of his pocket and wrapped both hands around the ends. Peterson did not acknowledge or seem to notice Toro as he entered and moved quickly behind him, wrapping the wire around Peterson's throat, and cinching it as tightly as possible. Peterson's eyes bulged out as he struggled for air. His hands went to his throat as he fought to relieve the pressure, and his pants fell to the ground as a result.

Toro pushed Peterson against the wall, but the DEA agent resisted by putting his left foot against the wall and trying to push back. The assassin continued to press forward, and the momentum caused Peterson's right knee to smash into the urinal, which broke off from the wall and crashed to the ground, shattering on impact, leaving urine spread across the bathroom floor. The crashing urinal and slippery floor surface caused Toro to momentarily slip and lose power behind his attack. Peterson pushed back with his legs against the wall with as much strength as possible. Maintaining the wire around Peterson's neck, Toro then used the DEA agent's own momentum to swing him over his back and onto the messy floor, all the while keeping the wire tightly wrapped around Peterson's throat. At that point, Peterson was face down on the floor, with Toro laying on top of his back, using his body weight to prevent any additional movements. Peterson's movements stopped and his eyes remained open as he succumbed to the infamous cartel assassin.

Just as the elder Peterson expired, the younger Peterson walked into the bathroom. Unable to comprehend what he was seeing, he looked at the broken urinal and then at the two men lying on the ground, not realizing that it was his brother lying motionless on the ground until it was too late. The younger Peterson was reaching for the gun concealed under his shirt on his right hip when Toro rushed forward, pinning him against the wall with his left hand and plunging a pocketknife into the man's heart. Toro swiped his left arm down forcefully, knocking away the younger Peterson's weapon out of his right hand. Toro used the same left hand and grabbed Peterson's forehead, pushing his head against the wall, exposing his neck. The trained killer then pulled his blade out of Peterson's chest and swiped it across his throat. The younger Peterson fell face down on the floor, his blood mixing with the urine that was already surrounding the elder Peterson. Toro wiped the blood from the blade on the side of his pants.

He removed a set of papers from the cargo pocket of his pants, and opened the folded papers, which were copies of the Informant paperwork that showed Peterson as the individual that authorized payment to Jose Padilla shortly after Padilla had poisoned El Jefe's wife.

Toro wanted the world to know that Peterson's death was not random. It was vengeance for the man's role in the death of his sister, El Jefe's wife. Toro stabbed the papers into Peterson's back. Whoever found his body would know the reason for the murder.

Toro turned and calmly walked out of the bathroom. Seeing nobody from the restaurant walking down the hallway, Toro went out the rear exit and into the Southern California night.

* * *

The black Toyota Camry parked on the side of Broadway Street just two businesses up from the Dragon's Lair was in the exact spot Vaquero had assured Toro it would be. Toro looked up and down the street at all the pedestrians, his senses on full alert for law enforcement or anybody coming out of the restaurant looking for him, but he believed he had successfully escaped unnoticed.

The rear driver's side door of the Camry was unlocked, and Toro reached underneath the black duffle bag on the floorboard and retrieved the car keys. As he sat the bag on the rear seat and raised up to close the door and move to the driver's seat, Toro froze. He made eye contact with a white male sitting in a vehicle parked on Broadway just four car lengths back, closer to the restaurant. The white male seemed to be talking to someone, although there was no one in the car with him. Toro noticed the individual immediately turn his glance from Toro, toward the front of the restaurant, and back at Toro.

The assassin breathed deeply as he stared at the man in the car, who again turned his glance toward him, confirming what Toro had hoped to be able to avoid, further confrontation with what he could only assume was law enforcement. The man in the vehicle appeared to be local law enforcement, possibly there for security. The man started to open the car door while staring at Toro. Before he could move more than a step away from his vehicle, Toro removed a rifle from the duffle bag that had been left in the Camry. He leveled the rifle at the man, set it on full auto, spraying bullets at the unlucky man who immediately fell to the ground just as he was pulling out his weapon, which fell harmlessly onto the street. At that time, a group of men burst out the front door of the Dragon's Lair. Toro recognized them as the men that had been having dinner with the Petersons. A quick burst of fire in their direction dropped each man in his tracks before any had the opportunity to return fire.

Knowing that his opportunity to leave in the Camry was gone, Toro knew he would have to go with Plan B, but before he even got to that, a windowless van screamed onto Broadway and stopped near the white male's vehicle. The side door to the van slid open as Toro saw three men armed with rifles preparing to get out even as the vehicle still moved. They weren't more than a step away from the van before the grenade that Toro had removed from the duffle bag and threw on the ground near the van detonated, sending a huge blast that not only instantly killed the three men exiting the van, but also caused the van to crash into the car parked on the other side of the street, leaving pure pandemonium in the area.

Before anyone else showed up, Toro grabbed the Glock handgun from the duffle bag and stuck it in his back waistband, running down the alley that connected to the other street that paralleled Broadway. In the exact location Vaquero had promised was a Kawasaki Ninja motorcycle, along with the keys and the helmet. As he got on the Ninja, Toro again made eye contact with someone, this time an Oriental man leaning against the wall of the nearest store on New High Street. The man, who Toro sensed was the lookout making sure the Ninja was not stolen, simply gave Toro a head nod.

The sirens were already blaring as police cars raced in the direction of the Dragon's Lair. As all the LAPD vehicles roared towards the restaurant, Toro sped towards them away from the restaurant, turning on Cesar Chavez and then getting on the 101 freeway.

Less than an hour later, Toro was in a private jet at the Van Nuys Airport, flying to Mexico City, with one more target remaining before he planned to retire from the lifestyle he had known since childhood.

Chapter 27
San Diego, California

Friday, September 8

The charge nurse working the morning shift at UC San Diego Hospital in downtown San Diego was going over discharge paperwork with Reuben when Tyler Jameson walked into the room. The look on his face was clear that the two men needed to speak immediately. When they were trapped in Tijuana, Tyler had not requested any explanation about how Reuben got into that predicament. Reuben knew that he owed Tyler an explanation, he just was not sure if the explanation was going to be provided to the authorities, resulting in his arrest. Tyler was a man of integrity, and Reuben knew he would not look the other way. Reuben patted the charge nurse on the shoulder and told her that he understood all the paperwork, but he needed ten minutes to speak with his co-worker and would then be ready to leave.

Reuben looked down at the floor in resignation as the nurse left the room, prepared to provide what little explanation he could regarding his involvement with Vaquero, a man he knew to be involved with the Cartel de Culiacan.

"Have you heard the news?" Tyler asked.

Reuben shook his head. "I haven't turned on the television or looked at the Internet since I got here."

"There is great news and awful news," Tyler said, sitting down in the chair underneath the television mounted on the wall. He looked at Reuben, who was sitting on the edge of the hospital bed.

"Give me the good news first. You can't lay the awful crap on me first," Reuben said, trying to make light of the situation.

Tyler nodded. "What do you remember about us getting out of Tijuana?"

"I remember we went to Chico's house, and he agreed to get us out through the tunnel. I remember leaving Chico's house to go to the tunnel, but I don't remember going in the tunnel."

"Okay," Tyler said. "As we were waiting to go into the tunnel, a guy working for Chico came out of the tunnel driving a load car that was taking money back to Chico's house for him to count."

"I remember Chico talking about that before. It was supposed to be $3 million, right?"

"Yes. During our conversations, Chico told us he was going to count the money that night and then transport it to another location in the morning."

"Right, but you agreed to let the money go if Chico helped us get back to San Diego."

"And I kept my word to Chico, I didn't have law enforcement swoop down on his house and seize that money, but I did leave my I-phone in the pocket of the passenger door so that the vehicle's location could be tracked."

"You left your I-phone? Are you crazy?" Reuben asked, laughing at the same time.

"Yeah, it was an older model anyways," Tyler said, grinning. "It was time to upgrade."

"So, you tracked your phone?" Reuben asked.

"I passed the location of my phone, which was in the money car, to Brandon Ledbetter in Mexico City. We met him at the SOD Conference a few weeks ago."

Reuben nodded his head, remembering Brandon.

"The vehicle traveled to La Paz. Brandon coordinated surveillance, and they observed Chico take out several bags containing the $3 million, and the bags went into the bottom section of a big yacht that was docked on the water. The surveillance team remained there after Chico left. They saw several additional deliveries of suspected money go into the yacht."

Reuben whistled. "So, did they stop the yacht or let it go somewhere?"

"They let it go to Mazatlán across the Gulf of California. From there, it went to a gated residence in the city. Brandon's FIU team sat on the residence and saw more vehicles coming and going, until they finally stopped one of the people leaving and the guy confirmed there were three rooms full of cash. Brandon's team served a search warrant on the residence last night, and they just got the count. It's $302 million."

Reuben's jaw dropped. "They seized over $300 million? Seriously?"

"Seriously."

"All because you dropped your I-phone in the vehicle coming out of the tunnel that was delivering money to Chico?"

"That started it, yes. Brandon and the FIU guys in Mexico City did the heavy lifting." Tyler grinned, but Reuben still sensed sadness in his partner's features.

"Amazing, simply amazing. Do you think the DEA will pay for you to get a new I-phone since you sacrificed yours for the greater good of the agency?"

"Doubtful," Tyler said, shaking his head. "Now, on a much more somber note, you need to know about what happened in Chinatown last night in Los Angeles. The Deputy DEA administrator was killed, along with his brother, and four FBI agents."

* * *

Reuben's heart dropped to his stomach when he heard the news about the death of the DEA Deputy Administrator and the other law enforcement officers in Chinatown. At the time he hadn't known why Vaquero had requested him to put the Deputy Administrator's name on the informant paperwork indicating that he had overseen a payment to the individual responsible for poisoning El Jefe's wife. Reuben had convinced himself that the man was safe, and never imagined Peterson's life might be in danger, not in the United States. He wasn't sure how, but he knew deep down, the paperwork that he had delivered to Toro at the bar in Tijuana, even though it was false, had sealed the man's fate.

Tyler noticed the color drain from Reuben's face when he mentioned Peterson's death in Chinatown. He hoped Reuben was just upset about the deaths of the law enforcement officers, but Tyler sensed there was more.

"It's time you know what happened, what I was doing in Tijuana," Reuben said.

"It doesn't have to be now; if you'd rather leave, we can talk about it outside."

"No, I need to say it now or else I might decide to keep it to myself." Tyler sat back in his chair and did not urge him on. He didn't want to hear what Reuben was about to say but knew that it was something he needed to know.

"There's a reason I've been so successful making lots of small seizures of drugs and money," Reuben started. "The reason is I've been getting information from certain people that direct me where and when to make those seizures."

"Like a regular informant?" Tyler asked. "What's wrong with that?"

"That's how I justified it. But the truth is, that the person giving me the information had ulterior motives. He was on El Jefe's payroll. He would tell me where 10 or 15 kilograms were so that a shipment of 200 kilograms coming through LA wouldn't get knocked off by law enforcement."

"What?" Tyler asked. Of all the things he had expected to hear from Reuben, that was not it. "You let dope shipments go? But how did you stop other agents from making the seizures?"

Reuben continued looking at the floor in shame. "I would get a license plate, or a phone number, or an address from my contact, a guy name Vaquero, and put it through LA FAST," he said, referring to the clearinghouse that all law enforcement officers in Los Angeles, used to de-conflict with other law enforcement agencies to make sure that the individual they were investigating was not already being investigated by another law enforcement entity, and if so, to make sure that both agencies knew about the other so that no law enforcement officer was mistaken for a criminal lookout.

"If I got a call from LA FAST telling me that another law enforcement group was working the phone or address, I'd get them to back off and convince them that I had the better case and was on top of the situation."

Tyler stood up, unable to believe what he heard, and disgusted with Reuben.

Reuben continued. "I justified that I was taking drugs and drug proceeds off the street, but I know it doesn't make up for allowing the bigger shipments of drugs and money to go."

Shaking his head, Tyler asked his friend, "What does that have to do with why you were in Tijuana?"

"The contact I had, Vaquero, requested me to do something I'd never done before. I didn't know why he wanted it, but now I know."

"What?" Tyler asked.

"Vaquero asked me to fill out Informant paperwork that made it seem like Jose Padilla was a DEA informant...and that he got paid by Allen Peterson. Vaquero had me deliver the paperwork to someone at a bar in Tijuana. That's why I was there."

Tyler's jaw dropped at the latest revelation. "Why would you do that, Reuben? The world will believe that Jose Padilla was a DEA informant, when he was not, and that Peterson paid him to kill El Jefe's wife, which he did not. You do realize that is likely why Peterson was killed last night! In retribution for the murder of El Jefe's wife."

Reuben could only nod. "I know. I don't know what to say. I never thought anything like that would happen. I don't know what I thought would happen, but it never involved Peterson getting killed."

"Why would Vaquero and the Cartel de Culiacan want you to fabricate DEA informant paperwork to implicate Padilla was an informant and that Peterson paid him as an informant?" Tyler asked.

"It must've been so that Toro would kill Deputy Administrator Peterson. I promise, I never thought that was a possibility, or I would have never agreed to do it."

"Then why would the Cartel want Peterson dead? What does that do?"

"I don't know, because it is going to cause the weight of the world to come down on El Jefe since he is the leader of the cartel."

"Maybe that's the intention."

"Why would the cartel do something that would cause law enforcement to take them out?"

"Because...American law enforcement is going to hold El Jefe accountable, *because* he is the head of the cartel. Whoever Vaquero was working for within the cartel wanted to create an incident which would lead to American law enforcement taking out El Jefe. Who stands to gain the most from El Jefe being removed from leadership with the cartel?"

"Montoya. The second in command."

Both men looked at each other in silence.

"You have to confess. Promise me you will, and I won't say anything."

Reuben nodded. "I will, first thing Monday."

"I don't know what to say to you. Everything I thought about you has been a lie. I can't be in here right now." Tyler opened the door of the hospital room to leave but was stopped in his tracks by four men in suits approaching the room.

The men had serious looks on their faces. Tyler had seen that look many times, and knew they were feds.

"Excuse me," the man in the lead said, brushing shoulders with Tyler and knocking him out of the doorway and back into the room. The man looked directly at Reuben sitting on the hospital bed.

"Reuben Valdez, I am FBI Special Agent Lionel Simmons. I'm the case agent on an international investigation that has resulted in the wiretap of a member of the Cartel de Culiacan you know as Vaquero. We began investigating Vaquero because of intelligence that indicated he was involved with human trafficking into Southern California. During our investigation, we intercepted you speaking with Vaquero. We know Vaquero provided you with information on large shipment of drugs and drug proceeds and that you made sure those drugs and proceeds were not seized by law enforcement. We also know Vaquero instructed you to deliver paperwork to a member of the Cartel in Tijuana indicating that DEA Deputy Administrator Allen Peterson was involved with paying Jose Padilla as a DEA informant, even though Padilla was not a DEA informant and Peterson did not pay Padilla when he arrived in Los Angeles. Allen Peterson was killed at a restaurant last night in Chinatown, strangled to death in the men's bathroom. The killer, who we believe to be a man known as Toro, the same individual you met with at the bar in Tijuana, was responsible for kidnapping DEA Special Agent Ana Lucia Rodriguez, and killing not just Peterson, but also Peterson's brother, the Chief of Police in Albuquerque, as well as four FBI agents that were on surveillance outside the restaurant. Based on your involvement with Vaquero and Toro, and the false documents you provided to Toro at the request of Vaquero, both known associates of the Cartel de Culiacan, you are being charged with multiple counts of Conspiracy to Commit Murder of a Federal Agent. You are under arrest."

Simmons walked over and placed Reuben in handcuffs, while Tyler looked on from the corner of the room, stunned at the turn of events. As Simmons walked Reuben out the door, he stopped and looked at Tyler.

"We know all about your hero journey into Tijuana to rescue Valdez. The federal prosecutors are determining whether they are going to charge you for anything, but after four of our agents were killed last night, we could not leave this scumbag free any longer. He will spend the rest of his life behind bars. You might join him. I have already spoken with the SAC from San Diego. I think he and OPR have a few questions for you, starting with how you allowed a robbery to occur, and that one of the guys that committed the robbery then drove drunk through Vegas and hit a pedestrian...that just died by the way. We know all about it, and we passed that information on to your OPR."

Simmons stormed out of the hospital, leaving a wake of surprised nurses and doctors staring at Reuben as he left the hospital in hand-cuffs.

Chapter 28
Mexiquillo, Durango, Mexico

Sunday, September 10

Nestled in the coniferous forest of Mexiquillo in the Mexican state of Durango, one of the most beautiful and best kept secrets in all of Mexico, was an 1800-square-foot cabin, so far off the beaten path that the nearest road, Federal Highway #40, was miles away. With 52 miles of forests and countless trees reaching hundreds of feet into the sky, it was a place to retreat from the world and all its troubles. That was exactly what El Jefe did following his near capture in La Paz. It was a location that even those closest to him did not know about.

Following the shootout in La Paz and El Jefe's gunshot wound, five of his bodyguards managed to get him to a boat on the Gulf of California that immediately transported him across the body of water to Mazatlán, where he was met by a physician on the cartel payroll. El Jefe refused to stay in Mazatlán and insisted on being transported to the location he considered most secure in Mexico. Nobody in his inner circle, or those that could have possible betrayed him in La Paz, knew about the residence in the forest. After La Paz, El Jefe's aura of invincibility was shattered, and he did not know who his friends or enemies were. All he knew was that he could not trust anybody until he was completely healed and ready to show the world that he still lived.

The physician provided as much assistance as possible in the van as the vehicle traveled east on Federal Highway 40 away from Mazatlán, but once it was time to exit, even El Jefe himself didn't trust the physician to go further. He took antibiotics and advised the doctor to return to Mazatlán and keep the events of that night to himself. El

Jefe was convinced that he was going to recover from the gunshot wound, which had entered his back on the right side, and exited from the right shoulder. The bullet didn't hit any vital organs or blood vessels, and other than being painful, he was convinced that he simply needed a couple weeks to recover and determine who was responsible for betraying him to law enforcement. In the meantime, he would recuperate in the cabin deep in the forest that only he and one other person alive on the earth knew belonged to the leader of the Cartel de Culiacan.

Unfortunately for El Jefe, the only other person in the world that knew of the existence of the cabin, was the very individual now intent on ending his life.

* * *

The first time Toro met El Jefe was during another period of El Jefe's reign in which others around him sought his demise. It happened many years earlier, before the Cartel de Culiacan had wiped away other smaller cartels in Tijuana and Juarez. The circumstances leading up to the events were not known by Toro at the time, but he later learned that it originated from the actions of El Jefe's son, Victor.

Even prior to his death at the hands of Juan Montoya's son, Carlos, Victor Rodriguez had established a reputation of unpredictable behavior. Addicted to the very cocaine that his father had created an empire selling, Victor was beloved by few people due to his harsh tongue and heavy hand. Those actions almost cost him and his father their lives after Victor stormed onto a small farm in Central Mexico and demanded use of the location to store a shipment of 2000 kilograms of cocaine that had come directly from Colombia. Those types of requests from the Cartel were common, and the individuals involved usually knew that it was in their best interest to look the other way while the Cartel did what they needed to do, or else they would pay with their lives. Thus, it was not Victor's request that set about the sequence of events that almost led to his death, it was what happened after he was allowed to use the property as a storage location.

On the night he oversaw the delivery of 2000 kilograms of cocaine, the 15-year old niece of the owner of the property caught his eye. The girl, whose father had ironically died after being caught in the crossfire of an execution by cartel members, had moved to her uncle's farm to escape the very type of men that now surrounded her.

Fancying himself an Alpha, Victor wished to take the girl for himself. When the girl's uncle, the owner of the farm, happened to walk in and see Victor raping his niece, he reacted with understandable rage and was only stopped by the bodyguards that rushed to Victor's aid.

The uncle of the teenage girl was subjected to extreme torture over the next three days, so much so that the teenage girl offered to give herself to Victor at any time he desired if he would stop, but at that point, his mind was set. The uncle finally succumbed to his injuries and died after three days.

Unknown to Victor and the other members of the Cartel at the farm, the uncle was a very beloved man in the nearby town, and news of his torture did not sit well with the locals. The day after the uncle's death, a group of locals from the surrounding area, along with several other mysterious individuals whose arrival was unexpected but welcomed, attacked the farm, intent on killing Victor Rodriguez. In the man's memory, the group named themselves, "Los Tios."

While Los Tios did not have the firepower of Victor and his crew of Cartel employees, they vastly outnumbered the drug traffickers, and they knew the area better and how to utilize it to spring traps. After three days of skirmishes, Victor and only two other bodyguards had survived, taking a vehicle to the nearby city of Durango, which just happened to be where Toro and El Jefe were located, for different reasons.

During the three days of fighting, Victor had been unable to send a message to his father advising him of the situation. Once El Jefe was made aware, he immediately got into a vehicle, surrounded by a dozen bodyguards, and started traveling in the same direction to meet his son and provide protection. Unknown to him, Los Tios had raised another faction in Durango, and they were traveling from the city to intercept Victor before he got to Durango. Toro was on the same freeway that night, alone, returning to Durango after completing another mission.

What resulted, when all the forces came together on a freeway on the outskirts of Durango, was as bloody a scene as Toro had ever witnessed. Pure chance placed Toro at the location at that time, and when he realized El Jefe was involved, he sprung to his assistance, eager to support the man that had provided him employment. Had Toro known of Victor's actions that led to the incident, Toro's response would have been much different, but on that day, El Jefe was a first-hand witness to Toro's amazing skill with weapons.

Toro walked away, unharmed, while El Jefe and Victor both suffered minor wounds. None of the bodyguards that accompanied El Jefe or Victor survived. Over 60 men from Los Tios were left dead in their wake, bodies strewn across the highway. It had been El Jefe's first true brush with death, and he was shaken. It had been the first time he didn't know what to do, so he instructed Toro to take him and Victor to a remote cabin in the forests of Mexiquillo, where they hid for a week before returning to the public spotlight.

That week of contemplation was what led to El Jefe's decision to wipe out all other drug cartels, other than the GDG in the eastern portion of Mexico. He did not know who the Los Tios were, but he knew that they had been supported by some entity other than angry farmers. Since he did not know who to extract revenge on, El Jefe decided to take no prisoners, and ordered the complete decimation of all rival cartels, other than the GDG. An agreement was made with the GDG to evenly split the shipping lanes in Mexico.

After that night, El Jefe had trusted Toro with his life, and was impressed with his skills. Neither man spoke about the cabin after that moment, with Toro continuing to serve the cartel like a faithful soldier.

But now, with El Jefe injured and once again on the run, unsure who to trust or where to turn, Toro knew exactly where the leader of the Cartel de Culiacan had retreated. With the cabin in sight, Toro moved forward to complete his final mission.

* * *

Toro made his move three hours past midnight. Having arrived at sunset the day before, continuous surveillance of the cabin revealed no more than five bodyguards, each taking turns with their positions, whether outside the cabin or inside. At that hour, only one guard patrolled the perimeter of the residence. Trying to stay awake, the man walked back and forth along the front of the house, extending from one side of the property to the other.

Toto recalled that there was only one way in and one way out for vehicular transportation, which meant Toro knew the direction El Jefe's black Chevrolet Suburban would take for a quick getaway.

Quietly creeping as close as he could get to the cabin without being detected, Toro lit the first Molotov cocktail and tossed it on the roof of the cabin. He immediately lit the second Molotov cocktail and tossed it on the opposite side of the roof. The bodyguard who was on the other side of the property never saw or heard where the device came from, but he saw its result, instantly lighting the small wooden cabin on fire. As the guard scanned to see where the attack was coming from, he knew he had to retreat to the cabin and extract El Jefe to get him to a safer location.

While the bodyguard rushed inside, Toro silently moved away from the cabin and down the path where the Suburban would be momentarily exiting. The experienced killer calmly waited for the bodyguards to lead El Jefe to the vehicle.

After what seemed like a long minute, with the aid of night vision goggles, Toro saw the five bodyguards rushing outside the property, surrounding an individual in the center that could only be El Jefe. Toro moved away as the Suburban cranked up and roared down the path, fleeing from the fires consuming the cabin.

Fifty yards from the cabin, the Suburban traveled over the portable land mine, recently placed by Toro. The explosion rocketed the huge SUV up into the air, with the vehicle landing upside down with a resounding thud, breaking all the windows and pushing in the roof where the only exit was through one of the broken windows.

Now came the moment of truth. Toro hoped that El Jefe had not been killed. He wanted one last opportunity to confront the man for his sins before ending his life. He slowly approached the smoking SUV as one of the bodyguards crawled out the window onto the ground. Toro noticed the man looking back at the cabin, but once he was certain that it was a bodyguard, Toro did not think twice before putting a bullet in his brain.

When Toro got close enough to the Suburban, he kneeled to look inside. What he saw pleased him. While four other men were motionless inside the vehicle, the unmistakable form of El Jefe was attempting to crawl out.

Toro held out his hand to the leader of the Cartel de Culiacan who grasped it eagerly as he was pulled out. Toro had thought about what to say to El Jefe in this moment, how best to avenge the memory of his sister and the life that was taken away from her. Before he had a chance to say anything, El Jefe pointed to the cabin, screaming the name of Esmerelda. El Jefe attempted to bring himself to his knees, but was unable, so he continued to pull himself forward with his arms, screaming the girl's name over and over.

Looking at Toro, and not understanding why he was standing there and not the bodyguard, El Jefe looked at the assassin and made a plea from the bottom of his heart. "My daughter! She is still in there! They took me out before and did not get her. Please save her!"

Toro's mindset instantly changed, and he looked back at the residence, knowing that El Jefe was referring to Toro's own niece, his sister's daughter, the only living person on this earth who was related to him, the 11-year old girl he had never met. Looking through the cracking fires, and focusing his senses, Toro could hear the screams of a young, scared girl.

* * *

For reasons that Toro never understood, the rescue of the pre-teenage girl from the burning house was never meant to be. His attempt was delayed not once but twice, first by a hole in the ground that resulted in a rolled left ankle, then by a stump that tripped his right foot and caused him to fall face first onto the ground in the forest. Adrenaline helped him push aside those injuries, but the slight delay in the rush to the cabin was the difference, for as he got within 20 yards of the residence and Esmerelda, who had just climbed out the window, the roof of the cabin caved in, causing the walls of the cabin to collapse to the ground.

The young girl fell to the ground and for the first time, Toro noticed the flames that had consumed her back and hair. The screams were those that would haunt a man's dreams for the rest of his life, but they also signified that the girl was still alive, whose survival instinct was at full throttle in an attempt to escape with her life, and in Toro's estimation life was better than death, so he pushed on toward her.

He never reached Esmerelda, as the thick branches of one of the tall trees in the forest fell from overhead, hitting Esmerelda as she tried to get up.

As haunting as the screams of the young girl were inside the burning house, the silencing of those screams was even worse. It was the most internally crushing and soul-deflating moment in Toro's life since the girl's mother had been kidnapped from in front of his eyes so many years earlier. Now he had failed the two people in his life who had needed him the most.

He was able to roll the branch off Esmerelda and drag her away from the flames, rolling her on the ground to get the flames to die out. Once he was a safe distance away, he inspected her closely. He looked at the lifeless face of the niece he had never known, and never would know.

Having withheld his emotions for so long, a requirement of someone whose job was to end the life of so many people, Toro wasn't sure how to react, but there was no denying the heaviness that he felt in his heart, and the tears that swelled in his eyes. It was something he could not control, emotions that had been withheld for decades. In that moment, Toro told himself that his niece's death, albeit unintentional, would be the last death he was responsible for bringing about.

Toro walked over to El Jefe, who was lying chest down on the ground, with his head turned to the side, eyes still open, but lifeless. The exact cause of El Jefe's death, whether from complications of the gun shot suffered in La Paz, or injuries from the explosion or the crash of the suburban, or a combination of those factors, Toro didn't know, and didn't care. He pulled his Glock handgun out of the holster and laid it down beside the recently deceased leader of the Cartel de Culiacan. He took nothing with him but his wallet and a knife and disappeared deep into the forest.

Chapter 29
Mexico City, Mexico

Monday, September 11

American law enforcement were already upset over the death of Daniel Benson during the shootout at the border in Juarez. Now they raged over the deaths of their brethren at Chinatown in Los Angeles the week before. Leaders put unprecedented pressure on all law enforcement and intelligence agencies to provide any information leading to the capture or death of the head of the Cartel de Culiacan, Julian Rodriguez. The American president personally spoke with the Mexican president about a renewed commitment to helping stem the flow of drug cartel violence, which had been rampant and ever present in Mexico for years. Now that important American law enforcement figures were victims, it became a high priority for the US.

News agencies from the United States and Mexico speculated on the law enforcement response that all knew was coming. News reports and newspapers disagreed on the target of the Chinatown massacre, as it was dubbed, with some claiming the Peterson brothers were at the center of the plot for another sinister and unknown motive, while others claimed the FBI agents killed were the center of attention for the murders, and that they were drawn out by killing the Peterson brothers, who were nothing more than pawns. Law enforcement did not reveal the document that was pinned to the chest of the DEA Deputy Administrator, the Informant paperwork indicating that Peterson had paid Jose Padilla as an informant days after Padilla was responsible for poisoning El Jefe's wife. Even though DEA now realized that one of their own, SA Reuben Valdez, had forged the documents, it was clear that the Cartel assassin had believed it was authentic, and the murder of Deputy Administrator Peterson was his vengeful response. They had no way to realize that Toro's true motive of killing Peterson was not vengeance for El Jefe, but for the assassin himself that mourned the loss and murder of the sister taken from him so many years before.

Before the sun rose Monday morning, Mexican news agencies were reporting the possible death of Julian Rodriguez in the forests of Mexiquillo, Mexico. If those reports were accurate, and Rodriguez was truly dead, then DEA Special Agent Brandon Ledbetter knew that this was going to be one of the greatest days in the history of law enforcement against the power structure of the Cartel de Culiacan, for in a few hours, Ledbetter was going to lead the culmination of an operation he had been working on since receiving the information from Juan Montoya, his "high-ranking confidential informant," of all the different phone numbers being used by members of the Cartel de Culiacan.

Since receiving the information from Montoya and obtaining the location of the telephone numbers being used by the individuals from the Cartel responsible for reporting information about the murder of El Jefe's wife, Ledbetter had coordinated with numerous law enforcement groups throughout Mexico and the United States. Members of the Cartel had been identified in Mexico from Mexico City, to Culiacan, to Juarez to Tijuana, and in southwestern US cities such as Los Angeles, San Diego, Phoenix, and El Paso. Whether the users of the phones and members of the Cartel de Culiacan were corrupt law enforcement, government officials, defense attorneys, prosecutors, or those responsible for the storage and movement of drugs or drug proceeds, the coordinated arrest of all these members of the Cartel de Culiacan, at the same time, could potentially dismantle the largest and most powerful drug cartel in the world. If El Jefe was truly dead as some media reports claimed, then this takedown would deliver a staggering blow that might finally result in the diminished power and reach of the world's strongest drug cartel.

The DEA's Intelligence Technician Specialist had the teleconference prepared when Brandon walked in the conference room at the Embassy in Mexico City. The screen at the front of the room showed video feeds from all the law enforcement groups Brandon had coordinated with over the previous weeks.

Each group spent several minutes discussing their part in the international operation, explaining where they were, who they were seeking to apprehend, what that individual's role was in the cartel, and up to date location information from the surveillance units.

The pressure put on Brandon and the Mexico City DEA office after the death of the Deputy Administrator had been enormous, and the demand from DEA Headquarters that Brandon take immediate action despite the fact that all the necessary parts might not be in place, had frustrated him. Coordinating an operation of this magnitude was no small feat and required extensive time and effort. Rushing something like that only set it up for failure, but to his amazement, everything had come together, as if it was meant to be.

Brandon finished the pre-brief for the operation scheduled to commence at noon local time in Mexico City, coordinated at that time for maximum exposure. Brandon explained he was going to be present in person for the arrest and search of one of the Cartel de Culiacan's most expansive drug warehouse overseers. Three days of continuous surveillance led Brandon's FIU team to believe that a substantial amount of cocaine was being stored at the facility in Mexico City.

After several days of working over 20 hours, Brandon's mind was tired but still sharp. He knew this was the pinnacle of his law enforcement career as he ended the pre-operation brief. Before exiting the conference room, Brandon was met by two serious looking men in dark suits.

"Are you Brandon Ledbetter?" one of the men asked.

Brandon looked at both men and turned to the group supervisor at his side with a curious expression. He shrugged his shoulders.

Brandon nodded. "Yes, why?"

"We are investigators with the DEA Office of Professional Responsibility. We have investigated an allegation that unfortunately requires removal from your position as a Special Agent, starting immediately. You are hereby suspended and not allowed to carry out the duties of a DEA Special Agent. Please hand in your gun and badge."

Brandon stormed past the two OPR investigators, but noticed the doorway was blocked by two other men that he recognized from the Diplomatic Security Service. Their responsibility was to ensure the safety of personnel inside the US Embassy.

"Please don't make this more difficult than it needs to be," one of the DSS agents said. "Go into the interview room down the hall."

The exasperated DEA agent turned to his group supervisor. "Does the Regional Director know about this?" he asked. The GS shrugged his shoulders.

"Actually, SA Ledbetter, I am aware of the situation." Regional Director Salvador Martinez walked into the room through the two DSS men. "The timing is unfortunate. I was aware that the OPR investigators were coming yesterday, but I was unaware of the focus of their investigation until I spoke with them last night."

"Do you understand that I am coordinating one of the most important operations in the history of this office?" Brandon asked, moving toward the leader of the DEA Mexico Field Office.

"I know, and I apologize, but this directive comes from Headquarters," Martinez said.

"The same DEA Headquarters that pressured us to carry out this operation before we were ready, now wants to put me on the sideline hours before the culmination. Why?"

"Come to the interview room and sit down with the OPR investigators so they can explain what is going on," Martinez said.

Brandon brushed past the OPR investigators, intentionally bumping shoulders with the man who moved out of the way too slowly and went straight to the open interview room. Before the OPR investigators entered the room, the DSS agents walked into the room behind the RD and reminded Brandon that he had to relinquish his firearm, out of safety concerns. He removed the holster from his side and placed it on the table with the Glock firearm still inside the holster and loaded.

The RD took the holster. "Brandon, we need your badge as well."

Brandon glared at the man. He pulled his DEA badge out of his pocket and placed it on the table. Martinez took the badge and walked out of the room without saying another word.

The two OPR investigators walked in and identified themselves as Harold and Stan, investigators from the OPR office in Washington D.C. Before the two men seated themselves, Brandon demanded to know what was going on.

Harold spoke first. "SA Ledbetter, do you know a Mexican national named Leticia Fernandez?"

The realization of the pending publicizing of his indiscretions came down on Brandon like a ton of bricks. "Yes, I do."

"Just so you're aware," Harold began, "a short time ago, this woman chained herself to the flagpole of the US Embassy. She took all her clothes off, protesting the United States, and your alleged involvement with members of the Cartel de Culiacan. She also indicated that you are involved in an extra-marital affair with her.

"Ms. Fernandez made allegations to DEA OPR last week, and we coordinated to meet with her yesterday. Apparently, she was not pleased that you were not immediately fired, which is why she is outside chained naked to the flagpole right now."

Brandon breathed deeply, thinking that the only way out of the predicament was to tell the truth, and that the OPR investigators and the powers that be at DEA would take into consideration his outstanding work history in any disciplinary proceeding that followed.

"Next," Stan said, speaking up in place of Harold. "Do you recognize this man?" He slid a picture on the table. It was a picture of Juan Montoya. Brandon immediately recognized the picture as one taken from his meeting with Montoya when Leticia picked him up from the airport after returning from the SOD meeting in California.

Brandon nodded, realizing the source of the photograph was his former mistress.

"Who is he?" Stan asked, already aware of the answer to his question.

"Juan Montoya."

"And he is involved in the Cartel de Culiacan?"

"Yes."

"In what role?"

"He is the second in command, behind Julian Rodriguez."

"Is there a reason you were meeting with the second in command of the Cartel de Culiacan immediately after returning from an SOD meeting in California? Was it to provide information to Montoya about international DEA operations?" Stan asked, getting to the point.

"Of course not! I'm not corrupt. Montoya was an informant working for the DEA."

The two OPR investigators did not make any indication what they were thinking.

"SA Ledbetter, we've looked through all the Informant paperwork here at the office, and Montoya's name is not listed anywhere."

"Of course not," Brandon said, looking at the two men. "There is no way we could put his name as a DEA informant. We had to use an alias."

"Is there any other DEA agent in this office that has been with you while you met with the individual you claim to be Juan Montoya?"

Brandon shook his head. "I've met him twice, both times it was only me, but I did communicate with him a lot by text message. Others know about that."

"You understand that DEA policy is for an agent to meet with informants in the presence of another agent, precisely so an allegation like this isn't made? It is a violation of DEA policy to meet with an informant by yourself."

"I understand that, but both instances were emergencies."

"Well, the allegations from Ms. Fernandez is not that Juan Montoya was a DEA informant, but instead that you were corrupt and working for him."

"That's insane. I didn't conceal my involvement with Montoya. Everyone knew about it. Ask my boss or the SOD Coordinator."

"So, there isn't anybody that you know who will confirm they were with you when you met with Juan Montoya? Other than a woman that you were having an extra-marital affair with?"

Brandon knew he was in trouble, and that the perfect trap had been set.

"Montoya informed me that El Jefe was in La Paz when he was almost apprehended, the same occasion when DEA seized $10 million cash. That information came from Montoya, he was an informant.

"Also, I was the lead agent for another operation that seized $302 million. If I were corrupt, then there is no way I would have allowed the DEA to seize $302 million. This is all absurd."

"I'm sorry, SA Ledbetter, but the allegation that you are providing information to the second in command of the Cartel de Culiacan is not something we can look past, especially since you have admitted to meeting with him without another agent present on multiple occasions, once when your mistress was present. These are serious violations of DEA policy. DEA simply cannot allow you to continue your duties until these allegations are investigated more thoroughly, especially since there is such a high-profile operation about to be conducted. It will still be carried out. There are plenty of capable DEA agents that will make sure it is successful."

"That's not the issue. I know it will be successful. The point is that I put the time and effort into making sure this operation will be successful, and now the opportunity to see the results of all the hard work is being taken from me. You guys, who have never actually done anything, are keeping me from it."

Silence hung in the air as the OPR investigators felt the sting of the last comment, but they did not want to escalate the situation further. Brandon continued, "If these allegations came in last week, and OPR was so concerned about whether or not I was providing information to the Cartel de Culiacan, then why didn't Headquarters take me off the case last week? They knew I was busy coordinating the details for this takedown. They waited to take me off the case until AFTER I made all the details, and BEFORE the operation took place," Brandon said, not trying to hide the disgust he felt from his voice.

"I understand your frustrations, SA Ledbetter, and I realize the time and effort you put into this operation."

"Let me interrupt you again," Brandon shot back. "Based on your last comments, I'm pretty sure you have never done a thing in your career other than ride the coattails of other hard-working agents. Only somebody like that would not find any problem with taking me off the case moments before an operation of this magnitude. You've never put in hard work, so you don't understand what it's like to have something snatched away from you that you have worked hard for."

The two OPR investigators realized they were not going to be able to rationalize their actions with the angry DEA agent. Stan said, "SA Ledbetter, I'm sorry to say, but you are suspended from your position as a DEA agent. You will be on an airplane back to the US tomorrow afternoon, please go home and gather your possessions. You will not be authorized inside your government living quarters after midnight tomorrow."

* * *

Much to Brandon's dismay, news reporters were stationed outside the gates of his gated apartment complex in Mexico City, waiting for the DEA agent's arrival. As part of his suspension, his official government vehicle had been taken, so he suffered even more humiliation by having to take a taxi to his residence. Seeing the American DEA agent in the back seat of the taxi, the news reporters pressed forward and pounded on the windows demanding a statement and whether Brandon admitted to an extra-marital affair or that he was secretly working with the Cartel de Culiacan. Having to exit the taxi outside the friendly confines of the gates of his apartment complex, the mob roared their fury at what they believed was a corrupt American federal law enforcement agent working with the very cartel members he was supposed to be in their country to apprehend.

The security guards at the complex were able to usher Brandon inside the gates and away from the throng of people that were frustrated they hadn't gotten an answer to the question that was being plastered across online and television reports throughout Mexico City: Did DEA Special Agent Brandon Ledbetter Work with the Cartel de Culiacan?

Brandon was hopeful that at worst, one of his co-workers would speak up for him and vouch for his character and inform the news reporters that the allegations against him weren't true, but deep down, another realization was beginning to take shape. There was no way the DEA would ever acknowledge that a DEA agent had worked with Juan Montoya, even if for the express purpose of capturing the leader of the Cartel de Culiacan. If there was evidence that Brandon met with Juan Montoya, the only conceivable justification would be that it was because Brandon must be corrupt. The DEA would not allow the public to believe they had authorized an agent to work with such a high-ranking member of the Cartel de Culiacan.

Brandon now had to face his wife and children. He was not sure what or how he was going to tell them. To explain the suspension would mean admitting to the affair, which was something that he knew would crush his wife, but the way he saw it, there was no way to avoid it.

When Brandon walked through the door into his spacious apartment complex, the first thing he saw were suitcases lined against the wall by the door. His daughter ran up to him and gave him a hug.

Wondering why his seven-year old was not in school, he looked at his wife who had walked up, and by the look on her face, knew that she was aware of everything. The pain in her eyes was evident, her eyelids swelling as they often did when she cried.

"How could you Brandon?" She said between sobs. "I never gave you anything other than love, encouragement, and support. I packed our family up and moved to another country for you. And how do you thank me? You sleep with some young Mexican woman! I've never been so humiliated and embarrassed in my life."

Seven-year old Chelsea stayed at her father's side, desperately clutching his leg as her mother yelled at her father. She was pulled away by her mother, who again directed her anger toward Brandon. "Your girlfriend sent me several videos and photographs just to make sure I knew the extent of your affair, so that you couldn't lie about how far you've gone and how long you've been doing it. I hate what you have done to our family, but I will not stand for it any longer! I pulled Chelsea out of school, and I have packed everything up from Benjamin's room, and we are leaving right now, without you." His wife carried their two-year old son in her right arm, and with her left hand, guided Chelsea outside the door.

Brandon finally found his voice. "You're leaving tonight? Can't we talk about this?"

"So, you have nothing to say about the fact that your mistress sent your wife photos and videos that you have been screwing another woman? Nothing to say about that! Just questioning when I'm leaving?"

"I don't know what to say," Brandon said, shaking his head. "I'll do whatever you want if we can just talk about this, please."

"What I wanted was for you to be faithful and not destroy our family, but it's too late. You think about that while you sit in this big apartment by yourself without your family. If you decide to come home to the US, maybe we can talk then. I'm not staying here any longer. I should have never come here in the first place. The kids and I will be back in Dallas with my parents." She told both children to hug their stunned father, whose head was spinning at the recent turn of events both personally and professionally. Before he knew it, the door slammed behind them, and he sat in the apartment, all alone, wondering how he managed to lose his job and his family all in the same day.

* * *

Brandon desperately wanted his wife and kids to stay, but he knew that his wife would not put up with his unfaithfulness, so any attempt to get her to stay was going to prove fruitless. He knew that his wife deserved better, and thought she was better off without him.

He wandered to the pantry and pulled out as much alcohol as he could carry with him back to his couch, where he plopped down and turned on the television, just in time to see breaking news stories about the massive law enforcement takedown that was taking place across cities throughout Mexico and the United States. Drowning his sorrows away with as much alcohol as possible, he continued to watch as the same criminals he had spent hundreds of hours investigating were paraded in front of the television in handcuffs, a list of their crimes and association with the Cartel de Culiacan on the television screen beside them. The facts displayed on the television were the very same facts that Brandon had typed up to pass out for dissemination days earlier.

Realizing he was not able to be present for this special moment only worsened when he saw the face of his Group Supervisor, John Jacobs, standing proudly with Brandon's FIU team outside a Mexico City warehouse. The reporter standing outside the warehouse breathlessly reported that Mexican law enforcement, combined with the efforts of the DEA, had seized 3,000 kilograms of cocaine from a warehouse in the capital city.

During his career, Brandon had not seized 3,000 kilograms of cocaine total, now this amount was surpassed in one seizure! He put all the hard work into this operation, yet the supervisor was going to get all the credit, for the arrests and for the drug seizures.

When he could not take it anymore, Brandon turned the television off. In the silence, Brandon started hearing all the sounds from his family's life in the apartment over the previous years. Chelsea bumped her head there. Benjamin vomited there. Family meals were eaten here. Now they were gone forever, and he was being banished back to the US in disgrace, despite all the hard work he had put in for the agency after graduating from the DEA Academy.

Needing to get out of the apartment, but not wanting to face the crowd of angry protestors outside the apartment gates, Brandon took as much alcohol as he could with him up to the roof of the 20-story apartment tower. He unfolded the chair he carried with him, and sat near the edge of the building, looking out over the city skyline, drinking away his worries, still stunned at the dramatic and sudden turn of events. Just 24 hours earlier, he had been a husband, father of two, a respected DEA agent who was coordinating the most important takedown in recent history. Now, he had missed the takedown. He faced what he knew would be a long road to proving that he was not a corrupt DEA agent, but worst of all, he knew that he was likely facing a divorce. His two children were likely going to be raised by their mother, who he was sure would re-marry at some point, and another man would be responsible for tucking his children in at night, reading them stories, watching the excitement on their face on Christmas morning. All these emotions overwhelmed Brandon. He wished he had considered them prior to his affair, but at that time, he had only been concerned about pleasing himself and his desires. Now, he had humiliated the one woman that he had ever loved. His career was tarnished, and as he continued to consume alcohol, Brandon decided that he did not think he could wake up to face the scrutiny of the coming morning. He could not face his wife. He could not face Chelsea or Benjamin. He could not face the throng of reporters that wanted to question him. He could not face his co-workers who would forever look at him with the stigma of someone that they might not be able to trust.

It was too much weighing on him, so without further thought, Brandon stood up from his folding chair. Intoxication caused him to sway slightly as he stood, but he managed to walk to the ledge of the building. As the sun was setting in the west ahead of him, Brandon stepped off the ledge, anxious to forget everything, and fell to the pavement 20 floors below.

Chapter 30
Englewood, Colorado

Wednesday, September 13

The transfer of Federal Prisoner 4598327 from FCI Mendota, a medium security prison 35 miles west of Fresno, California, to Englewood, Colorado, a low security prison less than ten miles south of Denver, was seemingly a blip on the radar, an inconsequential transfer of an inmate between prisons that was lost in the shuffle of all the significant events in the law enforcement community over the previous weeks. The media could not get enough of the dramatic events surrounding the previously perceived impenetrable Cartel de Culiacan. The law enforcement response to the Chinatown massacre was swift and efficient, with law enforcement seizing $302,000,000 from a residence in Mazatlán, the reported death of El Jefe in the forests of Mexiquillo, the seizure of 3,000 kilograms of cocaine from a warehouse in Mexico City, along with thousands of kilograms throughout other parts of Mexico, and the arrests of numerous members of the cartel throughout the US and Mexico. The Cartel de Culiacan was staggering, and on the ropes.

The American news welcomed a respite from the cycle of eye-rolling announcements by power hungry political figures in Washington D.C., and eagerly turned their sights toward the American southwest and away from the Beltway. As such, Federal Prisoner 4598327 left behind the 12 foot high razor fences of FCI Mendota in Central California for the fresh, crisp air of a much more relaxed prison life surrounded by white collar criminals and non-violent convicts that were not restricted with intimidating guards and tall fences, and for the most part were allowed to come and go in the area as they please with the expectation that they would be present at the prison for roll call at the end of the day. From the places the Federal Prisoner had seen, he was surprised this was even considered a prison by modern day standards. It was more like a hotel without the luxuries. But it was America.

Having been notified the day prior of the imminent transfer, Federal Prisoner 4598327 knew that wheels were in motion and that his return to a prominent role in his previous lifestyle was pending.

Hours after arrival at Englewood, after the sun had set in the west and cast the area in shadows and darkness, Federal Prisoner 4598327 followed the instructions of the letter that was given to him back at FCI Mendota, and walked out the doors and toward a small dirt path a mile and a half to the southwest. The low guard to inmate ratio of the minimum security prison had made it much easier for the few guards on shift to be paid off and make sure they were not in the certain location at the time Federal Prisoner 4598327 went on his evening walk. With headcount still several hours off, the absence of a prisoner that just arrived would not be noticed by any of the other inmates. Further, the proper payoffs had been made, and paperwork documenting how many inmates were supposed to be present was doctored to show the same amount that was there the day before Federal Prisoner 4598327 arrived, which assured that his absence would go unnoticed for a considerable length of time.

The dark SUV was in the exact place as promised, and without a word to the driver, Federal Prisoner 4598327 entered the rear passenger seat, and the vehicle immediately departed the area and traveled to a nearby private air field, where the occupants of the vehicle, to include two other passengers and a driver, all which were fully armed, exited the vehicle and entered a small jet. As the jet left the runway, Federal Prisoner 4598327 looked out the window and was pleased, that he would never set foot in the United States again, and that he was returning home.

* * *

Thursday, September 14
Mexicali, Mexico

The jet landed at a small airport on the Mexican border town of Mexicali, shortly after 2:00 a.m. Two of the individuals from the SUV were the first to get off the jet, with another staying behind with the prisoner, who looked through the window to see what was happening.

He observed a dark SUV pull on the tarmac of the private airport and stop 50 yards from the jet. One individual exited the passenger seat of the SUV and met with the two men from the jet. What appeared to be a short conversation ensued, and one of the two men from the jet turned around and motioned for the occupants inside the jet to join them on the tarmac.

Having coordinated this moment for a long time, but not intending all the collateral damage that resulted from his planning, CIA Case Officer Toby Phillips stood up and led Federal Prisoner 4598327 off the jet and to the group of people waiting a short distance away. Toby held his hand on the prisoner's arm while they awaited to see who would exit from the SUV that had just arrived.

A short time later, a middle-aged man exited the rear passenger seat of the SUV. He walked up to Toby and the Federal Prisoner with tears in his eyes.

"It's him, just like I promised," Toby said. "Where are the three men you agreed to exchange?"

The man quickly turned around and made a motion, and within 20 seconds another SUV pulled up, and a heavily armed man pulled three chained individuals out of the back seat.

"And just like I promised you," Juan Montoya said, "in exchange for your prisoner I will provide you with three terrorists from North Africa that you seem very interested in speaking with. Personally, I did not agree with Julian allowing terrorists and bombs to enter the United States through Cartel tunnels, no matter how much the terrorists pay. It was very short sighted. If the terrorists kill all the Americans, then who will we have left to consume our product?" Montoya produced a hearty laugh at his own wit.

Both Toby and Montoya kept the prisoners beside them prior to completing the exchange.

"You have no intention of allowing terrorists to have access to any Cartel tunnels?" Toby asked, wanting the answer to be documented on the recording device nearby.

"None," Montoya assured the CIA Case Officer.

"And what about the weapons?"

"I understand there was preliminarily an agreement to move a nuclear warhead and an electromagnetic bomb into Texas and California through our tunnels, but I assure you that will not happen."

Toby nodded in approval. "If you hear about that then you will let us know?"

"Of course."

"Since Julian's closest associates are in jail, what do you plan to do?"

"It works to my benefit that they are gone. They were loyal to Julian. I need people loyal to me."

"You really planned this thing out for a while, didn't you?" Toby asked, realizing the lengths Montoya had gone to assure himself of the opportunity to assume leadership of the Cartel de Culiacan and then ensure the prisoner exchange resulting in his son being released from prison.

"The Americans are not the only ones that look long-term," Montoya told Toby. "It is a shame what happened to SA Ledbetter. He deserved better than being suspended for a lie by a scorned woman."

Toby shook his head, still upset about Brandon's death. "The woman has been taken care of. She won't be a problem anymore." Earlier that day, Toby had used his considerable influence over a judge in Mexico City, to sign a court order sending Brandon's ex-mistress to a maximum security mental health facility, where she would be confined for the next 10 years.

"I told you this would work when you approached me," Montoya said, changing the subject. "Julian was always emotionally unstable and paranoid, but the only way to crack the tough exterior was going to be to get to someone close to him. It was unfortunate that Julian's wife had to die, but many innocent people have died in this drug war."

Toby nodded. "Including the DEA Deputy Administrator. What was the purpose of forging paperwork to make it appear he was involved? Of all the people you could have implicated, why Peterson?"

"Do you really want to know the answer to that question?"

"Yes."

"Allen Peterson was the reason my son was sent to a Medium Security prison in the United States, instead of a minimum-security prison as was previously agreed. Peterson refused to agree to that stipulation with the US Attorney's Office, or so I've heard."

"That's why you wanted Peterson dead?" Toby asked.

"Yes. Also, I knew the murder of an American law enforcement office would cause an uproar that would not be quieted until Julian was either killed or captured."

"Now Julian is dead, those loyal to him have been arrested, and you are the new leader free to put those in power that are loyal to you," the CIA case officer said, realizing the long game Montoya had played for months had finally produced the desired results.

"Yes," he said. "And you have three terrorists in jail and my promise to no longer allow terrorists access to Cartel tunnels. So, we both win. But there is one more thing, more important to me than any other, that has not yet come to fruition. Speaking of surrounding myself with those loyal to me..."

Without saying another word, Toby released the handcuffs of the man standing beside him, who immediately went to embrace Montoya. The new leader of the Cartel de Culiacan remarked with emotion, "It has been too long, my son."

Carlos Montoya hugged his father. Ever since he killed El Jefe's son after the man raped Carlos' sister, and the agreement between El Jefe and Juan Montoya that followed which spared Carlos' life but sent him to the United States to live the remainder of his days in prison, Carlos held out hope that he would one day return to Mexico and see his father. That day had finally come. Father and son kept their arms around each other, as they walked toward the waiting SUV. Juan Montoya had a lot of work to do, but now that he had his son by his side to help carry it out, he knew that they would be successful.

Once the prisoner exchange was complete, Toby and the other two individuals with him loaded up the three North African terrorists onto the jet, which left the area as quickly and quietly as it had when it arrived. As Toby looked out of the windows of the jet, he recognized that Montoya was now the unquestioned, "El Jefe Novo."

Epilogue
Woodstock, Georgia

The 7-8-year-old, Woodstock Wildcats gathered around their summer basketball league coach Tyler Jameson. His wife Jennie could not help but notice their son, Conner, looking up at his father with joy in his eyes that had not been there since he was a toddler. The Wildcats had won the Cherokee County summer league championship, and Conner was excelling on the basketball court with the extra time and attention he had been receiving from his father. Not only was Conner excelling on the basketball court, but at school as well. Having dad at home at night to go over homework and study for tests and help with projects was something that was not an option when his father was constantly working late nights as he had with his job with the DEA.

Tyler's suspension from the DEA following the revelation of his involvement with traveling to Tijuana to rescue Reuben Valdez, who was arrested by the FBI, was one of the most deeply humbling moments of their lives. When the OPR had accused Tyler of poor decision making that resulted in the death of innocent civilians, Tyler knew that his hope for reinstatement with the DEA were gone.

First, Tyler had allowed Chico and his brother Tito to travel to Los Angeles to commit a robbery, which was carried out when surveillance was unable to stay with the brothers. Tito had left and traveled back to Vegas, where he got drunk and hit and killed a pedestrian. While Tyler had not been directly involved with the individual's death, the OPR investigators both informed Tyler that had he arrested Tito and Chico prior to the robbery, then the pedestrian in Las Vegas would still be alive.

Second, the OPR investigators were visibly upset with Tyler's decision to allow Felipe and Tonio to travel to Los Angeles to murder

Jose Padilla. Once again, Tyler's inability to maintain surveillance of the targets at a crucial moment had given the killers just the time they needed to kill Padilla. Despite both of those things, Tyler had written a strong affidavit explaining his actions and why he felt they were warranted at the time. The DEA's Deciding Official told Tyler that his actions did not deserve termination, but that he might be demoted or face extended leave without pay. However, the media was able to obtain the information that Tyler allowed Felipe and Tonio to get to Padilla's residence, even when Tyler had plenty of opportunity to apprehend the two men prior to them getting to Los Angeles. Even though Padilla himself was a murderer that had poisoned an innocent woman in Mexico, Padilla's murder in Los Angeles, and more so Tyler seemingly allowing it to happen, caused the DEA to find itself under intense scrutiny about the actions of one of its best agents. After the publication of Tyler's role in the events, and the one-sided reporting that resulted, the DEA Deciding Official's tone changed. He later stopped responding to the phone calls of Tyler's attorney. Finally, the Deciding Official informed Tyler's attorney that he made the decision to remove Tyler from federal employment.

Tyler's previous cases and seizures, to include his role in the seizure of $302,000,000 in Mazatlán, was cast aside, and the only focus was that being portrayed by the media as a rouge DEA agent with poor decision making.

The family had to sell their home, and move to Jennie's family home in Woodstock, Georgia, while both Jennie and Tyler looked for employment. While Tyler's new job as a private investigator provided for the family and helped them get their own place and put food on the table, Jennie could tell Tyler missed his old job. Tyler knew he was not going back, so he instead focused time and effort on his parenting skills and his relationship with his wife, and as a result, those relationships had blossomed.

It was not the way that Jennie had hoped, but ultimately Tyler was now spending more time with his kids and wife. As Tyler picked up his son and hugged him following the team's championship win, he and his wife locked eyes. Both knew this was a moment that would have never happened had Tyler not lost his job with DEA. It was a moment that he, his wife, and his son, would remember and cherish for years to come.

* * *

Mclean, Virginia

Sitting at the head of a large table at Maggiano's Italian restaurant in Tyson's Galleria, Rod was as happy as he had been in months, since long before his suspension from DEA. It had been a tumultuous couple of months of allegations rampant from multiple news sources that Rod had accidentally shot and killed two civilians during the shootout in Juarez. Many of Rod's friends from El Paso stopped speaking with him, for reasons he could only assume were due to the negative reporting about his actions in Juarez. What hurt most was his co-workers also stopped all communication with him. Only Ana Lucia and Trevor had maintained contact, checking in to provide whatever encouragement and support possible.

Rod's suspension, much like that of Tyler's, extended from days, to weeks, to months, stretching for long periods of time without any contact from anybody in the DEA to provide updates about his employment status. Some days, Rod was convinced his employment was going to be terminated; other days he was sure that he was going to be given the opportunity to return to the DEA.

As he waited longer and longer, Rod's wife's faith never faltered, and even got stronger as she verbalized over and over that she was trusting in the Lord's provision for their family. Rod returned to his faith, and his insistence at leading the family in prayer in the mornings and at night was noticed by his youngest children, whose own faith remained strong with the example displayed by their parents. Absent from the family was Rod and Monique's eldest daughter who had run away from home months before and become ensnared in the life of drug abuse and prostitution. At some point, due to the media attention several weeks following the Juarez shootout, their daughter Keisha had become aware of her father's situation. She struggled whether or not to reach out to her father, for her decision to leave home was not due to a strain in the relationship with her parents, but resulted from her own bad choices and surrounding herself with the wrong people. For a time, her own humiliation and embarrassment stopped her from contacting her family. She knew that nobody from her family knew where she was. She also knew that her father and mother continued to look for her, as reports of their questions were relayed to her by other homeless friends. At some point a couple weeks earlier, she resolved to put aside what remained of her pride, and go to her parent's home, for no other reason than to check on her father.

Instead of seeing a broken and crushed man, what she saw surprised her. Her mother's steadfast faith in the face of adversity was expected, as she had always been the stalwart in the family keeping everything together, but the same example of faithfulness displayed by her father in spite of the circumstances was unexpected. He had been suspended by his job as a DEA Special Agent for almost nine months and had been without pay for six months. She was pleased to see her father doing well. The peace in her parents was something that she earnestly longed for in her own life. When her father held her hand in his and asked for her to spend the night under their roof, she considered it. Keisha saw her mother's eyes closed in prayer, and was overcome with the realization that despite their own financial hardship and employment difficulties, their sole focus and prayer in that moment was nothing more than for their eldest daughter to spend the night at their house.

She agreed. She stayed that night, and the next, and the one after that. Keisha began going to church with her parents. They helped her speak to counselors about her substance abuse problems. They went with her to the doctor to get medical checks for STDs. They began daily meetings with Pastor Jeremiah Banker. Before long, Keisha repented of her past sins, and the rebellion that had divided her from her family. She leaned on her parents and together they studied bible verses together and prayed together daily, all the while being unsure if Rod would ever get paid again. Savings built up during Rod's career were quickly depleted.

Finally, Rod received the news he had been waiting for. The OPR investigators had finally confirmed that the two civilians killed at the shootout in Juarez had not been killed by the bullets that came from Rod's gun, despite media reports to the contrary. For the time being, the media scrutiny about that incident subsided, but the DEA still refused to make a statement correcting the inaccurate reporting which claimed that bullets from Rod's gun had killed two innocent civilians. It was decided that Rod would be allowed to return to the DEA on the condition that he accepted a transfer to the DEA Training Academy in Quantico, Virginia.

The mandatory transfer to the DEA Training Academy was all but a demotion, an admonition that Rod was no longer trusted to make operational decisions in the field during surveillance or making arrests. It was an undeniable shot in the gut to the veteran DEA agent that had spent almost his entire life in the El Paso area, but it held the promise of a constant, and bulky paycheck, and that was something that Rod would not pass up, for he knew it was needed to provide for his family.

On the day before the family's departure from El Paso, Keisha made a public decision to restore her relationship with God and submit her life to Jesus. Keisha said she wanted to be baptized that same day, so Rod and Monique eagerly contacted Pastor Banker and the ceremony was performed late in the evening less than 24 hours before Rod and his family got on a plane to Regan National Airport in Washington D.C.

Upon arrival on the east coast, Rod and Monique picked up a rental car from the airport, and began to make the drive to Stafford, Virginia, where they would be staying in a temporary apartment until they found a residence to rent or purchase, but before their arrival, they stopped at the Tyson's Galleria, and had lunch at the Italian restaurant Maggiano's, in celebration of the start of a new phase of their life.

As Rod looked into the eyes of his first born, he recalled the words of Pastor Banker just after the baptism of his daughter. First, the pastor told him that God uses good things and bad things to make happen what He wants to happen. Only God Himself could see the big picture well enough to determine why bad things happened the way they did, most especially those bad events that cost some people their lives, as was the case with Rod's former DEA co-workers in Juarez and Mexico City. Second, Pastor Banker told Rod that if everything that had happened to him, all the embarrassment and humiliation, the frustration with his job, the abandonment of his friends, the loss of so much money, if Rod went through all that for no other reason than his daughter would to turn to Christ, then in the end it was worth it. In that moment, Rod agreed with Pastor Banker's sentiment. He would gladly go through all that again if it meant the salvation of his daughter was secure.

* * *

DEA Headquarters
Arlington, Virginia

"The Administrator's Individual Award for Excellence in the Field of Law Enforcement is presented to El Paso DEA Special Agent Ana Lucia Rodriguez."

A round of applause from all the guests in attendance in the conference room followed the announcement as Ana Lucia walked to the podium at the front of the room. She accepted the award from the Administrator and placed it on the podium as she pulled out a folded paper with several notes that she did not want to forget in her acceptance speech.

Most of those in attendance had not been on the street conducting an actual investigation in years, maybe decades. None of her co-workers from the El Paso Field Division had been included on the invitation and allowed to attend, although El Paso SAC Todd Morris was sure to be in attendance. Ana Lucia's request for Rod to come from Quantico a short distance down the interstate was denied.

SAC Morris stood proudly in the front of the room, alongside DEA Administrator Haskell, and many other senior level DEA management officials.

Ana Lucia had been approved to give a short acceptance speech but was instructed not to speak for longer than three minutes due to the very busy schedule of those upper management officials from DEA HQs. SAC Morris had requested Ana Lucia provide a copy of her speech for him to review and approve. She provided him a speech, but had no intention to follow along with it because there were a few issues that needed to be addressed to the DEA management who sat in their nice cushioned chairs in the air-conditioned offices at HQs across from the Pentagon, passing judgement and making questionable and ineffective command decisions far too often on the very agents they were supposed to support.

"I appreciate being presented with this award," Ana Lucia began. "When I started at the DEA Academy, I remember all the counselors and instructors consistently saying that the DEA was a family. They said the men and women we worked with were like our brothers and sisters. When I graduated from the DEA Academy, my goal was to report to the El Paso Field Division and establish my reputation as the most reliable and hard-working agent in the office. I did not want to let anybody in my DEA family down.

"What I saw when I reported to El Paso was that many of the senior investigators had no fire left in them. They had no desire to initiate drug trafficking investigations, and instead were content to sit around and collect a six-figure paycheck by working 9 – 5.

"I learned which agents did and did not want to work, so I surrounded myself with the agents that worked hard. Fortunately, I was placed in a good group, with a good boss, and a great partner, Rod Chambers."

At the mention of Chambers' name, SAC Morris shifted uncomfortably. He knew of Rodriguez' affection for Chambers and was aware of how upset she was that he had been placed on indefinite suspension without pay for such a long period of time.

"Together," Ana Lucia continued, "Rod and I had a special dynamic. He was trustworthy and the leader in enforcement operations but deferred to me in the investigative process to include informant operations, surveillance, and wiretaps. We made a formidable team, one that was responsible for making the most overall seizures of drugs and money in the El Paso Field Division, second in the southwest United States only to San Diego DEA Special Agent Tyler Jameson."

At the mention of the name of the second DEA agent who was suspended within the last year, Administrator Haskell's posture stiffened, and he noticeably turned his head to look at the El Paso SAC. The leader of the El Paso DEA office shrugged his shoulders and gave an expression that indicated this was not the speech he reviewed, and he had no idea what was going to be said next. They were in the awkward position of being unwilling to stop the acceptance speech of an agent awarded with the highest honor in DEA.

"SOD Coordinator Michael Winston was able to determine several connections between targets in Mexico that were responsible for supplying cocaine to our domestic targets in El Paso and San Diego, so we joined forces with several other hard-working and loyal DEA agents and set out to dismantle an organization, just like you guys always say you want us to do.

"I led my investigation in El Paso, but it would have not been successful without Rod. The SOD Operation would not have been successful without Tyler in San Diego, Daniel in Juarez, and Brandon Ledbetter in Mexico City.

DEA Administrator Haskell looked intently at Ana Lucia, attempting to determine the best course of action, but frozen in his decision making.

Ana Lucia smirked, and paused her speech for a moment. "I see some of you guys are contemplating what you should do right now. Stop my speech, or let me continue? That is a decision that you must make. While you stand in the office making a very inconsequential decision like that, the very agents you are supposed to lead are confronted with making split-second life or death decisions on the street. In most cases, like those of Special Agents Chambers and Jameson, there is no right choice, only the lesser of two evils, but a decision must be made. Indecision is NOT an option. Rod followed me into a gun battle at the border between El Paso and Juarez when I saw our informant murdered. Was the right decision to follow me into another country and help, or sit back and let me fend for myself? The sad truth is, based on the actions of DEA, if Rod had refused to help me and stayed in El Paso, he would still be working in his hometown, surrounded by his family, helping the DEA El Paso office make more seizures of drugs and money. But he made the decision to help, and now he has no life savings left, forced to spend it all while he was on unpaid leave. He has been shipped to Training and is working with a bunch of other people that wanted to escape the work on the streets."

SAC Morris attempted to step forward, "Ana Lucia, I think that's enough."

"For once, Todd," she said, clearly refusing to refer to the SAC's preferred and prideful title, "you're not the highest ranking individual in this room, so I don't have to abide by what you say."

The eyes of the onlookers widened in shock at the recipient of the DEA Administrator's Award speaking to her SAC in such a disrespectful manner, even though the majority in the room knew the man was nothing more than a figurehead and did nothing tangible for the Agency or the El Paso Field Division.

Since Administrator Haskell continued to remain silent, Ana Lucia continued her speech. "From what I understand, Tyler Jameson was likewise faced with a difficult decision after my kidnapping. He identified the individual that was going to kill the person who killed El Jefe's wife. Should he stop the murder before it happened, which would likely result in my death? Or should he allow the man to travel to the area where the killer was, so that he would be able to speak

325

to the assassin of El Jefe's wife and obtain the very information that might save my life? Just so you know, I spoke with Tyler many times by phone, but had only met him one time in my entire life, a couple weeks earlier at the SOD Conference in California, yet he did what he thought he had to do to save my life. I wonder if anybody in this room did a single thing to try and obtain the information requested by Toro in exchange for my life. Did anybody here do anything half as courageous and daring as SA Jameson?"

Nobody said a word, so Ana Lucia continued. "The fact that his actions weren't successful, doesn't take away from the attempt that was made for it to be successful. The decision to take away his job for a decision that nobody here would have made is a disgrace. It sends a message to the agents to not put their neck on the line in a situation where the outcome is not assured of being successful, and let me fill you guys in that haven't been on the street in decades, but none of the outcomes are assured of being successful. All this and I have not even spoken of the numerous seizures of money and dope that were made by operations he led. The $302,000,000 seizure down in Mazatlán that DEA still has plastered on its website... that was started by Tyler when he put his own personal I-phone into the vehicle that he knew was transporting drug proceeds into Mexico. Is there anybody here that would have had the wherewithal to make that kind of a split-second decision?"

Continued silence.

"What respect does he get from the agency that he worked so hard for? He is suspended, without pay, much like Rod, but instead of being demoted or sent to Training, he is fired, but not before DEA Deciding Official told Tyler that he was going to authorize his return to the agency, assuring Tyler and his family that they will once again get a paycheck to pay the bills and put food on the table. Yet what does the Deciding Official do? The exact opposite of what he said. He does not approve Tyler's return, as he told him he would do numerous times. Instead, he makes the decision to fire Tyler, the most successful agent in the entire Southwestern portion of the United States, for what everybody involved knows is because of the media attention that resulted."

Ana Lucia looked directly into the eyes of the Deciding Official who was also at the event. "Your title is Deciding Official. If it is your responsibility to decide, then make the decision yourself, and do NOT be influenced by others. If you do not have that authority, then stop speaking to the agents and giving them false hope. Tyler and his family spent all of their life savings paying for their house in the months that he was on unpaid leave, primarily because you told them that he was going to return to work in San Diego, but you changed your mind later. Say what you mean and mean what you say.

"Finally, and I will get off my soap box and return to El Paso," Ana Lucia said, "is the case of Brandon Ledbetter from Mexico City. Again, I only met him one time at the SOD Conference in California, but from everything I have heard and read, he was a phenomenal agent responsible for phenomenal seizures. He ran with the lead given to him by Tyler, and instead of making the easy seizure stopping a vehicle and getting a few million dollars, his FIU team followed the money vehicle to a boat in La Paz, and then to a residence in Mazatlán, where they got the biggest seizure of money in the HISTORY of law enforcement.

"Then, Brandon works up information provided to him by a DEA informant that just happens to be the second in command of the Cartel de Culiacan. Sure, this guy was trying to bump off El Jefe so that he could claim his spot, but at that point, DEA would have done ANYTHING to get El Jefe, including working with the person right under his command.

"Being a smart agent that would do whatever it takes to get things done, he complied with Montoya's request to use a false name on the informant paperwork. Doing otherwise would have shut down the operation before it started. As a result of Brandon's work, he retrieved information from Montoya that led to the arrest of most of the high-ranking members of the Cartel de Culiacan connected to El

Jefe. Yet, one false allegation is publicized by a scorned woman - which the DEA knows is false - and the agency fails to defend Brandon because of fear of the public's reaction if they found out the DEA was working with the second in command of the Cartel de Culiacan as an informant, instead of trying to arrest him, and the DEA is quick to suspend Brandon literally as he is walking out the door to lead the operation that DEA HQs requested him to do. While DEA Mexico City was off making seizures based on a case Brandon started, to include the 3,000 kilogram seizure that DEA still has plastered on their website, Brandon Ledbetter was shoved to the side out of fear of bad publicity, and the rest is history.

"Now, the four best DEA agents I have ever worked with are no longer in the field. Two are dead, one is fired, and one is banished to the confines of training. The DEA should be very proud of the agents that represent them, and ashamed of the way that they represent their agents. With all due respect, you can take this award back. I don't care what you do with it," Ana Lucia said, throwing the award to the unsuspecting Administrator who dropped it to the floor, which resulted in it breaking in pieces.

"I'll be back in the field in El Paso, or wherever you guys assign me since I just wounded your pride, but I will be there working hard, in honor of those that should be here but aren't."

Ana Lucia walked off the stage, and the crowd of people that had gathered to celebrate what they thought was going to be a joyous celebration, parted as she walked through them, out the door, and out of DEA HQs.